THE SHEPHERD'S ADVENTURE

—OR—
A PRACTICAL GUIDE TO PRINCESS RESCUING

THE SHEPHERD'S ADVENTURE

—OR—
A PRACTICAL GUIDE TO PRINCESS RESCUING

(A learned discourse concerning the ancient and oft-neglected art of Princess Rescuing, with a complete account of the foibles, follies, mistakes, and miscues which commonly result when the untutored layman attempts to enact such a scheme; told in the similitude of a story, complete with beautiful but unnecessary descriptions, remarkably strange characters, countless classical references, one or two effusions of poetry, several sage observations, and, the intriguing presence of a helpful yet mysterious coin. . . .)

Al Anderson

WINEPRESS WP PUBLISHING

Printed in the United States of America.

Packaged by WinePress Publishing, PO Box 428, Enumclaw, WA 98022. The views expressed or implied in this work do not necessarily reflect those of WinePress Publishing. Ultimate design, content, and editorial accuracy of this work is the responsibility of the author(s).

ISBN 1-57921-312-X
Library of Congress Catalog Card Number: 00-104838

To Beth, Lindsay, and Coach Clark

Contents

Introduction

Imagine reader, if you would,
Two bottles, labeled BAD and GOOD,
Both filled with fluid to the brim,
But different shades: one bright, one dim.

The surface of the BAD is bright
And bursts with bubbles, clean and light,
Everything to catch the eye
Is in this bottle, bubbling high.

The surface of the GOOD is very
Dim, and frankly, ordinary.
People who see it think it poor,
They take one glance, and then ignore.

But these dull folks don't understand,
That though the surface may be bland
And hasn't got a strong allure,
What's underneath might well be pure.

Shake each bottle, and then you'll see
A truer test of quality,
For only by testing can you know
The faults or virtues hid below.

Shake the BAD, and in dismay,
Watch its shimmer fade away;
The bubbles bubbling at the top
Last but a moment—then they pop.

The scum that rises soon holds sway
And turns angelic white to gray,
And golds and silvers change to blacks,
Shake once more—the bottle cracks.

Shake the GOOD, and then behold
What once looked meager, turn to gold;
Shake it harder, then you'll see
GOOD sparkle in its adversity.

No gaudy glitter here is found,
Just liquid pure, and clean, and sound,
Too rich and strong to melt in heat—
And if you taste it, it tastes sweet.

As with the bottles, so this tale
Shows badness strong and goodness pale,
But once we've read the final word
GOOD looks better—or so I've heard.

The story's filled with love and hate,
Princesses pure, and heroes late,
Amazing plots, athletic feats,
And drunken kings, and rogues, and cheats,

And sudden twists—the plot's careening—
(Below the surface is the meaning)
And evil plans and evil deeds
Spring up like plants from poisonous seeds.

Patient reader, I suppose
You'd like to read the rest in prose;
So turn the page—this won't take long—
Just quit this poem and come along.

Chapter I

An Introductory Chapter, Which Contains a Description of a Kingdom, a King, a Queen, a Princess, a Dog, and, as an Added Bonus, a Shepherd Lad

There was once a little country called Hoodahooda. Its origin has been a subject of much scholarly debate, and countless books and seminars have been devoted to this intriguing topic. However, the only independent account of Hoodahooda's origin can be found in the History of Frawd, an obscure, ancient chronicle. According to this fascinating work, the Kingdom of Hoodahooda was founded in the following way.

On one bright morning in the Dark Ages a tribal chieftain named Ragnar the Unimpressive was arrested and charged with three counts of Robbery, two counts of Extortion, and one count of Frightening the Transportation of a Minor. He was also accused of being flagrantly ugly in public. He was sent before the King.

"Ragnar," said the King, "your crimes are grievous and you must be punished. I'll give you two choices. You can either die by slow torture, or you can leave this land, taking your wife, your children, and your children's children, and embark on a dangerous yet fruitful voyage to discover a new land beyond the setting sun, a land where your hopes and dreams can be realized, a land where your children can grow up, strong and free, and a land where there is no war and violence, only year after year of peaceful solitude in the company of your happy, noisy children, and pleasant, talkative wife. Now, which shall it be?"

Ragnar chose the first option, but before the sentence could be carried out the King, who had never liked Ragnar, pardoned him. The story of Ragnar's behavior quickly became known throughout the land, and he became a laughingstock, and his family the butt of constant ridicule. This ridicule became so severe that Ragnar finally decided to take the King's advice and leave his country forever. With tears in their eyes, he and his family packed their belongings into a tiny ship and sailed toward the setting sun.

Two months later they struck land, marched inland for several days, and set up the pleasant little country of Hoodahooda.

A few centuries later the ruler of Hoodahooda was King Lars XIV, an enormously tall man with a bushy blond beard and a big red nose. Speaking of red, that was the color of most of the drapes on the windows of his castle, and, since this edifice has already been artfully woven into the fabric of the story, I shall attempt to describe it.

The King's castle was, as one might expect, a large stone building several stories high. It stood in a grove of trees at one end of the little village of Troddleheim. The castle had a moat, a solid mahogany drawbridge, several towers, and many rooms, 114 to be exact, each of which served a unique, specific function. Besides such conventional rooms as the Kitchen and the Master Bedroom, there were several unconventional rooms, such as the various recreation rooms where the King's courtiers could loosen up and have a little fun. There was the Axe room, the Searing Iron room, and, my personal favorite, the Cloak and Dagger room. There was also a Drawing room, where several of the top leaders of rival countries were quartered during their stay at the castle.

All of the rooms in the castle were interesting, but the most important room of all was The Great Hall. The Great Hall was, as the name suggests, a great hall, and this great hall was where King Lars could commonly be found during the day, sitting at his Great Table, stuffing freshly roasted chickens into his mouth, and jesting with a huge retinue of inebriated, belching retainers. Every day he would tell them the same Traveling Moneychanger jokes, every day they would laugh just as uproariously as the day before, and every day would conclude with the King dropping unconscious into a huge bowl of chicken and beer soup. Fortunately for the nation, someone would always pull him out, but never without first displaying some slight hesitation. King Lars also had a great fondness for dogs, and was usually surrounded by about thirty of them, although he sternly insisted that no more than five could stay on the table during dinner—yes, even the best of Kings can be arbitrary and capricious.

The castle also featured a large interior courtyard which contained the garden of Doctor Oldair, the greatest philosopher in the western world, and surely one of its finest gardeners as well. Around the castle were spacious grounds, which included a large park and the King's stables.

Now that you've been introduced to the country, seen the castle, and met the King, you might as well be told the story, which begins, like all the world's best stories, not in the sumptuous abode of a King, but at the humble setting of a stable.

Once upon a time, on a cheerful spring morning, the King's two coachman were sitting against one of the stable walls. The

Head Coachman was a burly man with a bald head and a quiet, world-weary manner. Sitting next to him was his assistant, a much younger man, who was fast asleep and snoring lustily. The assistant also had a bald head; not a naturally bald head, but one rather sloppily shaved in an effort to emulate his leader. The Head Coachman was dreamily studying the little tufts of hair that awkwardly sprouted out of his assistant's head, when suddenly he leaped to his feet.

"Get up!" he blurted to his assistant. "The Queen wants to go for a ride."

The Head Coachman had not gotten this information verbally, nor by letter, nor from divine inspiration; this was merely his interpretation of the rolling pin that had flown past his head and smashed into the wall behind him. The conclusion he drew from this phenomenon was quickly proven correct, for when he looked back toward the castle he saw the Queen staring down at him from one of the uppermost windows.

"I'm riding today!!" she shouted with typical subtlety and grace. "Prepare the horses!!"

The Head Coachman watched the Queen leave the window and knew she would soon be bounding down the stairs, out the side door, and across the moat, so he pulled his sleepy assistant to his feet and hurried over to the horses.

The day was so pleasant that all the horses were outside, frolicking in their pasture, and enjoying a moment of freedom. The Head Coachman leaped over the fence and, after flashing one of his rare smiles, politely spoke to the horses.

"I need six of you to come with me on a little trip. I know you'll enjoy it."

His countenance beamed with joy and goodwill.

"Yeah," added his naive assistant, "the Queen wants to go for a ride."

Oddly enough, immediately upon hearing this remark most of the horses suddenly became lame, and started hobbling off to the far side of the pasture—some were lame in two legs, and some in three, while others were not only lame but suffering from violent choking attacks as well, and one horse was lame in all four legs, and also his tail, which was an unusual sight to see. One horse was suddenly struck with violent convulsions and began spinning on the ground in paroxysms of agony; next to him another horse was desperately trying to stuff his hoof into his mouth, and one particularly melodramatic horse climbed up onto the edge of the water tank, and, while teetering, looked at the Head Coachman with a plaintive eye, intimating that he didn't want to, but would jump if forced.

"Where's my coach?!" the Queen thundered as she crossed the moat and strode up to the stables.

"Please?" the Head Coachman pleaded to the infirm quadrupeds, as they staggered around the pasture.

He eagerly tried to place a halter on a few of them, but whenever he came near, the ailing equines would experience a sudden burst of dexterity, and would take advantage of these temporary remissions by leaping playfully away. The Head Coachman finally gave up and stood in the middle of the pasture, frowning. Generally the horses didn't mind pulling a coach, unless the Queen was to be in it, for the Queen had a habit of having slow horses beaten, and, coincidentally, seldom rode with horses that she didn't consider unusually slow.

"Why aren't the horses ready?!!" asked a glass-shattering voice. "I want my coach ready now!!!"

The Head Coachman stared at the ground and thoughtfully rubbed his neck, as if he didn't expect to find it in such complete condition at anytime in the near future. His assistant, after deciding against joining the horse at the edge of the water tank, was busily scratching his Last Will and Testament onto a nearby tree.

"Purella!!" the Queen shouted, turning back toward the castle. "Hurry up! I told you you're riding with me today!"

"I'll be right down, mother!" came the reply from another of the castle's upper windows.

The mellifluous voice of Princess Purella was unmistakable, and the reaction to her voice was immediate. The horses wavered, the Head Coachman raised his head, and his assistant misspelled "executrix."

"Hurry!" the Queen repeated.

The horses were now in a quandary, for as much as they hated to pull the Queen, they loved to pull the Princess. This was because the Princess was notoriously nice, and was always certain to reward each of her four-legged friends with an apple and a piece of sugar. Better yet, the Queen had never had a horse beaten while the Princess was with her. At the sound of Princess Purella's girlish voice the horses stood transfixed; the Head Coachman took the opportunity to gather six of them, and, with the help of his assistant, began preparing the coach for the Queen. While they prepared it, the Queen waited for her daughter with unconcealed impatience.

Queen Gertrude was a slim woman with prematurely gray hair, whose face was wrinkled from too much frowning and angry words. However, she had once been beautiful, just as King Lars had once been handsome. And, just as Lars had revelled in performing the duties of a King, Gertrude had been happy in her role as Queen, supporting her husband and performing acts of charity throughout the kingdom.

But as the years went by the King began to feel that his courtier's jokes were more important than his country's laws, and that a full flagon of beer was more beautiful than his wife. In turn, Gertrude changed as well. She became embittered and demanding, and the responsibilities her husband abandoned she took over herself. She loved the feeling of power, and though she had never been much of a thinker before, her thoughts started becoming very, very big.

But alas! Thought is a heady drug, and should only be taken in regular, well-controlled doses. Unfortunately, the Queen ingested far too much all at once, and began vomiting out one bad decision after another. Her rule (for she was now the real ruler of Hoodahooda) was capricious, intolerant, and harsh, and if it wasn't for the love the people had for her only child, the Princess Purella, she probably would have provoked a revolution several years before.

"I'm sorry I'm so slow," said Purella, as she jogged up to her mother and curtseyed. She had run out of the small side door of the castle, across the moat, and to the stable with amazing speed, considering that her dress and shoes were designed for decoration rather than function.

"Never mind," said the Queen. "Just get in the coach."

"Can Floppy come too?" Purella asked.

"Oh, I suppose so," the Queen replied.

"Floppy!" Purella called.

Upon hearing his name, a little dog jumped out of a first-floor castle window and began running toward the coach. This dog, the celebrated Floppy, was Purella's faithful friend. He was an obvious member of the breed Canus Beeus Currus, or, in the vernacular, a mongrel. He had one brown eye and one blue eye, droopy ears, and a fuzzy tail, and the color of his fur (he was 5/8 shorthair and 3/8 longhair) was a sort of tortured orange, something like the color you would get if you crossed a lion with a zebra. Although the coach was only forty yards away from him, it took Floppy a good while to get there, because his form as a runner was less than ideal. He had the habit of stepping with both front legs at the same time, thus causing him to move up and down as much as forward, and making him look altogether like a tiny, fur-lined rocking horse. Eventually, however, he bounded into the coach and hopped onto Purella's lap.

"Remember Floppy, if you're going to sit in here you'll have to behave," she warned him.

"Arf," said Floppy, thus making the first of many important contributions to this story.

Finally the Head Coachman had the horses hitched and ready. Then, without further ado, he and his assistant hopped onto their seat, and soon the coach was rattling through the streets of Troddleheim.

After rolling through several cobblestone lanes lined with story-book houses and chatting villagers, the coach left Troddleheim behind and burst into the beautiful green countryside. Inside, Purella gazed happily out the window, admiring the day. Floppy sat on her lap and, in the great tradition of dogs who stick their heads out windows, had his mouth wide open, his tongue flapping in the wind like a streamer, and was breathing with great vehemence for no apparent reason.

Purella was (in case you were curious) very pretty, possibly even beautiful, which was actually standard among eighteen-year-old princesses from kingdoms such as Hoodahooda, and she had the standard-issue long blond hair. Not that Purella realized that she was an attractive young woman, of course, because if the people closest to you spend their time either ignoring you, or criticizing you, you naturally tend to have doubts about yourself, and Purella was not immune to this. For, in truth, in several ways her beauty and her behavior didn't conform to the ideal. For example, she was a few inches shorter than average, had a couple of slightly crooked teeth, and freckles instead of a tan.

But what really made her different from most princesses was that she didn't want to be a princess. She wanted to be one of the people, and spend her days outside, working, talking, laughing, and making friends. She loved the common people, and they loved her, because she was kind, honest, generous, virtuous, tender-hearted, and many other pleasant adjectives too numerous to mention.

One might suppose that her beauty and virtues would make her well-liked by her parents as well, but such was not the case. Her father, who had shown a great deal of interest in her for the few years following her arrival in the world, now completely ignored her, and was generally so intoxicated that he had a very confused idea about whether she existed at all.

The Queen thought her daughter was young and attractive, and refused to forgive her for it. She would nag and lecture at her continually, and though Purella's goodness of spirit would occasionally win the Queen over, the harmonious moments in their relationship were few and far between, although Purella always prayed for more.

Purella leaned over and gave Floppy a big hug. Except for her two maids, Floppy was her only close friend.

Suddenly the Head Coachman stopped the coach.

"What's wrong?" the Queen asked.

"A herd of sheep crossing the road, Your Majesty," the Head Coachman replied.

The Queen and the Princess looked out their respective windows and watched the herd of sheep being led across the road by a pale-faced but robust shepherd lad. He was a tall, gangly youth of about eighteen summers (and approximately the same number of winters), and he looked a little confused—in fact, it seemed as though the sheep were leading him, rather than the other way around.

"Hurry along, lad," said the Head Coachman.

At this point Floppy stuck his head out the coach window and said, imprudently, "Arf! Arf! Arf!"

The sheep obviously interpreted this as an insult. One could come to that conclusion for two reasons: first, the sheep collectively glared at Floppy, and second, when Floppy leaned over too far and fell out of the coach they began chasing him en masse.

Although it is not unusual to see a dog chasing sheep, seeing sheep chase a dog is quite another thing, and well worth seeing just for the experience. Fortunately, Lathan (for that was the name of the confused but robust shepherd lad) immediately sized up the situation. He saw his sheep chasing the dog around and around the coach, heard a mellifluous voice inside the coach say "Floppy! Floppy! Floppy!" and decided to effect a rescue. He raced over and (after tripping over one of his sheep and doing a spectacular somersault) scooped up Floppy, and then carried him over to the coach.

"Here's your dog," said Lathan, handing Floppy to Purella through the window.

"Thank you very much!" said the Princess, gratefully. "That was very kind of you. What's your name?"

At that moment Lathan suddenly realized that the cute girl and the frowning older woman beside her were none other than Princess Purella and Queen Gertrude, neither of whom he had ever seen up close before! Lathan turned beet red, and when he opened his mouth to answer Purella's question nothing came out but strange, half-stifled gurgling sounds, which seemed to belong to no language whatsoever.

"Drive on!" the Queen shouted.

Immediately the royal coach began to rumble down the road, leaving Lathan standing there, open-mouthed, in a cloud of dust. He kept his eyes fixed on the coach until it disappeared from sight.

"Did you see that?" Lathan said to his sheep (no, I'm not kidding, he said it to his sheep). "That was the royal coach! Princess Purella seemed really nice, just like they say."

The sheep were apparently not as impressed as Lathan, because even as he spoke they were continuing their long trek to the feeding grounds on the upper slopes near Brakehed Pass. Lathan, on the other hand, still stood staring at the road ahead, until finally he turned to stare at the spot where the little incident took place, in an effort to relive the experience. By the time he turned back to his sheep they were long gone, and he ran after them toward the upper slopes.

Chapter II

Wherein The Queen Gives a Lecture, Meets a Peddler, and Gets Real Mad

Meanwhile, the Queen was having a conversation with the Princess in her usual style—the Queen would talk, eventually wait for the Purella to reply, and then would cut her off in mid-sentence with some new thought.

The Queen's conversation, though fascinating to herself, was a bit tiresome, and conceivably could have been printed and marketed as the latest cure for insomnia. Nevertheless, Purella waited patiently until the Queen's little oration was over, and then resumed gazing out the window.

Meanwhile the Queen stared at the floor of the coach and smiled broadly, apparently overwhelmed by the massive entertainment value of everything she ever did and thought. However, the smile gradually faded from her lips as the serious discussion she wanted to have with her daughter crawled back into her mind.

Finally, after giving Purella a long, pity-filled stare, she opened the royal mouth and spoke.

"I've been thinking," said the Queen, with particular emphasis on the last word.

"Indeed, madam," Purella replied.

"Yes, yes, it's true. My daughter, I've been thinking that you are very unhappy."

Although obvious to a deep thinker like the Queen, Purella's despondency would not have been so apparent to a casual observer, and Purella and Floppy each gave the Queen a quizzical look.

"But I *am* happy," Purella said, scarcely believing that her mother was really showing some concern for her.

"No child, you are not," the Queen responded ominously. "In fact, you are the most unhappy, most miserable, most wretched, and most pathetic girl I've ever seen. But the solution to all your problems is obvious. It's clear that you must be married to Prince Charming of Skindeepia without delay."

"But I don't want to get married!"

"Nonsense! Every girl wants to get married."

"But I'm not in love!"

"Love? Love?! Love?!!" the Queen replied, as if she didn't know the meaning of the word, "I don't know the meaning of the word!!"

"But . . ."

"Listen to me child," the Queen interrupted, "love is completely unimportant. I've never cared one bit for love, and look where I am!"

"But I'm only eighteen! I'm not ready to marry."

"Nonsense! You've led a happy, innocent life for a long time now, and I think it's about time for you to have a change. Just eighteen! Why when I was your age I was twice as old as you are!"

"But why Prince Charming?"

"Because he's handsome for one thing; he's smart, he's fashionable, he knows how to eat with a fork, and his father's kingdom is much more respected than ours, and this alliance will give our country the prestige we need. Also, I happen to know that their treasury is getting low and Prince Charming needs your dowry to keep himself up in the style he's accustomed to. And besides that, he's tall. What more could you ask for? Of course, I don't think we should have the wedding right away. We'll have it, shall we say, next week?"

"Next week!"

"And that's not the half of it!" the Queen continued. "Take a look at this magazine!"

The Queen pulled out a copy of "Castle Beautiful" magazine from under her seat and flipped to an article entitled "10 Things You Can Do with Idols." The article told all about the Great Fish idol of Bubbylonia, the Great Lion of Motownto, and the Poodle idol of Prissovia.

"Idols are making a comeback," the Queen exclaimed with glee. "When I was a little girl everyone worshipped idols, and the idol of the great god Fungo was the center of the universe. It was so wonderful—the dancing, the sacrificing, the grovelling at the feet of the Queen in her official role as High Priestess— it was all so wonderful! Now we're infested with all these sick new religions with their invisible gods! Whatever happened to the good old days when everyone worshipped idols?"

"Well mother, thanks to 'Trollkiller' Sven Svensson those days are . . ."

"'Trollkiller' Sven Svensson!!!" the Queen shouted. "Don't ever mention that name to me again!"

("Trollkiller" Sven Svensson was a famous hero, as well as the founder of a notorious religion. I have an idea you will hear more about him later on.)

"Listen to me!" the Queen continued. "The Great Chamber of Fungo at our castle has remained sealed and empty for thirty-five years, ever since that maniac came in and desecrated the temple. What I think we should have is a new idol, a spectacular new idol, and your marriage with Prince Charming can be the first celebration of the new religion!"

"You know I can't do that, mother," Purella boldly replied. "I believe in the one God who created heaven and earth, and you and me and everyone else! I've been a faithful 'Trollerist' as you call us ever since my maids took me to visit their little church outside the village, and I will never, never have anything to do with an idol, because idols are just dumb, lifeless pieces of rock made by sinful men."

"Insolence!!" the Queen shouted. "I should have had your maids whipped! This Trollerism is worse than a plague!"

"Mother, you condemn 'Trollerism,' but you don't know anything about it! The very least you could do is look into it and see what it's all about! Couldn't you at least do that?"

Before the Queen could respond the coach hit a rough spot in the road, and the right-rear wheel came flying off. The horses didn't need much encouragement to come to a halt, and soon the Head Coachman and his assistant were busy repairing the wheel.

The tense little conversation inside the coach was over, but nevertheless Purella's last words planted a seed in the Queen's mind, where, since there was plenty of room for growth in that region, several new ideas began to sprout.

While the men worked, the Queen, Purella, and Floppy stepped out of the coach, crossed over to a large oak tree, and took a seat on some boulders in the shade. The Queen and Purella didn't speak to each other, but sat quietly apart. There were now far away from Troddleheim, in the middle of the Sweedle forest, a pleasant little wood dotted with oak trees, grassy meadows, and playful streams. The route they had chosen was circuitous, and they were as far from the castle as they would ever be. As soon as the wheel was fixed, they would rise through the hills to the left, cross Brakehed Pass, and head directly home.

The Head Coachman had a difficult time jacking up the coach, and an even worse time fitting the wheel back on, despite the valuable advice of his assistant, who sat watching his exertions with a look of profound sympathy.

Soon an hour came and went, and the wheel was still not on. The Queen was about to upbraid the two men for their slowness, but before she could speak her attention was distracted by clanging and banging sounds which came from down the road. Purella, also intrigued by these strange sounds, hopped off her boulder and went over to the road to look.

Coming up the road was a peculiar-looking wagon, piled high with various types of furniture, tools, and gadgets. Pots and pans were strung to the sides, crates full of bottles could be heard jangling together, and the whole thing shook and swayed back and forth with a great sense of urgency. This singular conveyance was pulled by a singular creature, who appeared to be a cross between a pony and some type of sheepdog. This sturdy beast was notable both for his shortness of stature and his inability to walk in a straight line. He apparently had a great interest in the drainage capacity of the area, for he would wander over and examine the ditches on either side of the road with great assiduity, and would occasionally exhibit unmistakable signs of desiring to curl up in one of them and fall asleep, presumably in order to get a first-hand idea of its volume. The driver prevented his steed from ever performing this experiment, not by threats and whippings, but rather with gentle pleadings, which would rouse the beast from his scientific contemplations and encourage him to continue the journey.

The driver of this wagon was as singular as his pony. He was a short, pudgy little man, wearing greasy clothes that were made long before he was born, and with the understanding that they would be worn by someone about a foot taller than their current owner. The little old man had line-less pink cheeks, sparkling blue eyes, and a dirty cap. Soon he pulled his wagon even with the Queen's coach and stopped, making sure everyone could see the huge pink sign on the side of his wagon, which said, "Oddities." When the wagon stopped, the pony, in an apparent attempt to determine the width of the road, instantaneously dropped to the ground, stretched out across the thoroughfare, and closed his eyes, probably in order to concentrate more fully on the mathematical calculations he intended to make. Meanwhile, the little old man climbed down from his wagon and, after ascertaining her high rank and contorting himself before her in a way which might be interpreted as a bow, addressed the Queen.

"Madam, Jack Crackback's my name, and oddities is my game! Potions, powders, lotions, chowders, wonders, blunders, chains, brains, and septic drains, all the wonders of earth, sea, and sky, most of the questions, and all of the answers are strapped onto the humble wagon you see before you, and are at your service!"

The Queen, instantly realizing that he was poor, looked at him with considerable contempt. The others, however, looked at him with great curiosity; to get a closer look at him, the Head Coachman's assistant temporarily let loose his grip on the wagon, causing the partial crushing of the Head Coachman, while Purella stepped forward to introduce herself.

"I'm Princess Purella of Hoodahooda," she said.

"Your Highness," Jack replied, "Jack Crackback's my name, and oddities is my game! Potions, powders, lotions, chowders..."

"We've heard that already!" blurted the Queen.

"Your nerves are unsteady?" Mr. Crackback replied. "Well I have a potion that would make your nerves so steady you could thread needles behind your back while hanging upside down."

"That's not what I said, you blithering fool!"

"I agree, Your Majesty. The weather *is* cool," Mr. Crackback earnestly replied.

"What are you babbling about?" the Queen demanded. "Are you deaf?"

"What?"

"I said, 'Are you deaf?'!!"

"What?"

"Are you deaf?!!!" she bellowed.

"There's no need to shout, Your Majesty. After all, I'm not deaf."

At this point the Queen began berating the unfortunate peddler with a wide variety of remarks not too complimentary of his personal appearance and level of intelligence.

Fortunately for Mr. Crackback, Purella interposed and, after several misunderstandings, managed to ask him where he was travelling, and if he had any items that might prove interesting to the Queen.

"I'm going over the pass to see if I can sell some stuff to the farmers in the next valley," he responded. "I can show you lots of things."

He guided Purella over to his wagon, while the Queen remained on her boulder, frowning.

"This is a rainmaker," he said as he shakily grabbed a weirdly-shaped metallic instrument. "You just fill it up with water, attach it to your roof, smear the tips with butter, wait for it to get hit once by lightning, and soon you'll have rain in no time. And over here I've got a left-handed cheese slicer, a book on snake charming, and a machine that turns tomatoes, grapefruits, and pomegranates into cucumbers."

"But don't you have anything my mother could use?" Purella asked.

"Like food for example!" shouted the Queen, who was listening from a distance, and gradually becoming famished by the exertions of the day.

"Absolutely right, Your Majesty," Jack solemnly replied, as he gazed at the cucumber converter he held in his hands. "Crude but ample."

Purella spent a minute browsing through the contents of the wagon, amazed at the variety and eccentricity of the merchandise.

"Do you really have most of the questions and all of the answers stuffed into this little wagon?" Purella asked, unable to suppress a smile.

"Answers for any question, and questions for any answer," Jack replied.

"All right," Purella playfully responded, "if Marcellus is three years old, and Sarah is four times as old as Marcellus will be in ten years, and Frank is . . ."

"Of course, I try to avoid answering questions that are too trivial," Jack hastily explained. "Not that I couldn't if I wanted to, of course."

"Oh, of course," replied the smiling Princess.

"I generally give answers to only really important questions, such as the meaning of life, the meaning of death, marriage . . ."

"Marriage?"

"Sure. I answer questions about things like marriage all the time, because I like to answer questions on subjects that are so important you can't afford to make a bad decision. After all, marriage is something you can't rush into—a hasty marriage can ruin your life. Why I remember one time . . ."

"I will hear no more of this!" demanded the big-eared Queen from her seat on the distant boulder. She didn't like the turn their conversation was taking.

"But Your Majesty, I, I, well," stammered Jack with a blush so red it was hardly credible, "I haven't known you long enough to give you a kiss."

Before the shocked Queen could compose herself and bury the poor peddler under a mound of expletives, Purella interposed once again and asked Jack if he had any special cleaning fluid which could take the dust and grime off the royal coach. Jack responded in the affirmative, and, after snatching up a dirty bottle of clear fluid from the depths of his wagon, followed Purella over to the stricken conveyance.

The coach was dirty, particularly on the right side, just below the window. This was Floppy's fault. He had sat for most of the time with his head sticking out the window, and, according to his habit when he was excited, emptied a considerable quantity of liquid out of his mouth, which soon adorned the side of the coach. The dust in the road, after being kicked up into the air by the coach's front wheels, quickly noted the presence of this fluid, and, since it is the ambition of every piece of dust to someday rise to the exalted position of mud, attached itself onto it with great enthusiasm, and soon the coat of arms on the side of the coach looked like a gigantic black smudge.

"BAP water," Jack pronounced after observing the coach's condition. "What I have here in my hands is not ordinary water, but BAP water, drawn from the purest well in the universe, and guaranteed to clean anything, and show it as it really is."

So saying, he opened the bottle and dramatically splashed most of its contents against the side of the coach.

Sure enough, the dirt quickly disappeared, and Purella and the coachman's assistant looked at Jack with admiring eyes. The Head Coachman missed this demonstration, however, because for some reason or other he was balancing the full weight of the coach on his head, while trying very unsuccessfully to gain the attention of his preoccupied assistant, who had wandered over to observe the BAP water experiment without giving prior notice. Floppy watched the cleaning process from a distance, embarrassed by his negligence in causing such a problem, while the Queen watched from her seat on the boulder, and expressed the opinion that she found it hard to believe that Mr. Jack Crackback could do anything right.

Unfortunately, in this instance the Queen's assessment of Jack's abilities proved correct, for as soon as the BAP water succeeded in removing the dirt, it felt obligated to continue and remove the coat of arms as well, and, not content to rest on its laurels, concluded by removing several underlying coats of paint. This operation produced a startling revelation, namely that the original color of the coach was pink and orange, and that its original owner had written on it in bold blue letters:

LUG-A-LOT INC.
Cut Rate Coaches, Wagons, and Battle Equipment
(Credit is our Middle Name!)

The Queen was not amused by the sight of her defaced coach. She jumped up and down, shouted unintelligibly, searched for a large rock, and gave every indication that she intended to apply one to Mr. Jack Crackback's face at the first opportunity. Purella hastily grabbed Jack by the arm and, after leading him back to his wagon, thanked him for all his help.

"It was a pleasure to be of service," Jack gallantly replied as he placed himself on his shaky perch. "I'm sorry I couldn't do more."

Several violent pulls on the reins brought Jack's pony to its feet, much to the indignation of that learned animal, who doubtless had been computing something of great import in his mind, which, due to this barbarous interruption, was now thrown into hopeless confusion. The pony was so incensed by this treatment that he gave every indication that he would never move again for the rest of his natural life, and, despite many tender pleas from Jack, stood as if locked in concrete. Finally, however, a look of philosophical resignation stole over the pony's face and, no doubt inspired by higher ideals of duty and loyalty (and a desire to get to a stable in time for dinner), the pony began marching bravely forward, and before long Jack Crackback and his wagon were out of sight.

Shortly thereafter, the sun, tired of floating over everybody's head, decided to start dropping toward the western hills, in the hope that it could rest for nine or ten hours before having to get up bright and early the next morning. As a result of this singular action, there were only a few hours left before sunset, and the coach was still not repaired.

The Queen was getting angry. More time passed.

"Someone will be punished for this," the Queen said.

The horses began to paw the ground nervously. The Head Coachman and his assistant each gulped. They began working on the wheel with renewed energy, and finally it was fixed.

"Ready to go, Your Majesty," the Head Coachman chimed with forced cheerfulness.

"If we're late for dinner, someone will pay," said the Queen ominously.

"Please don't talk like that, Mother," said Purella sweetly. "We'll get home in plenty of time."

She took her mother gently by the hand and escorted her into the coach. Then, after Floppy leaped inside, the coach rattled off toward Brakehed Pass.

The Head Coachman and his horses needed no encouragement to hurry, and proceeded vigorously forward, even though the road to Brakehed Pass was a treacherous road that often bordered the sides of huge cliffs. Still, the Queen was not satisfied by their progress.

"Late for dinner . . . late for dinner." she kept repeating. "Too slow! Too slow!"

She said the last words so loudly that the horses clearly overheard her. Though unable to understand the words, they could clearly recognize the tune, and frantically tried to speed up.

"Mother, please!" said Purella, "they're going as fast as they can!"

"Silence! Don't contradict me again! You've hurt me deeply today!" said the Queen, who really did look hurt.

"But Mother, how did I . . ."

"I have spent days, weeks thinking about the new idol we should have, and how you could marry Prince Charming and be so happy, and I finally tell you all my exciting plans and you scoff at them! You and your invisible God! Then, to top all, I must sit out in the middle of nowhere while some fools try to fix a wheel, and listen to the insults of a repulsive old peddler. And then my horses deliberately go slow so I'll be late for dinner! Don't try to deny it!! I know their game, and I have half a mind to stop the coach right now and have them all beaten!!"

That did it. The horses began running at breakneck speed, unmindful of the danger, and the Head Coachman could no longer control them.

The horses raced to the top of the pass. The road narrowed. Soon they were galloping along the side of a sheer cliff. Eight hundred feet below them, in a narrow, inaccessible gorge, one could see the white water of a river. The Head Coachman and his assistant closed their eyes. They rounded a turn, and for an instant one of the rear wheels swung off the road and hung over the edge of a cliff.

Chapter III

Contains an Accident and a Rescue, After Which Lathan Contracts a Debilitating, Yet Common Disease

Meanwhile, on the sunny side of a tall peak that overlooked Brakehed Pass, a herd of sheep was peacefully grazing, while their master, who was none other than Lathan, sat on a rock nearby and thought about the Princess.

Lathan didn't know much about girls. He was a shy, unassuming lad who lived with his grandmother in a snug little cottage in the woods, and, other than sheep-shearing festivals, he didn't get out much. He was popular with his sheep and with other shepherd lads—shepherd girls either treated him with disdain, or, more frequently, ignored him altogether. Princess Purella, though . . . hmm. She seemed different.

Lathan was roused from his reverie by the sound of galloping horses—this was something no one would expect to hear near dangerous Brakehed Pass.

Alarmed, he darted over to a spot where he could look down on the road. When he looked down he beheld a frightful sight: the runaway royal coach tearing up the road at breakneck speed. Lathan's astonishment turned to horror when he looked further up the road and saw, just around a sharp corner, a large wagon completely blocking the road. The driver of the wagon was tugging ineffectually on his reins, trying to encourage his pony to move forward. However, the pony remained standing very still, and looked abstractedly at the rock formations which bordered the road, apparently lost in geologic contemplations. In fact, a close observer would have noted that his eyes were closed, clearly in an effort to block out any extraneous data. But alas, his scholarliness proved his undoing, for just as the pony was about to determine the density of the roadbed by lying down on it, the royal coach careened around the corner and crashed into the stalled wagon.

A cloud of dust rose into the sky, obscuring the site of the accident. Lathan, horrified, scrambled down the steep mountain side as best he could, hoping he could be of some assistance.

Soon the dust cleared, and Lathan saw that the road was littered with papers, bottles, gadgets, and cooking utensils, all of which had fallen out of the wagon marked "Oddities," the remains of which were dangling precipitously over the edge of the cliff. The driver was vainly trying to pull his battered vehicle to safety, while his pony (who had somehow become unhitched) staggered around like a professor who had just been denied tenure. Sprawled next to the pony were six horses, who were each moaning, and inwardly vowing that they would never do this sort of thing again.

The royal coach looked only moderately damaged. Lathan climbed down almost to the road, but when he saw that there were no serious injuries, he stopped short. He looked ruefully down at his ragged clothes, and didn't come any closer.

The Queen and Purella climbed out of the coach to assess the damage. Purella suddenly began looking frantically about, and soon let out a scream.

"Floppy! Floppy! Where's Floppy?!!"

The sturdy pup was nowhere to be seen. Suddenly the air was split by the cry of a familiar voice.

"Arf!"

Purella ran over to the edge of the cliff and saw, twenty feet below her, (O horror to relate!) her faithful friend sprawled out on a narrow ledge above the sheer cliff. The impact of the collision had caused him to fly off Purella's lap, out of the window, and over the cliff, where only a freakish outgrowth of rock and some suspiciously good luck could save him.

"Oh, please save him!" cried Purella, looking at the Head Coachman and his assistant with stone-melting eyes.

The assistant took one look over the edge, and then began giving a rapid summary of his many physical disabilities, in surprisingly precise medical terminology, while the Head Coachman mumbled something about his job description.

Floppy's face was dotted with tiny beads of perspiration. He looked down. Eight hundred feet below him he could see the white water of the river raging through the gorge. A few hundred feet below him he could see buzzards, circling. They were looking up at him, and smiling.

"Oh, save him! Somebody save him! Help! Help! Help! Help! Help!" Purella shouted, without much originality of phrasing, but with unfeigned sincerity.

Lathan stood transfixed. He had been about to leave, fearful in the presence of royalty, when the pathetic cries of the Princess pierced his youthful breast. Without further ado, Lathan scrambled down to the roadway, and, without stopping to say a word to anyone, climbed down the cliff toward Floppy. He scooped up Floppy, scrambled back up the cliff, and soon stood panting on the safety of the roadbed, while Floppy ran over to his overjoyed mistress, who hugged and kissed him over and over.

Meanwhile, Lathan took a long look at the Princess, and was awestruck by her beauty and femininity. Everything about her dazzled him.

Compared to this vision, Lathan was an unimpressive sight, and Lathan was sadly aware of it. He knew very well that he looked like a basic, dirty (albeit robust) shepherd lad. He had two eyes, two ears, one nose, and one mouth, which are the amounts generally accepted in polite societies, but he had rather poor specimens of each, which often saddened him. His ears were big, his eyes were weak, his nose was red, and his mouth, which generally remained wide open whether he was talking or not, housed a high, rather squeaky voice. He was short, had knobby knees, skinny arms, foot fungus, one leg shorter than the other, allergies to six kinds of grasses, an occasional bladder problem, and three ingrown toenails. He was, however, quite robust.

Lathan considered quietly leaving to rejoin his sheep, but then Princess Purella, her face flushed with relief as well as admiration for the robust hero, set Floppy down and bounced happily over to Lathan to express her gratitude.

"I don't know how to thank you! This is the second time you've rescued my dog today! You're so good, brave, and wonderful!!!"

Lathan responded by turning crimson, repeatedly opening and closing his mouth with great rapidity, and staring fixedly on the ground in front of him as if it were the most interesting thing he could ever possibly see. Purella sensed his uneasiness, and, speaking in a gentler tone, asked him what his name was and where he lived.

It took Lathan about two minutes to respond to these questions, because for some reason he would repeat each word twice before going on to the next one.

"You live at the edge of the Sweedle forest!" Purella responded. "Why, I think that's the most beautiful place in Hoodahooda. Every Friday I make a special visit to the Trollerist church, and on the way I stop by Bonkers Wells. I love to just sit there and enjoy the day. Lots of times I go to Bonkers Wells and eat my lunch. You should join me sometime."

"My-my, grandmother-grandmother, is-is, also-also, a-a, Trollerist-Trollerist," said Lathan.

"Really? That's wonderful!" said the delighted Purella.

While engaging in this conversation Lathan never dared look at Purella's face, but behind her he did eventually notice her companions: the Queen, who stood outside the coach looking dazed and surprisingly passive, and two bald coachmen covered with dust, the elder looking at the battered coach with great resignation, and the younger looking blank.

"Why don't you come along with us, Lathan?" Purella asked. "I could show you the castle and introduce you to my father. He's really a fine man, and I'm sure he'll be pleased when I tell him how brave you are."

"Well, I, I, certainly, that is, that is, I mean, thanks, that is, I certainly will if you want, I mean, I want to of course, but that, that would be fine, of course," elucidated Lathan, while nodding his head up and down with great rapidity, as if attempting to fully demonstrate the elasticity of his neck.

"That's wonderful!" said Purella happily. "I can show you the castle and you can tell me all about being a shepherd. It can get lonely being a Princess, and it will be nice to have someone new to talk to."

"Let's go," the Queen said as she climbed back into the coach. The two coachmen quickly prepared the horses.

Lathan, whose face was crisscrossed with astonishment, was led over to the coach by the smiling Princess. He would have compared this situation to a dream, but Lathan's dreams were usually much more realistic. Not only had he met a beautiful Princess, but she was actually nice to him, and was even a believer in "Trollkiller" Sven Svensson just like his own grandmother! And now she was taking him to the castle! He had lived in Hoodahooda all his life, but had never come near the castle's threshold.

Purella led Lathan up to the coach, but just as he was about to take his seat Jack Crackback's wagon slid a foot further over the edge of the cliff and dangled even more precipitously than before. Jack moaned in despair, and his pony was so excited by this occurrence that he fell into a deep trance, somewhat resembling sleep.

"My goods, my life, my everything!" cried Jack. "Somebody help me pull it back from the cliff, or I'll lose all I have in the world!"

"Drive on," the Queen said.

"Mother, can't we stay and help him?" Purella pleaded.

"Drive on," the Queen repeated.

"But someone has to help him!" Purella cried.

The two coachmen hesitated. Lathan climbed down from the coach and ran over to help Jack.

"Drive on!" the Queen repeated firmly.

"But mother, we have to wait for Lathan!"

"I'm getting hungry and I. . ."

Before the Queen completed her sentence the Head Coachman, who needed no further prompting, started the horses racing toward home.

"Quick Lathan, jump aboard!" Purella called out as the coach began to rattle away.

Lathan, fearful of being left behind, ran after the coach until he was only a step or two behind it.

"I'll never get my wagon up!" cried Jack.

"Jump!" cried Purella.

"Everything—I've lost everything," Jack sobbed.

Lathan, whose hand could almost touch the back of the coach, slowed down and came to a stop. The coach quickly disappeared around a corner, and the dust it made blew back into his face. Half-smiling and half-frowning, Lathan turned and walked back to where Jack Crackback was standing, wringing his hands.

"Don't worry sir. I'll be glad to help you, if I can," said Lathan.

"What a fine lad!" Jack replied happily. "What's your name, my boy?"

"Lathan, sir."

"Well Nathan, Jack's my name and oddities is my game! Potions, powders, lotions, chowders . . ."

Before long Lathan and Jack had pulled the wagon to safety.

"I won't forget this, Laman," said Jack solemnly. "Now, do you think you could help me load it up again?"

It took quite awhile, but finally all the "oddities" were loaded back onto the wagon and Jack was ready to leave.

"Lad, you've saved an old man's life," Jack said as he gazed at his rescued vehicle. "I don't know how to thank you."

"Oh, forget it," Lathan said with a sigh. He was thinking about all he had missed by stopping to help the old man.

"Are you sure you don't need a ride somewhere?"

"No. Thanks anyway."

"My pony is a very smooth walker. Isn't that right?" said Jack, directing the question to his steed.

The pony gave a noncommittal neigh.

"No, thanks. Really."

Jack smiled, patted Lathan on the back, and slowly climbed up onto his perch. He put the reins in his hand, adjusted his cap, and looked back at Lathan.

"What did you say your name was, Mike?"

"No, it's Lathan."

"Well, if you ever need anything from me, don't hesitate to ask."

"That's all right," said Lathan. "I've seen all your things, and they're all very nice, but I don't think any of them could help me."

Jack thought for a moment.

"Well, you could be right. Still, you never know."

Jack urged the pony forward, and the wagon began to waddle away.

"I'm sorry you didn't get to visit the castle. But I have a feeling you'll see the Princess again," Jack called back to Lathan.

Lathan was surprised. Jack had appeared so upset by the potential loss of his wagon that Lathan didn't think he had even noticed the Princess, let alone hear what she and Lathan were talking about.

"Good-bye, Johnson, and thanks!" Jack called out as his wagon rounded the corner and disappeared from view.

"Good-bye," said Lathan.

The sun was setting. After spending a few minutes standing in the spot where Purella stood, Lathan climbed back up the mountain side and rejoined his sheep.

It was a warm night, even on the upper slopes, and most of Lathan's livestock were gathered around a little mountain pond; the fatter sheep were grazing, while the more athletic sheep were having a swim. When they saw Lathan trudge back toward them they snapped to attention.

Lathan's subsequent behavior was most inexplicable. Instead of guiding the sheep down to the lower slopes, he walked over to where they were sitting and collapsed in a heap. He then sighed, moaned, groaned, called himself an idiot, jumped up, paced feverishly back and forth, flopped down again, jumped up again, banged his head against a tree, carved a couple of names into the tree, sighed several hundred times more, kissed the tree, quickly apologized to the tree for being so forward, expressed the opinion that he couldn't help kissing the tree because of its great beauty, wandered aimlessly over to a nearby stream, mentioned repeatedly a polysyllabic name that started with a "p" and ended with an "a," completely melted, flowed downstream several hundred feet, came ashore and reconstituted himself in another flurry of sighs, and then, inexplicably, rose up into the air and floated all the way home.

The sheep were shocked, and concluded that their master was suffering from some pathetic, rare, and extremely debilitating disease. This assumption was only partially correct, for though the disease their master suffered from is indeed debilitating, it is certainly not rare, and over the centuries has ravaged a remarkable number of people, and has effectively turned many a vigorous six-footer into a grinning, bon-bon-buying babbler.

Meanwhile, the royal coach arrived home, and, although they were late for dinner, the Queen was still too dazed by the accident to have anyone punished. After dinner she went straight to bed and lay there thinking for some time. Purella had really annoyed her.

Invisible gods? Ha! she thought. *We'll see about that!*

Chapter IV

A Heavy Theological Chapter, Wherein the Major Religions of Hoodahooda are Objectively Discussed, and the Queen Makes a Decision

The next morning the Queen commanded her maid to bring her a copy of *The Complete Religions of Hoodahooda, Unabridged.* Upon receiving the book the Queen locked herself in her room and for the first time in her life began to study religion. She skipped Section A, "The Idols of Hoodahooda," because she knew their history fairly well. She found herself suddenly interested in religions that didn't use idols, so she went straight to Section B, "The Three Major Religions of Hoodahooda: The Invisible God."

The oldest major religion of Hoodahooda was called Calculism. It was popular with lawyers, bankers, and accountants, and anyone else who was mathematically inclined. It had an elaborate set of rules, and was remarkable for its precise use of statistics. In the Sixth Edition of *The Official Rules of Calculism: Enlarged and Updated,* there are no less than 1,539 prescriptive rules concerning personal conduct, over 5,000 non-prescriptive or "discretionary" rules (breakable if approved by a 6–4 vote of the arbitration board), and 30,000 non-binding suggestions. Each of these sets of rules was divided into seven sub-classifications and four sin-effectiveness groups, although a strong reform movement kept trying to reduce the number of sub-classifications to three, a cause of much dissension in the church. Each person's TSO (Total Sin Output) was tabulated every two months by the Department of Sins, Follies, and Other Flaws, a powerful organization which could only be overruled by the arbitration board. The department gave out statistics in twelve categories, so that by looking at a person's "numbers," one could know everything about that person; for example, one could learn if that person was a "power sinner," a "finesse sinner," etc. The most important figure in the TSO was the ESA (Earned Sin Average). This measured the amount of prescriptive and non-prescriptive sins committed on the average day. Anything below 8.00 was considered good, and if a person's ESA dipped below 3.50 that person was considered a candidate for sainthood. Each year the ESA champion would win a gold cup (the J.P. Schweinbaum Award) and a lead pencil, which was very useful in helping calculate faults and virtues.

The Queen was impressed by this very precise religion right away, but while examining the rule book she came across a minor stipulation that disturbed her greatly. This was *Chapter 4, article 3, subparagraph 7, rule No. 9A*, which I will quote for you as it is worded in the sixth edition of the rule book:

> All rules in this book are sacred and unchangeable, and each is essential for salvation and/or virtuous living; therefore, if anyone breaks even one of these rules he has broken all the rules, and whoever breaks all the rules will be forever damned. Whoever keeps all the rules, and never breaks a single one at any time, will live forever in eternal bliss.

At first the Queen thought this was a reasonable stipulation, but then, with typical penetration, it occurred to her that the J.P. Schweinbaum Award winner of the previous year boasted an ESA of 3.23, which averages out to approximately 22.5 major sins per week. In fact, in all recorded history there had never been anyone who had an ESA of even close to 0.00, the requirement for eternal life. The lowest ESA in recent memory belonged to one Agnar Flatts, an angelic individual who gave all his money to the poor, and was eventually burned at the stake for being too kind to foreigners. However, Agnar hated cats, and was occasionally irritable if bothered during dinner, which caused his ESA to soar to 0.39, thus sending him whirling to eternal damnation.

The Queen wasn't the first to notice the grave flaw in this precise system, but most of the practitioners of this religion hoped that "God" (for that was what they called their deity) would loosen up at the end of the world and let everyone under 6.50 slide by without much hassle. Some particularly hopeful people (generally those with an ESA of higher than 12.00) believed that "God" would let them go into Heaven merely because they took the time to keep their scores, for they felt that knowing about their religion was just as good as practicing it. The Queen, however, was not a particularly optimistic person, and found Chapter 4, article 3, subparagraph 7, rule No. 9A discouraging. She then shifted her attention to the second of the three religions, Pambyism.

Pambyism was easily the biggest religion in Hoodahooda, although no one was very enthusiastic about it. It was especially popular with three groups: respectable people, those who wanted to be respectable people, and servile politicians. In theory this religion had several rules, none of which was ever seriously followed. The two main precepts of this religion were to try to "be good," and never to criticize anyone for failing to live up to that standard. They believed in only one deity, whom they unimaginatively called "God." This "God" was a rather wishy-washy individual, who gave several commands but never expected them to be obeyed, who opposed sin but would forgive every sin of every person at all times whether they asked him to or not, and who created the world and everything in it, yet never liked to get closely involved. His main concern was that the world have "love," a word which he defined very loosely. His followers would generally ignore him, except on public occasions, when they would mention his name repeatedly, usually with an eyeful of tears.

The great beauty of this religion was that it allowed no distinction between vice and virtue; if you did good you were good, and if you did bad you were still good, because you were automatically forgiven whether you asked for it or not. This appealed to the Queen greatly, but she soon became conscious of the religion's main flaw: namely, that there was really no reason to believe in it. For, in fact, according to the Pambyists everyone was forgiven for all their sins even if they didn't believe in the religion, or never did one decent thing in their entire lives. Thus, the only practical use of the Pambyist church was to make people look respectable, and help organize ice cream socials. In the end the Queen utterly rejected this religion, partially because she was allergic to ice cream, but mostly because she wanted to see a religion that was a little flashier.

The last major religion was called Trollerism. It was especially popular with poor people and old people, although it had many adherents of widely differing backgrounds, including the Queen's own daughter, Princess Purella. This religion had been founded only forty years before by the famous "Trollkiller" Sven Svensson. This Svensson was an epic hero of almost mythic proportions, who conquered kingdoms, slayed dragons, and rescued helpless maidens with alarming frequency. Ironically, he was not physically impressive, nor would he ever stand out in a crowd; nevertheless he always succeeded in everything he attempted, and he defeated so many super-villains that their ranks were depleted for many years to come. However, it was because of his religious views that "Trollkiller" earned his greatest notoriety.

Hoodahooda was once a largely pagan country, and idols dotted the landscape. The temple of the great god Fungo, which was part of the royal palace, was the most revered pagan temple in the world—that is, until "Trollkiller" Sven Svensson came along. One day, during the Awesome and Most Sacred Fungo Festival, when thousands of worshippers paid homage before the sixty-foot image of the god, "Trollkiller" Sven Svensson sauntered into the temple. He walked straight up to the altar without bowing three times, painting his face red, or collapsing in a heap, all of which together being the prescribed method of approaching this most hallowed shrine. The high priests were shocked at the impudence of Trollkiller, and shouted at him that his rashness would be quickly punished by the angry god. However, Trollkiller was unperturbed, and boldly announced to the crowd that the monolithic figure they worshipped was not really a god, but was nothing more than a lifeless piece of granite that had been rather crudely chiselled into a face.

After making this announcement, he pulled out a couple of ropes and, faster than you could say "Jack Svensson," he had them looped around the head of the magnificent and all-seeing Fungo. Then, by using the principles of leverage and gravity, scientifically calculated in advance, he skillfully caused the god to topple over and smash into a thousand pieces, while the high priests looked on in horror, and bellowed that Fungo's revenge would be bloody and unmerciful.

Fortunately for Trollkiller, the god proved to be much more easygoing than was hitherto believed, and not only let his own demolition proceed with impunity, but also watched Trollkiller smash everything in his temple (including his high priests) in conspicuous silence. That very day paganism fell out of fashion, and the Awesome and Most Sacred Fungo Festival was never held again.

The name of "Trollkiller" Sven Svensson's deity was also "God;" however, this God was quite different from the gods of others, and was altogether a very idiosyncratic individual. He not only created the world, but he insisted on taking an active part in all earthly affairs, regardless of whether the participants wanted him involved or not. Nevertheless he was a stealthy fellow, and never allowed himself to be seen openly, although he gave sly proofs of his existence continually; in fact, these proofs were given so regularly and convincingly that they were always ignored, partially because of their familiarity, but mostly because no one wanted to believe in this God in the first place.

God was unpopular with many people because he was extremely strict on questions of morality, and was insensitive enough to label everyone as "sinners," regardless of the fact that all people of delicate sensibilities find that term offensive. God was willing to forgive anyone's sins, but only if they asked for forgiveness, and were sincere. This wrangling nit-picking on God's part was best demonstrated by the perverse emphasis he placed on justice and truth, traits which he valued as highly as love and mercy. He had a very fussy and exact idea about what was "right" and "wrong," and was so hardheaded that he refused to alter his opinions, despite the fact that times change, and a sizable portion of the population would always disagree with him. To sum up, although this "God" had several followers, he was generally not well-liked, and many people claimed, perhaps with some justification, that his laws were so unaccommodating and his attitudes so unchanging that he really seemed almost inhuman.

At first glance the Queen looked on this religion with some favor; after all, her daughter liked it, and it was certainly more exciting than the other two. She even liked the stories of the Trollkiller destroying idols; the idea of smashing things in public places appealed to her greatly. However, there were two things about this religion that bothered her.

First, there was the question of "Trollkiller" Sven Svensson's current status; namely, whether he was alive or dead. Most educated people felt that he was certainly dead; he had disappeared rather suddenly, and was rumored to have been brutally killed. His followers, however, adamantly believed that he was still alive and would someday return. Old-timers would often tell you (if you were ever unlucky enough to get caught alone with one) that Trollkiller was not only alive but was watching Hoodahooda closely, and that, if ever anyone set up an idol again, he would come roaring back like a lightning bolt and would knock it to the ground that same day.

The more sophisticated citizens scoffed at these tales, and over the years "Trollkiller" Sven Svensson became the object of a considerable amount of wit and ridicule. Indeed, in order to be considered "witty" or "clever" one was required to mock poor Trollkiller nearly every day. Doctor Oldair, who was very witty and extremely sophisticated (he often wore glasses), let loose a veritable torrent of flippancies whenever the famed hero was mentioned, much to the delight of the King and his courtiers. Occasionally the good Doctor's jests would reach such a high level of hilarity that everyone within earshot would be rolling on the ground with laughter, and the Doctor, who had a singular aversion to humility, would usually compliment himself and join in the laughter most heartily. However, a shrewd observer of these wit sessions would have noted something about the Doctor's behavior that was quite perplexing. For some reason, after every couple of "Trollkiller" Sven Svensson jokes he would turn and look nervously behind him, as if he half-expected to see someone standing there, watching.

The Queen rightly felt that it was somewhat irresponsible of a religion to have a central character who was not definitely alive or definitely dead. This, however, was a minor offense she could easily pardon, but this religion had still another unpleasing factor which forced her to reject it entirely.

Everyone is a sinner. These four words (as I hinted earlier) played an important part in the Trollerist religion. However, try as she might, the Queen just couldn't apply this proposition to her own case. She thought about it and thought about it, but she still couldn't think of a single thing she had ever done wrong.

"This religion could never apply to me," she said, "because I'm basically a good person."

On this note of sober judgement she concluded her analysis of the three major religions and speedily came to a conclusion: they were all foolish and out of date. Therefore she would proceed with her plan to start up a religion of her own, with a trendy new idol, where she would be High Priestess, and there would be lots of sacred feasts, sacrifices, fireworks displays, demanding rules, elaborate ceremonies, and thousands of people daily grovelling at her feet. Pleased with this prospect, she fired off a letter to Prince Charming of Skindeepia, inviting him to marry her daughter at one o'clock next Sunday afternoon, and then marched boldly down to The Great Hall.

Her entrance into The Great Hall did not go unnoticed. She stomped into the vast chamber, drop-kicked a few unfortunate dogs that got in her way, and marched up to The Great Table. She pulled the King out of his soup just as he was going down for the third time and accosted him thus:

"Listen you," (she often called him "you") "we've got to change a few things around here! What we need is a new religion, with a great big new idol! Everyone's going to have one at their castle except us!"

"But . . . but darling," the King replied, "last time we had an idol some guy smashed it."

"That's why we need a new one!" the Queen bellowed.

"Whatever you say, sweetheart," said the King as he slid under the table. Two burly servants helped him back into his chair.

"For this question," the red-faced monarch orated after re-
suming his seat, "I will need the advice of our friend Doctor
Oldair, the greatest philosopher in the western world."

A servant was instantly dispatched to find the good Doctor.
Doctor Oldair did not live in the castle, but rather in a cottage
on a nearby plot of land called Bushey ("that's pronounced, 'bu-
shay'!" the Doctor would always indignantly say). However, the
servant was wise enough to know that the Doctor wouldn't be
at home at that hour of the afternoon, and so headed straight for
the castle garden. The castle garden, which Doctor Oldair and
everyone else referred to as "Doctor Oldair's garden," was the
pride and joy of the Doctor's heart, and sure enough the servant
found him in the middle of it, working feverishly in the dirt.
The servant informed the Doctor of the King's command, and a
few minutes later the immortal philosopher prepared to make
his entrance into The Great Hall.

Chapter V

A Brief Description and History of That Great, Great Man: Doctor Oldair; Followed by an Account of That Learned Man's Conversations with the Queen

Doctor Oldair, the King's Chief Counselor (and Princess Purella's tutor), was the greatest philosopher in the western world, but was only rated number six in the eastern world, which greatly embarrassed him, and caused him to perpetually rail against the injustices of the rating system. He was a Doctor of Metaphysico-diestmo-existentiology, a science of which he was one of the founders, and the chairman of their annual convention, where each year the members would unanimously decide that they should get paid more, and should add another syllable to their science's name.

The Doctor was a gentleman of about sixty-five years of age, with long, uncombed gray hair and a gray beard. His face was etched by deep lines, the result of many years of habitual sneering, and his smile was so crooked that his face always looked as if it were in imminent danger of sliding into his left ear. He always stood slightly bent over, as if he were peering over a cliff, and his body was so thin and bony he appeared to be little more than an animated skeleton. His legs were crooked, his eyes were crossed, and his walk looked like a cross between a stumble and a swagger.

As the Doctor will play an important part in this history, a brief description of his background and character might prove useful.

Doctor Oldair's real name was Francis Martin Windee. The Windee family had once been very rich, but by the time of the little philosopher's birth they had lost everything but their pride, which fortunately remained immense. Little Francis's mother, a beautiful, sensitive woman, died shortly after seeing him for the first time, and he was raised by his father. Although Mr. Windee was a Book Reviewer, and naturally of a sullen and insolent temperament, he did try to instill in his offspring many of the Windee family values. Little Francis soon learned to dislike rich people, despise poor people, and distrust everyone else.

Mr. Windee was particularly fearful that some fanatic might brainwash his son into believing a religion, and so continually told his son that all religions were false, stupid, and dangerous, that God does not exist, that we can only believe what we see with our eyes, and that children should not be taught religion, but when they come of age they should decide for themselves if they want to believe in a religion or not.

Thus, when young Francis turned eighteen, his father called him into his study and asked him, now that he was old enough to think for himself, what he thought of religion. Young Francis freely replied that all religions were false, stupid, and dangerous, that God does not exist, that we can only believe what we see with our eyes, and that children should not be taught religion, but when they come of age they should decide for themselves if they want to believe in a religion or not. Pride swelled in Mr. Windee's breast.

"This is the happy result of an open-minded and liberal education," he said, beaming, "a young man who can think for himself!"

Shortly after this touching scene Mr. Windee choked to death on a turkey bone, and was buried in an unmarked grave with three or four other paupers, which effectively denied the world any further benefit from his lofty philosophical speculations.

Young Francis was greatly affected by his father's death, and shortly thereafter decided to have his name changed. This was when he took the name of Oldair, which means "Ancient Breeze."

Young Oldair was determined to make his fortune in the world as a playwright. In pursuit of this goal he furiously wrote play after play, each of which was a Tragedy in every sense of the word. Commercial success was denied him until his production of *The Blooming Buds of Boobleton,* which was the first play in Hoodahooda ever to have women on the stage. Young Oldair designed the actress's costumes himself, but unfortunately the budget wasn't large enough to provide all the necessary material, so the costumes had to be substantially abbreviated. Surprisingly, the play was greatly admired by King Lars XIII, who hitherto had shown little interest in drama, and soon Oldair's star rose rapidly in the world.

Oldair soon went on to write an epic poem in twelve parts, a history of Hoodahooda in three parts (loaded with royal flattery), several thousand poems, a few novels, and, finally, several books of philosophy. Eventually he became primarily known as a philosopher, and was awarded a doctorate. Shortly after producing *The Blooming Buds of Boobleton II*, the smash-hit sequel to his former play, he was appointed Chief Counselor to the King, a position he had now held for twenty-five years.

As a person, Doctor Oldair was notable mostly for the contempt he showed for others, which was a clear sign of his intellectual superiority, and caused him to be hailed as a genius everywhere. Generally he was a man of great sobriety (except when he was drunk), but he did have one overriding obsession: gardening. No matter how lofty his philosophical speculations were, one only had to point out to him a nearby patch of broccoli and he'd be grovelling in the dirt in no time. For him it was an all-consuming passion; day and night, night and day, he slaved away in his garden, tending his leafy friends with the tenderness of a mother, and the intensity of a fanatic. However, because of the King's refusal to eat anything that didn't drip blood, his efforts to found a Royal Vegetarian Society failed.

When Doctor Oldair entered The Great Hall a hush descended on the room (after several profound burps, which were perhaps intended as tokens of respect). Looking very much like a large spider that had just been poked with a stick, the Doctor ambled up to The Great Table and bowed before the King and Queen.

"You called, Your Majesty?" said Doctor Oldair dutifully.

"What?"

"I said, 'You called?'"

"I called you what? Oh, you mean I called," the King continued. "Uh, yes, I have a most important subject to discuss with you, most important."

"Which is?"

"Huh?"

"What is the subject, Your Majesty?"

(Doctor Oldair always treated the King and Queen with such servility and respect that few would have guessed that he secretly held them in contempt, and was continually sending money and other assistance to the Republic of El Limo, a perfect republic strongly supported by his philosophical society, where everyone was equal, and kings, titles, and private property were abolished.)

One of the courtiers managed to whisper in the King's ear that the subject was religion.

"The subject is religion," the King announced triumphantly. "We want a new one."

All eyes turned to Doctor Oldair. He stared above everyone's heads for a few moments, figuratively demonstrating to them where his thoughts were in relation to theirs, and then, with a melodramatic turn of the head, he spoke.

"Religion. Ah, religion."

After uttering this profound effusion, he condescended to gaze at the other mortals in the room, chuckled to himself, and smiled knowingly. The King decided he should smile too, but he didn't have the slightest idea why.

"The Queen has some ideas about a new religion, and my courtiers and I want your advice."

The Queen leaned against The Great Table and waited intently for the Doctor's reply, while the courtiers, who had first heard of this troubling question only five minutes before, either slid under the table, or belched. To be honest, most of them didn't even know what a religion was, except for a vague notion that it had something to do with putting money into tin plates. Doctor Oldair coughed majestically, and then gave his response.

"Your Majesties, I hate to see you promoting any kind of religion. Don't you know that religion is the cause of all the unhappiness in the world? Don't you realize that millions of people die each year just because of religion? And last year I lost a whole row of begonias, and I'm convinced it was the work of religious fanatics!"

(The religious fanatic in question was a certain Floppy, who had used the beautiful row of flowers as a sort of bone repository.)

"These fanatics are everywhere," continued the roused academician, "creeping into our daily lives, trying to force on us their values, their 'truth'! But I tell you there is no such thing as truth! Nothing in life is black and white, and nothing is good or bad. Existence is all there is. Everything in life is relative, and believe me that's the absolute truth!"

This impassioned speech roused the audience to several sympathetic belches, and even a protracted snore, although perhaps no one really understood it.

"Why do we need another religion? Do you want to spread hatred and violence, ignorance and death? Do you want to be ruled over by black-robed hypocrites, who glare at you with the cold eye of fanaticism, brainwashing your children, and forcing you to do their slightest whim?"

These were very telling points, for it's a well-known fact that religious-minded people are strongly in favor of all these things, and that these are the only purposes of religion. The courtiers belched in approval.

"When I behold these fine gentlemen in front of me, products of a free and open education," he said, gesturing to the courtiers in front of him, one of whom was so moved he threw up, "I wonder how anyone could favor enslaving us again to the foolishness of religion. I know I am against it, and on this issue I cannot compromise! In conclusion I'd like to suggest that instead of adding a new religion, let's destroy the ones we already have. After all, religions are mere superstitions believed only by the ignorant."

"Ignorant?!!" said the furious Queen. "I'm building a new idol if I have to build it over your dead body!"

"Oh, an idol! That's *different!* Idols can be incredibly wonderful," said Doctor Oldair, whose philosophy at times could be remarkably flexible.

"I want a new idol," said the Queen, "and I want it now!!"

"Heck, I can go along with that!" said the Doctor enthusiastically. "In fact, I think I have something back at my cottage that might solve all our problems."

When properly stimulated, the Doctor, despite his advanced years, could prove remarkably agile. While the Queen picked up a rolling pin and restlessly fingered it, the Doctor raced out of The Great Hall, out of the castle, over the moat, and into his cottage at Bushey, touching his feet to the ground about three times along the way. He ran to his bedroom, reached into his trash pail, grabbed something, left his cottage, and then recrossed the moat, reentered the castle, and stood before the Queen once more, holding in his hands a long, greasy piece of parchment.

"Your Majesty," he said, between contorted breaths, "I saw ... I saw this advertisement posted on the castle doors just yesterday, and took it down and put it in my cottage, meaning to present it to you later. I think it's just what you're looking for."

The Queen was intrigued. She ordered her maid to take her rolling pin away, and then woke up the King.

"Read it to us," she commanded the Doctor.

After clearing his throat the appropriate number of times (five), and assuming an appropriately grave expression, the Doctor read the document, which went like this:

CHECK THIS OUT!!!
Tired of bowing down before the same old deities? Need a new idol, supreme being, or object of veneration? If the answer is yes, try ***MOLD-A-GOD***!!!

MOLD-A-GOD WORKS!!!
MOLD-A-GOD, the latest in scientific religion, works for YOU!! Why? Because at ***MOLD-A-GOD*** we follow no RULES or GUIDELINES; your religion is designed and implemented by YOU!! Anything goes!! Want human sacrifice? We'll help build the altar!! Need to justify all your faults, no matter what they are? NO PROBLEM!! (Read our free pamphlets, "Virtue—How To Steal it and Use It" and "Inquisitions— Good Old-Fashioned Fun, or Just Plain Overrated?") CONCERNED about idols? ANXIOUS to know the latest trends? CHECK US OUT!! We have it all: Teraphims, Seraphims, Ephods, Custom-made Gold or Rock idols, Multi-media idols, and even the traditional Golden Calf, all at low, low prices!!!

COME ON DOWN!!!

Come down to our showroom now, or visit any one of our convenient locations throughout the world; we're carving idols for you 24 hours a day!!! LISTEN to what satisfied customers have been saying about **MOLD-A-GOD** for years:

"Before I discovered **MOLD-A-GOD** my life was a mess. I drank, smoked, and beat my wife daily. Now, with a little help from **MOLD-A-GOD**, my life has completely changed. I no longer feel bad about myself, and my weekly devotionals have improved my self-image immensely. The only problem I've had was last week when, after drinking several bottles of spiritual fluid, I accidentally set my bed on fire while attempting to smoke my sacred pipe. Half my house burned down, but happily no one was hurt; the spiritual waters prevented me from feeling any pain, and my wife was fortunately staying in the hospital at the time."
Flexard Q. Guzzel
Federal Judge

"After trying **MOLD-A-GOD** I lost over 25 pounds in only 14 days!"
Gladys Biffle
Homemaker and Liar

"Exciting . . . dazzling . . . one of the year's best . . ."
Dodger Fleebert
Metaphysics Tonight

ACT NOW!!!

Any questions? Please send all correspondence to:
MOLD-A-GOD
c/o Count Zandar the Unfriendly
666 Dead Dog Drive
The Dark Castle, Land of Doom, 66666

"It's amazing how many words they can fit onto a piece of parchment nowadays," the King commented.

"It's perfect!" the Queen said joyfully.

"It sounds like a very reputable company," Doctor Oldair asserted.

"Doctor," the Queen announced, "you must write to this Count Zandar at once, and tell him we need his help with the fabulous new religion I'm planning."

"Your Majesty, I don't believe that will be necessary," Doctor Oldair replied, "I was informed by the man who posted this advertisement that the worthy Count is at this moment touring in Skindeepia, and could be brought here in only a couple of days."

"Splendid," said the Queen, clapping her hands with delight. "Now let me see . . . today is Wednesday. If we send for him today he'll be here by Saturday morning. He can make and set up our idol on Saturday, and the first ceremony of the new religion can be the Princess's wedding on Sunday afternoon."

"Which Princess's wedding?" the King asked.

"Why your daughter, you knucklehead!"

"Don't you think she's a little young?" the concerned father exclaimed. "I mean, she's not even twelve years old."

"She's eighteen and a half!"

"Eighteen and a half? Oh well, I guess she would be thinking about marriage then. It's sad though. When a girl gets to a certain age all she thinks about is herself; she completely forgets about her old father, and doesn't even care if he's alive or dead."

After making this melancholy reflection, the teary-eyed King attempted to console himself by imbibing vast quantities of liquid, and soon The Great Hall returned to its usual atmosphere of drinking, eating, belching, and barking. The Queen immediately sent a messenger to Skindeepia to find Count Zandar the Unfriendly, and then departed with several of her maids to make plans for the wedding. Doctor Oldair remained in The Great Hall, talking to the steward, the only other sober person in the room.

"I don't like this idol business," said the Doctor. "I don't think you should believe in anything. I think everyone who worships an idol is a fool."

Just then a young servant lad named Scruppins rushed into The Great Hall.

"Doctor!! Doctor!!" Scruppins cried.

"What is it?" Doctor Oldair replied, grabbing him by the collar.

"Oh Doctor, I saw a gopher in your garden!!"

"You're mad!!!" the Doctor screeched in horror, as he held the unfortunate lad up against a wall.

"I swear it's true!!!!"

"Can this be?!" the Doctor groaned dismally. He looked imploringly at the ceiling, as if he shortly expected it to give him a definitive answer.

"I think there's only one, Doctor! Maybe you can get it with the hoe!"

"Egads, you're right!' the Doctor exclaimed. "What are we waiting for?!"

Doctor Oldair and Scruppins ran out of The Great Hall, raced down several hallways, hopped out into the main courtyard, and then darted into the tool shed. After grabbing all the brutal and sadistic implements of modern gardening they could lay their hands on, the two warriors staggered into the garden. There, at the summit of a mound of dirt, sat the gopher, in all the haughty splendor of his arrogance and pride. His eyes glistened with defiance, and rhododendron juice trickled down his chin.

"Villain!" Doctor Oldair cried.

He was on the presumptuous rodent in an instant. The gopher, unable to return to the safety of his hole, scurried across the garden, searching for sanctuary. The Doctor chased him, shouting curses and threats of an astonishing variety. The gopher spotted a hole in the courtyard wall and made a dash for it. The Doctor raced to cut him off. The gopher leaped for the exit, while Doctor Oldair raised the hoe above his head. The hoe came down with a crash! But it was too late. The gopher had escaped.

With Scruppins's help the Doctor plugged up the hole in the wall, and then started breathing easier.

"You're safe! You're safe!" he said, running around to each and every plant. "If anything had happened to you I would have died!!!"

He fell to his knees and kissed the ground of his garden with tremendous passion. After indulging in this brief emotional outburst, he slowly rose to his feet and looked over at the astonished lad. The Doctor smiled broadly. He didn't even care that his face was covered with mud.

Chapter VI

Returns Us to a Pastoral Setting, Where We Deal With the
Lowest of the Low, and Then Shifts to an Urban Setting, Where
We Deal With the Highest of the High

E ver since he had met Princess Purella, Lathan had been
behaving strangely. Every day, shortly before noon, he
would start marching off in the direction of Bonkers
Wells, and then would stop after about twenty yards, sit under
a tree, and groan. This strange behavior continued until that
Friday.

On Friday, Lathan spent most of the early morning gathering firewood. He searched through the forest for dead trees,
gathered up pieces of wood, and carried them back to the little
cottage he shared with his grandmother. The cottage was deep
inside the Sweedle forest, at one end of a large, sunny meadow.
When Lathan scooped up his last load of wood he started trudg-
ing back to the cottage, followed at a distance by several of his

most loyal sheep. Lathan passed through the meadow, crossed the stream that flowed by the cottage, and dumped the wood on the pile. He then looked to the east and saw that the sun was rising steadily higher. His reaction to this sight was most unusual. He took a deep breath, gritted his teeth, slapped himself in the face several times, went down to the stream, bathed, washed his clothes, and even made attempts to adjust the alignment of his hair, much to the shock of his sheepish observers, who were quickly nauseated by his powerful lack of smell. Lathan, ignoring the looks of disgust on their faces, put on his clothes and hopped back to the cottage, whistling happily.

The cottage consisted of a single room, which served as a combination kitchen, bedroom, living room, dining room, and guest room. It contained a little wooden table, two chairs, a rusty iron stove (which took up approximately one-fourth of the space), two rickety beds with mattresses so firm they were slightly harder than solid ground, two cupboards filled with various objects, and a badly-painted picture of the King on the far wall. When Lathan entered, his grandmother was sitting by the stove, preparing breakfast.

"Well, Grandma," Lathan chimed without looking her in the eye, "I've got to go!"

Lathan turned and started to race out the door.

"Lathan, you haven't eaten your breakfast," she said in a kind but authoritative voice.

Lathan stopped short.

"But I'm not hungry."

He didn't turn back and look at her directly, because Lathan's grandmother was one of those grandmothers who by looking at your eyes could see directly into your soul, and could tell, with ninety-nine percent accuracy, what you had been thinking, what you were thinking, and what you were going to think.

"Why are you in such a hurry? Are you meeting someone?" she asked, as if she hadn't already guessed. His recent interest in cleanliness, and his sudden habit of sighing and walking around in a listless daze had given him away. She got an even bigger hint when he very off-handedly asked her, only about four or five times per day, whether she had ever seen Princess Purella, and what she thought of her.

"Of course not, Grandma. I just want to get the sheep up to the high pasture early. Besides, who could I possibly be meeting?" he added, with a very feigned laugh.

"All right, Lathan," his grandmother said with a smile, "you can hurry them up to the pasture if you want. But try to be back for supper, and make sure you walk her home."

"You mean, 'them' home," corrected Lathan.

"Good-bye," his grandmother replied.

Lathan bolted out the door, gathered together his little flock, and started marching off in the direction of the upper pastures.

Eventually he and his flock came to a trail crossing, and, after pointing the sheep in the direction of the upper pastures, Lathan bid his fuzzy friends farewell and set out in the direction of Bonkers Wells. He chuckled to himself, but felt a little guilty too; he hated to fool his grandmother. Imagine what the look on her face would be if she found out he wasn't going to the upper slopes at all, but was actually going to try and meet Princess Purella!

Bonkers Wells was a pair of wells located on the side of a hill near a lush grove of trees. There was a beautiful waterfall just below the wells, and one could get a good view of the surrounding countryside. The wells were named after a couple of heroes of Hoodahooda history, Horatio and Eustace Bonkers, two interior decorators who once defeated an attacking Skindeepian army by naming them one of the ten worst-dressed armies of the year, which completely broke their spirit, and caused them to retreat to their homes in embarrassment. The water in Bonkers Wells, like victory, tasted sweet.

Lathan arrived at the wells, looked around, and, after waiting very patiently for at least ten seconds, decided he had waited long enough, and that Purella had probably already been there and left, and that it would certainly be much better to go away and try again some other time. He turned and started away, but just then his ears were pierced with the sound of a lovely, familiar voice.

"Arf!"

Then Purella, who also had a fairly lovely voice, called out, "Oh Lathan, I'm so glad to see you again!"

Lathan turned and soon beheld the object of his every waking thought, the beautiful Princess Purella, accompanied by her faithful friend, the inimitable Floppy.

It was a beautiful day. The three of them talked, waded in the stream, looked at the waterfall, chased sticks (Purella did the throwing), and talked even more. In fact, if Lathan hadn't accidentally fallen into the well three times it might have been a perfect day. Of course, at first their conversations were a bit awkward, for when Purella would say something to him Lathan would often respond in some strange foreign dialect, which was notable for its frequent use of stuttering and hesitation, and only understandable to himself and perhaps the residents of ancient Babylon. Lathan also appeared fascinated by Purella's feet, and looked at them with such fixed attention throughout their conversations that Purella more than once wondered whether the robust shepherd lad was secretly an aspiring podiatrist. However, as the day progressed Lathan grew less and less interested in Purella's feet, and not only began enunciating grammatical sentences, but even shot a few glances at his fair companion's face.

Lathan was incredibly happy. The Princess was so nice! Lathan had known other girls before, mostly shepherd girls, but they had all treated him quite differently. Instead of talking with him, they would generally throw things at him, criticize his appearance, or else simply walk past him with their noses in the air, carrying with them a certain air of superiority, which often smelled remarkably similar to unwashed sheep. Purella was just the opposite; she was kind to Lathan, and by the end of the day Lathan decided he definitely loved her, and that he would never be happy unless he proved himself worthy to be her husband.

Lathan would have been shocked to know it, but Purella really liked him. Despite his stuttering shyness, she really enjoyed Lathan's conversation. He was *real*. The words he spoke seemed to come right from his heart, and were quite unlike the slickly rehearsed lines of a courtier. Lathan carried with him an aura of goodness, innocence, and sincerity, traits which are not often appreciated in the world, but which at times can be perversely appealing. Exactly how much did Purella like Lathan? Well, it would be unchivalrous of me to take a lady's deepest and most private emotions and splatter them across the printed page like yesterday's burglaries; however, if you could have seen the expression on her face when Lathan robustly climbed a tree to put back a fallen bird's nest, or when he cheerily taught Floppy how to "roll over," or when he bravely waded out into the deepest part of the creek, you might have suspected Purella of more than mere indifference (of course, you should have also seen the expression on her face when she had to dive into the creek and pull him out).

Soon it was time to go home. As Lathan bade farewell, he was suddenly struck with the brilliant idea of walking the Princess back to the castle.

After congratulating himself on coming up with this wonderfully original idea, he announced to her his intention of walking her home. Purella consented, and, accompanied by the faithful Floppy, the two of them started back toward Troddleheim.

They passed through the forest until they came to the high road, which they followed into Troddleheim. The cobblestone streets were filled with townspeople, some milling about aimlessly, and others scurrying home for dinner. As Purella walked past, each citizen doffed his cap and greeted her respectfully, and, as soon as she and Lathan were a short distance away, joined in a lively conversation which sounded something like this:

"Buz . . . buz . . . buz . . . beautiful Princess . . . buz . . . buz . . . can't believe she's with him . . . buz . . . buz . . . little twerp . . . buz . . . buz . . . smells like sheep . . . buz . . . buz . . . buz . . . robust though!"

When Purella came in sight of the castle, she stopped short. There, parked on the side of the moat next to the drawbridge, was a large row of carriages and supply wagons marked, "Property of Skindeepia." Lathan's eyes were not only focused on the wagons, but on the enormous castle behind them. As he stared at the castle's sturdy walls, lofty towers, solid mahogany drawbridge, and the long row of beautiful carriages in front of it, his heart sank. The Princess lived in a beautiful world, and he was just a dirty shepherd lad.

"I wonder what a Skindeepian ambassador is doing here," Purella pondered out loud, "They're never up to much good. Still, we might as well go in and find out."

"You mean, inside the castle?" Lathan stammered.

"Of course. You can meet my father. He's not like what some people say (he's really a good man.)"

"G-G-Great," said Lathan.

"Well then, let's go."

"No, wait," said the nervous Lathan. "I've really got to go."

"But it'll be fun."

"I'll talk to you later," said Lathan. "Good-bye!"

In a flash he was gone, leaving nothing but a skid mark in his wake. Just then Purella's two maids-in-waiting ran across the drawbridge and accosted her.

"Your highness," they cried, "your fiance has arrived!"

"Fiance? What fiance?"

"Prince Charming of Skindeepia!"

Purella was completely abashed. The Queen, in her zeal to make the upcoming wedding the most spectacular event in human memory, had neglected to inform the bride-to-be. When her maids-in-waiting related to Purella that her wedding would take place in two days, at one o'clock on Sunday afternoon, and would be the first official ceremony of the new religion, Purella was more than miffed. With Floppy and the maids-in-waiting at her heels, she marched over the drawbridge, through the castle gates, down the entrance passage, and into The Great Hall. There, seated at The Great Table next to her sleeping husband and his sleeping courtiers, sat the Queen in all her regal glory, eating a salad. Purella marched up to The Great Table, curtseyed, and spoke.

"Madam," said Purella, addressing the Queen, "I have informed you once, and I am informing you again, that I will never marry a man I do not love, and who is not a fervent admirer of the great hero, 'Trollkiller' Sven Svensson."

The Queen, after hurling an artichoke heart in Purella's general direction, gave a long red-faced oration which included such phrases as "never seen such ingratitude," "worked my fingers to the bone," and "I'm glad your father wasn't awake to hear this." She then commanded Purella to go upstairs to the Guest Room and fall in love with Prince Charming of Skindeepia with all possible dispatch.

Purella didn't bother to respond. She looked at her mother in icy silence, curtseyed, and then slowly turned and walked upstairs. When she reached the top of the stairs she did not turn toward the Guest Room, but instead walked down to her own room at the other end of the hall. Her maids watched her as she walked past them with great dignity, stepped inside her room, and locked the door.

Once inside, Purella crossed the room and sat down on her canopied bed. Soon her rigid posture slumped, and the defiance in her eyes gradually turned to tears. Yes, even princesses cry, and Purella spent the next hour with her face in her hands, weeping because she felt trapped like a prisoner, and there was no way of escape.

Then there was a knock at the door. Purella quickly rose upright and wiped the tears from her eyes. There was another knock. Purella regained her composure. She took a deep breath, got up, and then crossed the room and opened the door.

Reader, have you ever made a huge bowl of fruit salad, let it ferment out in the hot sun for a few days, and then walked outside and smelled it? Well, if you ever do, the smell you would encounter would be about half as nauseating as that experienced by Purella when she opened the door, for as the door swung open her senses were bombarded by a whirlwind of exotic fumes, which caused her to cough vigorously, while the room filled with a dense, semi-tropical mist. Through this aromatic fog Purella managed to discern Prince Charming of Skindeepia standing at the door, basking in the balmy glories of the latest fashion in perfumes. He wore velvet shoes (with bells on the toes), purple pants, a silk shirt, a gold lame' jacket, and a powdered wig. His physical appearance was perfect. He was tall, handsome, and had one of those faces that looks like it's been chiselled out of a tan-colored rock.

"May I come in?" asked the odorous Prince suavely.

"All (cough). . .(cough). . .right," gasped Purella.

The Prince, with a supremely confident look on his face, strutted slowly into the room, with the mincing strides of a peacock with an ego problem. He gave Purella a touching look of pity.

"Ah," said he, "such beauty. And yet so alone. So alone."

He sighed.

"Fair maiden," he said as he stepped closer to her, "you are a beauteous flower wasted in a desert of mediocrity, a diamond in the midst of greasy stones, unknown, unloved, and unappreciated! O, just to think of it drives me mad!"

He crumbled to his knees before her.

"O lovely Princess, your beauty is beyond all earthly description, beyond what eye can see, and what ear can hear, and what tongue can say! O, woe is me! For my heart beats for an angel, not a human being! I blush to make my love known to you Princess, for you are so far above me I know such love can never be! O Princess, what shall I do?! O, tell me, tell me, what shall I do?!"

"How about not spitting when you talk? It's a little disgusting."

"Oh yeah, uh, sorry. Well, anyway Princess, what can I do, I'm not worthy of you!"

"That's your problem."

"Huh?" said the Prince, as he sat up in bewilderment. By this time the girl was usually desperately in love with him. He pulled a piece of paper out of his pocket and started consulting it.

"I was right," he said to himself as he glanced at the sheet, which was crammed with information under two headings entitled "Set-ups" and "Clinchers," "At this point she's supposed to get an idiotic grin on her face and jump into my arms. What did I say wrong?"

"Are you finished?" asked Purella coldly.

"Uh, well, no," said the Prince as he shoved the paper back into his pocket and jumped to his feet. "What I meant to say was, 'Has anyone ever told you you're the most beautiful girl in all the world?'"

"Yes."

"Uh, all right, how about lately?"

"Would you please leave?"

"This isn't right," said the Prince, shaking his head. He pulled out his piece of paper again and started reading.

"Let's see . . . 'Ah such beauty. And yet so alone. So alone. Fair madman' . . . no wait, that's 'maiden' . . . Fair maiden, you're a flower'. . ."

Purella snatched the paper out of his hands and ripped it up.

"If you're going to woo me I think you could at least use your own words," Purella scoffed.

"Those are my own words, I swear," the Prince insisted, "You didn't let me finish. I . . . I was just going to tell you that you're wasted."

"I beg your pardon?"

"Uh, wasted. Yeah, that's right, wasted. I just wanted to tell you that you're wasted and . . . and . . ." (he dropped to his knees again for greater effect) ". . . and that you're kind of like a greasy diamond or something. Yeah, that's right, a greasy diamond."

"Please leave,"

"And uh, ear can't speak . . . and eye can't hear . . . and . . . and my tongue is beating like crazy because . . . because you're like really good looking and everything!"

Purella smiled sarcastically. Although the Prince looked perfect in every respect, it was clear to Purella that he did possess at least one major flaw, which was located somewhere between his right and left ears. Unfortunately, when the face is chiselled, the brain has often been chiselled as well.

Purella walked slowly over to her bedroom window and looked out. It was a pleasant, warm evening. Far below her, on the other side of the moat, she could see some servants talking and joking happily. Birds were flying joyously about, and out in the distance she could see the peaks of the Brakehedian hills rising up from the Sweedle forest.

"Let's not kid each other, Prince," she said with a sigh. "I know you're only pretending to love me."

"But that's not true!" answered the Prince as he crawled around the floor, desperately trying to glue together the piece of paper she had ripped.

"Please don't lie to me," Purella said softly, as she watched some children swimming in the moat. "You probably care more about my father's wealth than you do about me."

"Ridiculous!" the Prince replied.

"No, it's true. I think all I mean to you is more money in the Skindeepian treasury, and nothing else."

She turned abruptly around and was surprised to see the Prince standing next to her silver cabinet with a test tube in his hand, pouring some strange liquid over one of the silver teaspoons in an apparent effort to determine its silver content.

"Why that's the most outrageous thing I've ever heard," said the Prince, while zealously studying the surface of the spoon.

"Leave my room at once!" the outraged Princess demanded.

The Prince, after spilling the test tube all over himself and then dropping it to the floor with a crash, was completely abashed. He had never failed with a girl before. Since his sure-fire lines were now destroyed, he was, like some third-rate, alcoholic actor, reduced to ad-libbing.

"But seriously, you're . . . uh . . . well . . . beautiful! Your eyes! Your lips! Your hair! Why . . . you have all three, and I really like that in a girl."

"Get out!"

"O Hildegard, how can you speak that way to someone who loves you deeply."

"My name is Purella."

"O, please, let's not quibble over details! After all, a rose by any other name would still smell a lot."

"Out!" Purella said, while grabbing the reeking specimen of royalty by the shirt and attempting to shove him out of the room. She had almost gotten him through the door when the Prince finally remembered that he was the stronger of the two and roughly pushed her away.

"Oh, so you don't like me, eh?" said the remarkably astute Prince. "Well, that doesn't matter because you're going to be mine anyway! Mine! Mine! Mine! Mine! Mine!"

"I never want to see your face again, you . . . you block-head!" Purella intoned with a very unladylike hint of dislike.

"Blockhead?!" said the Prince.

"Yes! Blockhead!"

Blockheads, as a rule, have an extreme hatred of being iden-tified as such by their fellow human beings, and are invariably tempted to respond to such accusations with violence.

"So I'm a blockhead, am I?" said the Prince menacingly. "You're going to regret you said that."

His eyes narrowed, his fist clenched, and he glared at her with cold, wolf-like eyes, obviously thinking about something very intently; drool slobbered from his mouth.

"Don't come any closer," Purella said with defiance, but not fear.

She retreated to her bed, and slowly reached down toward the scissors she kept on her nightstand. The Prince smirked.

"I'm telling your mom!" he blurted suddenly and snottily. "You'll be mine soon enough! You'll see!"

He then strutted out the door and back toward the Guest Room.

Purella let out a sigh of relief, and sat down on her bed and shuddered.

A short time later Purella heard footsteps coming down the hallway. She tiptoed over to the door and peeked out. In the hallway were two burly guards. One, who had an unusually red face, was trying valiantly and somewhat unsuccessfully to stand at attention, while the other was obviously trying to figure out what the strange tropical smell was in the hallway.

"What's going on here?" Purella asked.

"We're sorry P-Princess, but . . . but . . . you . . . you . . . you . . ." said the red-faced guard, who unfortunately swayed so far to one side that he toppled to the ground before he could find a suitable verb.

"We're not supposed to let you out of your room until your wedding, Princess—sorry," said the other guard.

Just then Floppy came bounding down the hall. Purella let him in the door and then shut it behind him.

She held him by the paws and looked in his eyes.

"I'm going to leave here, Floppy," Purella said softly. "I could never marry a man like the Prince. I want to become a simple shepherd girl, and live the rest of my life in the forest, poor but honest, ignored yet happy. If you could help me escape this place I would be very grateful, and . . . well . . . I know this would be a step down for you, but I was wondering if you'd go with me. I think we would have fun together, and it would be so lonely without you."

At first Floppy frowned (obviously, few royal hounds appreciate being demoted to sheepdog), but when he looked into Purella's eyes, she was impossible to resist. At least he and Purella could still be together, and after all, one of his great-grandparents was a sheepdog (or was that a sheep? He could never remember which).

"Arf," he said in agreement.

"Oh, thank you, Floppy!" Purella blurted as she gave him another hug. "Someday I'll make this up to you. I really will."

Gold is a fine thing, and diamonds are reputed to have splendor, but perhaps no substance in nature shines as brightly as a loyal friend. When Purella knew that Floppy was willing to join her in exile, her tears dried, her spirits cheered, and she stopped thinking about the possibilities of failure, and could only think of the possibilities of success.

She crossed over to the window and looked out. Out in the distance she could see the edge of the Sweedle forest. As the sun set she could still see the distant, solitary hill that marked the sight of Bonkers Wells. She smiled warmly.

"You'll see, Floppy," she said, "everything's going to be all right."

Meanwhile, at Bonkers Wells, a certain robust shepherd lad of our acquaintance was sitting in the dark by the side of the stream, looking glum.

"What a coward," he said to himself.

He had been too scared to go inside the castle, and now the Princess probably hated his guts. Just think, only a few hours earlier he was happier than he had ever been, and now his life was completely ruined and he was probably better off dead. Such are the trials of youth.

Finally, after berating himself for being a stinking, pathetic, wretched coward, Lathan started condemning himself for even talking to the Princess in the first place, for she was the sweet, beautiful, gentle daughter of the king, and he was a dirty, smelly, and excessively stupid shepherd lad. On this cheery note he started to slink back toward home. However, as he walked along and thought some more his attitude began to change, and just before he entered his cottage he stopped short and made a decision.

"I can't be a coward all my life," he said to himself. "If the Princess hates me she hates me, and if she forgives me she forgives me, but whatever she does I'm not going to be a coward anymore."

Lathan didn't sleep much that night. He vowed that he would go to the castle and visit the Princess the very next day.

Chapter VII

A Storm Blows in Some New Acquaintances, Some Construction Begins, and The King Proves Himself to be a Stern Disciplinarian

*T*hat night a storm blew in. The wind howled, the rain dropped in sheets, and lightning flashed across the sky. Just before dawn a strong hand knocked violently on the castle gate.

"Coming," said the Porter as he jumped up from his straw sleeping mat. He lighted a candle, and, after mumbling something about "time and a half," walked over and opened the gate.

Before him stood three hooded figures. The leader of the three stepped slowly inside, while the other two waited out in the rain.

"I am," said the figure ominously, "Count Zandar the Unfriendly."

The Porter stammered out an apology for being so slow in opening the gate, and then turned and started lighting the torches in the entrance way.

The Count lowered his hood and gestured for his two companions to enter.

"I must see the King and Queen—now," Count Zandar coolly announced.

"But they're asleep," the Porter replied, "and I have orders never to disturb . . ."

"*Now,*" the Count repeated in the rather sinister tone that was peculiar to him.

The Porter didn't need to be told again. He raced upstairs, woke up the King and Queen, and informed them that Count Zandar the Unfriendly had arrived. The Queen was so excited by this news she didn't even bother to whip the Porter, who was cringing at her feet, and sweating in brick-sized drops. The Porter was instead sent to wake the Steward, who was the only person who could officially announce visitors. Soon both the Porter and the Steward were down in The Great Hall, where a few moments later they were joined by the King and Queen, who sat down at The Great Table and waited to formally greet the founder and President of Mold-A-God, the latest in scientific religion. A few courtiers were also there (many had been there all night, and some all week), and even a few of the dogs were on hand to greet this venerable visitor.

"Count Zandar the Unfriendly!" the King's Steward announced boldly.

The Count strode into the center of the hall, followed by his two companions.

"And friends!" the Steward hastily added, a little unsure of what to say.

The Count had black shoes, black pants, a black shirt, a dark black moustache, and bleached-blond hair, about which he was somewhat vain. He was six feet tall, had powerful muscles, and a pair of duelling scars on his face. He was an expert on all religions, although he himself served only one god, whose name was Moloch, and whose temple was conveniently located in the

Count's place of residence, the Dark Castle. This Moloch was particularly fond of sacrifice by fire, and the Count burned hundreds of men and beasts on its altar every year. The god especially craved beautiful young maidens, and every year, during the international SIN (Society of Idolators and Necromancers) convention, the Count would sacrifice the most beautiful, innocent girl he could find, followed by about a hundred other helpless maidens, in order to appease the fiery desires of the hungry god. In fact, Mold-A-God was really just a hobby for the Count —the thing he really cared about was finding beautiful, innocent maidens for the annual sacrifice, especially maidens of noble blood. Everything that was innocent, pure, and good, the Count felt it was his religious duty to crush, humiliate, and destroy. The Count looked at the smug, self-important expression on the face of the Queen, and the completely vacant expression on the face of the King, and grinned diabolically.

The Queen leaned over to the King.

"I have a good feeling about this," she whispered. "I think this is a man we can completely trust."

The King nodded in agreement, even though his perpetual drinking made the Count and everyone else in the room seem to him little more than a blur.

The Count bowed, and then formally introduced himself and his two companions, who he described as his assistants.

The first was a short, elderly lady named Kaklina. She was rather heavier than her height might deem advisable, and had a face covered with many blemishes remarkable both for their size and variety. She also exhibited a somewhat unmelodious voice, which gave the impression that she had spent some time as a saw swallower, or in some other such professional occupation. All in all, she was what a less delicate author might describe as an "old bag"—a type of person that diabolical Counts can often put to good use.

Count Zandar's second assistant was called Og. He was about eight feet four inches tall, and weighed about 450 pounds. He had little or no intelligence. He was often quite amiable, although he did have an inordinate fondness for sitting on people and crushing the life out of them. It gave him great personal satisfaction, but he did lose many potential friends that way.

"I understand you wish me to embark immediately on the construction of a sacred, graven image," the Count said to the Queen with a slight bow.

"Well, Count, what we'd really like is for you to make us an idol," the Queen replied in her best business-like tone.

"I see."

"What we're looking for in an idol is something very impressive-looking that asks for a lot of sacrifices, a lot of hard rules to follow, and other stuff like that," said the Queen, who got so excited she nearly jumped out of her seat. "The peasants need to follow stricter standards, especially some of these upstart servant girls! I think we should make everyone worship the new idol at least three times a day, or die a horrible death. That's reasonable, isn't it?"

"Very," the Count replied.

"You see, this religion is not for me, but for my subjects. Oh, I'm sure it will be a comfort to me in the long run, but actually I'm basically a good person already."

Several of the courtiers suddenly began to experience violent fits of choking, and the Queen gave them each a threatening stare.

"By the way," the Count interjected, "I was wondering what type of idol you'd prefer. After all, we are running a special on Golden Calves."

"But Count, this idol has to be huge, so that thousands of peasants can worship it at the same time."

"Well then perhaps you'd like something in a moose."

A golden moose, even if tastefully done, could not quite match the grandeur of the Queen's vision.

"Perhaps you should see where it—I mean, where Our Lord —will be displayed. That will give you an idea of just how big he has to be."

The Queen took a set of rusty keys and led the Count and his two assistants down several winding hallways toward the castle's abandoned north wing. Finally they came to a huge, wooden door. The Queen put one of her rusty keys into the lock and opened it.

They entered a vast chamber, filled with dust and cobwebs. It was even bigger than The Great Hall, and had a general smell of decay. The windows were boarded up, and though the sun had just risen, very little light shone through.

This chamber was called, appropriately enough, The Great Chamber (the builders of the castle, though creative with archi- tecture, were much less so with names). The Great Chamber had been the religious center of pagan Hoodahooda, and was once the house of the immortal Fungo, guardian of the universe. The Queen showed her three visitors the gigantic pedestal on which that awe-inspiring deity sat, and the ornate booths from where his learned priests gave their pronouncements of doom. She then described, with great enthusiasm and a considerable amount of graphic illustration, how a certain hoodlum named "Trollkiller" Sven Svensson once entered the temple and smashed to pieces the all-powerful god.

"Shocking," said the Count.

"So you see," the Queen continued, "we need the new idol to be in Fungo's old place by one o'clock tomorrow afternoon. That's when we're having my daughter's wedding. In a few hours I'll have workers come in and completely redecorate the cham- ber. Then, once the idol is put in place, we'll all be set."

"You're asking for awfully fast work," said the Count, "but I think 500 extra gold coins will speed us along nicely."

"Done," the Queen replied.

"I think an animal figure would be very effective," the Count suggested as he looked at the gigantic pedestal, "Perhaps a giant rat with eyes that follow you everywhere you go, or even an overdeveloped frog."

"Animals are best," croaked Kaklina in agreement.

"I was thinking that it would be more natural to worship something that looks like a human," the Queen replied, "Besides, we had an animal last time; the great Fungo was a gigantic bat."

The Queen then repeated her assertion that building another animal idol would be a grave error, and she balked at the mere suggestion of it.

"But at my price an animal would be a steal," the Count argued, appealing to her base desires. "I'm the one who's making the sacrifice."

The Queen refused to listen to this pitch, however, and proclaimed that the god would consist of a gigantic human face with a massive pair of shoulders. The Count eventually agreed to this proposal, and vowed that he and his assistants would begin work at once. Meanwhile some of the Queen's servants came in and managed to open up some huge, thirty-foot high side doors that led to the outside, and had been sealed shut for years. The Count and his assistants strode out one of these doors and went back toward their equipment wagon, while hundreds of meek, hastily recruited laborers entered the chamber and began preparing it for the arrival of the god, and the wedding of the Princess.

The Count and his companions had brought with them a large, covered equipment wagon labelled "Mold-A-God," which was parked next to the Skindeepian carriages in front of the castle. The three idol makers walked up to their wagon and stepped inside.

"See what we need, tell the workers what materials they should gather, and then come back and mix the potion," the Count ordered Kaklina.

"As you wish, Master," rasped Kaklina, who then examined her black cauldron, cackled maniacally, and hobbled outside. The hilarity that Kaklina derived from looking at her cauldron escaped even the Count, but he was used to the eccentricities of his subordinates, and didn't much regard them. For example, Og was currently trying to eat a hammer, and rather than reprimand him for such behavior, he chose to leave Og to his own entertainment and decided to get a bit of fresh morning air by walking around the moat.

The Count had walked partway around the castle when he looked up and beheld an unusual sight. Hanging out of an upper window was a long white rope which very much resembled several bedsheets tied together end to end. Harnessed at the end of the rope was a small, oddly colored dog who was slowly being lowered to the ground. There was a six-foot-wide strip of land between the castle wall and the moat, and when the dog reached the ground he wriggled out of the sheets, dove into a little bush, waited a few moments, and then gave the rope two firm tugs with his teeth. This was unusual enough, but imagine the astonishment on the Count's face when he saw a beautiful princess climb out of the window and start scurrying down the rope. He stared at her with hawk-like eyes.

"She'd make a lovely flaming sacrifice," he thought, among other things.

The Princess and the dog (who my more perceptive readers will identify as a certain Floppy) still had to cross the moat. The Count watched from behind a tree while Purella pulled out a long wooden plank hidden in some weeds and placed it across the moat. As soon as Purella and Floppy were safely across, and were about to run for the woods, the Count leaped out in front of them.

"Going somewhere?"

Purella shrunk back.

"My, you're a pretty one," said the Count, twirling his waxy moustache. "I hope we get to know each other much, much better."

Floppy began to growl. Purella glared warily at this ominous-looking stranger, and when he tried to put a black-gloved hand on her shoulder she slapped it away.

"Now that's not very nice, Princess. You *are* the Princess, aren't you?"

Purella answered him by looking at him with a face that showed unmistakable signs of extreme hatred. The Count smiled.

"Allow me to introduce myself. I am Count Zandar the Unfriendly, Founder and President of Mold-A-God, the latest in scientific religion. And now, as I realize you have an important wedding to attend tomorrow, allow me to escort you back into the castle."

The Count was a big, dangerous-looking man, and so Purella had little choice. Keeping a safe distance away from the Count, she marched back over the drawbridge and into the castle, followed by the Count, with Floppy at his heels (actually, attached to his heels, for Floppy was endeavoring to bite off the Count's leg in defense of his fair mistress, which unfortunately went unnoticed by the Count, but which gave Floppy a sore jaw for many days thereafter).

The Count brought Purella back to the Queen, who was back in her place at The Great Table. When the Queen heard that Purella had tried to escape the castle, she was enraged.

"Ungrateful little wretch!' she screeched. "Take her up to her room and double the guard!"

"But Mother . . ."

"I don't think locking you in your room is enough for you," bellowed the infuriated Queen. "What you need is to be beaten, and beaten soundly, and I think Count Zandar is the man for the job!"

"I'm happy to do as you wish, Your Majesty," said the Count with extreme politeness. "After all, I have written a book on the subject: *Beatings, Maulings, and Maimings: A Layman's Guide.*"

"Why, thank you, Count!" said the delighted Queen. "I'm glad to know there's at least one real man around here."

She punctuated this last statement by giving a disdainful look at the King, who was seated in his usual place at The Great Table, searching desperately for his beer mug, which happened to be directly in front of him.

"Let her sit and stew in her room until evening, Count," said the Queen, "and then you may go up and beat her any way you like."

"Mother, how could you!" stammered Purella as two burly guards prepared to drag her away. "If you want to punish me, you should at least have my father do it, not some stranger!"

Meanwhile the King had slid under the table, but at the word "father" he stumbled to his feet on the table's opposite side and staggered over toward the conversation, vaguely remembering that the term "father" somehow applied to him.

"What an interesting idea," the Queen remarked. "Perhaps the King should be the one to punish his own daughter."

"If you wish, Your Majesty," said the Count, "but I assure you that punishing your daughter would be a great honor for me."

Though his senses were generally crushed beneath an ocean of alcoholic beverages, the King heard this reference to his daughter, vaguely remembered that he had one, and, imagining that perhaps that he was being insulted, had the temerity to grab the Count by the shirt.

"Who are you?" he asked forcefully. The rest of his body wobbled, but his hands held the Count in a vise-like grip.

"Majesty, you're wrinkling my clothes," the Count said softly. The Count was a big man, so I don't think the slight tremor in his voice was caused by fear. No, it couldn't have been.

"Why it's the Count, you fool," blurted the Queen as she pulled the King away from him, "What's wrong with you?!"

The King reassumed his usual posture of confused humility. "I . . . I just thought . . ."

"That's your problem! You think too much! Now get back to your seat! Or better yet, maybe you should be the one to punish our daughter. It's about time you fulfilled some of your responsibilities. When it gets dark I want you to go up there and give her a good thrashing. And no drinking until then! For once I want you to do something right!"

The King, looking rather beaten himself, sat down on the floor and sighed. The Count looked at him with an amused sneer. Purella was led away to her room.

"Well, Your Majesty, I must go," the Count said to the Queen. "I have plenty of business elsewhere."

Just then Og bounded into the room, munching on some sort of iron chain.

"Duh, you want me to get the rock now, boss?" he asked.

"Right. We have a long day ahead of us. You must find a rock quarry, and take some of the workers with you."

"Duh, all right."

"Well Your Majesty," said the Count as Og blundered away, "I probably won't see you again until the unveiling early tomorrow morning."

"Tell me, Count, you're not going to use rock from around here for the idol, are you? The local rocks are awfully dirty, and not nearly as divine as I would want."

"Fear not, your majesty," Count Zandar replied, "My assistant Kaklina is an expert in magic potions, and we have

80

brought with us a barrel of Deluxe High-Tone Ultra-Black Obsidian, a Mold-A-God specialty. When the rocks are assembled in The Great Chamber, she will pour over them this secret brew, which will turn an awkwardly-shaped pile of rock into a smooth, golden idol, worthy to be worshipped by even the most beautiful of Queens."

"Oh, you're just saying that!" replied the giggling Queen, accurately enough, as the Count dutifully kissed her hand. The Count bowed again, grinned broadly, and then strode away to begin his work.

It was a busy day at the castle, with action and excitement everywhere, but it started out as a quiet, introspective day for Lathan, who spent all of the morning and part of the afternoon sitting at Bonkers Wells, trying to work up enough courage to go and visit Purella. After giving this subject a great deal of thought (and accidentally falling into the well a couple of times), Lathan finally gritted his teeth and marched off in the direction of the castle.

When he arrived in the cobblestone streets of Troddleheim, he saw several groups of people gathered together, excitedly discussing something. When he got close enough to hear what they were saying, he received a tremendous shock.

"I don't know, it just seems awfully sudden," he could hear someone say.

"But it's so romantic!" a cute little barmaid interjected. "Just think, a royal wedding! Tomorrow at one o'clock our very own Princess Purella will be the wife of Prince Charming, the handsomest man in the world!"

She sighed deeply and nearly crumbled to the ground in ecstasy.

"I'm excited about the wedding, but I'm even more excited about the new idol," said a beefy butcher. "It'll be great to see, and talk about fun to worship! It'll be shaped like a man, and'll have a 24-hour continually burning altar, and all the latest in idol technology!"

The townspeople oohed, aahed, and loudly expressed their approval. They especially lauded the fact that the idol would benefit from all the current developments in divinity; after all, no one likes to worship a god who doesn't follow the latest trends.

Lathan was completely devastated.

"This can't be," he gulped. "The Princess would have told me if she was getting married. And what about this new idol? I've got to find out what's going on!"

He raced through the town, sped over to the castle, darted across the drawbridge, and was promptly thrown into the moat by the two guards who stood at the castle gates.

"Get away, runt," one of them said. "No one's allowed to come in until our new idol is finished."

Lathan swam out of the dirty water and dejectedly sat down on the edge of the moat. Soon, however, he decided to look for another way to get inside. He noticed, however, that on this particular day the castle had guards stationed everywhere, and there was no way to get in without being seen, especially in the daylight.

As he desperately circled the castle a second time he spotted a line of men with pickaxes and huge baskets marching out of the castle's north wing and into the nearby woods. With the vague idea that somehow these men could help him get into the castle, he followed cautiously behind.

The men marched for about two miles until they came to a rocky-looking ridge. Here they spread out in a line, heaved their pickaxes, and started smashing out huge chunks of rock. Lathan scrambled up to one of the men and asked him what they were doing.

"Breakin' rock for the new idol," the man replied, giving the robust shepherd lad a contemptuous look. "What's it to you?"

"I . . . I was just wondering if I could give you guys some help."

"Get lost, squirt."

Lathan ran over to the next worker and asked him if he could help load the broken rocks into the baskets.

"That's a man's job, kid," came the sneering reply.

Lathan, despite being a bit discouraged by these rebuffs, ran over to two bald-headed workers who were toiling away at the far end of the line. He was about to ask if he could help them, when suddenly he recognized them as those two worthy horsemen, the Head Coachman and his assistant, who had both been temporarily demoted to common laborers in order to help with the construction of the idol. The Head Coachman was wearily pounding away at the rocks, while his assistant, in between a few ineffectual blows with his pick-axe, gave him lengthy advice on pick-axing technique, and bombarded him with amiable chatter.

"Excuse me, sirs," said Lathan, "do you remember me? I'm the robust shepherd lad who rescued the Princess's dog."

They certainly did recognize the courageous youth, and said they were glad to see him.

"Tell me, is the Princess really getting married?" Lathan asked.

"I guess so," the Head Coachman replied.

"Well then, is it all right if I help break rocks with you?"

"Why would you want to do that?" the Head Coachman asked.

"Well, I want to get into the castle and see the Princess, and it looks like workers are the only people they let in."

"We're not going back till after dark," the Head Coachman explained.

"I don't mind working the rest of the day—that is, if you'll let me."

"Why, certainly!" the Head Coachman's assistant replied, handing Lathan his heavy pick-axe. "I don't mind getting a little relief."

The assistant added that this would give him a better chance to observe the Head Coachman's pick-axing form, and to give him more detailed advice on how to improve his stroke. The Head Coachman sighed deeply, lifted his pick-axe, and resumed work, while Lathan shouldered his heavy tool and began slowly picking away at the massive rocks. By nightfall the two of them, inspired no doubt by the assistant's encouraging speeches, had filled ten large baskets with rock.

Meanwhile, back at the castle, it was time for the King to go upstairs and punish Purella. The King paced up and down The Great Hall. He hadn't taken a drink all afternoon, and was feeling rather peculiar. Not only could he remember his name and who he was, but he could remember what he was supposed to do as well, and that scared him. He looked out a castle window (one of the ones with the red drapes) and watched the sunset.

"Have you punished that girl yet?!" a familiar voice thundered.

"Well . . . no dear, I was just . . ."

"Then get up there and do it!" the Queen commanded.

The Queen handed him a big paddle, and then bustled off to The Great Chamber to observe the installation of the idol. After her departure, the King walked slowly up the stairs. When he got to the top of the stairs he turned left for the first time in about seven years. He couldn't remember which room was Purella's, but after a few moments of confusion he realized that her room must be the one that was guarded by two armed men. He wandered over to the door, had a sudden attack of nervousness, and then knocked sheepishly. Purella opened the door, and he walked awkwardly inside.

When Purella shut the door she turned and looked at him with tearful defiance, while the King looked at her as if he had just seen her for the first time. He was surprised at her appearance; a full-grown woman, a real person, was standing in front of him. Her innocent, yet proud and noble face reminded him of someone he once knew, and once admired, but he couldn't remember who.

"She's beautiful," he thought. He was embarrassed to have a big stick in his hand, and dropped it to the floor.

"You may punish me any way you like," said Purella, "but I promise you I'll never marry a man I don't love."

"You mean you . . . you don't want to get married?"

"Oh father," she said, throwing her arms around him, "Don't force me to marry a man I despise! Let me marry someone I love!"

The King was confused. As he looked around the room his head cleared for a moment, and he recognized the miniature bow-and-arrow set he had once given her for her birthday, and he noticed her bed, which many years ago he had carried up to this room and reassembled by himself. He had forgotten about that afternoon, but for some reason he could suddenly remember it quite clearly. He remembered his little daughter laughing and clapping her hands as he set up the bed, and what a happy day that was. Then his thoughts turned back to the bow-and-arrow set; it occurred to him that that was a strange present to give to a girl. He remembered that he had always wanted a son, but now he couldn't remember why. He felt dizzy and had to sit down.

"Father," Purella said as she knelt before him, "if you only knew all the things I've been through while you've been downstairs drinking with your courtiers. I've been ridiculed for my loyalty to 'Trollkiller' Sven Svensson, I've been bullied by my own mother into marrying a man I despise, and today a total stranger laid his hands on me, leered at me, and threatened me with violence, while no one except Floppy lifted a hand to help me."

"Who dared to lay his hands on you?" the King asked, stirred to indignation for the first time in many years.

"That slimy wretch Count Zandar the Unfriendly," Purella replied. "Don't you remember him saying he would be happy to punish me?"

Although it had happened just a few hours before, the King could only vaguely remember; still, he clenched his fists in anger, and cursed himself for his drinking.

"Why didn't you use on him some of those self-defense tricks I used to teach you?" the King asked.

"You haven't practiced those with me in a long, long time," Purella replied.

In fact, the King hadn't done anything for anyone in a long, long time, and, for the first time in many years, he felt ashamed.

A couple of hours later the Queen marched up to Purella's room to see how the beatings were coming.

"Well, has he been thrashing her like I told him?" she asked the guards.

"Listen," they replied.

She listened, and suddenly heard a tremendous succession of crashes.

"Please, no more!" the Queen could hear Purella say.

"Oh no!" the King roared, "we're going to keep this up all night if we have to!"

The Queen then heard the sound of Purella sighing, followed by the sound of a body being prolifically slammed to the floor. The Queen was actually alarmed at this, and even feeling a little guilty, but tried not to show it.

"Sounds good," she said awkwardly, turning to the guards. "I . . . I . . . I guess I'll go back downstairs."

So saying, the Queen hurried back downstairs, and the guards celebrated her departure by pulling two bottles of wine out of their clothes.

"To the Princess," one of them toasted as he raised the bottle to his lips. "May her skin soon grow back!"

Meanwhile, inside the room, the Princess's skin remained as lovely as ever, but her face was etched with concern.

"Please, haven't I had enough?" she asked the King.

That gentleman, who was currently trying to pull himself up off the floor, grunted vociferously, turned his face to her, and replied in the negative.

"You're not leaving this room, young lady, until you slam me into the floor at least a hundred more times. And remember, follow through! That last time I didn't even black out!"

"But I don't like to use these self-defense tricks on you! I think we . . ."

"No 'buts' young lady! Let's run through it again."

The King straightened himself up and staggered over to Purella, who then grabbed him by the wrists, kicked him in the knee, twisted his arm, and, with remarkable efficiency, slammed him face first into the cold, stone floor.

"Grbaggghaba," said the King, with his face partially embedded in the floor.

"What did you say father?"

"I said, 'Keep your wrists straight,'" mumbled the King as he slowly regained his feet. "Now let's try it one more time."

"Father," Purella said, "I . . . I want you to know that I appreciate your caring enough to teach me these things again."

"I should be thanking you," the King replied, with a lump in his throat (which might very well have been one of his teeth). "Each time I hit the floor my head clears a little, and I realize how much I've let you down these past ten years or so. I hope that someday you can forgive me."

"Father, there's nothing to forgive," said Purella, with her face flushed with emotion. "I've always loved you, and I always will."

Then, as the tears welled in her eyes, Purella crossed over to her father, grabbed him by the wrists, and flung him into the bookcase.

Chapter VIII

The New Idol is Unveiled in All Its Glory, But Then a Pink Shadow Descends on the Scene

Meanwhile, it was dark outside, and time for the workers to return to the castle with the rock they had collected. The Head Coachman woke his assistant from a well-earned rest (his voice had been getting hoarse), and the two coachmen and Lathan went over and asked some of the other workers why no one was heading back, even though it was already dark.

"We can't go back until the Count's assistant goes back," a couple of them said.

"Where's he?" the Head Coachman asked.

"Over there," one of them said, pointing.

"Is his pile in front of that small mountain, or behind it?" Lathan asked.

"That small mountain is his pile," the man replied.

"Duh, time to go!" a voice bellowed in the distance, and suddenly the small mountain rose a little higher into the air and began moving toward the castle. Without further ado the workers lined up and began carrying their baskets of rock back to The Great Chamber.

When the workers passed through the huge, recently reopened outside doors of The Great Chamber with their loads of rock, they did not see the musty cavern of several hours before, but rather an ornate, impressive temple, which had been cleaned and refurbished by hundreds of forced laborers from the village. Tapestries were hung, bronze was polished, torches were lit, offertory plates were enlarged, and the huge, empty pedestal at the far end of the chamber was clean and ready to be filled by the magnificent new deity. Lathan shuffled over to the pedestal, and, along with the other workers, dumped his rocks onto it. When all the rock had been placed on the pedestal, the pile reached up to the ceiling. The Queen was unimpressed.

"It doesn't look anything like a god!"

"Of course, this isn't the finished product," Count Zandar explained to the distressed Queen. "This is just the beginning. Now, using our magic Deluxe High-Tone Ultra-Black Obsidian, we shall shape it into an awe-inspiring god."

This part of the operation was a trade secret, and the Count ordered a gigantic screen to be placed around the idol while Kaklina mixed the potion. While the workers scrambled around, trying to set up the curtain, Doctor Oldair entered The Great Chamber, having decided to take a rare break from his gardening. He was introduced to Count Zandar, and then, as usual, began looking at everything and everyone with amused disdain.

"Imagine," he said to himself, "all this fuss over a simple idol."

Just then a messenger burst through the crowd carrying a large crate.

"Special delivery for Doctor Oldair!" he called out.

"Can it be?" the Doctor cried.

The Doctor raced over, tossed the messenger aside, and then ripped open the crate with his teeth and bare hands.

"It is! It is!" he cried rapturously. "The only seeds of Flaming Pink Chrysopata Scummatta of Phylum Fulvibrata left in the world!"

"Doctor Oldair! What are you babbling about?" the Queen asked sternly.

"Oh, Your Majesty," the Doctor replied, delirious with joy, "you know how long I've strived to make my garden the greatest in the world, and it is the greatest in the world, despite the malicious envy of religious fanatics everywhere! Still, there has always been one thing missing: I have never had a specimen of Flaming Pink Chrysopata Scummatta of Phylum Fulvibrata, one of the rarest plants in all the world. For years I've sent messengers everywhere to search for it, and now I've been sent a crate containing all the seeds of Flaming Pink Chrysopata Scummatta of Phylum Fulvibrata known to be in existence. The greatness of my garden is assured!"

Doctor Oldair did a little dance around the crate, and even made several attempts to jump up and click his heels.

"Doctor, control yourself," the Queen reprimanded. "Put those plants aside for now. A philosopher should have more self-control."

"I apologize, Your Majesty," said the Doctor. "The triumph of this moment is too much for me."

"I must congratulate you, Doctor Oldair," said Count Zandar. "Now you will not only be known as the greatest philosopher in the western world, but the greatest gardener as well."

"Oh well, thank you, thank you, thank you!" said Doctor Oldair, still in a state of mild euphoria. "Are you a gardener yourself, Count Zandar?"

"Not at all," said the Count, "But I do love to collect rarities. I would be proud to have a few of those rare seeds to keep in a jar in my collection."

"Well then," said Doctor Oldair, reaching quickly into his crate, "take these five seeds as a present from me. I'm so happy I feel like sharing my joy with everyone."

"Thank you," said Count Zandar as he put the seeds into his pocket. "I hope someday I can return the favor."

"Doctor Oldair! Stop bothering the Count, and put that ridiculous crate of seeds aside," said the Queen. "We have important business to do."

Doctor Oldair laughed inwardly; how could anyone think that a new religion was more important than Flaming Pink Chrysopata Scummatta of Phylum Fulvibrata?! Nevertheless he ordered one of the workers to carry the crate over to the other side of the chamber, and spent the rest of the night nervously pacing back and forth behind the Queen, fantasizing of the moment when he would place the precious seeds into the tender soil of his garden.

Kaklina was having trouble putting the potion together by herself, and she croaked that she needed a helper. Some wise-guy shepherd lad pushed Lathan in her direction, and soon Lathan was busy sorting out eyes of newts, tongues of frogs, and droppings of bats, and was continually smacked with a stick for his incompetence.

The work continued all night. Finally, shortly before dawn, the potion was completely mixed and ready to be applied to the idol. The application process took about an hour, and only the Count, Og, and Kaklina were allowed behind the curtain. Everyone else stood and waited in eager anticipation.

"Another brilliant job," the Count coolly said to Kaklina as he gazed up at the finished idol. "But this is nothing. I have my sights set on bigger things than the gold coins due us."

"Like what, master?" croaked Kaklina.

"The King's daughter, the one who's to be married tomorrow, is very beautiful, sweet, and innocent—she'll be perfect as the main sacrifice at the SIN convention."

Og and Kaklina grinned.

"When do we snatch her?" Kaklina asked.

"We bide our time for the moment," said the Count. "First we get our gold, then we carry off the Princess sometime before the wedding. I'll work out the details later."

The sun rose. Inside Purella's room, the sound of violent crashes ceased.

"I think you've finally got it," said the King as he stumbled to his feet. "Now, remember to practice those tricks regularly, and make sure you get enough to eat so that you'll keep your strength up. Why, you look so thin right now it almost makes me cry."

Then, with the sudden impulse of fatherly affection, he stepped over and threw his arms around the bed post.

"Excuse me, father, but I'm over here," said Purella delicately.

"Uh? Who? Oh," said the King. "I guess I'm still a little dizzy."

He staggered over to Purella and gave her a hug.

"I don't care what Gertrude says, I'm going downstairs to tell everyone that your wedding is off."

"Oh, thank you, father!" said Purella. "I was thinking of running away and becoming a shepherd girl, but now I can stay here and we can become best friends again, just like we used to be."

"Purella, for all that you've suffered because of me, I'm very sorry."

The King hugged her one more time, stumbled out the door, and went off in the direction of The Great Chamber.

Purella walked dreamily to her window and looked out. It was morning again, and now that she knew she had the love of her father the sun seemed to shine a little brighter than usual. She could hear the sound of children laughing and playing next to the moat, and when she looked down toward the castle entrance she was surprised to see a small, furry pony sprawled across the drawbridge, either too tired to move on, or anxious to see his reflection in the moat. Whatever the case, he was attached to a large wagon marked "Oddities," which was driven by a funny little man whom Purella recognized at once.

"Get that animal off the drawbridge!" the guards shouted, in reference to the somnambulistic pony.

"Hello!" the driver of the wagon loudly replied, "Jack Crackback's the name, wedding presents for royal weddings is my game! Potions, powders, lotions, chowders. . ."

There was a knock at Purella's door. It was one of her maids.

"You've been ordered to come down now," the maid said breathlessly. "They're about to unveil the idol!"

Purella, accompanied by her maid and the two guards, walked solemnly down toward The Great Chamber, which was bustling with excitement.

"The time has come!" the Count shouted as he gestured to the closed curtain. The crowd hushed.

"Lower the curtain!" he commanded.

Just then the King strode into the chamber.

"Stop everything!" he shouted. "The wedding is off, and I'm not paying for a new idol!"

"What?!!" the Queen bellowed.

"I'm the ruler of this country," said the King, "and from now on I'll be giving the orders!"

A major uproar ensued. Purella and her little retinue entered the chamber.

"What have you done to your father, you vixen?!" the Queen demanded.

Count Zandar knew how to bring the royal arguing to a stop.

"Lower the curtain!" he commanded once more.

The workmen obeyed. The curtain dropped to the ground, and the sixty-foot idol was exposed for all to see. An awed silence descended on the room. The stern-faced idol, a golden figure of a man's upper body, was the most magnificent thing anyone had ever seen. Its eyes sparkled with mystery, its curly silver hair shown with beauty, its body oozed with power, and its face demanded respect. The townspeople and everyone except Purella dropped to their knees before it (even Lathan, who tripped over a bucket of newt's eyes and fell to the ground). The Queen was in her glory.

"This is the kind of idol I've always dreamed of," she rhapsodized. "Look at those beautiful arms, that massive chest, those sparkling eyes, that silver hair, that pink beard, that . . ."

"Pink beard?" everyone asked.

There was definitely something wrong with the worthy deity, for even as the Queen spoke some gaily-covered whiskers were sprouting all over its face.

"They're flowers!" shouted a sharp-eyed youngster who stood at the base of the idol. "He has flowers growing out of his face!"

The townspeople started to laugh.

"What's the meaning of this?!!!" the Queen demanded of the bewildered Count, who for the first time in his life looked surprised.

Doctor Oldair chuckled. The idol looked ridiculous.

"A pink beard of flowers!" he chortled. "I've never heard of such a thing. They could have at least used brown flowers—those flowers are almost the same color as my . . ."

The Doctor paused. He ran over to his crate. He looked inside. He screamed.

"They're gone! The last specimens of Flaming Pink Chrysopata Scummatta of Phylum Fulvibrata are gone! But how could this be?!!"

Lathan, who was sitting rather conspicuously between the Doctor's crate and Kaklina's mixing pot, soon became the center of the Doctor's attention.

"You didn't take anything from my crate and put it into the mixing pot, did you?" the Doctor asked in a steady, measured tone.

"Well gosh," Lathan replied, "I'm really kinda confused. Let's see . . . she said the bat's eyes were in a crate, and so I saw that crate there and . . ."

The Doctor's learned hands were soon firmly grasped around Lathan's throat, and he began uttering epithets far too creative to fit comfortably into this work. Purella, who was stunned to see Lathan in The Great Chamber, ordered her two guards to pry Doctor Oldair away.

In the confusion, Purella took Lathan by the hand and quickly led him out of The Great Chamber. Lathan offered no resistance; one touch of Purella's hand quickly put him in a dreamy, trance-like condition.

She led him down a castle hallway, and then pulled him behind a big, potted plant where they couldn't be seen.

"What are you doing here, Lathan?" she asked breathlessly. "Anyone caught in the castle without permission is supposed to be killed!"

"I-I came to rescue you," he replied. "I heard about the wedding, and I figured you were being forced into it, so I pretended to be one of the workers so I could get inside and save you."

"Oh Lathan, you're very sweet," she said. (Here Lathan blushed and knocked over the potted plant.) "But you shouldn't have put yourself in such danger on my account."

"I don't mind," said Lathan, as he tried frantically to straighten the plant. "I did it because I luh . . . I luh . . ."

"Because you luh?"

"Because I love . . . adventure."

"Well, Lathan, since you're here, I might want to escape with you after all," said Purella. "My father is on my side, but my mother is so determined to see me married that I'm afraid I

96

might be forced into it anyway. If I can escape for a few days, it might give my father a chance to stop her."

"Then what are we waiting for?" said Lathan. "Let's go!"

"I have to do one more thing before we go," Purella replied. "I don't want that new idol in our castle another minute, and I intend to do something about it."

While Lathan remained hidden behind the potted plant, Purella returned to The Great Chamber in time to hear Count Zandar address the Queen.

"Your Majesty," he said, "the work is finished. Now it's time for us to receive payment, so we can return home."

"Finished!" the Queen bellowed. "My idol has a beard of pink flowers! My daughter's wedding will be ruined! You're not getting one farthing until that block of rock gets a shave!"

"Once the flowers have been mixed into the potion, no power in the universe can remove them from the idol," the Count coolly explained.

"No flowers or no money!" the Queen replied.

The Count glared at her ominously.

"Beware, lest you anger me," he said.

Suddenly Purella stepped forward to offer a solution to this impasse.

"There's no need to argue," she said. "There's a man just outside the castle gate who can clear the idol of those flowers in no time."

"I'm telling you, it can't be done," said the Count.

"Bring the man in!" the Queen ordered.

Purella left The Great Chamber, returned to Lathan, and hurried with him back through the castle toward the main gate. They arrived at the gate just in time to observe Mr. Jack Crackback being thrown bodily into the moat by the two guards, who instantaneously thereafter were deposited in that same body of water by the rear feet of the pony, who suddenly roused himself from his slumbers and applied the basic physics principles of force versus motion against them with remarkable efficiency.

When the three men came out of the water, Purella scolded the two guards and apologized to Jack for their rudeness.

"I hope you remember me," she continued, "I'm Princess Purella of Hoodahooda."

"Why I certainly do! Jack's my name, and wedding presents is my game! Potions, powders, lotions, chowders . . ."

"We remember," said Lathan.

"And I remember you too," Jack said, "Ernie, isn't it?"

"No sir, it's Lathan."

"Oh, that's right," Jack answered. "Ernie sure is a fine name though."

"We're in the middle of an emergency," Purella explained. "Our new idol was accidentally given a beard of pink flowers, and we were wondering if we could borrow some of your famous BAP water to remove it."

"Surely! It would be an honor," said Jack as he hopped over his once again sleeping pony and pulled the bottle of liquid from his wagon.

"Tell me, Mr. Crackback," said Purella, "I want to make sure of something before we go inside. Didn't you say that the BAP water would clean things off so well that only its true appearance would remain?"

"That's right," said Jack. "After you put this stuff on something you see it as it really is."

Purella smiled.

"Let's go," she said.

They left the pony snoring on the drawbridge, and the two guards trying to dry their clothes with a torch, and made their way through the castle toward The Great Chamber. When they arrived the townspeople were still tittering at the idol, Doctor Oldair was still weeping into an empty crate, the Queen and the Count were still arguing over the bill, and, most marvelous of all, the King was walking around in straight lines, much to the astonishment of his pie-eyed courtiers. When everyone saw that Purella's solution to the idol controversy was a little old man with a greasy cap and a dirty bottle of water, they were considerably disappointed. The Queen, who recognized Jack immediately, was outraged.

"This man can't work on our idol! He's an idiot!" she cried.

However, no one else seemed to think that was a sufficient reason to disqualify him.

"Give the old guy a chance!" a few townspeople cried.

"My flowers! My beautiful flowers!" the Doctor kept crying.

"I tell you those flowers can never be removed," the Count insisted.

But the will of the crowd prevailed. Soon Jack, with the bottle of BAP water in his hand, was attached to several sturdy ropes and hoisted up by pulley to the top of the idol. He firmly grasped onto the idol's silver haircut, and slowly prepared to pour the cleanser over its flower-afflicted face. When he pulled the cork out of the bottle a hush descended on the room. All eyes were fixed on Jack as he leaned over and poured some of the BAP water on the gaily-colored intruders.

"Look! The flowers are melting away!" the townspeople began to shout a few moments later.

Sure enough, the BAP water did its job; the flowers melted away, and the idol was clean-shaven once more.

"He's a genius!" the Queen exclaimed.

"Hooray!" said the crowd.

Lathan looked over to Purella, who kept her eyes firmly on the idol's face. From his precarious position on top of the idol's head Jack made an awkward bow. This happy scene was interrupted by a shout from a sharp-eyed onlooker.

"Look!" he said. "Something's wrong with its face!"

Alas, it was too true, for the BAP water, whose idea of its role as a cleansing agent was apparently quite liberal, began eating into the idol's face with all possible dispatch. The idol's nose was quickly transformed from aquiline to button, and its cheeks from full to sunken. Its mouth and lips wore rapidly away, until the idol appeared to be sticking out its tongue in a very undignified manner. In every place touched by the BAP water the idol began turning a very festive shade of green, and its bulky arms were worn down to mere toothpicks when touched by stray rivulets of the hearty water. In less than a minute the magnificent idol was turned into a sickly-looking rock. Most of the townspeople who were in awe of it before laughed at it now, while the rest merely shook their heads at such a pathetic sight.

"He dies! He dies! He dies!" said the Queen, with the pronoun apparently referring to the overly-efficient Mr. Crackback, who was still perched on top of the idol, and looking a bit perplexed.

"It's not his fault," Purella interjected. "The BAP water just shows thing as they really are, that's all."

"He dies, I tell you! Bring him down from there! Bring him down at once!"

Jack, perceiving that the Queen and a good portion of the population on the floor below him desired to do him harm, stuffed the BAP water bottle back into his pocket and hung on as tightly as he could to the idol's green, misshapen head.

"Grab the ropes and pull him down!" the Queen commanded.

Several eager youths grabbed the ropes by which he had been hoisted up and tried to pull him down.

"Pull, lads!!"

The young men heaved with all their might, but none of their efforts could pry Jack loose. Soon Jack's unwillingness to be pulled off the idol and plunge to a certain death had the crowd frustrated, and scores of onlookers joined the young men in trying to shake him off. Eventually the combined strength of hundreds of people pulling on the ropes left Jack barely hanging on to the part in the idol's hair, and the idol itself, though weighing many tons, began to sway back and forth like an old, creaking rocking chair.

"Pull harder!" the Queen commanded.

More eager townspeople streamed to the ropes. The idol was now swaying back and forth and from side to side like a gigantic top.

"Pull harder!!!" everyone yelled.

"Whooooooaaaaaahhhhhh!!!!" said Jack, not unemphatically.

Swaying, like all things in this life, must someday come to an end. Thus it was that the idol, after leaning forward at a 45-degree angle, suddenly gave every indication that it no longer intended to sway back to a reciprocal position. To put it less eloquently, they pulled the idol so far forward that it began to fall; the crowd scattered, Jack Crackback went flying through the air, and the celebrated new idol crashed face-first into the floor, hitting the exact same spot that the all-seeing Fungo had hit so many years before.

It was a chaotic scene. Dust filled the air, women were screaming and fainting, men were yelling and cursing, and everything that didn't belong to the latter two categories was in relatively poor shape as well. Jack had flown across the chamber and landed in the wedding cake, with a rope around his neck and the bottle of BAP water still unbroken in his pocket. Purella and Lathan hurried over and asked him if he was all right.

"Lotions, chowders, chosen, louders . . ."

"You're not bleeding, are you?" Purella asked.

"Don't worry, I've got plenty more where that came from," said Jack dizzily. "I'm just sorry I couldn't be of any help."

"I should apologize to you, Mr. Crackback," Purella replied. "Your BAP water worked just as I hoped it would."

"Well, that's wonderful, then!" said Jack happily as Lathan pulled him to his feet. "Why, I'll even make you a present of the rest of it. Don't worry, I've got more bottles of it back in the wagon."

When the dust finally settled The Great Chamber had been transformed from a magnificent temple into something resembling a coal mine. People with blackened faces wandered aimlessly about, dirt and rubble were strewn everywhere, and the only sounds that could be heard were groans, the loudest of which tumbled out of the mouth of the Queen.

"Ruined!" she groaned, "My beautiful religion! My beautiful wedding! Ruined! Ruined! Ruined!"

Meanwhile the Count ordered Og and Kaklina to pack up their equipment and haul it outside to the wagon. While they began carrying out his orders he coolly sauntered over to the distraught Queen, who was kicking the head of the fallen idol in a very energetic fashion.

"Our work is done," the Count announced calmly. "Pay us our fee and we'll leave you at once."

"What?!" the Queen shouted, turning fiercely toward him. "You build us an idol that has flowers in its beard, turns green, and then falls on its face, and you expect to be paid?!!"

"Don't toy with me," came the icy reply. "Pay me, or live to regret it."

"You'll not get one farthing from me!" the Queen bellowed.

The King, heady with sobriety, stepped boldly forward and told the Count to depart, never to return. In the ensuing tumult Purella and Lathan took the opportunity to slip out of The Great Chamber once more.

They snuck down a hallway and once more hid for a moment behind a potted plant.

"Here's our chance to escape, Lathan," said Purella. "We'll go upstairs, get Floppy out of the kennel, climb down the bedsheets that are hanging out of my window, and cross the moat. I'm really looking forward to being a shepherdess, at least for a while—it's terrible being a princess. Do you mind if I come and live in the forest with you?"

"Well . . . I . . . er . . . ah . . . uh," came the stout reply.

"Then what are we waiting for?!" she exclaimed.

Purella grabbed Lathan by the hand, and then went down the hallway, through the portrait gallery, and upstairs to get Floppy out of his private kennel.

Then, they raced to Purella's room. Once there, Purella set the bottle of BAP water on her bed and prepared to climb down the sheets, but then remembered that the plank she had used to cross the moat was now on the opposite shore.

"We'll have to swim across," said Purella. "That is, unless we can think of some way to get past the guards at the main gate."

A few moments later the two guards at the main gate heard a voice shout "Free beer in The Great Chamber!"

This announcement not only caused the speedy departure of the two guards, but also caused Jack Crackback's pony to rouse himself from his slumbers on the drawbridge and attempt to take himself and the "Oddities" wagon right into the castle after them. Fortunately, at that moment Mr. Crackback himself stumbled out of the main gate, and it took all of his great eloquence to convince the pony that the free beer was just a pious fraud, upon which revelation the pony collapsed into a heap once more, and gave every indication that he did not intend to move again in this lifetime. Although Purella and Lathan had no time to lose, because everyone would soon notice that Purella was missing, they didn't leave until Jack had coaxed the pony back to its feet.

"Take the Northeastern highway, Mr. Crackback," said Purella. "No one will follow you there. We have to go now, but I just want to thank you for your help. God bless you, and I hope we'll all meet again someday."

"God bless you, Princess," Jack replied.

He climbed up to his lofty perch on the "Oddities" wagon.

"Oh, and you too, Dave," he called out to Lathan.

Taking this as a cue to depart, Purella clasped Lathan by the hand once more, and, with Floppy at their heels, they ran off in the direction of the woods, trying to avoid the streets of Troddleheim as much as possible.

As they ran Purella's mind was filled with thoughts of the new life she was going to lead. No more would she be "The Princess;" she was going to be a real person, who would live and be loved for herself, and not for the title she bore. She felt the sweaty hand of the robust shepherd lads in hers, and realized that his was the world in which she wanted to live, where people were flesh and blood, not painted butterflies, and where feelings mattered more than gold. As she ran and thought these thoughts her whole body was flushed with excitement, and she looked more beautiful than ever before.

Lathan's head was a little flushed too—in fact, he felt it spinning vigorously. He couldn't believe he was actually holding the sacred hand of the Princess, and was running too fast to effectively pinch himself to see if he was awake. He kept thinking about how he was going to explain all this to his grandmother. Poor Lathan. It's easy to like a princess, but very complicated to have one like you in return.

Meanwhile, back in The Great Chamber, the Queen remained obstinate. She refused to pay for a deformed and smashed idol.

"Let me assure you, you will pay," the Count warned ominously.

"Get out!" the Queen demanded.

Count Zandar took another look around the once magnificent chamber, and watched the sheepish townspeople, with dust and grime on their clothes and faces, file meekly outside. As he surveyed them, Og bounded through the door and told him that the wagon was ready. The Count turned to the Queen for the last time.

"You will pay," he said. He turned, and with Og at his heels, walked coolly outside.

The Count strode toward his wagon, walking along the edge of the moat. It was a clear, beautiful day, which made the Count uneasy. He looked up at the hills on the other side of Troddleheim. The Count had excellent vision, and way off in the distance he could see two people running across the side of a barren hill, followed by a tiny dog. He stared at these figures until they moved out of sight. He turned and looked back at the castle. His eyes fixed first on Purella's room, and then moved down to the moat. The plank Purella had used to cross the moat during her escape attempt still lay along the shore. The Count sauntered over to it and casually kicked it into the water. He smiled.

"You will pay," he said aloud.

Chapter IX

A Tragic Occurrence, and a Startling Revelation

Nothing could surprise Lathan's grandmother. When Lathan arrived with Purella and Floppy, and somewhat incoherently explained the situation to her, she was not discomposed in the least, and actually behaved as if their appearance was not at all out of the ordinary, and that she generally conversed with two or three princesses per day. Although they didn't belong to the same congregation, their Trollerism gave them much in common, and soon Lathan's grandmother was chatting away amiably with the Princess, feeding Floppy some choice biscuits, and sending Lathan to go collect firewood. After that, Lathan's grandmother set up a new bed for the Princess, and very kindly offered Floppy Lathan's bed, which forced Lathan to spend the night in a ditch with some of his sheep. Still, Lathan was in ecstasy. Now he could see Purella every day, and he looked forward to teaching her the honest yet subtle art of shepherding.

The next morning Lathan hopped out of his ditch, washed his face in the stream, wiped it on a sheep, and walked nervously into the cottage, where Purella was helping his grandmother cook breakfast.

When Lathan entered, he saw that Purella was no longer in her royal dress, but rather in a dress of Lathan's mother when she was a girl. His eyes opened wide as he saw Purella standing before him, with her hair dishevelled and her face flushed, daintily placing the bacon on the stove, and laughing with girlish laughter.

The effect this cruel display of blooming femininity had on Lathan was extremely severe, for it not only caused his head to turn light and lose all faculties of reason, but it almost certainly contributed to his banging his head against a cupboard, his placing his hand on the red-hot stove, and his sitting on Floppy three separate times. The proximity of the beautiful Princess gave Lathan a sensation far worse, however. Sadly, it gave him an even clearer sense of his own inferiority.

That morning, as he attempted to teach Purella the fine art of shepherding, this feeling became more and more acute. He carried his shepherd's staff clumsily, while she held hers gracefully. While he slipped and fell twice crossing the same stream, she crossed it nimbly in one skillful leap. All the tricks and subtleties of sheep control, which had taken Lathan many backbreaking years to learn, Purella picked up in fifteen minutes of light practice. All this, coupled with the fact that Purella was the loveliest creature on earth, while he was, at best, markedly below average, had Lathan depressed. He asked Purella to take the sheep a little farther into the forest while he sat down on a stump to rest. As soon as she was out of sight he felt like crying, and almost did.

Lathan remained at the stump until mid-afternoon, thinking depressing thoughts, when he finally pulled himself to his feet and dejectedly followed the trail of the sheep. Soon he found them, grazing at one end of a little meadow. Lathan saw Floppy curled up against a tree, fast asleep, while Purella stood with her back to him, watching the sheep, her soft blond hair blowing gently in the cool breeze. Lathan walked up behind her, and blurted out that he didn't deserve to be near her anymore, because he was beneath her.

"Oh, Lathan, how can I convince you that you're not beneath me?"

"Well, maybe if you took your foot off my throat . . ." Lathan gasped as he lay sprawled in the dirt.

"Oh, sorry, Lathan. You shouldn't have come up behind me like that. My father had me practice those self-defense tricks so much I used them without thinking."

"That's all right," said Lathan as he stumbled to his feet, "but I wish you hadn't kicked me in the ribs when I was down. That was really unfair."

"Getting back to the subject," said Purella, "I want you to know that you're not beneath me, not at all. I like you, and I admire you very much."

"Princess," said Lathan, "you've been very sweet to me, and I want you to know that I . . . I really like you. And even though I'm just a poor shepherd lad, no matter what happens I'll always be your friend."

"Lathan," Purella replied, "I feel I'm very lucky to have a friend like you."

And then Lathan and Purella talked. They talked about what their lives had been like, and what they felt, and asked each other questions, and, even though no more than an hour passed by, they really got to know each other well. And the more they learned about each other, the more they liked each other.

Unfortunately they were not alone.

About thirty yards away, hidden behind a blighted oak tree and a patch of poisonous berries, stood the menacing figures of Count Zandar the Unfriendly and his gigantic assistant, Og.

Behind them the Count's horse and Og's horses (he always rode two tied together) grazed contentedly on some deadly mushrooms and a nest of spiders, which was their usual diet at The Dark Castle, and which they had sorely missed during their travels abroad.

The Count gazed fixedly at Purella, smacked his lips, and began thinking of lust, violence, and other related topics.

"The time has come," the Count whispered, "The King and Queen will regret not giving us our money, when we take something they should value more: their only heir."

Og grinned stupidly.

"This is better than selling a hundred idols," the Count continued. "A sweet innocent princess to be the featured attraction at this year's sacrifice to Moloch."

He turned to Og and smiled.

"Let's grab her," he said.

"Duh, all right," said Og.

The two brutes then leaped out onto the trail and confronted Lathan and the unfortunate Princess.

O Villainy, hast thou no ending?!!! O Violence, canst thou never be conquered?!!! O Lust, canst thou never be quenched?!!! These are all very pertinent questions, and, if I might add, very eloquently phrased, but since none of these abstract concepts is liable to step forward and answer them (that's the way abstract concepts are), I will refrain from further philosophical discourse and will faithfully report what Count Zandar said to Purella when he grabbed her by the shoulders and stared into her startled eyes.

"You're pretty. I can tell I'll enjoy your company immensely," he added with a diabolic leer.

Lathan, who was badly startled by the sudden appearance of the two men, quickly leaped to the rescue.

"Unhand her!" he cried as he jumped on Count Zandar. The Count picked him up with one hand and slammed him into the ground.

"Get lost," he said with a sneer.

Lathan jumped back up, the Count threw him back down, and the process was repeated several times before Lathan finally dropped unconscious.

"Lathan! Lathan, speak to me!" Purella cried.

There was no answer.

"So much for your boyfriend," said the Count, chuckling.

The words had hardly escaped his lips before Count Zandar found himself flat on his back, being pummeled unmercifully by the fair Purella, who started applying her father's self-defense techniques with tremendous effect. In fact, the Count found himself being kicked in the head so prolifically that he became quite red in the face; whether from embarrassment or internal bleeding is difficult to determine. Purella also gave several well-aimed blows to a certain portion of the anatomy generally considered off-limits to more polite brawlers, and the Count would have protested this breach of decorum most vigorously, if he had not been bent over double at the time, with his face in the dirt, and throwing up prodigiously. Purella was winning an unconditional victory until Og snuck up behind her and hit her over the back of the head with one of Lathan's sheep. The sheep ran off unhurt, but the beautiful Purella was knocked unconscious.

"Can I crush the life out of this guy?" Og pleaded to the Count, pointing at Lathan, "Can I, can I, can I?!!!"

"We don't have time," the Count said as he staggered to his feet. "Go get the horses."

Og went back to the blighted oak tree and retrieved the horses. As he was returning he felt a leaf stuck in his shoe, and reached down to brush it away. Much to his amazement, the leaf in question felt as if it were covered with fur. He held the leaf up to his face for closer inspection and soon realized that he was holding not a leaf, but a certain apprentice sheepdog named Floppy. Floppy had risen from his sleep a few moments earlier, had quickly and ferociously fastened himself onto Og's ankle, and had remained unnoticed ever since. Og quickly tied the feisty pup to a nearby tree, and then tied the forlorn Princess onto the back of his villainous master's saddle. This done, the two fiends mounted their horses and were preparing to ride away when Lathan regained consciousness and stumbled to his feet.

"Stop, villains!!!" he yelled as he ran up to the Count's horse.

The Count dismounted. Lathan darted past him and was trying to pull Purella off the horse when the Count grabbed him by the scruff of the neck and, holding him out in front of him, lifted him off the ground.

"Listen, twerp," said the Count, "I don't know why the Princess even speaks to a little rat like you, but if you ever come near her again I'll reach down your throat and pull your guts out."

The Count then proceeded to throw Lathan some several feet into the air, and, after performing a couple of awkward midair somersaults, Lathan plunged into the ground head first.

"Ha, ha, ha," said the Count.

The Count strode over to Lathan and once again picked him up by the scruff of the neck.

"Now remember, boy," the Count said to the half-conscious Lathan, "I know you're not going to be stupid enough to follow us, but I also want you to never tell that you saw us kidnap the Princess. Understand?"

"Yes," Lathan gasped.

"Yes, what?!" the Count bellowed.

"Yes, sir!" Lathan cried, with tears running down his cheeks.

"You're a miserable little coward, aren't you?" said the Count.

He picked Lathan up and threw him to the ground one last time.

"Duh huh, duh huh, duh huh," said Og.

"And don't worry about your pretty little Princess," said the Count. "She'll add a touch of femininity to my castle, and we won't harm her a bit—that is, until we burn her alive."

"Duh huh, duh huh, duh huh," said Og.

"Let's go!" the Count shouted, and with Purella strapped safely to his horse, he and Og began riding back to where they had hidden their wagon, so they could immediately start their long journey back to the Dark Castle.

Lathan lay sprawled in the dirt. He was conscious, but he didn't feel like moving. His sheep slowly gathered around him in a little circle and silently watched, with perhaps even a few tears running down their woolly faces. Even the birds stopped singing at this melancholy sight, and the wood became so silent you could hear a pin drop. Finally a little lamb, the littlest lamb in the flock, walked bravely up to Lathan and licked him in the face. With this encouragement Lathan slowly lifted his face out of the dust and rose to his feet. His face was red from crying. He looked at his little friends and sighed.

Meanwhile, a helpful sheep had chewed through the ropes that bound Floppy to the tree, and the stout pup immediately raced off in the direction of the two villains, hoping they were still somewhere in sight. He scampered through the woods for a while, searching very doggedly (as one might easily suppose), but nowhere could he find a trace of the ruffians who had kidnapped his beloved Purella. Realizing he couldn't find Purella on his own, he raced back toward Lathan, and, shortly after the robust shepherd lad had risen to his feet, bounded in front of him.

"Arf, arf," said Floppy with his usual conciseness, neatly summarizing the entire situation in two words.

"You mean that the Princess is long gone by now, and you and I are the only ones that can save her?"

"Arf, arf," said Floppy, affirming the fact and commending Lathan for his remarkable perceptivity.

"But I can't save the Princess," Lathan sobbed. "The Count was right. I'm just a stupid, peasant coward. What could a piece of trash like me and a little dog like you do against a man like the Count?"

"Arf, arf, arf, arf," the loquacious pup replied, listing several favorable options.

"I can't," Lathan moaned, "I can't."

"Arf!" said Floppy sternly.

Nevertheless Lathan stood there with his face in his hands, sobbing like a child. Floppy gave him a last, pitying look, and then turned and ran madly after Purella.

When Lathan saw that Floppy was gone, he picked up his shepherd's staff and started to limp toward home. On his way he stopped for a drink at a little lake. He stared at his reflection in the water, and he felt he was the ugliest thing he had ever seen.

"Why did I ever think that a Princess could love me?" he thought. "And now because of me she's been kidnapped, and there's nothing I can do. I'm just too ugly, too weak, and too stupid."

With this thought in mind he crossed over a little hill and came to the meadow where his cottage lay. He trudged up to it, set down his shepherd's staff, and stepped inside.

His grandmother was sitting on her stool next to the giant cooking pot. She was sewing something, and was reading a faded book of the sayings of "Trollkiller" Sven Svensson. Lathan walked slowly into the room and sat in the chair opposite his grandmother. He buried his head in his hands.

"What's the matter, Lathan?" his grandmother asked. "Where's the Princess?"

Lathan haltingly told her the whole story from beginning to end. When he was finished he put his head back in his hands, but his grandmother was charged with excitement.

"Well, don't just sit there, boy! You've got to go rescue the Princess! It's your duty to save her!"

"I can't!" Lathan whined.

"What do you mean, you can't?" his grandmother asked.

"Don't you see, Grandma? Look at me. I'm a weak, spineless, ugly nobody."

"You're very robust."

"But that's *all* I am, Grandma. Other than that I'm just a cowardly piece of trash."

"Well, I never thought I'd see the day when my own grandson would say something like that."

Lathan didn't answer. He just sat there, staring at the floor. His grandmother didn't speak again for a long time.

"Lathan," she said finally, in a soft tone of voice, "I'm gonna tell you something I've put off telling you for many, many years. I wasn't gonna tell you until you became a full-grown man, but now I think that the time has come."

Lathan watched her as she reached back to the little obscure shelf above the stove and pulled out a rusty tin box. She opened up the box and with a melodramatic flourish pulled out a rusty little chain. Hooked onto the chain was an old gold coin. His grandmother put the box away, leaned over, and put the chain around Lathan's neck.

"What is it?" Lathan asked, fingering the coin.

"It's the very first gold coin ever minted in this realm, and because of that it's very special to me," she answered. "It belonged to your father."

"But how did my father ever get a coin like this! You told me he was just a poor honest shepherd!"

Lathan studied the coin closely. It was badly worn, but it looked like the coin pictured an old man with an extremely bushy beard. Above the picture was a long inscription. The first two letters were "T" and "r", and the last two letters were "o" and "n", but all the letters in between were too faded to distinguish.

"Your father wasn't a poor shepherd," his grandmother excitedly explained. "Why, your father was none other than 'Trollkiller' Sven Svensson!"

"But that can't be!" Lathan gasped.

"I'm afraid it's true," his grandmother replied. "The blood of 'Trollkiller' Sven Svensson flows through your veins."

115

"But 'Trollkiller' Sven Svensson was a famous hero! I can't be his son! Look at me! I'm short, I have a high voice, I'm a slow runner, I'm really quite weak (albeit robust), and I'm very stupid, and extremely ugly!"

"None of that means a thing," his grandmother scoffed. "What do you think 'Trollkiller' looked like? Why, old 'Trollkiller' was even shorter than you are!"

"Really?!!"

"Sure. And he had kind of a high voice, just like you, and most of the children in the village could run as fast as he could. But I'll tell you one thing; even though there were many men bigger, faster, and stronger, there was no one on earth that he couldn't beat. He could be attacked by a hundred vicious assassins and still find some way to win out in the end. A captured princess could be guarded by ten thousand dragons, yet old 'Trollkiller' would always find a way to get her home."

"But how, Grandma?!" said Lathan, whose mind had been driven into a state of feverish confusion by these sudden revelations. "How could he have been such a great hero if he wasn't big, or fast, or strong?"

"Because he was a good man, and he knew that if he dug deep down inside himself, and put his trust in his God, he could find the strength to win out at anything. Trusting in God is the first and most important step, because without God's help, nothing is possible. And whenever 'Trollkiller' felt very low, and sometimes he did, like all men, he would just grasp that coin, and feel how worn it was, and it would remind him that everything in life decays and fades away except for the power and love of God, and the instant he grasped it he would come aglow with energy, and his confidence would return. He would be filled with courage, would trust in his God, and would remember that he was 'Trollkiller' Sven Svensson, and nothing was impossible if only he trusted God with his whole heart."

Lathan was too excited to reply. He stood up, clasped the coin tightly in his hand, and felt a surge of power roar through his body.

"You're right, Grandma! The blood of 'Trollkiller' Sven Svensson does flow through my veins!" he shouted. "I'll show that lousy Count who he's dealing with! I'm gonna rescue the Princess!!!"

"Wait a little, Lathan," said his grandmother, trying to calm him. "You just can't rush off toward the Dark Castle and rescue the Princess. You have to have a plan first."

Lathan admitted this hero business was still kind of new to him.

"That's no excuse for reckless behavior," his grandmother scolded. "First you have to know where you're going."

His grandmother reached to the back of another shelf and pulled out a folded, dusty piece of paper. She carefully unfolded it and spread it out on the little table. It was a map.

"Here's Troddleheim, Lathan," she said, pointing to a tiny dot on the bottom left corner of the map. "The Dark Castle must be up here, at the far end of the Land of Doom."

This idyllic-sounding "land" was in the map's upper right-hand corner.

"Now, to get to the Land of Doom the Count first has to cross the ocean. His ship must either be at Aftly at the end of the Main Highway, or Scuttleton at the end of the Northeastern Highway; those are the only two possible places, and by horse they're only a couple of days away. If you're ever going to stop him, you have to stop him before he sets sail, because the ocean is huge and difficult to cross even in a big ship, and even if you could cross it there are so many kingdoms and treacherous deserts to pass through before you reach the Land of Doom it would be almost impossible to survive."

"I care not!" Lathan shouted in the diction of a true hero, as he jumped up and hit his head on a crossbeam. "I'm the son of

'Trollkiller' Sven Svensson, and I'll rescue the Princess or die in the attempt!!!"

"Still, I think the first thing you should do is go to the castle and get the help of the King and his courtiers. They've probably just discovered that the Princess is gone, and are searching for her right now."

"I'll go there at once!" Lathan stoutly replied. "With this magic coin I cannot fail!"

His grandmother's advice was so cool and sensible that Lathan, if he hadn't known better, might have suspected that she had once been in a few adventures herself. He bolted for the door.

"Remember, trusting in God comes first," his grandmother warned, "and don't lose that coin."

"I won't, Grandma! And thanks, Grandma!" Lathan joyously shouted.

He raced out the door, waved a quick good-bye to his flock, and was soon three-quarters of the way to the castle.

Chapter X

Strange Surprises at the Castle

As Lathan ran along he thought of how distraught everyone must be at the castle, and how furious they would be when they learned that Count Zandar had kidnapped the Princess.

"The King's probably gathering an army to chase him right now," Lathan said to himself.

Lathan raced up to the castle drawbridge and stopped short. There was no sign of the vengeful army he expected to see. In fact, everything looked absurdly normal; the guards stood sleepily at the gates, an occasional courtier sauntered in and out, and a few boys swam in the sandy section of the moat, throwing mud pies at each other with reckless abandon. Lathan paused for a moment, took a puzzled look in every direction, and then raced across the drawbridge and addressed one of the guards.

"Have you heard about the Princess?' Lathan asked. "Has anyone heard about the Princess?"

"Yeah, sure," the guard said dully. "It's a beautiful thing."

"Yeah, beautiful," the other guard added with a yawn.

"I've always agreed that a wedding is a beautiful thing," the first guard continued, "but when they keep calling it off and then calling it on again like this it gets kinda confusing."

They didn't even know the Princess was kidnapped! They thought there was still going to be a wedding!

"You've got to let me in to see the King," Lathan pleaded. "I have something urgent to tell him!!"

"You can't bother him now," the first guard said. "He sounds kinda busy."

For the first time Lathan noted the sounds of drunken revelry which emanated from inside.

"But I've got to see the King!" Lathan insisted. "They don't know about the Princess! They don't know!"

"Well, I don't suppose it would hurt to let him in," said the second guard as he leaned back against the castle wall. "They'll probably never notice him."

"All right, go in," the first guard said.

Lathan bolted into the castle and dashed off toward The Great Hall.

The Great Hall was crammed with courtiers, servants, jugglers, and dogs; all of them were intoxicated, and about half were either asleep or unconscious. The half that still held their heads in an upright position more than made up for the silence of the others by laughing, singing, belching, and barking with admirable enthusiasm. The King and Queen sat at The Great Table, the Queen drinking with heroic fervor, and the King staring awkwardly at his cup, not quite sure whether he needed a drink or not.

Lathan couldn't figure out why everyone was in such high spirits. After all, he thought the royal wedding had been called off. Still, he had an important announcement to make.

"People! Listen to me! The Princess has been . . ."

A couple of drunks shoved him out of the way before he could finish, and three or four others told the "runt" to "get lost."

"But this is important!" Lathan cried.

He had barely completed the sentence when some wise guy, who refused to let sleeping dogs lie, picked up a sleeping dog and threw it at him; while trying to avoid this unusual missile, Lathan tripped and fell over a pile of equally sleeping courtiers.

Lathan rested for a moment on this rather indecorous mound of human debilitation, and then, after clutching his coin and feeling a new surge of energy roar through his body, he leaped to his feet and jumped boldly onto The Great Table.

"Silence!" Lathan shouted. "You must know that I am Lathan, son of 'Trollkiller' Sven Svensson, and I have come to tell you that Princess Purella has been kidnapped by that treacherous fiend, Count Zandar the Unfriendly!!!"

"But that's impossible!" the King cried, rising to his feet.

Everyone looked at Lathan as if he were crazy.

"But I tell you it's true! I saw it with my own eyes! The Princess was walking with me in the woods, and the Count and his servant captured her and carried her away, and said they were going to sacrifice her to their god! I swear to you that this is the truth! I swear with my whole heart and soul that this is the absolute truth!!!"

Just then Purella walked down the stairs and strolled into The Great Hall.

Suddenly Lathan felt quite small.

"Get this blithering idiot off my table!" the Queen commanded.

This stern order proved unnecessary, for as soon as Purella appeared safe and unhurt the indignant courtiers pelted the blithering idiot in question with a vast array of chicken bones, wineskins, serving implements, old newspapers, and most everything else that was throwable, knocking Lathan unceremoniously to the floor.

"Kill the wretch!" several voices cried, and for a moment or two the prospect of total physical dismemberment loomed large in Lathan's future. Fortunately, however, one rather heavily shod courtier booted the robust shepherd lad over to where Purella was standing, and she immediately effected his pardon.

"Leave this poor shepherd lad alone," she said, gently but firmly. "He hasn't done anything."

Purella's wishes were obeyed. The courtiers grumbled a little, and then quietly resumed drinking.

Lathan cast his eyes up to his fair protectress, who seemed to him more beautiful than ever before. The face that gazed down at him beamed with celestial radiance, and the voice that rescued him seemed not to be a human voice, but the voice of an angel.

"But Princess, how were you saved?" Lathan faltered. "How did you ever escape from the clutches of that wicked Count?"

Purella paused before replying, and gazed at Lathan with her flashing, ocean-blue eyes. Finally she spoke.

"Ha! Ha! Ha! Ha! Ha!" she said.

This reply was somewhat unexpected. Therefore, after making several unsuccessful attempts at grinning (which is the least you can do when a Princess laughs), Lathan repeated his inquiries, this time with much clearer diction, and a prolific amount of gestures.

"Ha! Ha! Ha! Ha! Ha!" Purella replied once more. "Oh Lathan, if only you knew how stupid you look right now. Ha! Ha! Ha!"

Actually Lathan had a pretty good idea of how stupid he looked, but was trying his best not to think about it.

"You look like you just crawled in out of a gutter," said Purella, bubbling with delight. "You're covered with dirt, your clothes are torn, and you have blood all over your face!"

"I've never seen an uglier little rat," one of the courtiers exclaimed.

"Ha! Ha! Ha!" several others said.

"Oh, and you smell, too," Purella added. "Never come in here without bathing first, Lathan! Your stench is unbearable!"

Lathan turned red, made a couple more half-hearted attempts at grinning, and then stammered his original question once again.

"But . . . but seriously Princess, how did you escape from the Count?"

Purella abruptly stopped laughing, let the meaning of his question sink in fully, and then began laughing twice as loudly as before.

"What an imagination these peasants have!" Purella squealed to all the listening courtiers. "Really Lathan! Telling lies is one thing, but to make up lies and then worry your King and Queen with them is another!"

"Why do you even allow the little vermin to speak to you?" the Queen demanded.

"Let's beat him up and break his arms and legs," a few courtiers suggested, not in an enraged way (they were far too drunk for that), but matter-of-factly, much like someone else would say, "Let's play darts."

"Oh, I don't mind him at all," said Purella. "Of course, I wouldn't want him hanging around here during the wedding."

"W-Wedding?" Lathan stuttered.

"Of course wedding, fool," intoned the Queen. "She's decided to marry Prince Charming after all."

The courtiers let out a hoarse, unsynchronized cheer.

"Speaking of which, I have a million things to do in order to prepare for next Sunday," said the Queen, who promptly leaped out of her seat and marched happily out of the hall.

Lathan was so dazed he might as well have been as drunk as everybody else. He stared at Purella, speechless, searching for answers in the glow of her beautiful face.

"I'm so glad you're safe, Purella," said the King, softly. "At first I thought the lad might be telling the truth. We never should have hired that Count. Never."

It suddenly occurred to Lathan that he hadn't seen the King drinking the whole time he had been in The Great Hall. The King had merely been playing with his cup, and looking sadly and uneasily at the drink within.

"Oh, don't mind Lathan, father," said Purella with a laugh. "All these shepherds lie."

Lathan blushed fiercely at this point, and tried vainly to hold back some tears of confusion, which was doubtless very artful of him, and a sure sign that he was a habitual liar. Meanwhile, Purella slinked over to her father.

"I haven't seen you take a drink all day, father," she said, pouting. "I hope it's not because of something I said. I hate to see you deprive yourself of something that always gave you joy."

The King squirmed under his daughter's gaze and started to look as confused as Lathan.

"But . . . but Purella, I thought you told me that I shouldn't . . ."

"Drink quite so much? Why yes, that's very true, but you didn't think I meant you should stop drinking completely, did you? Why that's silly! Drinking is one of the greatest pleasures a man can have. It breaks my heart not to see you drink."

"But . . . but Purella, everything is . . . is much clearer now, and . . . and . . ."

"You need a drink to steady your nerves," said Purella. "If you don't take a drink right now I'll burst into tears. I will, truly."

The King slowly picked up his cup, looking like an old ox ready for the slaughter. He looked helplessly around the room, his eyes gazing grimly at the piles of debauched courtiers that were strewn all around him. He sighed, and started to think of that day he had carried little Purella's bed up to her room, and wondered again at how he could have forgotten it.

"Drink, father."

His hands wavered as he raised the cup to his lips. He looked at Purella, saw her beautiful face smiling at him, and drank.

Lathan was also looking at Purella's face, and as the King drank he was startled to see a monkey-like grin spread across it, a grin of triumph. Lathan would rather have been kicked in the stomach a thousand times than see that evil look on her face. He turned and walked sadly out of the castle.

When he stepped outdoors the world was, in reality, exactly the same as it was when he entered the castle ten minutes before. The same two guards stood at the castle gates, the same sun still floated up in the sky, the same trees dropped their shade down to the earth, and the same boys were splashing about in the moat, throwing the same mud pies at each other with the same reckless abandon. But to Lathan nothing was the same. Purella was not nice; she was mean, and despised him, and that realization turned Lathan's world upside-down and inside-out. If the sun suddenly started wandering east instead of west, or if the guards suddenly turned into flying gorillas and flew from tree to tree, or if one of the trees came up to him and asked him for the correct time, and then jumped into the moat and started throwing mud pies at the boys, it wouldn't have surprised Lathan in the least.

There was nothing true or solid in the world anymore, and when Lathan crossed the drawbridge and touched the ground on the other side he thought the very earth beneath his feet felt weirdly unreal, and he imagined that the sky was a vast blue weight that was trying to crush him to the dust. He turned back toward the castle, looked at it with red, streaming eyes, and sighed. Then he got hit in the face with a mud pie.

Although he didn't feel like it, Lathan knew that the dictates of civilization obligated him to find someone to beat up for this offense, preferably the perpetrator, but, if that individual couldn't be found, any person of reasonably short stature would do. With this in mind, he walked wearily over to the edge of the moat, hoping that one of the boys would immediately leap out of the water and apologize to him. Unfortunately, the mud pie battlers were having too much fun to notice him, and, since Lathan was too tired to try to get their attention, he just stood there until the mud on his face turned to dirt, and then walked away.

He walked along the edge of the moat for a short distance and found a place to sit along the edge of the water. He slouched over, looked at the water, and began wondering if drowning were an unpleasant way to die. As he looked down into the dirty water of the moat the coin of "Trollkiller" Sven Svensson slipped out of his shirt and dangled before him. He sat up straight and fingered the mysterious coin.

He thought about how the coin should remind him to trust in God, and that it belonged to his father, "Trollkiller" Sven Svensson, and that perhaps it was really a magic coin, and the more he stared at it and felt it, the more he was convinced that that was true.

"A lot of strange things have happened to me today," said Lathan, "but I'm still the son of 'Trollkiller' Sven Svensson, and I should never give up no matter what happens. So please, magic coin, give me strength and understanding so I'll know what I should do."

Lathan grasped the coin with both hands and squeezed it with all his might.

"Arf!"

Lathan immediately released his grip on the coin, thinking that he had squeezed it too hard.

"Arf!"

Lathan suddenly recognized the voice of Floppy. Floppy repeated a certain euphonious monosyllable three more times, until Lathan finally spotted the worthy pup gazing down at him from one of the castle's upper windows. Floppy immediately stepped out to the very edge of the window, and Lathan noticed that a rope of tied-together bedsheets hung from it to the ground.

Lathan had no idea whether the loquacious pup was barking out of anger, friendship, or merely for vocal exercise, but eventually he got the idea.

"You want me to climb up there?" Lathan asked.

Floppy howled, wagged his tail, and did three consecutive somersaults on the dangerous window ledge, which Lathan took to be an answer in the affirmative.

"I'd like to see what you want to show me, Floppy, but really I think it might be better if I go home and drop dead instead. You see, you don't know it, but the Princess doesn't like me anymore."

This time Floppy responded by howling even louder, kicking his feet together, shaking his head spasmodically, and doing three sets of triple somersaults on the window ledge, each with two twists, in the pike position.

"Well, if you insist," said Lathan, "but I don't know what you want me for."

Lathan didn't really feel like swimming across the moat, but fortunately he saw a large plank sticking out of the water which he quickly pulled out and used as a bridge. He walked carefully across the plank, and then started to climb up the bedsheets.

Lathan, though robust, was no expert with ropes, and twice nearly succeeded in hanging himself before he even got close to the window. However, after making several superhuman efforts to untangle himself and climb higher, he managed to reach the open window and flopped inside.

Lathan found himself in a spacious bedroom, which contained neatly arranged books, sewing equipment, a large mirror, a silver plate set, a miniature bow-and-arrow set, several paintings, a biography of "Trollkiller" Sven Svensson, and various feminine trinkets, and Lathan quickly realized he was in Purella's room. Meanwhile, Floppy jumped on Purella's bed and began dancing around a corked bottle of water that lay on top.

"Floppy, I shouldn't be here!" Lathan said as he finally extricated himself from the bedsheets. "The Princess doesn't like me anymore, and they'd probably have me killed if they caught me here!"

"Arf! Arf!" said Floppy, still dancing around the bottle.

Lathan reached over and picked it up.

"Don't get excited, Floppy," said Lathan. "It's just a bottle of water."

There was more light over by Purella's dressing table, so Lathan brought the bottle over there to give it a closer inspection. He sat in her chair and held it up in front of her mirror. He then unplugged the cork and sniffed its contents.

"I'm sure it's only water," Lathan repeated to the apprehensive pup, "and I'm glad it is, cause that's exactly what I need."

Lathan had caught a glimpse of his face in Purella's mirror, and noticed that it was still blotched by several dried fragments of mud pie. He therefore poured a little of the water into his left hand and applied it to his face, while Floppy vocalized frantically. Lathan's face was soon clean, but Floppy still jumped and yelped hysterically.

"Don't make so much noise, Floppy, they'll hear us."

Floppy, whose eyes were fixed firmly on the bottle, continued to let out apprehensive yelps.

"Look, it's just water," said Lathan as he held up the bottle for Floppy's inspection. As he held it up he suddenly noticed that there were three letters painted on its side: B, A, and P.

"BAP?" said Lathan quizzically.

Floppy moaned.

"BAP!!" Lathan blurted, suddenly realizing that he held in his hands Mr. Jack Crackback's sure-fire cleansing agent, which is (to all attentive readers) well-known for its excessive potency.

He moaned even louder than Floppy, set the bottle down, grabbed his nose (to make sure it was still there), and looked into Purella's mirror. Fortunately, the only effect the BAP water had on his face was to make it cleaner, and, unlike the unfortunate idol, his face showed no signs of deterioration. Lathan breathed a sigh of relief.

"He said this stuff would clean off anything, and it sure did, but he also said it showed everything as it really was, so either this is what I really look like, or this water's gotten stale and lost its zip."

Before Floppy could opine a reply, the bedroom door swung open. Purella darted quickly inside and hastily shut the door. Once the door was safely shut she took a deep breath, turned slowly around, and saw Lathan and Floppy standing in front of her. Purella shrunk back, startled.

"Purella—I mean, Princess—I'm so sorry, I um, we didn't mean . . . um . . . we . . . um . . ." said Lathan.

Lathan's deferential manner (he was once again paying very close attention to the attractions of Purella's feet) took the fear out of Purella's eyes. She straightened up, and began to look at the two intruders as if they were intruders indeed, and not her two most loyal friends.

"I cannot have mutts and shepherd lads prowling around my room as if they owned it," Purella said imperially. "It produces a bad image—very bad. Therefore I must ask you both to go downstairs and prepare to be executed at once."

She punctuated this sentence by sitting on her bed, adjusting her lovely hair, and looking at them both with supreme contempt. Lathan had nothing to say in reply. His enjoyment of life had dropped so precipitously in the last few hours that Purella's command almost pleased him, and he meekly began leaving the room in order to get his head lopped off as promptly as possible. Floppy, however, responded to her command differently. He jumped up on her bed and started barking at her.

"Get away, you smelly mutt!" she cried.

Floppy then did a strange thing. He leaped off the bed, bounded over to Purella's dressing table, and knocked over the bottle of BAP water so that it began spilling all over the floor.

"He's gone mad!" Purella cried.

Lathan stopped in his tracks and watched as Floppy put his mouth to the bottle and began feverishly drinking the precious water. Then Floppy leaped back onto Purella's bed, jumped into her lap, and spat BAP water all over her face.

Purella screeched, covered her face with her hands, and hopped to her feet, while Floppy stood a short distance away, wagging his tail and staring intently at her face.

"I'm ruined!" shrieked Purella as a horrible burning smell pervaded the room. Gray smoke could be seen seeping through the fingers that covered her face.

Lathan rushed to her assistance.

"Please, Purella, let me help!"

He raced up to her, pulled her hands away from her face, and saw the most ghastly sight he had ever seen.

Her face was melting. Lathan watched in horror as her beautiful left cheek oozed off her face and plopped to the floor, her beautiful right eye began climbing across her nose to mingle with her beautiful left eye, and several more of her loveliest features began melting into formlessness.

"Curses!" said Purella.

"Arf! Arf!" Floppy remarked to Lathan, gesturing at the left side of Purella's face.

O horrors! The left side of Purella's face had fallen completely to the floor, and underneath its last vestiges Lathan could see the wrinkled features of an old woman.

"You meddlers! I could have been the Princess!" said Purella as her lips fell off. "No one would have ever known! No one!"

Although part of her face was still exquisitely lovely, her voice had now been transformed from a mellifluous soprano to an ugly croak. Floppy raced over, took another drink of BAP water, and spit it all over the rest of her face. Soon all her beauty was gone, and the dog and the shepherd lad found themselves staring at the twisted features of Kaklina, who glared at them with sneering hate.

"Hey, wait a minute, you're not the Princess!" said Lathan.

"That's right, and you'll never see your precious Princess again!" Kaklina croaked.

"Where is she?!! What have you done with her?!!" Lathan demanded.

"You'll never find out from me!" she croaked with malevolent glee. She didn't realize that Lathan had a magic coin around his neck, and the feel of its precious metal touching against his chest was filling him with surprising courage.

"I am the son of 'Trollkiller' Sven Svensson!" he shouted as he jumped over and pinned the astonished Kaklina against the wall. "Tell me where the Princess is, or else!!!"

"Or else" is usually a rather vague threat, but from the fierce glint in Lathan's eyes, "else" seemed in this case to consist of some type of severe physical injury, which caused Kaklina to reconsider her position regarding her desire to give information.

"Count Zandar is taking her to the Dark Castle to sacrifice her to our god! But you'll never find them! By now they're well on their way to the ship!"

"Where is the ship?! What road are they taking?!" Lathan asked fiercely.

Kaklina hesitated. Lathan, who had never raised his voice at anyone in his life, was overwhelmed by the energy he felt surging through his body.

"I am the son of 'Trollkiller' Sven Svensson!" he shouted again, mainly because this announcement seemed to have the effect of redoubling his courage, "and I will not rest until you've told me everything you know!! Everything!!"

Kaklina, who had lived all her life in the Count's country, had actually never heard of Lathan's father before, but the name "Trollkiller" Sven Svensson sounded rather ominous to her, and since she figured Lathan's dad might be hanging around outside somewhere, she decided to tell Lathan everything, and soon the worthy shepherd lad discovered that the Count's ship was docked at the harbor of Scuttleton, an out-of-the-way fishing village at the far end of the Northeastern Highway.

"Watch her, Floppy, and make sure she doesn't get away!" Lathan ordered the ingenious pup. "I have to go downstairs and tell the King. We'll have an army after them in no time!"

Lathan darted out of the room, and raced downstairs and into The Great Hall. He dodged the sleeping bodies, leaped over a few empty casks, and finally reached The Great Table, where the King was lying slumped in his seat.

"Your Majesty, you've been deceived!" Lathan cried. "The real Princess has been taken, and the one you thought was the Princess was really an imposter!!!"

This startling announcement had no effect on anyone, since everyone in the hall was either asleep, unconscious, or unable to hear Lathan over the sound of hundreds of snoring courtiers. Lathan climbed up onto the thick table and tried to shake the King awake.

"They used some sort of magic potion!" Lathan said. "It was his assistant the whole time! I've got her upstairs! She'll tell you everything!"

The King finally lifted his head. He gave Lathan a long, perplexed look, and then reached over to take another drink.

"Your Majesty, no!" Lathan said, stopping him. "We don't have time to waste; he's carrying her to his ship right now!"

The King turned toward Lathan. He tried to focus his eyes on Lathan, but couldn't; he tried to it up straight and look majestic, but couldn't; and he tried to reprimand Lathan for touching him, but couldn't. In fact, all he could do was belch, roll his eyes around a few times, hiccup, and then collapse to the table once more.

"I-I was hoping for an army," Lathan said sadly. The King couldn't help him.

Lathan jumped off the table, skirted around a stack of sleeping dogs, and raced back upstairs. When he got back to Purella's room he found Floppy all alone, staring out the window, with a huge piece of dress in his mouth. Lathan ran over and looked out the window, but Kaklina was already long gone, never to be heard from again. Floppy looked very apologetic.

"Well, at least you tried, Floppy," said Lathan as he took the piece of dress out of the pup's mouth, "but we can forget about her. It looks like we have to rescue the Princess all by ourselves."

He related to Floppy everything that happened downstairs, and how they could expect no help from the King or his courtiers. Floppy looked glum. They knew they needed help, but didn't know where they could get it.

"Wait! What about the Prince who was going to marry her?" Lathan asked. "Isn't he in the castle? Wouldn't he want to help us?"

Floppy looked very skeptical. However, after a few moments his expression changed to a look of resignation. He realized they didn't have much choice—by themselves, a mongrel and a shepherd lad could be no match for a powerful nobleman like the Count.

"Arf," said Floppy finally, and then ran out of the room and down the hall. Lathan quickly followed, and soon they arrived at the room of Prince Charming.

Chapter XI

*A Recruiting Chapter, Filled With Heartwarming Examples
of Noble-Mindedness and Self-Sacrifice*

*A*ll the other doors in the castle were of unfinished
wood, but Prince Charming's door was different.
It had been very recently been painted purple, pink,
and gold, and was carved with figures of dancing maidens, and
decorated with liberal amounts of lace and ribbons. However,
Lathan was so worried about Purella that he barely noticed any
of this, and pushed open the door and rushed inside without
even bothering to knock.

The inside of the room was even more unique than the
door. The walls were covered with paintings of provocatively
dressed women, there were fashionable clothes hanging from
every piece of furniture, and the floor was strewn with bou-
quets and empty perfume bottles. The air was filled with an
extremely thick and aromatic mist, giving the room the atmosphere of a dense, tropical jungle.

In the far corner of the room was a huge, sumptuous, awning-covered bed, in which rested Purella's faithful lover, Prince Charming, propped up by several large, fluffy pillows. In the room with him were two young maids, who each held a platter of grapes, and fought constantly over who would have the honor of dropping the next grape into the Prince's mouth, for even though the Prince appeared to be in an unusually lethargic mood, he still had his rock-hewn face, his roguish air, and a smile that a girl could die for.

Lathan, after choking a few times on the equatorial air, dashed over to the Prince's bedside and made his startling announcement.

"The Princess has been kidnapped by Count Zandar! He's taking her to be sacrificed at his castle on the Far Northern Sea! You've got to come and help us save her!"

Unfortunately, Prince Charming was completely oblivious to everything Lathan had said, for he was right in the middle of giving the taller of the two maids one of his most killing looks.

"Did you say your name was Sandra?" he asked, his eyes burning into her.

"Yes, Your Highness," Sandra stammered, blushing, curtseying, and fumbling.

"Well, Sandra, I want you to know you're looking fine. Real fine," he added with heavy emphasis.

Sandra couldn't answer, because her whole body was trembling with ecstasy, and her brain could no longer operate.

"We have no time to waste!" Lathan cried.

The shorter maid was now insanely jealous, and, shoving her hated rival out of the way (they had been best friends the day before), she dropped a particularly juicy grape into the Prince's mouth.

"Would you like to squeeze a grape of your own, Your Highness?" she humbly asked.

The Prince turned his gaze on her, and even touched her with his hand, which soon reduced her to a quivering mass of fluttery emotions.

"Grapes are fine," he said, without averting his gaze, "but there are other things I like to squeeze besides grapes."

She blushed spectacularly, and began giggling uncontrollably over this extremely clever comment.

"Your Highness, you must listen to me!" Lathan continued frantically. "The Princess is in extreme danger!"

The Prince was still giving the shorter maid a devastating look, which apparently had to be of a certain duration in order to achieve its full effect. Finally, however, he turned away his gaze and shook his head as if he had just come out of a trance. For the first time he noticed that a robust shepherd lad was shouting at him, and a little dog of obviously poor breeding was standing by the door, smirking. Prince Charming immediately plugged his nose.

"Get out of here, you putrid little wretches!" he squealed. "Your stench is unbearable!"

The maids noticed the two intruders for the first time as well.

"Impudent boy . . . filthy swine . . . I've never . . . how dare such trash . . . the presence of a Prince . . . nothing better than death . . . kill the scum . . ." and various other colorful epithets were shouted out by the two innocent maidens, who were quite incensed that their grape distribution program had been interrupted.

"Listen to me!" Lathan pleaded. "The Princess has been kidnapped by Count Zandar, and we need you to help us rescue her!"

"Nonsense!" the Prince replied. "I just saw the little minx an hour ago when she came in to apologize for her shocking behavior to me. Of course, I knew she'd come crawling back to me. Some of them fight it for a while, but soon they all give in to the magnificence of the superior male. Oh, yes, their little hearts can never resist greatness."

Prince Charming punctuated this last comment by touching each of the maids on the hand, which sent them both trembling with joy once more.

The Prince's discourse was largely unintelligible to the innocent young shepherd lad, but it was clear to Lathan that the Prince had been deceived by Kaklina.

"The Princess you talked to was an imposter," Lathan explained. "The real Princess is being taken to Count Zandar's ship at Scuttleton. They're well on their way there right now!"

"She can't be kidnapped. We're supposed to get married next Sunday."

"We have to leave at once, or we'll never be able to stop them!"

"Go away, boy! Can't you see you're disturbing the Prince?" the shorter maid said, with a look of the highest moral indignation.

"But Your Highness, we . . ."

"No no, she's right, boy, go away, go away," said the Prince, awkwardly gesturing Lathan away. "I can't go around chasing people. It would probably make me all sweaty and everything. Besides, that Count is supposed to be very . . . well, of course I'm not afraid or anything, but I've got business here."

He then reached over, grabbed a huge bunch of grapes, and stuffed them into his mouth.

Lathan slowly began to leave. When he reached the door he turned and made one last remark.

"Farewell Prince. I guess the Princess's hand in marriage and the entire Hoodahooda treasury will go to someone else."

Lathan and Floppy stepped out into the hallway, closed the door behind them, and then began walking back to Purella's room. Lathan was afraid that he and Floppy would have to rescue her all by themselves.

Just then they heard a door burst open behind them, and turned around to see Prince Charming, grapes in hand, stumble out into the hallway.

"Excuse me, what was that you just said?" Prince Charming asked.

"Well, since the Princess is the King's only heir, I'm sure that the nobleman who rescues the Princess will get her hand in marriage and half the Kingdom of Hoodahooda, which is worth hundreds of thousands of talents in gold."

"You know, you're right, and my dad'll kill me if I blow this deal," the Prince replied. (His father, a pot-bellied gentleman named King Charming XII, was notoriously hot-tempered.) "If we don't get more gold back into the Skindeepian economy, our next debutante season could be seriously affected. See if you can get some more help, and I'll meet you down at the stables."

Floppy smirked a great deal at this, but Lathan was very pleased by the enthusiasm of the new recruit, and immediately sped downstairs to see if he could find another. However, since the Queen and her servants were in another part of the castle preparing for the wedding, and the King and all his courtiers were not in a state of high physical readiness, the only person Lathan could find who was still standing on two feet was the King's Steward.

"Well, I really have to stay here in case the King ever wakes up," said the Steward, "and the guards have to stay here too. The only other person who could help you is Doctor Oldair."

"Where is Doctor Oldair?" Lathan asked.

"In his garden—where else?" the Steward replied.

"Thanks! Come on Floppy!"

Lathan darted off, then darted back to ask the Steward where the garden was, and then darted off again. He went down a hall, found the side door that led into the garden, and burst outside. Doctor Oldair and his young assistant, Scruppins, were in the center of the garden, standing solemnly in front of a little mound of dirt with their hats in their hands.

With Floppy at his heels Lathan ran up to them.

"Doctor Oldair, the Princess has been . . ."

"Silence, boy!" Doctor Oldair said, cutting Lathan short. "Can't you see we're busy? This is a memorial service."

Lathan and Floppy stopped short and for the first time took a look at their surroundings. The garden was in a shambles. There were remnants of parsnips, potatoes, and carrots strewn everywhere, and many of the flowers had been crushed and marked with tiny footprints. Around the edge of the garden, along the stone wall, and in several other locations there were sharpened knives sticking out of the ground, pits lined with spikes, and arsenic-laced cargo nets; there were enough defenses to stop a small army. There were at least two steel traps placed around each hole in the wall or in the ground, and tiny nooses hung from strategic locations, designed to lynch any tiny heads that might try to peek at one of the Doctor's precious vegetables. Lathan thought these brutal and elaborate defenses seemed a bit excessive, until he saw a large, well-fed gopher sitting on one of the steel traps, solemnly chewing a carrot, and apparently deeply moved by the Doctor's memorial service. Soon, with quavering voice, the Doctor began to speak once more.

"This garden, my garden, the most excellent in the world, was last night ravaged and almost destroyed by enemies. It is obvious that this was the work of religious fanatics. Their narrow-minded bigotry and envy of my gardening skills has gone too far! But it is not of them I wish to speak. Today we come to pay tribute to those who have fallen."

"First there were my azaleas, who were trampled and beaten, though they had offended no one, and had always flourished, even with inconsistent watering; then there were my pomegranates, so majestic and red; then my tulips, my daisies, my violets, my peaches (they were young, so young!), my plums, my pears, my kumquats, and my apples, both red and . . . and green."

His voice cracked with emotion. Scruppins patted him on the back, but the Doctor gestured that he was all right.

"Then there were my dates, my figs, my squash of six different varieties, and lastly, my raspberries."

Doctor Oldair sighed and turned slowly toward his youthful assistant.

"Is there anyone I've forgotten?" he asked feebly.

"Doctor Oldair, I'm afraid you forgot . . . I'm sorry . . . the pansies."

"No, no," cried Doctor Oldair, "did they get the pansies too?"

Scruppins ruefully hung his head. The Doctor crumbled to his knees on top of the memorial mound.

"No! No!" he cried, putting his hands over his eyes, "not the pansies!"

For the first time Lathan noticed that there was a large wooden plaque on the mound which said:

In Memory of All the Plants Demolished
By Religious Fanatics in Their
Unbelievable Arrogance and Pride

—Erected by Doctor Oldair
Chief Counselor to the King
Outstanding Poet and Dramatist
Award-Winning Gardener
And the Number-One-Ranked
Philosopher in the Western World
(and, according to the latest polls,
rapidly gaining ground in the east)

After a few moments of extravagant weeping, Doctor Oldair began commenting on an even more painful subject.

"I vowed I would never say its name again," he said, "but on this sad occasion I cannot help but break my vow and mention once more the greatest loss in my life, a loss even worse than the loss of all these plants combined; yes, I speak of the loss of the last seeds of Flaming Pink Chrysopata Scumatta of Phylum Fulvibrata. O Flaming Pink Chrysopata Scumatta of Phylum Fulvibrata, you are gone forever, and all our lives are the worse for it!"

It seemed hardly possible, but Doctor Oldair concluded this pathetic speech by weeping twice as extravagantly as before, which caused Scruppins to jump to attention, since his sober meditation had been rapidly turning into sleep (after all, he had spent the entire afternoon erecting the plaque that was Erected by Doctor Oldair). Young Scruppins felt he should say something to comfort his master.

"We'll put this garden together again, Doctor Oldair," he said. "Why, maybe it wasn't religious fanatics who did this after all, but maybe it was that darn gopher that came back and brought a bunch of others with him."

Alas young Scruppins, it's an awkward policy to try to comfort people by telling them the truth; to many people, the truth is never comforting.

"Don't be absurd," the Doctor snapped. "I know a bit more about these religious fanatics than you do. Gophers! With all the scientifically advanced traps I've set up no gopher would *dare* come near these walls! So next time you give an opinion, young man, try not to be so narrow-minded."

Scruppins stammered out an apology and vowed he would try to be as open-minded as Doctor Oldair in the future. Meanwhile, Floppy wandered over to where the gopher was sitting and started to share a carrot with him. Floppy soon noticed about two dozen other gophers lying in the ditch behind them; they had flowers in their hair, and pieces of vegetables in their mouths, and were lazily soaking up the sun. They didn't look quite as fanatical as Doctor Oldair might have supposed, but they were in a state that did seem to border on religious ecstasy.

Lathan was anxious to tell Doctor Oldair about Purella, but wisely waited until the memorial service was over. When he saw how devastated the Doctor could be over the loss of a few flowers and vegetables, he shuddered to think what his reaction would be when he heard about the abduction of his favorite pupil.

The service ended, and Doctor Oldair sat on the memorial mound, weeping. Lathan gulped, and then stepped forward to tell the Doctor the horrible news as tactfully as he could.

"Doctor Oldair," he said, "I-I have something to tell you—something awful."

Doctor Oldair scrambled to his feet and stared at Lathan, his eyes bulging with terror.

"No, no! Not the rhododendrons! Please tell me it's not the rhododendrons!"

"No, it's not the rhododendrons at all," replied Lathan, a bit shaken by the Doctor's look of wild desperation.

Doctor Oldair breathed a sigh of relief.

"It's something worse!" said Lathan, and the Doctor's fears quickly redoubled.

"I don't know how to tell you this, Doctor," said Lathan, "but the Princess has been kidnapped!!"

"And?"

"And? And . . . and the Count has her, and he's going to take her to his castle on the Far Northern Sea and sacrifice her to his god!!!"

"Go on," said Doctor Oldair, after an awkward pause.

"Well, uh, that's it," said Lathan, a little confused. "Oh, and there's no one who can save her except me, Floppy, and Prince

Charming, so we were hoping, because she was your favorite pupil, that you'd come with us!"

"My son," Doctor Oldair said benignly, putting his hand on Lathan's shoulder, "misfortunes in life are many, but you must learn to transcend your problems, and bear them with dignity and courage."

"But . . . but if we don't chase after them she'll be killed!"

Doctor Oldair brushed this thought away with a wave of his hand. The philosophical resignation that the Doctor showed on this occasion was truly admirable.

"How do you know that she's been kidnapped?" Doctor Oldair asked.

"Because we saw them take her . . . and there was an imposter . . . and we can show . . ."

"Tell me, how do you even know there *is* a Princess?" the Doctor cut in, with a triumphant gleam in his eye.

"Huh?" said Lathan.

"In fact, how do you even know that I exist?" the Doctor continued. "Perhaps this whole conversation is a figment of your imagination."

"I . . . I . . . well . . . I . . . I . . ." stammered Lathan, who was finding himself being rudely dunked into the deep pool of Metaphysico-diestmo-existentiology.

"You see?" said the Doctor, smiling. "You don't know what exists and what does not. Therefore you must greet setbacks in your life with stoicism, and ignore the foolish trivialities that surround you. (By the way, Scruppins, go see if the rhododendrons are all right.) Otherwise look what might happen. You might have me chasing after a non-existent Princess, who's been kidnapped by a non-existent Count."

"But they do exist!"

"But how do you know? You have no proof whether they exist or not. I'll bet you never even considered the possibility that they don't exist."

"Of course I've never considered it," said Lathan, "because . . . because it's obvious that they do."

"Obvious? Oh yes, yes, obvious," said Doctor Oldair, smiling at Lathan's simplicity.

The Doctor put his arm around Lathan, paused dramatically, and then asked:

"Do you have a garden?"

"I beg your pardon?"

"I said, 'Do you have a garden?'"

"Uh, no," said Lathan. He was sweating in agony, because he realized that each moment's delay might be fatal to Purella.

"You must get your own garden," the Doctor said, as he took his arm away from Lathan and began strutting around. "You must get your own garden, and tend it."

"Please, Doctor Oldair," said Lathan, unable to contain himself, "we can't wait any longer! The Princess needs our . . ."

"Tend your *own* garden, young man," Doctor Oldair interposed.

"But . . ."

"Tend your *own* garden," the Doctor repeated, and was so struck by this phrase that he repeated it several times, and vowed to put it in his latest book, which was called *The Alexanderiad*, and was about how some religious fanatics tried to destroy the garden of Alexander the Great, but were discovered and severely punished by that monarch, who, even though he was a brutal and vicious conqueror, was really a good guy at heart, mostly because he didn't believe in any religion, loved gardening, and had grave doubts about everyone else's existence.

"Sir, I don't have time to make a garden, or to tend it," said Lathan. "I hate to disappoint you, but I really intend to rescue the Princess anyway, whether she exists or not."

The Doctor shook his head.

"When you get to my age, young man, you will realize that I am right about everything."

"Well, thank you anyway, Doctor," said Lathan as he and Floppy began to awkwardly take their leave. "And I'm very sorry about what happened to your Flaming Pink Chrysopata Scumatta of Phylum . . . of Phylum . . . whatever. If there's any way I can make it up to you, please let me know."

"What do you mean?" Doctor Oldair asked.

"Don't you remember?" said Lathan. "I was the one who mixed up your seeds with the Count's potion. I'm really sorry if I . . ."

"I knew I had seen you before!" Doctor Oldair bellowed. "You . . . you idiot!!!"

Doctor Oldair immediately grabbed his hoe and began chasing Lathan around the garden, apparently determined that his philosophy would make a mark on Lathan one way or another. The Doctor was not in the best of training, however, and eventually stood panting in the center of the garden, waving his hoe at Lathan and repeating the word "idiot" as often as his breath would allow.

"Please, Doctor," said Lathan, trying to placate the sage, "if you come with us, I promise you we can not only rescue the Princess, but we might also get back your seeds at the same time."

"What 'seeds' are you talking about?!!" Doctor Oldair asked angrily.

"The seeds of Flaming Full Scumatta of Phylum . . . of Phylum . . . you know," said Lathan. "The ones you gave to the Count when your crate arrived. Gosh, I guess those are now the last seeds of that flower left in the world."

What remained of the doctor's hair stood on end for a moment, including his beard, while the memory of his graciously giving the Count a few seeds raced back into his head. The Doctor's look of astonishment gradually changed to a look of thoughtfulness; his hair dropped back to its usual position, and he walked over to Lathan and put his arm around him.

"What's your name, young man?" Doctor Oldair asked.

"Lathan, sir."

"Lathan, I've given this a great deal of thought," said the Doctor, just like someone who had given something a great deal of thought, "and I think that it's our duty to rescue the Princess. Lathan, she and I were close, very close (I wish we had been closer), and it pains me more than you can imagine to realize that she is gone. Oh, no doubt you'll think me a foolish old man, but I say we should try to rescue her at once, for even though I realize, as you very clearly pointed out to me, that there is a possibility that she doesn't exist; still, even though what you say is all very logical and reasonable, I can't help believing that she really does exist, and that we can rescue her if we try."

"Gosh, I . . . I really didn't mean to say that," said Lathan, confused. "I'm not even sure how I thought of it."

"No, no, no, don't apologize," Doctor Oldair replied. "You said what you thought was right, and I respect you for it."

Lathan thanked the Doctor for his magnanimity.

"I've always been very open-minded," the Doctor explained. He turned to his youthful assistant.

"You're in charge of the garden while I'm away, Scruppins," Doctor Oldair said. "Be kind to the rhododendrons, and show no mercy to the fanatics. And now, we have a Princess to rescue!"

With these stirring words the Doctor, Lathan, and Floppy hastily exited the garden, whereupon the faithful Scruppins ran over to an apricot tree and greedily devoured every fruit, while various gophers occasionally ran between his legs, carrying away carrots, artichokes, and other assorted delicacies. By sundown the garden was stripped bare, and although Scruppins and all the gophers were sick for the next week, they all agreed they had a very good time while it lasted.

Meanwhile Doctor Oldair, Lathan, and Floppy hurried to the stables and met Prince Charming, who looked resplendent in a purple and green velvet sequined shirt and pants, and a blue hunting cap with a long pink feather. It was the feather that was particularly bewitching to the ladies, for there were about fifteen ladies of various ages gathered around the Prince, all of whom were giggling, blushing, and admiring his feather very much, and saying that whoever would wear a feather like that must be a very great and wonderful man indeed. The Prince accepted all these comments with great complacency, but when he saw Doctor Oldair arriving he broke out of his little mob of admirers and walked over to greet that famous sage.

"Doctor Oldair, you're looking wonderful! Are you going to assist me in rescuing the Princess? This whole situation is such a frightful tragedy. I'm ever so upset."

"Your Highness, we must learn to bear it," the Doctor said solemnly.

"Boy," said Prince Charming, addressing Lathan, "why don't you help those two wretches catch us some horses? We can't get started until we have something to ride."

The two wretches in question were none other than the Head Coachman and his assistant, who were both unsuccessfully engaged in their usual occupation of horse-gathering. The Head Coachman was unsuccessful because each time he brought a horse to Prince Charming the Prince would reject it because it clashed with his outfit. After six or seven rejections the Prince finally confided to the Head Coachman that he wanted a horse that had "a hint of chartreuse." The Head Coachman received this intelligence very gravely, and after venting a sigh or two, wearily began his search for such a singular beast.

While the Head Coachman searched for this colorful steed, his assistant was pursuing another horse which, despite all of the assistant's tricks, refused to have a rope put around his neck. Each sly maneuver the assistant made was countered by an even trickier maneuver on the part of the horse. Soon this horse led the assistant to a variety of places, and not only led the assistant to the watering hole at the farthest end of the pasture, but also made him drink.

Eventually the Head Coachman wearied of his search for a colorful horse, and, using a high degree of artfulness, took the first horse he could catch, brought it to Prince Charming, and explained that this was the only horse he could find that had a "hint of chartreuse." Prince Charming inspected it carefully.

"No, no, my good man," the Prince remonstrated, "this horse is too chartreuse; it's positively blinding! I said a 'hint,' not a 'dash'!"

Meanwhile, the assistant finally caught the elusive horse he had been pursuing and brought it proudly to the Head Coachman, who had to disappoint the assistant by informing him that the horse he had been chasing for the past half hour was deaf, dumb, and three-quarters blind. The assistant smiled weakly, asked the Head Coachman if he couldn't take a joke, and then went glumly off in search of another steed.

Despite all these setbacks, the Head Coachman (with the valuable help of his assistant) finally did manage to collect three horses; one for Doctor Oldair, one for Prince Charming (which had a universally admired streak of beige), and one for Lathan and Floppy. Soon their saddle bags were loaded with provisions, and the four Princess Rescuers were ready to mount up.

Lathan looked out at the dusty road ahead of them, and then turned to look back at the castle. He knew he was setting out on a dangerous journey, and he might never see his country again. He thought of the King, and remembered something Purella once said to him, "He's not what some people say; he's really a good man."

Lathan decided that he owed the King one last chance.

"Excuse me, sirs," said Lathan to Doctor Oldair and the Prince. "Please don't leave yet. I need to go back in the castle."

"What's the meaning of this, boy?" Prince Charming asked.

"I'm sure the King loves his daughter very much," said Lathan, "and I think we should give him one last chance to join us."

"Don't be absurd, boy. If you can't drink it, he doesn't care about it."

By the way, it was perfectly natural for Prince Charming to call Lathan "boy," since he was at least four years older than Lathan, and possibly five.

"I won't be long," said Lathan, who then darted back toward the castle's main gate. He crossed the moat, zipped past the two sleepy guards, and raced into The Great Hall.

The Great Hall remained much as he had left it. He dodged the various bodies, leaped up on The Great Table, and tried to shake the slumped-over King awake.

"Please wake up, Your Majesty," he said. "Your daughter has been kidnapped and we need your help."

The King woke up. He looked at Lathan.

"Daughter?"

"Yes, yes, Purella!" said Lathan. "We need the help of you and your men very badly, because all we have so far is Prince Charming, Doctor Oldair, me, and Floppy, and the Count is very evil, and very tough!"

The King slowly reached over and grabbed his cup with both hands, as if he were about to fall off a cliff, and that was the rope that could save him.

"Your Majesty, no!" said Lathan as he tried to pry the King's hands from the cup.

"Leave me alone!" said the King.

"But Your Majesty, she's your daughter!"

"Leave me alone!"

"Don't you care about your daughter at all?" Lathan asked.

The King's hands remained wrapped around the cup, but his eyes slowly moved away from it, and he began staring at the staircase on the opposite side of the hall. He tried to speak, but it took a long while for the words to come out.

"Carried the bed . . .," he said, "carried it right up."

Lathan couldn't understand what the King was saying. He sighed, jumped off the table, and then ran out of the castle. The King was still looking at the staircase.

"How could I have forgotten?" he said.

He looked down at the contents of his cup. The liquid glimmered in the torchlight of the hall, and he stared at it for a long, long time.

Chapter XII

Adventures on the Northeastern Highway

When Lathan arrived back at the stables, Prince Charming and Doctor Oldair were mounted and ready to go. Lathan, who knew more than anyone that there was no time to waste, immediately mounted the little gray horse that was provided for him, and, after placing Floppy on his lap, announced that he also was ready to go. Before long the four adventurers found themselves riding toward the Northeastern Highway, and soon the castle was far behind them.

The Northeastern Highway was a dusty road about thirty feet wide which led from Troddleheim to the little port of Scuttleton, which was about fifty miles away. For the first twenty miles the road travelled through a forest, for the next twenty miles it passed through a brushy, mostly treeless region, and for the last ten miles it passed through a marshy region that was cool, foggy, and misty most of the year. It was never a very crowded road, and the four Princess Rescuers saw no fellow travelers.

They had not travelled far when the sun set, and although Lathan pleaded that they continue riding all night long, Doctor Oldair scoffed at the idea. He said that although he himself would gladly ride night and day to rescue the Princess, he was concerned that the horses might need their rest. The Doctor then asked Lathan to try not to think of himself so much, and Lathan apologized.

All this riding was proving very ruinous to Prince Charming's hair, and he also insisted they stop and rest as soon as possible. Soon he spotted a small cottage near the side of the road, and the four travelers rode up to it, dismounted, and informed its inhabitants, a humble farmer and his wife, that they were staying for the night. After tossing the two peasants a couple of coins, the Doctor and the Prince immediately took over the premises. The Doctor quickly transformed a good portion of the cottage's food supply into a state of non-existence, while Prince Charming sat in the farmer's good chair, and ordered the farmer's wife to get for him a number of indispensable items, most of which she had never heard of (the items being very fashionable), and had no hope of finding.

A little later the Prince told their inquisitive landlady where they were heading, and asked her how far they had to go. When informed they had travelled a full two and a half miles from the King's castle, the Prince expressed his satisfaction, but told the farmer's wife that he would have gladly travelled twice, nay, even three times that far if it could help rescue the Princess. When the farmer's wife heard that the Prince was on his way to rescue a Princess, she called him an angel, felt very guilty about not having any of the things he had asked for, and immediately set out in search of a deluxe, multi-sprocketed hair-curling iron.

While their heroic friends were enjoying the comforts of the cottage, Lathan and Floppy stayed outside to tend the horses. In fact, Lathan and Floppy were too worried and excited to sleep, and stayed outside all night, waiting anxiously for dawn.

At the first ray of light Lathan slipped into the cottage and woke up his two compatriots, who tried vainly to convince him that he was mistaken about the time, and that it was actually the middle of the night. Lathan, however, was obstinate. He realized that if they didn't leave at once it might be too late to rescue the Princess; Count Zandar might be almost to his ship by now, and the Princess condemned to his cruel mercy. Lathan was determined to prevent this, and soon he, Floppy, and their two grumbling companions once again began galloping along the Northeastern Highway, bound for the port of Scuttleton.

I use the term "galloping" rather loosely in this context, for in actuality the progress they made during this journey was erratic, due to a number of factors, but primarily because of Doctor Oldair's unusual riding technique.

Shortly after setting out from the cottage it became apparent to Lathan that the Doctor's celebrated freethinking extended even into the realm of horseback riding. An impartial observer might have had some premonition of this when they had first mounted up at the castle the day before, for while Prince Charming and Lathan had mounted their steeds immediately, the Doctor spent a long time staring uneasily at his horse, with a sickened expression on his face. An enemy of the Doctor (supposing he were ever to have one) might have charged that the Doctor was afraid of his horse, and had never ridden one in his life. Coincidentally, this thought occurred to Lathan as well, and halfway through the first day's ride he had asked the Doctor if he had ever ridden before.

"Ridden before?!" Doctor Oldair scoffed. "Why, forty years ago I won the Piddling Cup, the Canterer's Open, the Slapleather Derby, and the Hoodahooda Horseman of the Year award, all in the same year!"

This had reassured Lathan, although Lathan was surprised by the horseback riding technique apparently used in the Doctor's heyday, which consisted of holding onto the saddle horn with both hands, sitting hunched over the horse's neck, and looking ahead with an expression of perpetual astonishment.

"I guess styles change," Lathan had mused. Besides, he had learned to ride at a sheep shearing festival many years before, and perhaps hadn't learned a very aristocratic style.

The first day's ride had been so short that the Doctor experienced few difficulties in his riding, but problems began shortly after they left the cottage on the second day. Doctor Oldair's horse, like many other horses, was a great judge of human flesh. For the first day's ride he had been cautiously obedient, but, feeling the nervousness in his master's hand, he now decided to put the good Doctor through a few tests.

Thus, as the three horses were galloping along, the Doctor's horse suddenly slowed down and began to walk. Lathan and Prince Charming stopped and galloped back to see what was wrong.

"Doctor, Doctor, why have you slowed down?" Lathan asked breathlessly.

"Isn't it obvious?" Doctor Oldair asked, after fishing for something to say for a moment or two. "I've noticed some irregularities in this animal's hoofbeats. I think it's essential that he walks for a short distance to regain his strength."

"But Doctor Oldair, the Princess . . . .."

"Silence boy! I believe I know a bit more about horses than you do," the Doctor snapped, "and I beg you to remember your position!"

"Yes, try to remember your position, you impudent little rat," Prince Charming said indignantly, as he doused himself with a fresh bottle of perfume.

Soon the three horses were walking toward Scuttleton, with Lathan's horse walking ten yards to the rear, as befitting the horse of a peasant.

Ordinarily Lathan would have been humbled by Doctor Oldair's rebuke, but now, because he had a magic coin around his neck and the blood of a certain famous hero flowing through his veins, as well as a Princess to rescue, his reaction was actually bordering on anger, and he began to wonder whether enlisting the help of Doctor Oldair and the Prince had been such a good idea after all. Floppy was sure it wasn't a good idea, and it took all of Lathan's strength to keep the stout pup from jumping off his lap and biting not only the Doctor, but his horse as well. Fortunately, however, they hadn't gone far before the Doctor's horse, without any warning, began galloping ahead as fast as he could go, and soon Lathan and Prince Charming were trying gamely to catch up.

This sudden burst of speed brought them out of the forest and into more open country, where the Doctor's horse suddenly stopped once more, and began eating some grass at the side of the road. When the others arrived, Doctor Oldair began explaining that proper nutrition was essential to a growing horse, when the Doctor's horse suddenly began galloping forward ahead. Shortly thereafter he ran off the road for half a mile to get a drink of water, then he ran back to the road, galloped the wrong way for a quarter of a mile, then turned around and galloped back, occasionally stopping for a particularly fine-looking piece of grass along the way. When everyone finally caught up with him again, Doctor Oldair gave several logical explanations for this erratic behavior, and when Lathan humbly implied that the Doctor might take more control of his horse, Doctor Oldair accused him of being intolerant of other species, and their needs and desires. The Doctor's horse seemed to actually smirk at Lathan while the Doctor made this speech, and then suddenly galloped off toward Scuttleton as fast as he could go.

For a while the Princess Rescuers made good progress, despite the fact that Prince Charming was several times attacked by swarms of bees, which made vigorous attempts to pollinate him. As they travelled further and further north the trees grew sparser, the skies grew darker, and the air became cold and misty.

There were four taverns on the highway, one twenty miles from Scuttleton, one ten miles away, one five miles away, and one three miles away. At 11 o'clock the four adventurers arrived at the Noisy Boar tavern, the sight of which informed them they were only twenty miles away from their destination. Lathan and Prince Charming would have continued on, but Doctor Oldair insisted on stopping and getting some information, so while Lathan, Floppy, and the Prince waited outside, Doctor Oldair went inside and had a very extensive conversation with the barkeeper. When Doctor Oldair came outside again his face looked very flushed, and Lathan, fearing the worst, asked him what he had found out.

"You don't want to know," Doctor Oldair answered, ominously shaking his head, and then hiccuping, "We'll have to stop off at the next tavern to see if their information is any better."

The four Princess Rescuers rode on with new vigor (particularly the Doctor). When they arrived at the next tavern, The Waterlogged Beaver, the Doctor went inside and had an even more intensive talk with its barkeeper, and came out with an even redder face and a very grim aspect. When asked if the information in this tavern was any better than the information in the last tavern, the Doctor shook his head and said he would have to test the information in the next tavern before making a decision. At the next tavern, The Clumsy Ox, Doctor Oldair stayed twice as long as before, and when he came out he was not only red-faced, but literally staggering under the impact of all the information he had received. When Lathan hesitantly asked him what he had discovered, Doctor Oldair shook his head once more, burped, and then rode off toward the next tavern.

Unfortunately, the gathering of all this sensitive information made Doctor Oldair unsteady, and had an adverse effect on his riding abilities. He and his comrades were only a few miles from the ocean when they encountered a tiny stream that crossed the road. The Doctor's horse immediately stopped, realizing that it might be in danger of getting its hooves muddy. However, when the fastidious beast observed his two fellow horses crossing, he decided he would try it too. He stepped back a few paces and then crossed the stream with a graceful leap, but unfortunately the Doctor (who was downright reeling over the information he had lately received) did not get a chance to fully enjoy the beauty of this leap, because he fell off the horse in mid-air and landed in the stream.

Lathan immediately dismounted and ran to Doctor Oldair's assistance.

"Doctor, are you all right?" he asked as he propped up the Doctor's head.

"I . . . I think so," the Doctor replied with a cough.

"Thank goodness!" said Lathan. "I was scared when I saw the horse throw you."

"Throw me? Don't be ridiculous," Doctor Oldair mumbled. "If I hadn't jumped when I did the horse would have surely twisted its ankle on the loose rock. My quick thinking probably saved its life."

After enlightening Lathan on this point, Doctor Oldair passed out.

Fortunately Lathan saw that there was another tavern about half a mile down the road. After flopping Doctor Oldair across the saddle of his horse, an action that required every bit of Lathan's strength (Prince Charming would have helped, but his hands were sticky), Lathan walked his horse and the Doctor's horse toward the tavern, which bore the sign of a Silly Sow.

Chapter XIII

A Stopover at The Silly Sow

The Tavern of The Silly Sow (or "Pig Inn" as it was known to the locals) was run by the Slurp family. Mr. and Mrs. Slurp were plump, had red round faces, and, contrary to all the rules of nature, were nevertheless not jolly. The Slurps had five daughters, ranging in age from twelve to twenty. Mrs. Slurp was a great reader of cheap romantic novels, so her daughters were named Sapphira, Xenoluvla, Pomphilia, Kendall, and Sylvania. These girls were not lovely in the strictest sense of the word, although they were all very healthy, had unusually strong arms, and very powerful vocal cords.

The eldest daughter, Sylvania, was sweeping up some rubbish near the entrance of the tavern when she saw Prince Charming riding toward her, with Lathan walking beside him, leading two horses, one carrying Doctor Oldair, and the other carrying Floppy. Princes are fairly easy to recognize, especially if dressed as resplendently as Prince Charming, and soon the eldest Miss

Slurp was squealing with delight and shouting to everyone in hearing distance that the biggest hunk of a Prince she had ever seen in her life was coming up the road. Soon there were five Miss Slurps, one Mr. Slurp, one Mrs. Slurp, two fishermen, a travelling salesman, and three seamstresses standing in front of the Silly Sow, gawking at Prince Charming. The first glimpse of his rock-hewn, sun-tanned face and the gorgeous pink feather in his cap sent every female heart a-fluttering, and when he came close enough for them to smell his fashionable perfume (which was about a quarter of a mile away) the women were all driven into a state of ecstasy.

When he arrived at the tavern a couple of the girls threw themselves in front of the horse's feet, while everyone else raced up to him and asked if they could be of some service, pushing Lathan out of the road and nearly trampling him to death in the process.

"It's very kind of you to offer your services," Prince Charming told the attentive group, "but, at present, I really have no use for them. Sorry,"

("He's *so* nice!" Miss Sylvania Slurp said to herself.)

"Right now I'm on a quest to rescue a princess," he continued, "and I don't have any time for delays."

("He's *so* brave!" Miss Kendall Slurp gasped to herself.)

"However, my great and worthy friend Doctor Oldair—he's on one of the horses the boy is holding—has been injured in a little mishap. In fact, you might say he had a 'falling out' with his horse."

Everyone laughed uproariously.

("He's *so* witty!" Sapphira, Xenoluvla, and Pomphilia sighed.)

"And so, if it's not too much trouble," the Prince concluded, "I think we'd better get the Doctor inside and see if he's all right."

Lathan was already trying to pull the Doctor off the horse when—amidst cries of "Get out of the way, boy!" and "Watch it clumsy, you'll hurt him!"—the Doctor was rudely pulled out of Lathan's grasp by Miss Sylvania and Miss Kendall Slurp, who carried the Doctor over to the tavern as if he were a football. The two maidens had a great argument over who would have the honor of carrying Doctor Oldair over the threshold, and the poor Doctor was nearly torn limb from limb until the fair Sylvania managed to pull him from her sister's grasp and carry him inside to the nearest chair. Soon everyone was inside the tavern, gathered around Doctor Oldair, except for two regular customers who stared calmly at the scene from the back of the room, and Floppy, who was not allowed inside.

"Who did you say this man was?" Mr. Slurp asked as he examined the patient.

"This is the great philosopher Doctor Oldair, the greatest philosopher in the Western world!" Lathan responded forcefully. He had had a hard time pushing his way into the room.

"Who did you say this man was?" Mr. Slurp asked again, as if he hadn't asked before.

"This is Doctor Oldair, the great philosopher," Prince Charming replied.

"My goodness! The great philosopher!" Mr. Slurp cried as he looked down at his stricken guest. The room buzzed with excitement at the news. Imagine, the great philosopher in The Silly Sow!

"He fell off his horse, and please see if you can help him, because we're in a terrible hurry!" said Lathan, after which there was an awkward silence.

"Tell me," Mr. Slurp asked, as he bent down to examine the Doctor once more, "How did the Doctor hurt himself?"

"He fell off his horse," Prince Charming replied.

A few of the young ladies screamed at this announcement, and the men shook their heads direfully, while Mrs. Slurp stated that no horse could be trusted anymore. Horses weren't like this in her day, she said.

Lathan, who at this point might have had some reason to doubt the effectiveness of his communication skills, nevertheless spoke up once more.

"Please, could you tell us how far it is to Scuttleton from here?" he said. "We're on our way to rescue Princess Purella of Hoodahooda, and there's no time to waste!"

This plea was followed by a prolonged silence, which was finally broken by Mr. Slurp.

"I don't want to seem too inquisitive," he said, "but I'm curious to know why you've come here, and where you're heading."

"That's no secret," said Prince Charming (as indeed, it wasn't). "We're on our way to the port of Scuttleton, in an effort to rescue Princess Purella of Hoodahooda."

This startling revelation thrilled everyone, and even the two regulars in the back of the tavern came forward to shake the Prince's hand. The Prince was quickly deluged with information; Scuttleton was only three miles away, it was all downhill, you could practically see the ocean from here, rescuing the Princess would be no problem for a brave man like the Prince, etc., etc.

Meanwhile Lathan, seeing that his input into the situation was not much desired, was beginning to slip outside when he heard Mr. Slurp say, "I think a strong cup of brandy will bring the good Doctor around."

"Brandy! But that contains alcohol!" Lathan said to himself. Lathan fought his way back inside.

"Don't give him brandy," Lathan implored. "Doctor Oldair is a great philosopher. I'm sure he'd never forgive you if you forced him to drink alcohol!"

Mr. Slurp reacted to this warning by filling a cup with brandy, and carrying it over to Doctor Oldair.

Just as he was about to pour a few drops of the fluid onto Doctor Oldair's lips, Lathan lunged forward and physically intervened, taking the cup of brandy out of Mr. Slurp's hand. Everyone, especially Mr. Slurp, was deeply shocked, and looked at Lathan

as if he had just dropped down from the sky, and they were noticing him for the first time. Everyone roundly cursed the "impudent boy," asked him who he thought he was, and threatened him
with physical violence. Lathan, however, stood firm.

"Doctor Oldair is too good a man to touch alcohol," Lathan
exclaimed, "and I won't let you force him."

Fortunately for all concerned, Doctor Oldair suddenly regained consciousness and asked what was going on.

"Doctor Oldair, they were going to make you drink brandy!"
Lathan exclaimed.

"No!" said Doctor Oldair.

"I told them you wouldn't want any. After all, that stuff has
alcohol in it!"

"You know, I believe it does," Doctor Oldair replied.

"Still," Doctor Oldair added after a pause, "even though I
might despise the thought of tasting alcohol, it might insult
our hosts if I refuse, and some recent scientific studies have in-
dicated that it may have some medicinal value after all."

"But Doctor . . .."

"No, no Lathan," said Doctor Oldair, in the tones of a mar-
tyr, "I'm an old man, I've seen much of life, and I'm not afraid to
suffer in a good cause."

Doctor Oldair then took the cup out of Lathan's hand and
drank it down in one vigorous swallow, so that Lathan could
only admire the Doctor's deep philosophical resignation.

Shortly after Mr. and Mrs. Slurp persuaded the Doctor to
take a second cup, Lathan was told by various people in the
room that: one, his face was not pleasing to them; two, he didn't
grovel properly to his superiors (who, theoretically I suppose,
comprised every person in the room); and three, he smelled (and
they must have had very good noses indeed to smell anything
beyond the fruitful aroma of Prince Charming). In short, they
didn't want him inside the tavern anymore, and shoved him
outside, telling him to watch the horses.

Since watching the horses was not a particularly thrilling activity (considering that the horses were all hitched to a post, and too tired to move), Lathan decided this would be a good opportunity to scout around. He had heard them say the ocean was close by, and wanted to see it as quickly as possible.

"If we can get a look at the ocean, we can see if the Count's ship is on it," he explained to Floppy. "If we don't see any ships, then the Count probably hasn't sailed and we still have a chance to rescue the Princess."

About a half-mile up the road, and several hundred yards to the right, there was a high, treeless hill which looked like it held a commanding view of the country beyond. Lathan and Floppy dashed over to it as fast as they could go, and, after a good fifteen-minute climb (the hill was much steeper than they thought) they reached the top. They soon discovered that this hill, instead of having a commanding view of the entire region, actually had only a commanding view of a larger hill about 500 yards further away. Undaunted, Lathan and Floppy ran down into the canyon between the two hills and up the other side. There, at the top of the second hill, they were greeted with the most spectacular view that each of them had ever seen.

The hill was about a thousand feet above sea level, and far below, about three miles away, the ocean stretched out before them, sinking into the distant horizon. Neither Lathan nor Floppy had seen the ocean before, and it was a scary sight for Lathan, for when he saw the restlessness of its surface and its incredible vastness, and imagined what sort of creatures might lurk in its icy depths, it seemed to him that the ocean was something living and dangerous, and not the larger species of pond he had always imagined.

"Arf!" said Floppy.

"You're right, Floppy," Lathan answered, "I don't see a ship on the whole ocean."

After gazing around for a few moments more Lathan did see a few boats very near the shore, which he thought were just small dinghies, but were actually large fishing boats. Lathan quite logically assumed that the Count would sail in a large ship, and so he knew that the Count had either sailed much earlier (which didn't seem possible), or not yet.

To his left, on the shore just beyond the fishing boats, Lathan spotted the port of Scuttleton and its little harbor. Beyond the town was a long stretch of windy beaches leading to the north.

Lathan's heart began beating loudly and insistently. Lathan knew that Purella was down there somewhere, praying to be rescued from the villainous Count. Lathan touched his magic coin lightly, for he had somehow gotten the idea that if he squeezed it too much it might lose some of its power, and he would need that power later on.

Then Lathan imagined himself to be in hand-to-hand combat with Count Zandar, then he imagined Purella kissing him in gratitude, then he imagined getting married to Purella (Prince Charming having decided to drop his claims because "Lathan truly deserves her"), and he was at the point of making decisions about his grandchildren's education when he was forcefully nudged by Floppy, who practically had to bite him to get him out of his reverie.

"Arf!" said Floppy bluntly, and with a slightly sarcastic air.

"Oh, sorry, Floppy," said Lathan, coming back abruptly to reality. "Well, this is it! Let's get the Doctor and the Prince, and save the Princess!"

"Arf!" said Floppy, seconding the motion, and the two of them raced back to The Silly Sow.

Back at The Silly Sow, Doctor Oldair had quite recovered, and, because of the respect shown him by Prince Charming, was treated by everyone as if he were an exceedingly wonderful person. Meanwhile, most of the ladies were giving Prince

Charming a complete tour of the tavern. Just as they were admiring the huge sign which gave the tavern its name (and which pictured a cheerful pig, which wore on its head something resembling a lamp shade), Lathan and Floppy ran up, announced to the Prince that the ocean was close by, and informed him that they should leave at once. Miss Sylvania Slurp responded to this announcement by kicking Lathan in the shin and telling him to go away. Floppy answered for his robust friend by grasping Miss Slurp firmly around the ankle with his teeth, and biting vigorously. Naturally a great uproar ensued, but when the dust finally settled Prince Charming announced that, yes, they truly had to leave. Soon he and Lathan and Floppy were mounted on their horses, waiting for Doctor Oldair, who said he would come out shortly, just as soon as he gathered one more bit of information.

While they waited, Lathan was literally shaking with excitement (and worry) over the thought of rescuing the fair Purella.

"She's so good, so kind, so beautiful!" Lathan couldn't help blurting out.

"Which one?" Prince Charming asked, as he ogled the line of admiring females who stood beside them, evaluating and ranking the appearance of each one with mathematical accuracy.

"No, not them!" Lathan replied with some warmth. "I mean Princess Purella, the most beautiful girl in the whole world."

"Her? The most beautiful?" Prince Charming sceptically replied. "What about her protruding lower lip?"

Prince Charming then further proceeded to describe to Lathan several physical flaws he had noted in the Princess, listing them in technical language, and a wealth of anatomical detail. The definitiveness of Prince Charming's evaluation was remarkable, considering he had only seen the subject once, and not under the best of circumstances. He concluded his analysis by reviewing in great detail her four most serious flaws (namely, a protruding lower lip, inadequate height, a slightly crooked front tooth, and hideously short eyelashes), and then announcing that on the Official Skindeepian 0-10 Beauty Scale he could only give her a 6.7.

Lathan was terribly shocked by the Prince's cool evaluation, and was eager to protest this mediocre review. He had casually noticed that Purella had a protruding lip and a crooked tooth (his dull observation had utterly failed to note her intolerably short eyelashes), but he thought these slight blemishes were themselves beautiful, because they helped to remind him that she was actually human, a fact about which he occasionally had grave doubts. Lathan, however, realized that to argue with the Prince over points of physical beauty was useless, and so he decided to praise Purella in another way.

"Well, the Princess is still better than any other girl in the world," Lathan boldly informed the Prince. "She's nice, kind, and brave, and she's got the best personality in the world."

"I didn't think much of her personality," the Prince said coldly. "I know you'll deny it, but she seems pretty independent-minded if you ask me."

"Well, what kind of personality do you look for in a girl?" Lathan asked, a little stung by the Prince's answer.

"What?"

"I said, 'What kind of personality do you look for in a girl?'."

"Personality?" said the Prince, who found the question baffling. "Oh, I don't know . . . just . . . just regular I guess."

He noticed the puzzled look on Lathan's face.

"Well, actually I like 'em kinda quiet. In fact, very quiet," he added after a pause.

Meanwhile Doctor Oldair, who was thoroughly awash with information, came stumbling out of the tavern and climbed onto his horse. Before they could leave, Prince Charming had to go through the ceremony of having his hand kissed or shaken by every person in the immediate vicinity. In the meantime Miss Sylvania Slurp was in a panic, because she had lost a valuable ring (an engagement ring actually; for on the following Saturday Miss Slurp was scheduled to form an indissoluble union with one Hezekiah Spittle, a local furniture polisher). Lathan, who really had enough on his mind worrying about Purella, was nevertheless so moved by her distress that he leaped off his horse and found the ring lying in the dusty road, where it had fallen while Miss Sylvania and Miss Kendall Slurp were scuffling over who would carry Doctor Oldair. Lathan picked up the ring and presented it to Miss Sylvania, who looked at him with great condescension, nodded her head at him in thanks, and told him that he was "lucky to find it." Lathan said she was quite welcome, and then mounted his horse once more. Finally Doctor Oldair and Prince Charming rode off, and Lathan followed the prescribed ten yards behind.

Miss Sylvania Slurp was embarrassed that a mere peasant like Lathan had recovered the ring for her, and just as he was riding away he could hear her say, "Did you see that skinny wretch give me the eye? He probably stole my ring from me just to give it back. Pathetic! Why can't a god like the Prince fall in love with me, instead of a pimply-faced little swine like that!"

A few days earlier comments like these would have had Lathan wallowing in a pit of self-condemnation, but in the last few days his whole outlook on life had changed, and he actually smiled at what she said, because she thought he was a nobody and tried to insult him, and had no idea that he was actually the son of "Trollkiller" Sven Svensson, and the possessor of a magic coin.

"What a silly girl," he said to himself.

Chapter XIV

The Arrival at Scuttleton, Followed by Desperate Plans and Desperate Actions

J ust beyond The Silly Sow the road headed steeply down hill, following a long series of switchbacks. When the Princess Rescuers finally reached the bottom of the hill, there was still a mile of flat, wooded ground between them and the prosperous little port of Scuttleton, a wind-beaten, fishy-smelling town, a large portion of which sat on pillars overhanging the ocean. When they realized they were near their destination Lathan practically shouted with excitement, while Doctor Oldair and Prince Charming, who suddenly realized that they were shortly expected to do something heroic, immediately slowed their horses to a walk, looked very grim, and began talking about the necessity of doing extensive reconnoitering before doing anything else. Doctor Oldair also began muttering something about "the things he did for gardens," while Prince Charming began estimating the Gross National Product of Hoodahooda on the corner of his saddle, and calculated how much a theoretical husband of a theoretical Hoodahoodan princess might earn annually in ready money.

As they neared the suburbs of Scuttleton (which consisted
of four badly-plowed fields, an orchard, three pumpkin patches,
two cottages, a dog, and an asthmatic billy goat) they passed
two boys and a girl playing by the side of the road. Actually,
only the girl was really playing; the two boys (who were smaller
than her, and very raggedly dressed) each held an end of a long
jump rope, which they grimly turned over and over while the
girl happily and effortlessly jumped. Apparently no one else was
allowed to jump until she missed, and, since this prospect was
nowhere in sight, the boys were using as many unethical meth-
ods as possible to make her miss, none of which was successful.
As Lathan rode past he noted that they looked at the girl as
sullenly as if they were captured slaves.

"Three thousand one hundred and thirty-six, three thousand one hundred and thirty-seven, three thousand one hundred and thirty-eight . . ." he could hear the girl saying until
her voice faded into the distance.

"I don't think we want to see any other people just yet,"
Doctor Oldair said. "Let's go over into the brush and think for a
bit."

They rode the horses into a large brushy area near a creek
and dismounted. Doctor Oldair then outlined what needed to
be done before they could rescue the Princess.

"First," he said, "we'll need to have someone go out and
reconnoiter, and find out what the situation is. Now let's see,
who should we have do that little job? Hmm. Well, I guess
Lathan would do all right."

He chose Lathan as if he were one of thirty well-qualified
candidates, who were each clambering for the job.

"Lathan," Doctor Oldair continued, "I want you to go into
the town, find out where Count Zandar's ship is docked, find
out when they plan to leave, and how many men they have—
and try not to get captured and killed while you're at it; meanwhile Prince Charming and I will stay here, make an analysis

of the entire situation, and take everything we know under advisement."

Lathan shook the Doctor's hand warmly and thanked the Doctor for giving him such an important responsibility. Lathan was now secretly glad that someone as wise as the Doctor was with them, for with Purella so near and in such danger it would have never occurred to him to sit in the brush all day and take things "under advisement."

Thus, after inwardly lamenting once more his lack of formal education, Lathan set out on his dangerous quest for information. Naturally he was accompanied by Floppy, who insisted on coming along because of his great love for Purella, and his great dislike of Prince Charming and Doctor Oldair. It seemed as if Floppy now strongly regretted bringing them along, and if there were any way to rescue Purella without them, Floppy would have abandoned them in an instant.

Lathan and Floppy hadn't walked far before they found themselves in the main square of Scuttleton. The strong smell of fish in the air practically slapped them in the face, and they gazed with wonder at the barnacle-encrusted docks, and the taverns, and the little shops of nautical equipment that lined the main square. Groups of weather-beaten loungers in funny caps were sprawled in various places, picking their teeth with splintered fragments of whalebone, and nodding their heads thoughtfully as they gravely discussed the fickleness of the weather, or the quality of the local beer. Lathan and Floppy, after going over to look at some fishing nets that were piled near the water, soon realized that several of the locals were staring at them, because there were never many strangers in Scuttleton, and Lathan and Floppy had a "landlubberly" appearance. Lathan, deciding that he should get the business of reconnoitering over as soon as possible, went up to a sailor who sat in a chair next to the nets and asked him if he knew where Count Zandar's ship was docked.

The sailor, a mature gentleman of about fifty, wore black greasy pants, a striped woolen shirt, and a blue, battered cap, and smoked a pipe that was about the length of Lathan's arm. His hair was thin, his eyes were bright, and his face was brown and deeply wrinkled, so that it looked as if he spent at least one hour a day being roasted over a slow fire.

This sailor was apparently not a very social individual, for when Lathan addressed him he looked at Lathan with some astonishment, as if to have a person walk up and actually speak to him was unique in his experience, and very difficult to believe. He gave Lathan a long, healthy stare (which made Lathan feel very awkward), but then his expression gradually softened, as if he had decided that although speaking was certainly a novelty, he was a man of the world and was willing to try anything once.

"So," he said after about a half-minute's pause, and then paused for a half-minute more, "yer lookin' to eyeball the Count's bark, eh?"

"Uh, yes, that's right," said Lathan. "Oh please tell us he hasn't already sailed!"

The sailor thoughtfully took a couple more puffs on his pipe, stared at the ground for a couple of minutes, and then continued the conversation as if it had never been interrupted.

"Sailed? Lad, ye sound a bit new-rigged. Ye can eyeball the sky, can't ye?"

Lathan certainly could eyeball the sky, and in fact had eyeballed it every day of his life, but no matter how hard he eyeballed it he couldn't eyeball anything in it that was unusual, except perhaps for a few extra clouds, which looked a bit darker than normal. Lathan told this to the sailor, who replied by puffing fiercely on his pipe, and not saying anything for the next minute and a half.

"Look 'ee lad," the sailor eventually continued, "either your main sail's ripped, or you never stepped between stem and stern not to know that there's a sou'easter comin' on!"

"There's going to be a storm?"

"Don't lag astern, lad," the grizzled tar replied. "What did I just say? A sou'easter!"

"Does that mean that no ships have sailed, or will sail?" Lathan asked.

The sailor replied that any swab that weighed anchor in a sou'easter had ballast where his crow's nest should be.

"Then the Count's ship is still here!" Lathan exclaimed.

"'Tis not here exactly, lad," the sailor replied. "She's berthed in a cove about two miles up the coast."

The sailor, weary of all the chattering he had been doing, sighed deeply, stared at the ground, and thoughtfully resumed smoking.

"Thank you very much! You've been a great help!" said Lathan to the loquacious old salt, who acknowledged his thanks by giving a minuscule nod of the head, and taking a thoughtful puff on his pipe.

Lathan and Floppy immediately raced off to find the Count's ship. They ran out of the main square, down several gravelly streets (there were not many streets in Scuttleton), and ended up at the northernmost limits of the town. No roads led to the north, and Lathan and Floppy crossed over the rocks on the edge of the ocean as best they could. They passed a couple of picturesque cottages, and finally came upon a wide, wind-swept beach that stretched on toward the misty, uninhabited north.

They ran beside the stunted trees at the edge of the beach so they would have a chance to hide if they were spotted by one of Count Zandar's men. When they had run for what Lathan thought was at least two miles they saw some cliffs and steep hills in front of them.

"The cove must be just up ahead, Floppy," said Lathan. "We'd better be careful and stay in these trees."

Moving carefully through trees, brush, and rocks, they climbed up one of the steep hills that overlooked the cove and looked down.

Anchored in the cove was a big black ship, with big black sails, a bank of big black oars on either side, and a big black dragon as its figurehead. Scattered both on ship and shore were about thirty burly men; the ones on the ship were entertaining themselves by spitting into the water, while the ones on shore were gleefully throwing ants and spiders into their campfire.

"I wonder where they've got her," Lathan whispered to Floppy.

Just then they heard rustling in the brush about thirty yards below them. The hill which rose above the cove was steep but not unclimbable, and soon Lathan saw two men come out of the bushes, a location they were inspired to go to by an excessive consumption of beer. Lathan and Floppy could overhear their conversation.

"So, she scratched you in the face too, eh?" one of the men said to the other.

The other mumbled a reply.

"And then she cut you on the hand? Ha!" the first man replied. "She's a feisty one, but pretty!"

The second man mumbled something inaudible.

"Don't make me laugh," the first man replied. "The Count has her locked in the hold for your protection, not hers. I tell you, for a Princess, she's vicious!"

So, she was in the ship's hold! Lathan had a strong urge to run down the hill, jump in the water, swim to the ship, and rescue her right then and there, but he realized this might be a bit impractical, and comforted himself with the thought that the Count's ship wouldn't leave for several days because of the incoming storm.

"You! Up there!"

Lathan and Floppy froze. They recognized the voice very well.

"At your service, Count Zandar!" said one of the men below them.

"Get down from there! We have to get the ship ready to sail!"

"Yes, sir!"

Count Zandar was walking along the beach with his usual menacing strides. Og ambled behind him, chewing on a starfish.

"But Count, there's a storm coming in," Lathan heard one of the men say.

"All the better," said the Count. "I hate calm weather—it makes me seasick. Stow the gear! We sail in one hour!"

One hour! Lathan and Floppy practically fell over backwards at the news, and tidal waves of sweat began rolling off their faces. One hour! How were they going to rescue Purella?!

Lathan watched the men as they began piling the gear on the beach, and when they saw that much of their equipment consisted of knives, axes, and other lethal weapons of all sizes and descriptions, his heart sank. The Count's men were all big, strong, and noisy, and looked anxious to crush anything that crossed their path.

"Floppy, what do we do?" Lathan asked.

Floppy, who usually had a recommendation for everything, was conspicuously silent, except for the sound of his heart beating away like a drum. Lathan stared helplessly at the Count's men, and when he thought of Purella being in their clutches, he felt very sick.

"Floppy, we've got to go back and get Doctor Oldair and the Prince. They'll know what to do. Come on!"

Lathan and Floppy scrambled back the way they came and raced back toward Scuttleton. They passed through its streets and sprinted to the brushy area where Doctor Oldair and the Prince were taking everything "under advisement." They found both men in a state of profound meditation, with their eyes closed, and their bare feet cooling off in the water of the little creek.

"Doctor! Doctor! The Princess is locked away in the ship a couple of miles away, and they're going to sail in less than an hour!"

The Doctor opened his eyes.

"Indeed?" said the Doctor, in the cool, non-committal tone that only a philosopher can exhibit.

"Yes, and we have to go at once!"

Lathan quickly explained the entire situation to Doctor Oldair, and described in great detail the brutal appearance of the Count's men. After hearing this description Prince Charming opened his eyes, gulped, and looked pleadingly at Doctor Oldair.

"Lathan, I'm afraid rescuing the Princess will be impossible," Doctor Oldair said matter-of-factly. "We gave it our best try though, and we'll have to be content with that."

"What do you mean?" asked Lathan, flabbergasted.

"Something's come up, that's all," the Doctor replied. "Take a look."

Doctor Oldair brushed some branches aside and showed Lathan several pieces of bright green fungus that were growing on a tree stump.

"That's Green Phantasia of Phylum Funjungatta," the Doctor explained. "It's very rare, and if I don't gather it soon it might turn brown and die. Since it will take me about an hour to gather all this, I don't see how we can rescue the Princess."

"But the Princess is more important than a plant!" Lathan exclaimed.

Floppy growled.

"You may think so now," the noted philosophical horticulturist replied, "but when you get to my age, young man, you'll realize that I'm absolutely right about everything."

"But I can't wait that long!" said Lathan.

"Don't be impertinent, boy," Prince Charming interjected. "If Doctor Oldair wants to collect his mung, or whatever you call it, let him do it. Naturally I'd rather rescue Princess Putrella . . ."

"That's 'Purella'," corrected Lathan.

". . . but it's Doctor Oldair who really knows best, and I'm willing to do whatever he says."

"Please, Doctor," Lathan begged, with tears welling in his eyes, "time is running out!"

Doctor Oldair was rather amused to see this display of emotion on Lathan's part.

"Come on, bear up, boy," Doctor Oldair said with manly good nature. "You don't see me breaking down over this, do you?"

The Doctor then skipped over to the tree trunk and started collecting fungus.

"These are beautiful specimens," Doctor Oldair rhapsodized as he began stuffing the fungus into his shirt. "Their color would have made them match beautifully with my specimens of. . . of. . ."

"Flaming Pink Chrysopata Scumatta of Phylum Fulvibrata?" said Lathan helpfully, miraculously remembering the name.

"Don't mention that name!" said Doctor Oldair, suddenly agitated. "I never want to hear that name again."

"Don't worry Doctor," said Lathan sadly, "in less than an hour the last seeds of it will sail away forever."

Doctor Oldair half-heartedly resumed fungus-collecting for a moment, but then abruptly stopped.

"I've been giving this a great deal of thought," he said to Lathan. "I hate to see you upset like this, so I think we might as well go and rescue the Princess. Oh, sure, I know she might not really exist, and I know you're going to feel guilty and insist that I stay here and collect fungus, and tell me that I've done more than enough already, and you'd be right too; still, I'm a sentimental old man, and I just can't resist making young people happy."

Lathan was overcome with joy. He thanked Doctor Oldair profusely, commended him for his generosity of spirit, and apologized for his own selfishness.

"Don't mention it," Doctor Oldair replied, with great magnanimity. "And now, let's be off!"

Meanwhile, Prince Charming was stuttering and briskly shaking his head.

"What's wrong, Your Highness?" Doctor Oldair asked.

"You're . . . you're sure you don't want to collect fungus instead?" the Prince asked.

"Quite sure," Doctor Oldair replied.

"You see, the problem is, I can't go out in public now. My hair is a mess."

"I'm sorry, Your Highness," said the Doctor, "but we don't have time to waste."

Before long they were riding toward the Count's ship, and soon arrived at the cove. They tied their horses to some stunted trees, went to the place where Lathan and Floppy had hid earlier, and stared down at the Count's ship below.

On the beach most of the Count's men were still stacking supplies, while a few others were rowing them out to the ship.

"What we need now is a diversion," said Doctor Oldair, obviously relying on many years of philosophical experience, "One of us must divert all the men, while the rest of us sneak over to where the supplies are, hide under the tarps, and get rowed out to the ship. Now, let's see, which one of us would be the best choice to create the diversion. Hmmm."

Doctor Oldair and Prince Charming each stared at Lathan as if he were a mirror. Floppy frowned.

"I suppose I could try," said Lathan.

"You?" said Doctor Oldair, astounded at this unexpected idea. "Well, I guess it's all right, but I hope you realize that even though you would be saving the life of a beautiful and completely helpless princess, it still might be dangerous."

"Dangerous or not, I'll do it!" Lathan cried.

"All right then, if you insist," said Doctor Oldair, shaking his head as he considered the impetuosity of youth.

Without further delay Lathan proceeded to scoop up a large pile of rocks and scramble down the hill toward the beach.

"I am Lathan, robust shepherd lad and son of 'Trollkiller' Sven Svensson," he shouted, "and I call you all cowards, villains, and fools!"

Lathan climaxed this speech by hurling rocks at every coward, villain, and fool that happened to be in range. He even shouted "Death to tyrants!" several times, but his outburst unfortunately did not achieve its intended effect, for most of the neighboring tyrants didn't even notice him, or feel the rocks that bounced off their muscular bodies. Those few who did notice him thought he was quite amusing, and playfully threw the rocks back at him, which on more than one occasion came close to giving Lathan a sudden skull fracture. Soon even these playful fellows ignored him and resumed their work.

"You are the lowest form of vermin I have ever seen!" Lathan shouted.

No response.

"When I first saw all of you I thought this was a basket-weaving seminar!" Lathan continued.

No response.

Lathan walked over to two big kegs that were sitting in the sand nearby. He played around with their nozzles for a moment or two, and then spoke once more.

"I have just emptied all of your beer onto the beach!"

The words had hardly escaped his lips when a deluge of spears and at least one flaming arrow came flying at him, which he evaded with the utmost difficulty. A score of burly men came running at him, with weapons in their hands and vengeance in their hearts.

Lathan, delighted that his diversion was working, but conscious of the fact that it's possible to have too much of a good thing, darted into the nearby woods as fast as he could go. After pausing to inspect the empty kegs (an examination which caused more than one stout warrior to burst into tears), the Count's men began pursuing Lathan with redoubled energy, muttering curses and highly detailed threats as they ran.

Not all of the Count's men were chasing after Lathan. The Count and Og were nowhere to be seen, the three men in the boat were still slowly moving supplies from the beach to the ship, and there was still one man on the beach guarding the supplies.

Doctor Oldair frowned; the lone guard was ruining his plans. Most of the supplies were covered by canvas tarps, so it would be easy to hide among the supplies and get rowed to the ship if the one guard would only leave. However, this faithful watchman showed no sign of leaving his post, and in fact (after checking to see if any of his comrades were in sight) pulled out an sleeveless lavender sweater and began sewing joyfully. Prince Charming was delighted to see a sailor indulging in such a beneficial activity, but the Doctor frowned even more.

Floppy came up with a solution. He didn't trust the Doctor or the Prince, but he knew that someone had to get Purella out of that ship right away. He ran down to the beach, walked up to the guard, barked pleasantly, wagged his tail, and then grabbed the guard's sweater and ran off down the beach.

"Hey, that's mine!" said the burly seamster, accurately. He leaped to his feet and chased after Floppy.

"Here's our chance," said Doctor Oldair.

Grabbing Prince Charming by the arm, he led the reluctant hero down to the beach, where they immediately hid themselves among the supplies.

"Stay under the tarp and try to get into one of the crates," Doctor Oldair whispered. "Make sure you keep still when they come to load us onto the boat."

Meanwhile, Lathan was still partaking in his highly successful diversion, for even though he had run about two miles inland (through a brushy, rocky region with no trails) he was still being followed closely by the Count's vengeful men, who did not approve of Lathan's imposing on them a beer-free diet. It has been noted earlier in this history that Lathan was not a fast runner; however, the rocks and arrows that flew past his head, and the many threats of physical injury that accompanied them, inspired Lathan almost as much as his magic coin, and helped lengthen his stride considerably. In fact, Lathan became convinced he was pulling away from his pursuers. Their voices were fading away, and his face was beginning to brighten with hope, when suddenly he saw two of the Count's men run out of the trees in front of him.

"There he is!" one of them shouted.

"We've finally cut him off!" the other replied.

Lathan heard more voices behind him.

"Good work, men! That's the way!"

Rats! They had seen the direction he was heading and had managed to surround him.

Lathan ran to his left, but even more of the Count's men came bounding out of the woods on that side. He turned and ran back to the right, the only direction that remained. Their voices sounded almost on top of him now, and he could sense them slowly converging on him. He ran forward, desperately pushing bush and tree limbs out of his way, and went down to the bottom of a small canyon. When he reached the little creek that flowed through the canyon, he stopped short. The creek was not very wide, but there were sheer fifteen-foot rock walls on either side of it. He had no time to climb down into the creek and climb up the other side. The only thing he could do was try to jump across.

"This is near where we went this morning!" he heard one of his pursuers say.

"Look, he's right there!" another one shouted.

Lathan had no time to waste. He took a running start and leaped across the creek. He made it! Barely, however, for he was hanging by his arms from the ledge on the other side, trying feverishly not to lose his grip.

"Get him! Get him!" the voices shouted.

Lathan was struck in the shoulder by a rock. He tried to pull himself up, but his arms were too weak. Desperately he tried to reach down and touch his magic coin, but before he could he lost his grip and fell into the creek. He banged his head on a rock when he landed, and his legs and lower torso plunged into the icy water. His body ached and his vision blurred, but he thought he could see some figures standing above him. He heard a roar of laughter, and then everything went black.

Chapter XV

*Contains Too Many Adventures to be Easily Described in a
Single Chapter Heading*

Doctor Oldair and Prince Charming stayed hidden in
the supplies for a long time, but were eventually rewarded for their patience. The three boatmen, who in
the meanwhile had come to shore and loaded up other crates,
finally came to the crates where the two rescuers were hiding
and loaded them onto the boat.

"Hey, some of these crates stink," said a sailor as he tried to
peek under one of the tarps. "What's in here, rancid fruit?"

"Don't worry about it," another sailor said. "It's probably
just a dead rat."

Soon the sailors reached the ship, and with the help of a
crewman on board and a few heavy-duty pulleys they loaded the
crate on board. They carried the crate down into the hold, and
then returned to the deck. As soon as the sailors left the hold
Doctor Oldair fumbled his way out of his crate.

"You look around down here," he whispered to a particularly malodorous crate nearby. "I'll see if I can find anything up above."

"But I thought they said she was in the hold," a voice from the malodorous crate replied.

"If she's here I can't see her. She could be anywhere."

Soon Doctor Oldair found the ladder that led out of the hold and climbed to the upper levels. The ship was a galley, fitted with both sails and oars, and after moving through the rowing area and carefully avoiding any straggling sailors, he made his way up to the officer's quarters.

He searched each cabin thoroughly, perhaps too thoroughly, for he seemed to have the idea that he might find Purella in some very unusual places. For example, he searched in every drawer and every planter box that he came across, despite the fact that the chances of finding a full-sized princess sequestered in either of those locations was very remote. After searching each cabin he snuck back down to the hold.

"Your Highness," the Doctor whispered as he crept over to the Prince's crate, "have you finished searching down here?"

"It's too dark," Prince Charming whispered as he finally managed to pull himself out of the crate, "I can't see a thing."

"Why don't you go up top and find something we can use as a torch," Doctor Oldair said, "We'll search every inch of this ship if we have to."

"It shouldn't be that hard to find a princess," Prince Charming said.

"You never know," Doctor Oldair replied.

Doctor Oldair guided Prince Charming over to the ladder, but then the Prince hesitated.

"What happens if I get caught?" Prince Charming asked.

"They'll probably feed you to the sharks," a low voice in the opposite corner of the hold suggested.

Prince Charming and Doctor Oldair froze. Suddenly they saw the sparks fly from five pieces of flint, and soon the hold was orange with torchlight. Count Zandar sat placidly in a corner, accompanied by Og and four other torchbearing guards. The Count smiled coldly at the two intruders, and Prince Charming took the opportunity to dive head first back into his crate. Doctor Oldair cringed spasmodically.

"Doctor, this is an honor," said the Count.

"Duh huh, duh huh, duh huh," said Og.

While Doctor Oldair was suffering extreme mental pain, his dear comrade Lathan was wracked with physical pain, and was continually lapsing in and out of consciousness. Lathan had the sensation that he was being carried, and he thought he could hear voices which said, "It's a little farther," "Is he tied good?," and "They stay there in the day and leave at night."

Lathan heard hearty bursts of laughter coming from all around him, and then he felt someone kicking him in the side.

"Get up," he heard someone say.

At first Lathan thought he was dreaming, but after four or five more kicks the reality of the situation became apparent. Lathan opened his eyes.

He was, as he suspected, surrounded by a large group of the Count's men, who laughed gleefully as he opened his eyes. Lathan looked around and saw that they were in a flat area among a grove of oak trees. He was lying next to a huge pit, which had a circular opening about twenty feet across. Nearby sat a massive oak tree, whose thick branches spread out over the pit, and Lathan was disconcerted to see that a rope had been hung over one of the overhanging branches, one end of which was tied to his right foot.

"He's ready!" the man who had kicked him said.

One of the men swung the free end of the rope across the pit, where the first man caught it and handed the end to Lathan, so that now one end of the rope was attached to Lathan's foot, and the other end was in his hands.

"We put knots into the rope so you could hold onto it easier," the man said, referring to the rope in Lathan's hands, "but remember, if you let go of the rope you die."

After giving this final recommendation, he picked Lathan up off the ground and hurled him into the pit.

Lathan plunged about ten feet into the darkness, until the rope finally jerked taut. He was hanging so tightly to the knotted rope in his hands that his fall was arrested completely, although he nearly dislocated both his shoulders in the process. Soon he found himself hanging upside-down in gloomy darkness, clutching tightly to the rope in his arms, while he could hear the branch above creaking ominously under his weight.

Although he was staring at the bottom of the pit he couldn't see it at first, because his eyes hadn't adjusted to the darkness. After a moment or two his eyes did adjust, and he thought he saw the bottom of the pit some twenty feet further below. It was hard to tell, but he thought he saw something moving at the bottom of the pit, and he decided that there must be an underground stream flowing through. Suddenly, from the top of the pit, he heard a familiar voice.

"So shepherd lad, you chose to disobey me."

The ominous voice of Count Zandar was unmistakable.

"Peasant! See where your foolishness has brought you! I discussed this with your two friends just a short time ago—it's unfortunate that you'll never see those fine gentlemen again."

Lathan gritted his teeth, and tried fiercely not to lose his grip on the rope.

"Oh, and don't worry about the Princess," the Count added. "I'm sure she and I will get along very well."

"You leave her alone!" Lathan shouted, but considering his posture and present situation, this was not a very threatening admonition.

"I am the son of 'Trollkiller' Sven Svensson," Lathan announced proudly, which caused the chuckling above him to convert to uproarious laughter, "and I promise you that even if I fall into this pit and break both my legs I'll still find a way out of it, and I'll come back to save the Princess!"

"Oh my, that is brave of you. I'm sure your 'dad' would be proud to hear it."

The Count's men erupted with further peals of laughter.

"However, young man," the Count continued, "I fear that you misapprehend the dangers of your situation. Allow me to clarify things for you."

Suddenly two burning branches hurtled past him and landed on the floor of the pit below. The burning branches illuminated the bottom of the pit, and Lathan thought he saw the water in the pit actually shrink away from the fire. When his eyes became further adjusted he realized that it wasn't water at all; tens of thousands of spiders were massed at the bottom of the pit.

"Interesting, aren't they?" said the Count. "They tell me they're quite poisonous too. It would be a shame to break your leg in the bottom of this pit."

The perspiration rolled off Lathan's face as he watched the hairy little creatures swarming beneath him. He thought he saw them looking up at him with their beady little eyes, licking their greedy lips in anticipation of a sumptuous feast. Lathan's hands and arms were numb from holding the rope, and for an instant his grip slipped and he almost fell.

"Now, now, don't fall," the Count instructed. "Just think of the consequences."

Lathan struggled to get a better grip on the rope. He heard the Count's men talking cheerfully above him, obviously enjoying the macabre spectacle of a shepherd lad hanging upside-down over a pit of spiders. Lathan assumed that they would stay and watch until he fell and was gnawed to death by the spiders, which shows how little he knew of the world, and how unfamiliar he was with the ways of super-villains.

When a common villain sees an enemy he will generally shoot or stab him on the spot, without so much as saying hello or good-bye. However, unlike common villains, the average super-villain is never this crude, and, in fact, killing an enemy in such an easy and commonplace fashion almost never occurs to him. Instead, he will incapacitate his victim temporarily, and then spend many hours of thought, several days of hard work, and sometimes large sums of money devising an elaborate method to kill his adversary. This elaborate method sometimes involves tying the victim to a conveyer belt which slowly carries him to some gruesome fate, or often the victim is tied next to some barrels of gunpowder, and as soon as the sun rises its reflection will hit a mirror which will ignite a long fuse, which will slowly burn toward the explosive barrels, etc., etc. The variations that can be played on this theme are endless, and some super-villains design deaths so elaborate that six hours—and seven different stages—must take place before the victim is finally killed.

Nevertheless it is a fixed rule among the super-villain fraternity that as soon as the complicated killing machinery has been set in motion, and the victim has been informed of all the gruesome occurrences that are about to take place, the super-villain will then look at his watch, or some other time-piece, and suddenly remember that he has to be somewhere else in five minutes. He then wishes the victim good day, chuckles fiendishly, and then leaves the premises with all of his men, not bothering to watch the result of the many hours of diligent preparation. Lathan, however, was unaware of this standard procedure, and so a chill went down his spine when he heard the word "farewell," and the sound of the voices above him fading away. Soon all Lathan could hear was the wind whistling through the oaks.

"Help!" he shouted, while he adjusted his hands to get a better grip on the rope.

There was no answer. Although they were his enemies, the sound of the Count's men talking above him had been something of a comfort. But now he was all alone.

He twisted himself so he could see the top of the pit out of the corner of his left eye. The gnarled oak branches, like the twisted fingers of an elderly giant, loomed over the pit, and Lathan could only see a few patches of the red sky beyond.

"Help!" he shouted once more.

His hands slipped. The knotted portion of the rope came out of his hands and for an instant he started to plunge into the pit. He grabbed wildly at the rope, finally getting it into his grasp once more. He had slipped a further five feet into the pit, and his hands were throbbing with rope burn.

He now hung only fifteen feet above the spiders. The branches had burned out, so he couldn't see the spiders anymore, but he knew they were there, and shuddered. Soon he was trembling violently, and the perspiration was flowing into his eyes and stinging them. He awkwardly looked back at the top of the pit, but he could no longer see the red sky. The sun had set; it was night, and he was very alone.

"I am the son of 'Trollkiller' Sven Svensson," he said brokenly, trying to reassure himself.

He couldn't hold on much longer. He tried to touch his magic coin with his left hand, but then lost his grip and fell.

"Purella," he said as he plunged through the darkness, just before striking the bottom of the pit.

Chapter XVI

Wherein Lathan Dies a Horrible Death, or Some Relatively Unbelievable Occurrences Must Take Place

Because Lathan had slipped further down the rope before he fell, his landing, though painful, produced no broken bones. He was shaken momentarily, but when he came to his senses the thought of the spiders swarming all over him made him jump to his feet, screaming in terror. He danced around wildly for a full minute, until he slipped and fell to the ground once more, his panic having made him almost bereft of his senses. Suddenly, however, he sat still. His hands, which rested on the ground before him, felt no spiders at all, only dust. Quickly he felt all over his body. There were no spiders on him anywhere.

Lathan was confused. He felt carefully around in the darkness, but still could feel no spiders, and couldn't understand why. For awhile he wondered if he had somehow fallen into the wrong pit, until he felt the two burnt branches, and the huge pile of rope that had fallen in with him. He slipped the rope off his foot and began pondering where the spiders might be—not that he was at all anxious to find them.

He sat for a long time, elated about still being alive, and very perplexed about why. Suddenly something someone said while he was half-conscious came to mind, "They stay there in the day, and leave at night."

"That's it. He was talking about the spiders," Lathan said to himself.

He jumped to his feet and began investigating the pit, wary lest he run into any eight-legged straggler who hadn't yet made his departure. After satisfying himself that all the spiders were gone, and sadly discovering that the pit contained no avenues of departure for anyone greater than three inches tall, he took a seat in the center of the pit and began thinking. In about seven hours the spiders would be back.

"It would probably take my father ten minutes to escape from here, but I'm sure it'll take me a little longer," Lathan said to himself as he grasped his magic coin. "Still, with the blood of 'Trollkiller' Sven Svensson flowing through my veins I cannot fail!"

Six and a half hours later Lathan was still sitting at the bottom of the pit, feeling like the very epitome of failure.

He had tried everything; climbing the walls, digging for secret passages, throwing the heavy rope back over the overhanging oak branch (his best throw came about forty feet short), and shouting for help with great volubility. The result of all his efforts was a dirty face, a wrenched shoulder, and a hoarse voice.

He sat down on the tangle of rope, exhausted. He rested for a few minutes, but then, realizing that he had little time to waste, tried to climb to his feet, but his foot got caught in the rope and he fell down. When he fell his hands touched something he had surprisingly missed in his first inspection of the pit: bones. Lathan shrunk back. He remembered that the Count had said something about his two "friends." Perhaps while he was still unconscious, they had been . . . they had been . . .

Lathan jumped to his feet and shouted for help even louder than before. He looked up, and it seemed to him that the sky wasn't as dark as it was before. He heard a bird sing in the distance, and he felt a strange rumbling sound in the earth beneath him.

"Help! Help!" he cried.

He looked up at the sky once more, and his heart sank. A red tint was creeping into the night's blackness.

He grasped his magic coin and yelled louder and louder. He felt a rumbling movement all around him, which he instinctively knew signaled the return of the spiders. He looked desperately up at the sky once more, and no sooner did he look up than he was hit full in the face by a gallon of water.

"Gotcha!" squealed a little voice from above.

"Help! Help!" Lathan shouted.

The sky was growing redder still when Lathan saw a young female face peeking down into the pit.

"You can't get mad at me, you know, cause you're not supposed to be playing there anyway."

"Help! Help!" said Lathan. He noticed the bucket in the girl's hand, and recognized her as the girl who was jumping rope when he first arrived in Scuttleton.

"Hey, I hope you know there are spiders down there," the girl said saucily.

Lathan mentioned that he was aware of the fact.

"They're poisonous, you know," she continued, in the tone of an expert witness. "They're so poisonous, it's disgusting. I saw a cow that was killed by them once. It was disgusting. Its eyeballs were all chewed out and everything. I took one look at it and I was disgusted. It was real disgusting."

Lathan was not as impressed by these nuggets of information as the girl had expected, and he proceeded to shout "help" to her with quadrupled volume. The girl became confused.

"Why don't you just get out the same way you got in?" she asked, dropping her superior tone.

Lathan said that it was easy to fall in, but not so easy to fall out, or words to that effect.

"You want me to help you get out?" she asked.

"Yes! Yes! And hurry! The spiders will be here soon!"

"I've got my jump rope," said the girl excitedly, suddenly realizing she was in the middle of an adventure, "It's not long enough, but maybe I can tie something on the end of it."

"Quick!" Lathan shouted.

A tiny ray of light shone down from above and struck the floor of the pit. Instantaneously Lathan saw a horde of spiders pop out of a hole in front of him like water out of a fountain. Suddenly spiders were popping out of little holes all around him, dancing toward him, and looking up at him with their red, hungry eyes.

"Quick!" Lathan yelled. Lathan stood on the tangled pile of rope while thousands of spiders swarmed around him.

"Ready!" the girl called out from above. "I tied one end of my rope around the oak tree, and I tied a branch to the other end so it'll reach you."

"Quick!" was the only response Lathan could think of giving to this pertinent information.

The rope Lathan stood on was being climbed by the voracious spiders.

"Watch your head!" the girl shouted from above. She shoved the large branch she had attached to her jump rope over the edge. The branch came down within about three inches of Lathan's head, nearly putting him, as well as this story, to an abrupt end. Fortunately it didn't strike him, and he latched onto the branch and began climbing as fast as he could.

He made it to where the branch was connected to the rope, and continued climbing by bracing his feet against the wall, out of which an occasional spider would pop out and encourage Lathan to climb faster. Eventually, in the true "Trollkiller" Sven Svensson tradition, Lathan made it to the top of the pit, crawled a few yards away from it, and then collapsed in a heap, trembling at the closeness of his escape.

Meanwhile his rescuer stared at him uneasily, unsure of what to say. She was approximately twelve years old, and although she knew how to treat boys of her own age and younger (namely, with imperious scorn), she was not at all sure of how to behave toward Lathan, who looked at least five years her senior.

When Lathan's trembling fit ended he sat up and looked at his rescuer. She had red hair and freckles, and her hair was adorned in that popular style known as "pigtails," although the part in her hair was not even, and one "tail" was considerably longer than the other. She wore no shoes, and her dress, if it can be so described, strongly resembled a sewn-together collection of dish towels. Fortunately, Lathan was not a devotee of fashion, and thought she looked very nice.

Lathan, although glad to be rescued, was unsure how to express his gratitude to the girl. Some people are trained early in life to warmly hug, kiss, and fawn over people they are actually indifferent about, or to continually say "I love you" and "I could never live without you" to people they despise and would like to leave at the first possible opportunity. Lathan, on the other hand, was trained according to the opposite school, wherein you don't hug or kiss someone you love with all your heart, soul, and mind, but instead show your affection by being kind and attentive to them, and occasionally bestowing on them a pleasant nod of the head. Consequently, Lathan showed his gratitude to his rescuer by saying, "Thank you for rescuing me, Miss," and shaking her hand.

The girl, who had also been trained according to Lathan's school of thought, was embarrassed by this display of emotion, and quickly changed the subject.

"I come out here to the creek every morning at sunrise," she said. "That's the best time to catch crawdads."

For the first time Lathan noticed that she had with her a little sack of implements relative to the above-mentioned scientific pursuit.

"It's a good thing I heard you yell. I thought you were just playing. I'm glad you got out, because those are disgusting spiders."

"Real disgusting," she added after a pause.

"Yeah," said Lathan earnestly, not knowing how else to follow up this topic.

When the shock of his narrow escape finally subsided, Lathan remembered that the Count's ship might have sailed, or might be sailing that very minute.

"Thanks for everything, but I've got to run!" Lathan said.

"You can't go yet!" the girl replied, reassuming her imperious manner. "My jump rope is hanging into the pit, and because that branch is attached to it I need you to help me pull it out!"

Lathan, despite being in a rush, was very anxious to show his gratitude, particularly if he could do it without any hugging or kissing. Soon he was pulling manfully on the rope, but the branch was so heavy he couldn't pull it out. While he paused to consider what to do, the knot slipped and the branch went crashing into the pit.

"Well, I'm so bad with knots it's a wonder it didn't fall off while you were climbing," said the girl as she happily pulled up the rope. Lathan gulped.

"Well, I have to run, Miss uh . . . well, what is your name?"

"You can just keep calling me 'Miss.' I think that has a ring to it. My real name's disgusting."

Lathan thanked "Miss" once more, and informed her that he must leave immediately to rescue a princess.

"Rescue a princess!" Miss replied, "I wanta see that!"

So saying, she quickly gathered up her jump rope and crawdad-catching equipment and ran with Lathan back toward the beach.

Lathan had no trouble finding his way back. He ran back exactly the way he came, and soon ran out onto the beach.

The ship was gone. The ship was gone, the stack of supplies was gone, and the men were gone, and there was no evidence that they had ever been there, or had ever existed. Vainly Lathan ran out to the edge of the water, as if the ship were really there after all, but he was still too far away to see it. He stared pathetically at the choppy water of the ocean, which seem to stretch out in front of him to infinity. He listened to the waves lap against the beach, and it sounded to him like the waves were saying, "Ha . . . ha . . . ha . . ."

"Well, where's this princess you're supposed to be rescuing?" asked Miss in a slightly mocking tone. If Lathan had been merely pulling her leg about the Princess, she wanted him to know that she had never really believed it in the first place.

"Floppy! Floppy!" Lathan called out, looking wildly in every direction. There was no answer.

"Are you all right?" Miss asked.

Lathan suddenly started running along the beach. Perhaps he had come to the wrong spot. He ran almost half-way back to Scuttleton before he gave up in despair.

Miss had run behind him with her equipment in her arms, half-confused and half-exhilarated by this strange adventure. Lathan finally stopped, looked sadly out over the ocean, and then sat in the sand. Miss stopped running as well, and approached him very cautiously, as if he were some sort of exotic animal. She sat down in the sand a few feet away.

"Are you sure you're all right?" she asked. "I mean, you look very disgusted."

Lathan grunted, looked forlornly at the ocean, started to make a very pathetic sand castle, and didn't say a word for the next quarter of an hour.

Miss kept thoughtfully silent as well, but, after building a fine sand castle of her own, she suddenly came up with an exciting suggestion.

"I know what you need. You need something to cheer you up. Something like . . . like . . ." (here she stopped and appeared to consider several hundreds of possibilities) ". . . like jumping rope for example!"

Miss clapped her hands with glee over this original and wholly unexpected idea.

"And what luck! I happen to be carrying a jump rope with me!"

Lathan was not nearly as overjoyed at this discovery as Miss was, but even in his numbed state of mind he couldn't help smiling at this remarkable coincidence.

"Come on, it'll be good for you!" Miss insisted.

Lathan sighed wearily. Nothing seemed to matter much anymore. There was nothing he could do to save the Princess now.

"If you want to," Lathan finally replied, and he slowly rose to his feet.

"Great! This will help you a lot!" Miss said breathlessly as she took Lathan by the hand. "I know the perfect place!"

She led him away from the beach and down a few country lanes until they came to a spot very near to where Lathan had seen her jumping rope before. This spot was "perfect" because it was a flat, open area near a tall fence, and, since there were only two of them, Miss could tie one end of the jump rope to the fence. They drew straws to see who would jump rope first. Lathan lost, which made Miss very sad, but rules are rules, and she couldn't change them even if she wanted to, and so she would unfortunately have to jump first. Lathan didn't mind, because he remained in a complete daze, and so before he knew it the words, "One thousand and forty-seven, one thousand and forty-eight, one thousand and forty-nine" were ringing in his ears.

Lathan had no idea that he had committed himself to an activity with a minimum duration of three hours, but he was in such a zombie-like condition that even if he had known this information it would have had little effect on him. He simply stood there, stared at the ground, and mechanically turned the rope.

Finally, at number three thousand, four hundred and sixty-two, Miss looked over at Lathan and for the first time noticed his pitiable appearance. A few jumps later a miracle happened: Miss missed.

"Gosh," said Miss as mechanically as Lathan had been turning the rope, "I don't know how I missed that one. I guess it's your turn now."

Lathan, who had snapped to attention and looked frantically around as if he had just woken from a dream, said not to worry about it, and told her that he didn't mind letting her have another chance.

Miss set down the rope and looked concerned.

"Are you sure you're all right?" she asked.

"Uh-huh," said Lathan, who then walked a few steps away and sat glumly on a tree stump. Now Miss was very concerned. She sauntered over and sat down next to him on the edge of the stump.

"I don't really feel like jumping rope anymore," said Miss gently, but nearly gagging on the words. "If you want to tell me about the Princess, I'd really like to hear it."

"Have you ever heard of 'Trollkiller' Sven Svensson?" Lathan softly asked her.

"Everyone's heard of him," Miss replied. "He's the one in all those jokes, isn't he?"

Lathan frowned.

"Wait, hold on," said Miss, who, realizing she had given an inappropriate answer, scoured her brain for a better one.

"You're right, I heard he was something else before he got into all those jokes . . . hmmm . . . I think . . . no . . . wait . . . that's right . . . He was a famous hero, wasn't he, or was he the guy who travelled around everywhere selling things?"

"He was the famous hero," was Lathan's melancholy reply.

"Sure, that's right. Everybody knows that."

"Well," said Lathan glumly, "I'm his son."

Miss was not quite sure if Lathan should be congratulated for this or condemned, and so remained silent until she could get further information. After a long moment of silence, Lathan partially lifted up his head and told Miss the whole story, mumblingly at first, but with more and more emotion as he went on.

First, he gave her a short biography of "Trollkiller" Sven Svensson, which impressed her greatly, and caused her to vocally label that worthy hero's opponents as "really disgusting" on more than one occasion.

Lathan then summarized the major events of his life before the last week (which took approximately a minute and a half, including three awkward pauses), told Miss of his great love for Princess Purella (which caused him to suddenly turn beet-red in spite of his world-weary demeanor), and informed Miss of the Princess's great beauty and great virtues, such as kindness, goodness, sweetness, gentleness, mercy, etc., etc., ad infinitum. He then told Miss of the strange and wonderful events of the last week, much more succinctly than I have done, but without the precise descriptions, learned commentary, and polysyllabic verbiage so appreciated by my faithful readers.

He concluded this oration by giving an account of all his adventures in Scuttleton until the episode of the spiders, briefly thanked God for all of his help, and then lavished high praise on his magic coin, which, although the extent of its magical powers was always ill-defined, had never failed to guide him and be an inspiration to him in all his troubles. He then burst into tears.

"Don't do that!" said Miss, who was so captivated by the story of his adventures and was so concerned for the beautiful Princess that she strutted around him like a little general.

"You can't just sit here! There's a Princess waiting to be rescued!"

"But they're on their way across the ocean," said Lathan glumly. "I don't have a ship, I can barely swim, and there's a storm coming in."

Miss looked up at the darkened skies, and for the first time noticed the wind gusting through the trees. She sat back down on the tree stump and looked as glum as Lathan.

"My Uncle John's pretty smart," she said after a while. "Maybe he could tell you what you should do."

Lathan was too sunk in despair to make a reply, but after Miss had gathered together all her things he let her take him by the hand and lead him, without any resistance, to the cottage of her Uncle John.

Chapter XVII

A Chat with Uncle John

Uncle John lived in a little cottage at the edge of the beach about a mile south of Scuttleton. His cottage, which might be more accurately described as an over-sized shack, was constructed out of many oddly shaped beams and curved boards, and even a person as inexperienced as Lathan could see that it was made entirely from old, wrecked ships. The cottage had four little windows, all of which were round, and a little chimney which was used as an exit by a steady stream of gray smoke. Miss boldly led Lathan up to the unsymmetrically cut front door.

"Go ahead and knock," she said.

Lathan knocked, and immediately Miss ran around to the side of the cottage and hid. Lathan, who had been partially in a daze for quite awhile, suddenly sprang to life and ran after her.

"What are you doing?" he asked, as he found a hiding place next to her, and heard the sound of mumbling coming from inside the cottage.

"Didn't I tell you? Uncle John doesn't like little girls. He thinks they're disgusting," said Miss, saying her favorite adjective as fervently as if she thought the same way herself. "If you show up with me, he'll think you're just playin', so don't tell him I sent you."

She then pushed Lathan back in front of the door, and once again ran around the corner and hid. Soon Lathan heard footsteps coming to the cottage door. Miss rushed back over to him.

"Confidentially," she whispered, "he's kinda sour."

She then raced back to her hiding place.

Lathan had no time to consider this latest information, for soon the door creaked open and he was greeted by a meek-looking, simply-dressed, middle-aged woman. She looked at Lathan deferentially, as if he were some sort of local potentate, and asked what she could do for him.

"I'm here to see Uncle John," said Lathan carefully.

"You want to see Uncle John?" she repeated, apparently wanting to make sure she had heard correctly. Just then a pillow was hurled against the door from behind her, just missing her head.

"Confound . . . whadya think he said . . . gar . . . bilge brain . . . drive tar crazy . . . gar . . . mumble, mumble, mumble!" a voice intoned from within.

"John will see you now," said the woman as she picked up the pillow and quickly shrank back inside.

Lathan, as one might easily surmise, did not walk through the door brimming with confidence, but he did walk through.

He entered a room which looked like a Captain's cabin on a ship, and might be described as a sitting room, because it had two chairs, along with a table, and in the chairs were two people, sitting. The woman who had answered the door was one of these people, for as soon as she had let Lathan in she had dashed over to her chair and began sewing as if her life depended on it. On the opposite end of the room, next to a very smoke-blackened little fireplace, sat a man wrapped in blankets, who was none other than Uncle John.

"A lad!" said Uncle John as Lathan walked into the room. "Confound . . . deal with tadpoles . . . gar . . . no time for swabs . . . his age . . . I worked all day . . . I'm blowed if I didn't . . . tarnation . . . mumble, mumble, mumble!"

Uncle John's mode of expression made the first sailor Lathan had met in Scuttleton seem a genuine grammarian by comparison, and Lathan was hard-pressed to understand even a single syllable of anything that Uncle John said. However, Lathan quickly recognized that Uncle John's constitutional dislike of girls was commendably balanced by a constitutional dislike of boys as well, which showed that he was an equal opportunity grumbler, and was in all respects truly liberal. Uncle John was apparently a perpetual invalid, but struck Lathan as being an unusual invalid, because he had dark black hair, huge, iron-hard arms, and looked little more than forty-five years old. John's wife, the woman who had answered the door, and who was sewing as frantically as if she shortly expected someone to yell at her for being slow, was about ten years older; at least, she looked about ten years older.

"Well, spew, lad, or shear off," Uncle John growled at the hesitant Lathan. "Can't waste day . . . full sail . . . crossed line . . . Cap'n . . . ten years I was, by gar . . . stuck mud . . . white caps . . . tarnation . . . spew, boy, spew . . . mumble, mumble, mumble!"

Lathan looked over to John's wife for interpretation. She meekly looked up from her sewing, and said that Uncle John was a ship's Captain of great experience, had no time to waste, and was ready to hear his story. She then immediately resumed sewing at a tremendous pace, perhaps noticing that Uncle John had just picked up another pillow.

Lathan, much as he had done a little earlier with Miss, told Uncle John his whole story from beginning to end. Since this was his second performance of the story he told it much better than the first time, despite being frequently interrupted by such comments as "confound," "tarnation," "stow that," "heave to, laddie," and other such nautical comments. Also, at the point in the story where Lathan mentioned that he was the son of "Trollkiller" Sven Svensson, Uncle John happened to fall off his chair and into the fireplace, from which he was extricated with great difficulty. Finally, however, Lathan finished the story, making sure to eliminate all references to Miss, as she had suggested, and as the sound of someone kicking the side of the cottage just before he mentioned her name helped to remind him.

When finished, Lathan asked Uncle John what he should do, while Uncle John looked at him with the non-committal look of the professional listener, who might believe your story, but probably did not. Mrs. Uncle John, on the other hand, was greatly affected by any tale that had the slightest element of romance in it, and was weeping profusely. After flinging another pillow at his blubbering wife, Uncle John looked Lathan square in the eye and gave him this candid answer.

"Consarn fairy tale . . . no Svensson's son? . . . you? . . . gar . . . Princess sunk . . . return to port . . . tarnation . . . no one the wiser . . . forget . . . ridiculous . . . go back to port or go blazes!"

It didn't sound too hopeful. Lathan turned to Mrs. Uncle John for the translation.

"He says that you're not the son of 'Trollkiller' Sven Svensson, and it's impossible for you to rescue the Princess," said Mrs. Uncle John carefully, as if she were translating holy writ. "Since no one knows you were following the Princess, and all your companions are dead, no one will ever know that you failed to rescue her. Uncle John says to either go home or go to . . . a warmer climate."

"But I *am* the son of 'Trollkiller' Sven Svensson," said Lathan. Uncle John shook his head.

"Return to port lad . . . tarnation . . . and don't try Lump . . . you'll drown sure . . . gar . . . and it's no use . . . mumble, mumble, mumble!"

Mrs. Uncle John to Lathan:

"He says to go home, and don't think of trying to get to the island of Lump, because you probably won't make it, and it wouldn't be of any use anyway."

"Why would I want to go to this island of Lump?" Lathan asked.

"Haven't you ever heard of the ancient Oracle?" Mrs. Uncle John asked.

"Oracle?" said Lathan.

"Consarn . . . tarnation!" said Uncle John, as he looked around for a pillow to throw at Lathan, to punish him for his ignorance.

"Why, the Oracle is on the island of Lump, 200 miles out to sea," Mrs. Uncle John explained in a meek but semi-romantic tone. "If you present the Oracle with a problem, it will know the right answer, and tell you exactly what to do. It never fails."

"Well, thank you very much for all your help," said Lathan politely. "I'll be leaving at once."

"Lad, return to port," said Uncle John, with a slight trace of thoughtfulness in his voice. He then turned his chair toward the fire to signify that their discussion was at an end.

Lathan turned to leave.

"You'd better head back home like John says," Mrs. Uncle John whispered to Lathan. "Rescuing princesses is fun to think about, and I used to think about things like that myself, but eventually you have to come back to reality. If I hadn't started thinking realistically, where would I be today?"

She would have said more, but yet another pillow came flying past her head, and soon she was sewing frantically. Lathan mumbled a quick good-bye and walked outside.

The skies were now very dark, and a cold wind gusted across the beach. Miss jumped up out of her hiding place and hopped over to Lathan.

"What'de say? What'de say?"

"He told me to go home," Lathan said. He started walking slowly along the beach.

"You're not going to, are you?" Miss asked as she followed behind him.

Lathan didn't answer. He walked on until he came to a little mound of sand near the water, where he sat down. Miss sat down next to him. They both looked out over the ocean.

"I don't know what to do," Lathan said.

Far out in the distance they could hear the sound of thunder.

"Doctor Oldair (the greatest philosopher in the western world) once told me that the Princess might not really exist," said Lathan, "and sitting here now it seems like everything that's happened to me is a dream, and I can almost believe that Doctor Oldair, Prince Charming, Count Zandar, and all the rest of them truly don't exist, and are just characters in my imagination."

"But you know that they do exist," Miss said.

Lathan sadly nodded his head.

"Still, like your Uncle John says, if I went home now no one would ever blame me. My grandmother would know, but . . . but I'm sure she'd understand."

"But what about your dad?" Miss asked.

"What do you mean?"

"You know, the 'Trollkiller' guy. You told me how he always rescued everybody no matter what, and he gave you a really swell magic coin and everything, so I bet if he finds out you gave up on this you're gonna catch it!"

Lathan had never looked at the situation in that light before. He pulled out his magic coin, studied it for a moment, and then squeezed it until he could feel its energy surging through his body. He leaped to his feet.

"I don't know what came over me," he said to Miss. "Of course I have to rescue the Princess, and I'm going to rescue the Princess, Count or no Count! Oh, if I only had a boat!"

"I've got a boat!" said Miss.

"Show it to me!" said Lathan, "I'll sail at once."

"But what about the storm?!"

"Forget the storm!" shouted Lathan, as he raised the magic coin high above his head. "I am the son of 'Trollkiller' Sven Svensson, and I sail now, storm or no storm!"

After this triumphant outburst, Lathan slipped, fell off the sand dune, and tumbled all the way to the water. After Miss helped pull him to his feet, the two of them raced off toward her boat.

Miss's boat was hidden in some brush on the edge of the beach, and was rather unlike the spacious clipper that Lathan had sanguinely envisioned. It was, in fact, a leaky wooden boat about eight feet by four feet, with a sturdy wooden paddle, and a long broomstick that stuck up out of its center and was intended to impersonate a mast. The sail, which was unfurled at the bottom of the boat, consisted of old, worn-out clothes very creatively sewn together. Also in the bottom of the boat was a jug of fresh water, and some rudimentary fishing equipment. Lathan, after his initial disappointment passed away, was so stimulated by his magic coin that he pronounced this humble vessel fit for a king, and with Miss's help, proceeded to drag it to the water.

"But Lathan," said Miss, as they finally reached the surf, "how are you going to find the Count's castle when you get across the ocean? You don't even have a map!"

"Uncle John said that there's an island out there called the island of Lump, and there's an oracle there that can tell me what to do."

Lathan pushed the boat out into the surf, and quickly climbed aboard. Lathan stayed in the boat for at least three seconds before he indecorously exited the vessel at the insistence of a large wave, which obstinately crashed on his head. Lathan quickly discovered that although the boat was fit for a king, the king it was fit for must have been an extraordinarily small monarch, with a remarkable sense of balance. Finally, after several false starts which left Lathan thoroughly soaked (yet undaunted), Lathan managed to paddle his boat away from the beach and into the open sea. Miss stood on the beach with the water up to her knees, shouting encouragement.

Lathan, in all the excitement, hadn't had a chance to thank Miss and say good-bye, which was something of a relief to him, because the school of thought that does not allow for elaborate emotional displays is firmly against teary good-byes. Nevertheless, on the inside Lathan was bursting with gratitude, and felt that some slight external display of emotion might be appropriate on this occasion. Therefore he sat up straight, waved back at the ever-more-distant figure of Miss, and shouted "Good-bye!"

"Good-bye!" her answer came faintly back. He could see her waving her arms.

"Thank you!" Lathan shouted with somewhat less volume than before, and no answer came back.

"I'll probably have a chance to thank her some other time," he said to himself. Suddenly he was struck with a thought.

"Hey, you never told me your real name!" he shouted, as loudly as he could. "What's your real name?!"

Her answer came back faintly, and he couldn't understand it. Eventually she faded from view, but even when he was far from shore he still thought he could see her arms, waving.

Soon Lathan was struggling to paddle his tiny craft over the rough, rude sea. The farther into the ocean he went, the rougher the ocean became, and he knew that the expected storm was not far away. The imminence of the storm inspired Lathan to feverish bursts of paddling, and he made tremendous progress. He was many miles from shore when he was suddenly struck with an unpleasant thought: although he was trying to sail to the island of Lump, he had no idea where it was. He knew that it was 200 miles from shore, but, as the shore extended some thousands of miles in either direction, finding the exact location of the island might be problematic. Nevertheless, after taking another grip of his magic coin and reminding himself that the blood of "Trollkiller" Sven Svensson flowed through his veins, he decided to paddle gamely forward. But soon the skies grew black, the wind howled, and the ocean was buffeted by the storm.

Chapter XVIII

Back to Purella, Followed by Adventures on the Island of Lump

Many readers are doubtless concerned about Purella, and are ready to condemn me for seeming to ignore her. However, nothing could be further from the truth. Like Lathan, I too have a great deal of admiration for the ground on which Purella walks, and the air in which she breathes I find quite delightful as well. However, Purella has been excluded from the last eight chapters of this history for two simple reasons.

First, consider that when Purella was captured she was put in a gunny sack, tied up, and placed in the back of the Count's wagon. She travelled this way until the Count and Og arrived at their ship, where she was transferred out of the sack and into a cage. I think that even my most contentious reader will concede that an account of Purella's experiences inside her gunny sack would have proven less than exhilarating, and that if I had interrupted Lathan's adventures with an account of how Purella caught a fly while in her cage, and how she noticed that her cage had rust on the third bar down on the north side, it would not have been welcomed by a majority of readers.

My second reason for excluding Purella is more embarrassing. To tell the absolute truth, Purella has (I blush to say it) not behaved properly for a Princess in her position, and turns out to be not as perfect a heroine as a history of this dignity would seem to require. Naturally, her behavior, which shows a lack of femininity too conspicuous to ignore, pains me very much, and almost certainly mars the perfection of this narrative. However, I will hide nothing from you reader, but will tell you the whole sorry affair exactly as it happened.

Purella had little opportunity to perform mischief while she was in the gunny sack, but when she was put aboard the ship the Count let her out of the sack and placed her on deck in a small iron cage. When the Count's men saw the sad-faced, blond-tressed Princess in the cage, several of them immediately stuck their hands through the bars and attempted to touch various parts of her anatomy, obviously intending to console the helpless female in her hour of distress. However, when these sympathetic gentlemen took their hands away they noticed that these appendages were bleeding profusely, each having been efficiently cut into by a sharp object,

"She's got a knife!" they shrieked, as each man danced around and wrapped his hand in his shirt.

Many onlookers didn't believe that anyone as sweet and innocent as Purella would do such a thing, and so, out of curiosity, stuck their hands into the cage as well. Sad to relate, their actions incurred the same result, and their hands soon acquired the reddish hue so often seen near major lacerations.

There was much speculation about where Purella had acquired a knife, until one of the Count's men, on closer inspection (which nearly cost him the tip of his nose) discovered that it was not a knife but a piece of sharp metal that she had somehow pried off the Count's saddle.

"What's going on here?" said the Count as he strode out onto the deck.

One of the men, whose chances for a career in violin-playing had diminished considerably due to Purella's carving skills, informed the Count of the situation, whereupon the Count ordered that Purella should be taken down to languish in the deepest recesses of the hold.

"Fear not, Princess, you will not be harmed—now," said the Count with a malevolent leer as his men prepared to carry her away. "After we've crossed the ocean, the Great Desert, and several mountains and valleys, we will reach the Land of Doom, where you will relax in my home, the Dark Castle. You'll get to know me better there, and although I have a few faults, you'll find that I'm basically a good person."

Purella accepted this information with a very unladylike sneer.

"Unfortunately your stay in my castle will be brief," the Count continued. "Two weeks from today is the SIN convention and the feast for the great god Moloch, and I'm afraid you're the main attraction at our sacrifice."

The Count smiled.

Soon, with great difficulty and the loss of several pints of whole blood, the Count's men placed Purella's cage in the murkiest corner of the hold, and they were ordered, partially for their own safety, never to come near her again.

I realize that most romantic heroines don't have such strong tendencies toward violence, and are usually pallid and passive, which I can't deny are traits that everyone admires in a heroine. Nevertheless I, at least, am still quite fond of Purella, because despite the occasional unladylike outburst, she was still a sensitive person, for as soon as they shut the trapdoor above her, and she was alone in the dreary hold, Purella, who before looked and behaved as fearless as a tigress, dropped her sharp piece of metal, sunk to the bottom of the cage, and began to weep. After a while she fought off her tears, and sat quietly, although the tears were never far away, and the only time they went away completely was when Og came down to give her some food; at that time her eyes dried up immediately, and until he left she looked at the fumbling Og with an icy glare.

She had been in the hold for only a day when she suddenly heard the voices of Doctor Oldair and Prince Charming. Instead of greeting these two men as her rescuers, however, she crouched down in the bottom of the cage, and sat there as still and silent as a statue—knowing their characters, she thought they might be in league with the Count, and when she heard the Count capture them she wasn't exactly overcome with remorse.

Soon the ship sailed. Purella sat in the stifling gloom of the hold for a long, sad hour, hearing only the sound of the ocean slapping against the ship, and the screams of men being punished for inadequate knot-tying, and other serious offenses. The sound of screaming men, though pleasant to the Count's ears, was not very comforting to Purella, and after a while the phenomenon of tears appearing on her cheek began occurring once again.

"Arf!"

Purella snapped to attention. She heard some rustling in a stack of crates on the other side of the hold. Suddenly, from out of the midst of the cargo squirmed a four-legged, part short-haired, part long-haired figure, who bounded over to Purella's cage and flopped himself in front of it.

"Arf!" said Floppy, spitting the word into Purella's face, which was his habit when he was excited. To Purella, this shower of greeting felt as pleasant as the gentlest spring rain.

"Floppy, how did you get here?" Purella asked, while attempting to hug her beloved companion through the bars of the cage.

"Arf! Arf!" said Floppy succinctly, and without much extraneous detail. Suffice it to say that after he had led the Count's guard away from the beach, he had circled back and climbed into a crate, in emulation of Doctor Oldair and Prince Charming, and had been carried aboard the ship. Unlike those two worthy individuals, he kept quietly hidden until he was sure the ship had sailed.

"Floppy, the Count is going to sacrifice me to his idol! Is my father on the way to rescue me?"

Floppy hung his head.

"Isn't there anyone trying to rescue me?"

"Arf," said Floppy hesitantly.

She looked hard into Floppy's face and knew immediately who her rescuer was.

"Oh, Floppy, no! Poor Lathan will be killed! If anything happens to him I'll never be able to forgive myself."

"Arf!" said Floppy, trying to drive these gloomy thoughts away.

"Well, Floppy, at least we're together again. We'll get through this somehow, you'll see."

"Arf!" said Floppy warmly, and from then on the air in the hold seemed cleaner, and the passage over the ocean smooth.

Meanwhile Lathan struggled over the storm-swept seas, his brittle barge battered brutally by bodacious, boisterous blasts, searching, searching for the island of Lump. Bounced up and down thirty-foot swells, and drenched by horizontal hail, Lathan still paddled madly forward. Finally, at the point when any non-relative of "Trollkiller" Sven Svensson would have given up in despair, Lathan sighted land. He peered through the hail and fog and mist and saw, far off in the distance, a brightly lit sign which said:

WELCOME TO LUMP
Land of Many Uses
(Please Put Trash in Receptacles—
Help Keep Our Oracle Clean)

Lathan gave a hearty shout, paddled furiously to shore, and hopped up onto the beach. He had been dreaming of shelter for a long time, and immediately ran under a tree to protect himself from the elements. As luck would have it, as soon as he made it under the tree the rain stopped, and the sky turned blue again. Although Lathan might have wished the weather had cleared a little sooner, he was pleased by this turn of events, and slipped out from under the tree, ready for action.

The first thing he did was walk over and take a closer look at the sign.

"This is the place," he said to himself after re-reading the sign. "Now all I have to do is find the Oracle."

This proved relatively easy, for as soon as he left the beach a bespectacled short guy approached him and tried to sell him an Oracle T-shirt. Lathan had no money (except his coin), so he had to forego the shirt, but he did manage to find out the location of the main road. This thoroughfare ran down the center of the island, and was bustling with sailors, students, gossipy women, families with unruly kids, and other tourists of every country and every description, all on their way to see the Oracle. Lathan tried to hurry through the crowd, but his way was slowed considerably by the throngs of concessionaires who tried to sell him Oracle pennants, Oracle pictures, Oracle buttons, Oracle shoes, and even an Oracle dinette set, which included a free bag of fortune cookies with every purchase. However, after two hours of twisting and side-stepping through the mob, Lathan finally arrived at the Oracle building, a huge stone structure built into a gigantic rock. It was surrounded by guards and boasted two immense iron doors. Lathan, inspired once more by his family heritage, marched boldly up to the two doors and was quickly confronted by two of the guards.

"I'm the son of 'Trollkiller' Sven Svensson," Lathan explained, "and I've come to speak with the Oracle."

"Get lost," the guards said.

Lathan was a little disheartened by their response, and was even more disheartened when they picked him up and threw him against the tourist information booth. Nevertheless, Lathan, recalling that the blood of "Trollkiller" Sven Svensson flowed through his veins (and out of his nose at this particular moment), decided to confront the guards one more time, this time using a healthy amount of Trollkillerarian ingenuity.

"Didn't you hear us? You can't come in," the guards snarled as Lathan approached once more. Lathan slyly noted that to the left of the big iron doors was a little green button.

"But the guy with the diamonds said I could," Lathan insisted.

"What are you talking about?" the guards asked.

"That guy behind that tree over there is giving away free Oracle diamonds. Can't you see him? He's right in front of the guy giving away something called 'free power tools.'"

While the guards were racing over to the tree in world-record time, Lathan darted over to the little green button and gave it a push. Sure enough, the huge doors swung open and Lathan ducked inside.

Once inside, Lathan tiptoed down several torch-lit corridors until he finally came to the vast inner chamber that housed the ancient Oracle. He stepped boldly into the room and stared at the gaudily decorated altar. Finally, summoning his courage, he spoke.

"O ancient Oracle, I am Lathan, robust shepherd lad and son of 'Trollkiller' Sven Svensson, and I have come to ask for your advice."

The ground rumbled, a mighty wind blew, and a disembodied voice called out in a dry, nasal tone, "Two farthings for two minutes please."

"But I don't have any money," Lathan replied.

"I'm sorry sir. Two farthings for two minutes please," the voice snottily repeated.

Just then Lathan had another ingenious thought.

"Oh, my mistake. I do have two farthings," Lathan said loudly.

He walked up to the money slot, took the chain off his neck, and lowered the magic coin into the slot. When he heard a click he slowly pulled the coin back up and repeated the process. After it clicked for the second time the disembodied voice spoke.

"Thank you, sir. Welcome to the Ancient Oracle. Don't forget: on weekdays there is a complete tour of the Oracle grounds at 12, 2, and 4 o'clock: admission is three farthings for adults, two farthings for children, and children under four, free. Now, may I have your question?"

"Uh, yes," said Lathan, clearing his throat. He quickly summed up the whole problem for the Oracle, and humbly asked how he might rescue the Princess. After a few moments pause the Oracle gave its response.

"We oracles generally don't like to give straight answers," it said, "but in this case I'll make an exception. Lathan, you're in big trouble. The Count is brave, strong, and intelligent, while you are a dirty, ignorant (albeit robust) shepherd lad. My official prediction is this: if you get some magical help, the advice of a great philosopher, and an army of Wabonian dwarfs, you will have a 2.3 percent chance of defeating the Count. If not, forget it."

Lathan grasped his magic coin, thankful that he at least had the first of the three recommendations. If Doctor Oldair hadn't been killed, all he would have needed were the dwarfs.

The Oracle explained its decision.

"You need magical help for the simple reason that what you're trying to do is impossible. You need the advice of a great philosopher because the Count is deep and secretive, and you need the insights of someone equally deep to defeat him.

Finally, you will need a brilliant plan, and the Wabonian dwarfs are the greatest plotters in the world. In this case, I'd suggest recruiting a large army of them."

"Where do I find these Wabonian dwarfs?" Lathan asked stoutly.

"You can look anywhere you want, but I think *Wabonia* might be the most likely place," replied the Oracle with its famous acidic wit.

"Thank you, Oracle," Lathan replied. "I'll proceed without further delay."

"There's one more thing I feel obligated to tell you," the Oracle answered. "When you hear it you might want to give all this up right now. You see, you're not . . ."

"Yes? Yes? I'm not what?"

"Two farthings for two minutes please," the Oracle whined once again.

"Oh, all right," Lathan answered.

He walked over to the money slot and lowered in his coin once more. However, as luck would have it, a little bald-headed man with glasses stuck his head out of the curtain behind the Oracle and saw Lathan commit this fraudulent act.

"Hey, this guy's putting a slug into the Oracle!" the man shouted.

Instantly a buzzer went off, and Lathan heard the big iron doors starting to close. He raced out of the room and down the corridors, and just before the doors shut he leaped through them and landed safely outside. The alarm had spread, however, and soon guards were running at him from all directions. Lathan fought his way through the crowds of tourists, running as fast as he could back to his little boat. Behind him he could hear people yelling, "He cheated the Oracle! He cheated the Oracle!"

Lathan ran like a madman, and never looked behind him. Finally he reached the beach, grabbed his boat, and pushed out to sea. The angry islanders shook their fists at him as he sailed slowly away. When he was a safe distance from shore Lathan stood up in his little boat and yelled, "I am Lathan, robust shepherd lad and son of 'Trollkiller' Sven Svensson, and I have proved today that I am as brave, strong, and intelligent as my father!"

Well, maybe he wasn't as intelligent, for Lathan hadn't gotten very far before he realized he had left his only paddle on shore.

This unfortunate occurrence gave Lathan the opportunity of spending the next few days floating aimlessly over the now placid ocean. He cursed his stupidity in forgetting the paddle, and was depressed by the last statement of the Oracle.

"It said, 'You're not . . .' and then the time ran out," Lathan mused. "I know what it was going to say. It was going to say, 'You're not going to succeed.'"

Lathan moped over this for two full days, but then finally roused himself from his depression, and gripped his coin particularly tight.

"Even if I am going to fail I've still got to try," he said. "That's what 'Trollkiller' would do. He wouldn't give up no matter what. Even if the odds were ten million to one he'd still think he could win out in the end, and that's what I've got to think too."

Then, seemingly in answer to this little outburst, the wind started blowing again. Lathan adjusted his sail, and was soon sailing rapidly across the sea.

Chapter XIX

The Count's Ship Lands at Scagabash, and Lathan Tours a Prison

To a person locked in the hold, long sailing trips are seldom fun. Thus, though Purella was glad to be separated from the Count's men during the voyage, she was very pleased to hear the words "Land ho!" being shouted on the decks above her. Before long several of the Count's men (each wearing heavy gloves, and a sheepish expression) climbed down into the hold to carry her cage outside. After cleverly sticking two long poles through the cage, they managed to carry her out on deck sedan-chair style, without suffering much bodily harm. Floppy was discovered down below shortly thereafter, and after a plea from Purella, (which sounded somewhat like a threat as well) he was placed next to her in a little iron cage of his own.

The ship was docked at the lively little port town of Scagabash, a town notable for its hundred taverns, and for the sound of bottles and chairs breaking, which could be heard at any location in the town, twenty-four hours a day.

On shore, some of the Count's men from the Dark Castle were waiting for the ship with several empty wagons. They had been waiting in Scagabash for over a week, and although their faces were covered with bottle and chair marks, they looked happy enough, and seemed to have enjoyed their little vacation thoroughly. Before long everything was loaded onto the wagons, including Purella and Floppy, and the long ride to the Dark Castle was about to begin.

"Two hundred miles to the Dark Castle," said the Count with oily cheerfulness. "We'll make it in plenty of time for the convention: I can hardly wait."

Purella didn't respond. She just sat quietly in her cage, fixed her eyes on the heavens, and wondered if Lathan was all right.

Meanwhile, Lathan was in a beautiful field of pink daisies. In the middle of the field was a watermelon tree. Lathan skipped over to the watermelon tree and picked the biggest watermelon he could find. Unfortunately, a blue tiger hiding among the daisies heard the tinkling of the little bells on Lathan's shoes, and saw Lathan's striped leotards clash against the green of the watermelon tree.

The tiger smiled. With two powerful leaps he bounded across the meadow toward Lathan. Lathan turned and saw him. He dropped the watermelon! The tiger leaped!

Crash!!!

Lathan went tumbling out of his boat and onto a beach. It was the middle of the night, and, although he looked frantically around, there were no tigers in sight.

"I've got to stop eating all those blowfish before I go to sleep," Lathan said to himself.

Lathan looked around and saw that he was in some strange desert region, and he was convinced it was the mainland. Too tired to rejoice, he dragged his boat up onto the beach, flopped down next to it, and fell asleep.

Early the next morning Lathan hid his boat in a large bush and went out in search of civilization. He was near the equator and the heat was oppressive, but yet he pushed himself onward. He climbed up on the bluffs that overlooked the ocean and walked along them, gradually going more and more inland as he went. Finally, after about a fifteen-mile walk, he looked down from the top of a giant sand dune and saw a little city.

The name of this city, which had been founded by nomads centuries before, was Fredscashthree. Lathan stumbled into the town, and, after nearly buying a rug from a persistent salesman, found his way to the mayor of the city, the Pishaw, to whom he explained that he was a traveller from Hoodahooda who was searching for a place called Wabonia. The Pishaw, after congratulating Lathan on not buying the rug and assuring him that he himself could give Lathan a much better deal, addressed him as follows:

"You are still a long way from Wabonia, my son. It is 1,500 miles due east, but to get there you must cross the Great Desert, the Not-So-Great Desert, and then you must pass through an impenetrable jungle inhabited only by thieves and vicious animals, a cursed and vile place with stinking air and putrid water, a sewer of the earth fit only for he lowest forms of humanity."

"Gosh, what's that place called?"

"We call it 'Cleveland.'"

"Sounds horrible."

"Oh, it's worse than it sounds. But you have to go through it to get to Wabonia. Of course, Wabonia's almost as bad."

"Really?"

"Certainly. Wabonia's just a glorified patch of desert. Haven't you ever heard the old wives saying:

> *That desert land no herb can stand,*
> *No pansy or begonia,*
> *Flowers can grow in hell, you know*
> *But never in Wabonia.*

"Some of those old wives were awfully clever," Lathan commented.

"I don't know. Rhyming 'Wabonia' with 'begonia' is pretty lame if you ask me. But, then again, what can you expect from an old wife."

"It'll take me months to get to Wabonia," Lathan said with a sigh. "I need some Wabonian dwarfs right away."

"Wait a moment," the Pishaw responded. "If you just need a few Wabonian dwarfs, I think I can help you."

After quickly showing Lathan about twenty or thirty rugs in all sizes, shapes, and colors, and at low, low prices, the Pishaw took Lathan across the city to the local prison. They went inside, walked out into the prison courtyard, and beheld six of the sorriest looking Wabonian dwarfs the world has ever seen. They had messy clothes, unshaved faces, and sat around in a lazy torpor.

"They don't look like it, but they really are ingenious plotters," the Pishaw explained to Lathan. "They came here with no money, and it looked as if they might starve. But then they came up with a clever plan. They went to the main square, called several of our leading citizens greasy sand-diggers, and got sentenced to prison for life. Now, instead of starving to death, they get to be fed by the city for the rest of their lives. And you should see how much they eat! If we don't get rid of them soon there won't be a piece of stale bread left in the country."

"If they want to go with me, will you let them?" Lathan asked.

"By all means," the Pishaw hastily replied.

Without further ado Lathan presented himself to the dwarfs and explained to them the situation. The prospect of going on an adventure was tremendously exciting to the dwarfs, especially since they were starting to experience a few doubts about the wisdom of their last scheme. After listening carefully to

Lathan's speech, the leader of the dwarfs, Bingo, took his pipe out of his mouth and candidly expressed his opinion.

"This is a very complicated problem," he said, "but, with the aid of a typically brilliant Wabonian plot, it should be easily solvable."

The other five dwarfs couldn't help grinning with pride at this mention of their fabled ingeniousness.

"I've considered the problem for at least a half a minute already, and I think I've got an idea. Listen: we march up to the castle, taking along with us (hidden in potato sacks) a thousand Siamese-twin jugglers. When we get to the castle, we let them out of the sacks and have them start juggling knives, or better yet, toasters. The Count will be so distracted by this unusual sight that we can grab the Princess without any trouble."

Bingo's fellow dwarfs cheered this plan enthusiastically, and complimented its artful design.

"But," said Lathan slowly, "don't you think it will be a little difficult to get a thousand Siamese-twin jugglers to come to the Dark Castle?"

"You're right," Bingo responded with a frown. "Most of them belong to the Union. I guess we'll have to think up something more complicated."

While the Pishaw went off to inspect the Prison Entertainment Center (which consisted of a can of marbles and a pool cue), Lathan got better acquainted with the dwarfs, who, besides Bingo, were named Bulbo, Plottle, Slipper, Tripper, and Rex. These five dwarfs were difficult to distinguish from each other, and were notable mainly for the way they grinned uncontrollably whenever their plotting skills were discussed. Bingo was distinguished from the others by the pipe that was in his mouth, and the perpetually thoughtful expression on his face. He also tried never to grin like the others, but was occasionally unsuccessful.

"Chow!" some voices shouted from another part of the prison, which signified either that a large group of Italians was leaving the premises, or that it was time for lunch.

Shortly thereafter several men wearing ridiculously large white hats began carrying trays of food into the courtyard, which verified the correctness of the latter supposition. Each portion of food was wrapped up in what was apparently a piece of newspaper.

"Attention!" shouted one of the cooks as he stood up on a dusty pedestal in the center of the courtyard. "Because of yesterday's riot" (a begging blind prisoner had thrown his tin cup at the Prison Commissioner when he discovered that the commissioner had given him a carriage token instead of a coin) "there will be no stale bread today. Instead, we will have punishment rations."

"What is it? What is it?" the prisoners asked as they gathered around the food trays. Some of them picked up the newspaper-covered parcels and looked to see what was inside.

Heaven preserve us! Broccoli quiche!

"Not that! Anything but that!" the prisoners screeched, backing away in horror.

"And no dessert until you've eaten every bit of it!" the cooks shouted. To prevent the inmates from unlawfully disposing of their meals, all the potted plants in the courtyard (both of them) were removed.

Shortly thereafter the Pishaw returned from the Prison Entertainment Center, and, after excitedly telling everyone about the new set of jacks that was then in use at that popular recreation spot, he informed the dwarfs that he would now go upstairs and fill out the papers for their release, which could be effected in about half an hour. Lathan and the dwarfs thanked the Pishaw, and then, having nothing better to do, sat down to eat.

"What kind of newspaper is this?" Bulbo asked as he opened up the package of quiche, "It looks like it's written in rhyme."

Lathan looked at his own newspaper and, after noticing there were characters' names on the side of the page, realized that he was looking at part of a play. The scene Lathan had was marked "Act III, scene 5," and on the top of the page he could see that the title of the play was "Zepholephylee, or, Fungus in the Garden of Joy."

"I guess they wrapped up the quiche in an old play," said Lathan.

"Read it to us!" said Bulbo, Plottle, Slipper, Tripper, and Rex simultaneously. "Let's see what it's about."

Lathan wiped some of the quiche stains off the paper and carefully began to read the following masterpiece.

Chapter XX

A Theatrical Specimen is Read to Universal Applause

Act III, Scene 5
The Garden of the Palace, Near a Philodendron Plant

(Enter Queen Ladamushea.)

QUEEN.   Alas!
          Like Bacterial Fungus, which no man sees
          Or an orchard rife with Dutch Elm Disease
          Our Kingdom rots, infected from within,
          By hypocritic rogues, who call pleasure sin.
          So what if my husband is my father's son?
          Who cares if he tortures peasants for fun?
          If with each soldier I've had an affair
          It's none of their business, what should they care?
          Yet now these fanatics approach our gates!
          How pointless their passions! How fickle the fates!

(Enter Crumbles and Thumbles, two inseparable courtiers who have just returned from the battle, and happen to be going to the council chamber by way of the garden.)

QUEEN.   Crumbles! Thumbles!

CRUM. &
THUM.   Your Majesty!

QUEEN.   What news?

CRUM.   When you ask so nicely, who can refuse?
Great Zepholephylee . . .

QUEEN.   (aside) My love! My life!

CRUM.   Fights like a madman, disdaining the strife,
Yet at the gates the rebels are giving him fits.

QUEEN.   At the gates! Is't possible?

CRUM.   Yes, it's!

QUEEN.   Your news of battle does much to grieve me,
So quit your gawking, and kindly leave me!

(Exit Crumbles and Thumbles.)

QUEEN.   My heart feels empty, like a vine unwatered,
Its leaves turned dusty, its grape stake, tottered.
Gnawed at by rodents whose hates soon harden
Their eyes from pity, and their paws from pardon.
But soft! A rumble sounds from far without,
Screams for pity, and a victorious shout.

I hope Zepholephylee has given some licks
To those vile rogues, those religious fanatics!

(Enter Zepholephylee in battle gear, his bloody sword brandished, and his helmet lined with flowers.)

ZEPH.   Hail womanly fruit tree, of whom I'm the sap,
You I knock up, but your enemies rap;
From my thorn-like sword, and photosynthetic eyes
Those outside weeds wither, and their fungus, flies.
To speak more plainly, I've won the fight,
Our hopes have blossomed, my budding delight!
So drop all modesty, and lip to lip,
Let's recommence our relationship!

(They embrace. Enter, climbing over the back wall, Villin, the leader of the Religious Fanatics. He is wearing all black, is covered with battle wounds, and is foaming at the mouth. In his right hand he is carrying a blood-stained meat cleaver, and in his left hand a satchel of religious pamphlets. He spies the two lovers, and immediately hides behind a twisted azalea plant.)

QUEEN.   Be silent bold hero! If my husband hears
He'll discover that I have cheated for years;
Such unpleasant news would make him furious—
To find his wife false, and his sons, spurious.

ZEPH.   It grieves me my love, that your husband's voice
Should deny you my love, and your freedom of choice,
For when nature calls should we deny it?
My answer is this—no way! Let's try it!

(They embrace and exit. Villin comes forth from his hiding place and speaks.)

VILLIN.   (in an evil, narrow-minded tone of voice)
              Like overripe melons, foul and unwashed,
              These "lovers" are sickening, fit to be squashed!
              O that the sound of their sloppy kisses
              Would transform to tears, and groans, and hisses!

"I've never been to a play in my life," Lathan commented after reading this drama-laden scene. "Still, for some reason this all sounds kind of familiar."

The dwarfs thought the play was wonderful, except for Bingo, who had a strange tendency to choke on his quiche at the close of every couplet.

"Hey, I think I've got the next page," said Rex happily as he handed Lathan another quiche-stained piece of foolscap.

Sure enough, it was the continuation of Villin's speech, which rose to heights of biological metaphor never before achieved by the mind of man. As it turned out, each of the dwarfs had a page of the script, so Lathan was able to continue reading the play all the way through Act V, scene 1. The following is a brief synopsis of those subsequent pages:

Villin, after concluding his speech, spies a helpless old woman planting a daisy in the corner of the garden, and immediately comes over and extorts a Love Offering from her. He uses the money to shave and buy himself a new set of clothes, and then, disguised as a happy-go-lucky Lieutenant (with a flower in his lapel) named Whiffle, he gets a job as Zepholephylee's chief advisor.

Meanwhile, Villin sends King Borosmore an anonymous letter telling of his wife's adultery. Even though a new army of Religious Fanatics has arrived at the city gates, the King vows to kill Zepholephylee, his greatest general. Fortunately, Zepholephylee's faithful servant Congo hears of the plot just in time, and, after accidentally encountering the King in the castle garden, Zepholephylee is able to strangle the jealous monarch with a long piece of asparagus.

Meanwhile, Zepholephylee has locked his beloved mistress, Queen Ladamushea, in an isolated castle tower where Congo is the only one able to communicate with her. Villin artfully tricks Zepholephylee into believing that the Queen and Congo are having a passionate love affair, and are laughing at Zepholephylee behind his back. After learning of this, Zepholephylee lures them both to the castle garden, and, in a fit of jealous rage, smothers Queen Ladamushea with a gigantic cauliflower, runs Congo through with a sharpened grape stake, and kills several innocent bystanders in an effort to assuage his troubled feelings.

While Zepholephylee is having this tantrum, Villin opens up the gates of the city and lets in the army of the Religious Fanatics. Villin then reveals his true character to the astonished Zepholephylee, and Zepholephylee realizes that he has made a fatal mistake. At the close of Act V, scene 1, Villin has tied Zepholephylee up in the middle of the garden and is trying to crush him in the pages of a giant prayer book by having some overweight monks sit on the cover.

"How exciting can you get?!" said Bulbo, Plottle, Slipper, Tripper, and Rex after Lathan finished the reading.

"King Borosmore has the busiest garden I've ever heard of," Bingo remarked.

"It certainly is!" the other dwarfs replied in admiration.

"There must be another scene somewhere," said Lathan. "I wonder where we can find it."

He asked one of the cooks.

"Who knows? They might have sent the rest of it with the quiche that went down to the torture chamber," the cook replied. "I thought I heard someone down there yelling something about international copyright."

Encouraged by this news, Lathan and the dwarfs decided to go down to the torture chamber, with only Bingo showing a lack of enthusiasm.

Following the directions of one of the guards, the little group of theatrical enthusiasts passed through a large metal door, and descended down a twisting, damp stone staircase. At the bottom of this tortuous staircase was a large, incredibly humid room, with moss growing on the walls, and rusty chains and torturing equipment everywhere. At first it was difficult to see in the gloom of the torture chamber, but as they entered Lathan and the dwarfs could hear several of the prisoners screaming, "No more! No more!"

"Silence! You'll not only hear more, but you'll hear it to the end, and that's that!" a voice pronounced sternly from the torture chamber's far wall.

Lathan recognized the voice immediately, and was struck dumb with amazement. He raced across the torture chamber toward the voice, but unfortunately tripped over a ball-and-chain that was lying carelessly in his way. When he jumped back to his feet he looked up and saw the man who had spoken chained to the wall by his legs. His hair was long and dirty, his face was unshaved, his eyes were bloodshot, his clothes were rags, and his body was emaciated, so that he looked in all respects remarkably similar to the author of this narrative; nevertheless Lathan had no trouble recognizing him as Doctor Oldair, the greatest philosopher in the western world.

"Doctor Oldair!"

"Silence!" the Doctor replied, as he held in his hands a quiche-stained piece of paper. "Wait until I've read the final scene."

"No! Please!" several prisoners begged.

The Doctor was unmoved by their pleas, and proceeded thus:

(Enter Tolerina, Queen Ladamushea's maid. She sees Zepholephylee being crushed by the monks in a giant prayer book, and laments his downfall.)

TOLER.   Alas my lord, your intellectual fires
         Are being crushed with words, and overweight Friars.
         Like a sun-ripened orange, fit to be picked,
         You'll be gone in a jiffy, I predict.

(Tolerina sees a group of other monks in the far corner of the garden, zealously burning biology books. She impulsively grabs some of their book-burning equipment, and, before the monks can stop her, she sets fire to the giant prayer book. The giant prayer book quickly bursts into flames, and the fat monks jump away.)

TOLER.   Avaunt fat friars, whose pudgy form
         No tolerance thins, and no mercy warms.
         Though you've put my master in cruel confines
         (His life to be read between the lines)
         With my last bit of strength, and final breath,
         I'll save this great hero, or join him in death.

ZEPH.   (From inside the book)
         Thanks kind (cough, cough) maid, it's getting warmer,
         Your last suggestion's fine, but I prefer the former.

(Tolerina helps Zepholephylee out of the burning book. Meanwhile, the fire spreads throughout the castle, and the army of the Religious Fanatics runs away. Zepholephylee and Tolerina, however, hide under a towering plum tree, where they are safe from the flames. Soon the flames burn out, and the Religious Fanatics have been defeated by their own arrogance and pride.

Arm in arm with Tolerina, Zepholephylee marches up to center stage.)

ZEPH.   Now I, alive, by Tolerina stand,
          The fanatics crushed, and forced to disband;
          No more by maggots will we be tortured,
          We've pruned our vineyard, we've sprayed our orchard!
          Now you, bold auditors, who here have seen
          A ravaged Kingdom, and a slaughtered Queen,
          Think of the things religion has destroyed,
          The thousands murdered (and millions annoyed),
          And know that you can avoid its furtive glance
          By loving tolerance, and truth, and plants!

Doctor Oldair delivered this theatrical coup with a flushed face, a booming voice, and a relish for every word which would have been very difficult for most performers to duplicate. The conclusion of his performance was greeted by the sound of a few chains rattling, and the hesitant clapping of Lathan and the dwarfs, followed by an awkward silence. Nevertheless, Doctor Oldair took the opportunity to make several dignified bows (at least, as dignified as his chains would allow him). Lathan rushed up to congratulate him.

"Oh, Doctor, it was a wonderful play, but I'm really glad and amazed to see you. I thought you had been killed in the pit of spiders! How did you ever escape?!"

"Well, I'd say the play is only moderately wonderful," Doctor Oldair mused. "I think the one word you could use to describe this play is . . . is . . . "

"Interesting?" Bingo suggested.

"Interesting, yes," Doctor Oldair replied. "You may be right."

Lathan took the opportunity to introduce Doctor Oldair to the six Wabonian dwarfs.

"An honor to meet devotees of Great Literature," said the Doctor, bowing once more.

"Now tell us, Doctor, how did you escape from the pit of spiders, and how did you get here of all places?" Lathan asked.

"The thing that perplexes me is how my play ever got mixed with paper that was used to wrap quiche. Somewhere a switch was made, and now there must be a theatrical company somewhere that has lost their copy of my play. Think of the agony they must be suffering!"

"I'm sure they'll learn to bear it," said Bingo.

"I'm really not sorry the mistake was made, however," the Doctor continued. "The play is so noble, so open-minded, and so uplifting and encouraging that I think a torture chamber might really be an appropriate place for it."

"I think it's very appropriate for a torture chamber," Bingo concurred.

"Critics have commented on the play's multi-layered plot, complex imagery, and use of symbolism, but actually the play's basic ideas are quite simple."

"Very simple," Bingo agreed.

"But tell us Doctor, how did you . . ."

"These chains are terribly uncomfortable," said the Doctor, as if he were just noticing them for the first time. "I think it would be easier to talk without them."

"Don't worry, Doctor Oldair," said Lathan. "I'll have you out of here at once."

Lathan, followed by the Wabonian dwarfs, hastily climbed up out of the torture chamber searching for the Pishaw. They found him in the prison courtyard, chewing on some broccoli, with their release papers in his hand. Lathan explained to the Pishaw that Doctor Oldair, the greatest philosopher in the western world, was currently lodged in the torture chamber, surely because of some monstrous misunderstanding, and Lathan humbly begged that the good Doctor might be released. The Pishaw, ever good-natured, included Doctor Oldair's name in the release papers, and before long the Pishaw was outside the prison gates with Lathan, the Wabonian dwarfs, and Doctor Oldair, who were now as free as the four winds.

"Well, friends, I know you are anxious to be on your way," said the Pishaw. "Remember to stay on the main trail, or you might run into some trouble. If you stay on the trail you'll go straight to the Dark Castle. I give you these mules as a parting gift, my friends. Take care of yourselves, and good luck."

The Pishaw hugged everyone, and couldn't resist selling Lathan a gigantic rug, on credit, and at very reasonable terms. After packing this awkward load onto his mule, Lathan thanked the Pishaw once more, and soon Lathan, Doctor Oldair, and the Wabonian dwarfs were outside the city walls, following a desert trail that led in the direction of the Dark Castle.

"Well, Doctor Oldair," said Lathan, as the mules plodded forward, "now that we're on our way, perhaps you can tell us about your miraculous escape from the spiders, and how you ended up clear across the ocean in a prison."

"Prince Charming and I had no trouble escaping from the pit of spiders, because we were never thrown into it in the first place," Doctor Oldair explained, "When we were captured on board the ship the Count threatened to put us there, but after a few words from me he didn't have the guts to do it."

"What did you say to him?" Lathan breathlessly asked.

"I said, 'Just try it, Count! I'm an old man now, but I've broken better men than you, and I'll break you too!' Then he said, 'But Doctor Oldair, please I . . .' and I said, 'Don't give me any of your lip! Either fight it out with me or let us go!'"

Lathan was overwhelmed by Doctor Oldair's bravery. He didn't think anyone could stand up to Count Zandar.

"So what happened—did you fight him?" Lathan asked.

"Not exactly," said Doctor Oldair.

Doctor Oldair had become highly excited when he recounted the proceeding dialogue, but now sounded a bit more subdued.

"Unfortunately, Prince Charming was doing so much whining and complaining that I lost my concentration, and soon someone snuck up on us and tied us up. After we began sailing they hung us upside-down from the masthead for a couple of days. Of course, Prince Charming was upset about this, but I had an idea. Oh sure, I knew the waters were infested with sharks, but I also knew I could out-swim them; after all, I was the Troddleheim Double-Pump Flutter Kick swimming champion fourteen years in a row."

Lathan whistled in admiration. Bingo, despite having finished his broccoli quiche a long time before, had a sudden choking attack.

"Finally they took us down and untied us, just to give us a rest. This was our big chance. I threw Prince Charming into the water and jumped in after him. When the sharks saw Prince Charming in the water they began to converge on him, but when they saw me swimming with him (doubtless noting my professional stroke) they veered away in fear. We wasted no time and swam briskly toward shore, with me helping the Prince along as best I could. Soon the ship was out of sight, and before long we saw the main dock at Scuttleton, and soon were safely on it."

"What an incredible escape!" Lathan exclaimed.

"Almost unbelievable," Bingo added.

"We decided to unwind from our adventure by going into one of the local taverns. We were drinking down a couple of bottles of—spring water—when some sailors came up and asked us why we looked so wet and weary. Prince Charming told them our story, and the sailors were so sympathetic they bought us another bottle. I was about halfway finished with this bottle when all of a sudden everything went black. When I finally woke up again Prince Charming and I were out in the middle of the ocean, stranded on a . . . on a . . .”

“On a what?” Bingo asked.

(Inaudible response.)

“I'm sorry, I can't hear . . .”

“A pickle barge!” Doctor Oldair repeated loudly.

“You were shanghaied onto a pickle barge?” Lathan asked.

“Yes, and believe me it was an ordeal. The Pickle Master was very mean to us. He made us stay in the hold the whole time and fill jars with gourmet pickles. The Pickle Society has a strict rule about jar-filling; each jar must be filled with so much pickle juice that it will spill all over the first person to open the jar. This has been a pickle tradition from time immemorial, and let me tell you, it's not easy overfilling those jars! The Prince could never get it right, and the Pickle Master punished him by sending him through the dilling machine three times!”

“Tell me,” asked Bingo, “did the Head Pickle . . .”

“That's ‘Pickle Master’!”

“Oh, I mean, did the Pickle Master tell you where he was sailing?”

“Certainly. He said he was going around the world, and Prince Charming and I had no interest in going there. We were planning a mutiny when a storm blew in and the ship was smashed to pieces. I clung to some wreckage, and was the only survivor. When I hit the water I saw Prince Charming astride a gigantic pickle mutation we were developing, trying desperately to hang on. Suddenly he slipped and flopped into the water, and I never saw him again.”

Lathan, forgetting his romantic rivalry with the Prince, bowed his head in sadness.

“So that's about it. I was washed up on shore, and walked a few miles until I made it to that city back there. I was there for three days.”

"But why did they put you in prison?" Lathan asked.

"Is that an oasis I see over there?" said Doctor Oldair.

It was an oasis, and, since it was late in the day, they decided to stay there for the night. As they rode in, Lathan recounted to Doctor Oldair all of the adventures he had had since they had last seen each other, particularly emphasizing what the Oracle had told him, and for the first time explained to Doctor Oldair that he was the son of the noble "Trollkiller" Sven Svensson.

"Oh, no! A religious fanatic!" the Doctor exclaimed with righteous indignation. "This is too much to bear!"

While the dwarfs dismounted and jumped into the lake in the center of the oasis, Doctor Oldair remained on his mule and berated Lathan unmercifully. He explained to Lathan that "Trollkiller" Sven Svensson was a fraud, that religion caused the death of thousands daily, and further explained that as soon as Lathan reached the Doctor's age he would realize that everything the Doctor ever told him was right.

As soon as they had set up camp the sun set, and they spent a little time sitting around a fire. Doctor Oldair, with his prison experiences now safely behind him, began treating everyone with great condescension. Lathan naturally looked up to Doctor Oldair as his superior, but the dwarfs felt that Lathan was the leader, and were befuddled about how to behave to the Doctor. All in all their's was a strained society, despite the natural good nature of the dwarfs, and things weren't helped when Bingo kept asking Doctor Oldair why he had been thrown in prison.

"Please, I don't want to sound too heroic, so I'd really rather not say," said Doctor Oldair, with laudable humility. "Let me just say that I was performing a noble act, but the vile authorities, jealous of my noble-mindedness, arrested me out of malice and envy."

Soon everyone except Bingo lay down near the fire and fell asleep. Bingo, still enamoured with the idea of distracting the

Count with toaster juggling, stared into the fire, thinking hard about how to overcome the minor obstacles in his plan.

He was sitting next to the sleeping Doctor, and couldn't help but overhear the Doctor mumbling in his sleep, ". . . Pickle Vending without a license? . . . I've never heard of . . . unhand me . . . all right, take my pickles . . . just let me go . . . let me go . . . let me go . . ."

Bingo smirked, and then kept pondering the efficacy of toaster juggling as a means of rescuing princesses until finally he too fell asleep.

Chapter XXI

The Prisoners Arrive at the Dark Castle, and the Princess Rescuers Visit an Empire

T he Count, his retinue, and his prisoners departed Scagabash and began a relatively uneventful journey back to the Dark Castle. Purella and Floppy had been locked in the ship's hold for so long that they actually enjoyed the first day's travelling, despite the fact that they still remained locked in their cages. In fact, they seemed to enjoy it so much that the Count ordered a tarp to be thrown over their cages, so that they never saw each other or anything else again until they arrived at the Dark Castle.

When the tarp was finally removed from her cage Purella found herself in a spacious, but incredibly gloomy, dungeon, which had recently been fitted with a bed, a dressing table, a mirror, and a few chairs to ensure the comfort of a royal prisoner. The dungeon was notable for the ornately carved heads of screaming demons that stuck out of the walls, each having glassy eyes that followed you wherever you walked.

"You'll be sacrificed in five days. Meanwhile," said the Count gesturing around the newly redecorated dungeon, "enjoy!"

The Count bowed, and then left Purella to herself. Purella wondered what they had done with Floppy, not realizing that the Dark Castle was so well equipped that it even had a kennel-sized dungeon for traitorous dogs, in which her faithful follower had been sequestered. After thoroughly inspecting the dungeon for secret exits, and finding none, Purella sat on the bed, and, since there wasn't much point in crying, even though she felt like it, stared at the stone floor in front of her. Little did she know that a great philosopher, a robust shepherd lad, and six Wabonian dwarfs were on their way to rescue her. Of course, even that news might not have cheered her. She was to be sacrificed in five days, and her rescuers were in an oasis several hundred long miles away, sleeping next to a smoldering fire.

The next day the roseate sun climbed up the steps of dewy-eyed morn, sending a myriad of colors cascading onto the verdant world beneath, and old Sol, inebriated with the power of light, joyfully ordered his luminescent beams to tiptoe merrily across the abodes of the sons of men; but what all this has to do with our story, or with any story at all for that matter, is difficult to understand. At any rate it was daytime, and everybody woke up.

"We have no time to lose!" Lathan exhorted. "The Princess needs our help!"

Two days later, after a wearying ride through the desert, the little band of rescuers arrived at the base of a mountain range. Unfortunately, the narrow little trail they were following continued straight ahead, heading directly over steep slopes as if they weren't there. On the other hand, if they left the trail and went to their right, there was a broad, gently sloping route which seemed to circumvent the difficult climbing. They debated over which route they should take.

"The Pishaw told us this trail would take us to the Dark Castle, so I think we should follow it, whether it's difficult or not," Lathan opined.

Doctor Oldair looked amused.

"I admit it looks like a rough trail," said Bingo, "but I suppose we should follow it anyway. Of course, in Wabonia we would have had a tunnel through mountains like this years ago, or who knows, possibly even a bridge over the top."

The Wabonian dwarfs grinned at the thought of their own ingenuity. The Doctor continued to look amused.

"My friends," he said finally, "this trail, albeit straight, is obviously the wrong trail."

He paused so that the realization of their ignorance would sink in as deeply as possible.

"Obviously this trail was blazed by a fool, since its perfect straightness goes against nature. Remember—trust nature. Always follow nature's simple course—it will never steer you wrong."

He gestured toward the broad sloping path to their right.

"My friends, nature leads us in this direction, on this gentle path. Let us not spurn her assistance."

Assured by this persuasive speech, Lathan and the dwarfs agreed to be guided by the Doctor.

They followed him down the gently-sloping trail, which gradually turned a little steeper, then much steeper, then unreturnably steep, until the mules all panicked and ran away, and the Princess Rescuers ended up in a jungle, sinking in quicksand, and being slowly surrounded by deadly, disease-ridden snakes.

"Well, obviously that gently sloping path was man-made," said Doctor Oldair just as his face began to sink into the goo.

Fortunately for the Doctor, there were six Wabonian dwarfs nearby, ready to put their world-renowned problem-solving skills to good use. Cleverly, the dwarfs began waving their arms, kicking their legs, and screaming frantically, which not only scared the deadly snakes away, but also displaced the quicksand so much that Bingo was able to paddle safely over to solid ground.

"Keep panicking," said Bingo. "I'll find a vine."

After twice mistaking the tail of a deadly snake for a vine, Bingo found a real vine and hurled one end of it into the quicksand. The dwarfs scrambled onto the vine, which unfortunately was too short to reach Lathan and Doctor Oldair, who were at the far end of the pit. With Bingo pulling hard at the end of the rope, all of the dwarfs soon made it to safety.

"Help!" said Lathan, who was up to his neck in quicksand. "Doctor Oldair is already under!"

"We'll have to get a longer vine!" said Bingo.

"Wait there!" Rex advised Lathan.

Soon the dwarfs disappeared into the jungle.

"Hurry!" said Lathan.

Soon Lathan's face sank beneath the surface. Keeping his right arm above the surface of the quicksand, he reached down with his left hand and grasped the magic coin. If ever he needed its help he needed it now, but as the quicksand enveloped his head all he could think of was Purella, and how he was failing her.

Just as his right arm was sinking he felt something touch against it. He grasped for it desperately, and soon found himself holding onto a vine. Quickly he took his other hand off his coin and reached down to find Doctor Oldair. The Doctor was already several feet under, but Lathan was able to find his arm and hold on. Soon the two of them were dragged to safety and lay on solid ground, completely caked with quicksand.

"Good work, Bingo," Lathan mumbled.

He and Doctor Oldair wiped the muck from their eyes, and found themselves surrounded by thirty-seven bronze-clad female warriors, each one carrying a spear, a good tan, and a fierce expression. There wasn't a dwarf in sight.

"Men!" one of them shouted. Several of them growled.

"Allow me to . . . phew . . . phew . . . intro . . . phew . . . duce . . . myself," said the Doctor, while spitting the quicksand out of his mouth. "I'm Doctor Oldair, the greatest . . . phew . . . phew . . . sopher in the western world."

"Silence!" said one of the warriors. "You men must be interrogated by our Empress."

A trumpet sounded. Suddenly a six-foot-tall blond woman wearing elaborate armor and peacock feathers came marching out of the jungle, followed by two slightly shorter attendants.

"*Men*, Your Majesty," said several of the warriors, pronouncing the first word as if it were a synonym of "vermin."

The Empress gave Doctor Oldair and Lathan a quick look, and was apparently not enamoured of what she saw.

"I am Helga, Empress of the Amazons," she said. "We will take you to our city, torture you until you tell us why you've come, and then you will die a horrible death. Shall we be going?"

"Now see here . . ." Doctor Oldair began. Suddenly there were thirty-seven spears pointed at his face.

"After you, Your Majesty," he continued.

Lathan and the Doctor were unceremoniously tied to wooden poles and carried a few hundred yards away to a wide, muddy river. Lathan kept calling out Bingo's name, but there was never a response. Soon they were in a long outrigger canoe, being paddled up a hippopotamus-infested river toward the city of the Amazons.

The city of the Amazons had a long and varied history, and resembled many other warrior cities, except for the fact that everything was spotlessly clean. Also, the Arena, the torture chambers, and most of the other public buildings were painted in bright pastels, and there were lace curtains everywhere. Lathan and Doctor Oldair were thrown into a prison cell for the night, where they spent their time bemoaning their fate, and picking the leaves off some tastefully arranged ferns.

"But what do you think happened to Bingo and the dwarfs?" Lathan asked the Doctor. "I thought they were right there."

"Oh please, don't be so naive," the Doctor replied, scoffing. "Those dwarfs never intended to give us any help. They used you to get out of prison, and then left us at the first opportunity, leaving us to die in the quicksand."

"But I thought . . ."

"Naive," said Doctor Oldair, shaking his head. "So naive."

Lathan sadly picked another leaf off a fern.

"Of course, it's strictly academic by now," said the Doctor. "The Princess will be sacrificed to the great god Moloch at the SIN convention, which is only three days from now, and we're still hundreds of miles away."

Lathan jumped to his feet.

"You mean we only have three days left?! We've gotta find some way out of here!" said Lathan as he jumped around and looked helplessly out the barred window.

"Naive," repeated Doctor Oldair. "So naive."

Lathan tried to squeeze himself between the bars in the windows, and was spectacularly unsuccessful. He took a seat for a second or two, and then started pacing restlessly.

"My boy," said Doctor Oldair, "there is nothing you can do to save the Princess, so you must learn to forget about her. In three days the precious flower that you love so much will be plucked, uprooted, and shredded. Here's what I recommend you do: go home, purchase a garden, and then tend it. The world would be a better place if everyone stayed home and tended their own garden, believe me."

Doctor Oldair was so inspired by his own little speech that he began plucking the ferns with great fervor. Just then a key turned in the lock, and the cell door swung open. The Empress of the Amazons and two of her blond-maned guards strode inside.

"On your knees, you men!" she ordered. Lathan and Doctor Oldair quickly obeyed.

"Your Majesty," said Doctor Oldair, "I feel that . . ."

She stuffed a fern into his mouth.

"I don't need your lip," she said. "I just want to find out why you've come, and then butcher you alive."

This didn't sound too hopeful, but Lathan was not reluctant to speak.

"I'm Lathan, and this is Doctor Oldair, the greatest philosopher in the western world, and we're on our way to rescue Princess Purella of Hoodahooda, who's about to be sacrificed by Count Zandar, the most evil man in the world. Oh please, let us go so we can save her! Help us, help us, help us!!!"

"That's a likely story," said the Empress. "You men are all alike; you'll say anything to save your skins. No doubt you're on a mission to trap and enslave women everywhere. Well, it's not going to work. You will be horribly punished for your insolence toward our sex."

At this point one of the guards dropped her spear. Lathan rushed over, picked it up, handed it back to her, politely said, "Here you go, miss; I don't think it's broken," and then went back to his former position. For some reason, this courteous display aggravated the Empress.

"Take them to the execution block!" she ordered the guards.

As Doctor Oldair and Lathan were being led out, Lathan stopped to hold the door open for the Empress, which further provoked her fury.

"Be merciless!" she ordered the guards, after shoving Lathan through the door in front of her.

Lathan and Doctor Oldair were led out of the prison and taken to the city's main square, which was the site of all public executions. Soon they found themselves next to a chopping block in the middle of the square, surrounded by a huge throng of statuesque warriors.

"Bring out the axe!" the Empress commanded.

The axe, which was so heavy that two Amazons were required to carry it, was brought out into the square.

"But we haven't done anything!" said Lathan.

"Silence!" said the Empress. "Spies like you are . . ."

"We're not spies, and we don't have time for this!" shouted Lathan in an unusually fiery manner. "I've got a princess to rescue, and you're not going to stop me!"

The Amazons were struck dumb with amazement.

"How dare you speak that way to me, you ugly, pathetic wretch!" said the Empress. "No one talks to me like that! No one!"

She slapped Lathan across the face, but Lathan was undaunted.

"You must have some laws in this land that protect foreigners. I appeal to the highest court in the land."

"I *am* the highest court in the land," the Empress answered with a sneer, "except for, of course . . . the Emperor."

At the mention of the word, "Emperor," the hundreds of Amazons in the square became silent, dropped down to one knee, sighed romantically, and then rose back to their feet.

"Emperor?" Lathan asked.

Everyone dropped to their knees, sighed romantically, and then popped back up again.

"That's right," the Empress replied.

"An Emperor, eh?" said Lathan, who then paused until everyone could become upright again. "You mean you're ruled by a man?"

"He's much more than a *man*," the Empress indignantly replied, with a slight trace of stars in her eyes. "He's the summit of human magnificence, the pinnacle of power, and the epitome of superiority. He is, in short, our Emperor."

Looking around him, Lathan could see that too much discussion of the Emperor would cause many of the Amazons chronic knee problems in later life; nevertheless he boldly announced that on behalf of Doctor Oldair and himself he was appealing to the Emperor. Throughout all this dialogue, Doctor Oldair said nothing, but merely stared at the axe and chopping block, looking rather ill.

"Don't be ridiculous," said the Empress. "The Emperor" (sound of knees creaking) "is unmerciful, and even I tremble when I speak to him. I will not bother the Emperor" (creak, creak) "with a matter as trivial as this."

"I beg your pardon, Your Majesty," said an Amazon with pointy-rimmed glasses (obviously a librarian), "but according to our law, if he appeals to the Emperor" (creak, creak) "to the Emperor" (creak, creak) "he must go."

"You talk to the Emperor for me, Lathan," whispered Doctor Oldair with a slight tremble, "I think I'll just stay here and . . . meditate. It's really not dignified for a philosopher to beg for mercy."

Based on the Empress's description, Doctor Oldair was not anxious to meet the Emperor.

"I understand, Doctor," said Lathan, who really didn't understand, but didn't want the Doctor to think he was naive by questioning him about it.

On the far side of the square was a huge palatial building with hundreds of steps leading up to the massive colonnade in front of its entrance. This building had every reason in the world to be palatial, since it was, in fact, the Palace.

While Doctor Oldair remained at the chopping block, heavily guarded by dutiful Amazons, Lathan was led to the foot of the broad, stone steps.

"Call for the Emperor!" the Empress ordered.

A thousand Amazon trumpeters lined up on the sides of the steps and blew their trumpets in an elaborate fanfare. Several adolescent Amazons raced up and down the steps sprinkling flowers over the area where the Emperor would walk.

"Here he comes!" someone said, and soon everyone dropped to their knees.

Lathan grasped his magic coin once more. No matter how tough, how strong, or how cruel this Emperor was, Lathan was determined to talk him into letting Doctor Oldair and him go.

All heads were bowed. A hush fell on the scene, as the heavy strides of the Emperor could be heard on the steps above. The Emperor slowly descended the steps. Just as Lathan was thinking that the adolescent Amazons had thrown too many flowers, because their smell was extraordinarily strong, he looked up and saw before him, in a badly-fitted silk Emperor's costume and a furry, golden Emperor's hat, none other than Prince Charming, formerly of Skindeepia.

"Your Awesomeness," said the Empress as she threw herself at the Prince's feet, "I and your citizens greet you."

"Hi!" said the Prince.

"Your Awesomeness," said the Empress, in a little girlish voice quite unlike the voice she used when dealing with her two captives, "this vile wretch and his accomplice have appealed to you for mercy, and the law says they have that right. I really hate to disturb you, and it's not my fault!"

She looked like she was about to cry. Lathan, whose mouth had been wide open with astonishment the whole time, finally blurted out, "Prince Charming!"

"Hey, that's 'Emperor' Charming, and don't you forget it, buddy!" said the Prince, turning fiercely toward Lathan. Then, after an awkward pause, he recognized him.

"Hey, I know this guy!"

"You mean you know this villain?" asked the Empress.

"Silence!" Prince Charming commanded her.

She quickly bowed her head. He looked around at the other Amazons and they quickly bowed their heads too. Satisfied, Prince Charming walked down to Lathan.

Though Prince Charming was always relaxed and confident when speaking with females, he always felt a little awkward in the presence of other males, never quite knowing what to say, but always trying unsuccessfully to convey an attitude of good fellowship.

"Hey, you're looking fine, real . . . I mean, you look all right," Prince Charming said while giving Lathan a pat on the back. "So what've you been up to? By the way, I don't know how to tell you this, but our old friend Oldair kicked off."

Lathan quickly assured the Prince that Doctor Oldair was not only still alive, but was sitting next to the chopping block in the middle of the main square.

"Really? The last time I saw him he was bouncing over the waves, trying to hang onto a Mr. Pickle Portable Pickle Wagon."

"But Prince, how did you escape from the sinking pickle barge, and how did you get here?" asked Lathan while sneezing repeatedly, for the Prince's dunk in the ocean hadn't done much to tone down his pungent aroma.

"I'll tell you the whole story. As soon as we were captured by the Count, Doctor Oldair started howling. I've never heard a guy howl like that before. Anyway, between howls he would beg for mercy, but they still decided to torture us. They hung us from the masthead for a while, and then the Count said he was going to throw us to the sharks. Doctor Oldair howled and begged for mercy about thirty times, and then they picked him up and tossed him into the ocean.

"Well, I guess howling attracts sharks, because soon there were about thirty of them swimming right toward him. Then they threw me in. Things were looking bad, but then a funny thing happened. I guess sharks can sense royalty, because after I hit the water all the sharks stopped, sniffed for a little bit, stuck their noses out of the water, and then swam away as fast as they could go. Two of the sharks tried to come closer, but when they got near me they started sneezing and suddenly went belly up. I still can't figure it out."

"It's a (sneeze . . . sneeze) real (choke . . . sneeze) mystery," sputtered Lathan, as his nose and eyes began to run. He tried his best to stay upwind of the Prince.

"Fortunately we were only about a few miles from shore, and were able to float to shore on a couple of barrels the sailors had tossed overboard a little earlier. Then we went to a tavern where they gave us each a Triple Snake Blaster, on the rocks."

"I believe it was actually spring water," said Lathan. He was amused that the Prince kept mixing up the details of the story.

"Well, that must have been some spring. Anyway, that's when we got knocked over the head and got stuck on that pickle barge. Look what they did to me with their dilling machine."

He showed Lathan the back of his neck, which had green stripes on it and looked crispy enough to chew.

"That's horrible, Prince," said Lathan. "But tell me, how did you escape from the sinking pickle barge?"

"At first I had a good grip on a giant, mutated pickle, but then I slipped and fell back into the ocean. Things looked bad. I sunk very deep, but then for some reason I felt myself slowly rising back to the surface.

"Suddenly I popped up above the water and found myself floating on a huge mound of pickle relish. The air bubbles in the relish caused it to float, and I rode on a soft green mattress of it until I was finally washed up on shore.

"After I got to shore I fell asleep on the beach. When I woke up I found myself arm in arm with a native girl dressed in white. Standing in front of us was an old guy with a black book in his hand, and behind him was a fatherly type who carried a spear in one hand and a badly-wrapped present, about the size of a cookbook, in the other. Next to him was an old hag who was crying her eyes out with joy. I decided I should leave. I ran along the beach, and even though I heard a lot of crying and yelling behind me I didn't look back. After about a mile I came to a marshy spot where a big muddy river flowed into the ocean. I saw an abandoned canoe along the shore and started paddling up the river. The people chasing me couldn't follow, and pretty soon the sound of their voices faded away.

"That night I slept on the river bank, and when I woke up the next morning I was surrounded by Amazon warriors. They quickly laid their hands on me, then they laid their hands on me again, and then again, and then they took me to their Empress. She laid her hands on me, apologized for the inconvenience her warriors caused me, and then offered me the vacant job of Emperor for Life. So that's the whole story. I didn't really have anything better to do, and it's really a pretty good job."

He and Lathan looked back to the Empress and the other Amazons on the steps, who still had their heads bowed in total submission.

"Of course, I do wish there were better opportunities for advancement," the Prince commented.

Prince Charming and Lathan walked over to Doctor Oldair. All the Amazons that were guarding him bowed deeply.

"Hi, Doctor Oldair," said the new Emperor, greeting his former comrade.

"No need for emotion, Your Highness," said the Doctor, just after his eyes had lit up and he had leaped to his feet on recognizing the Prince. "I am not just an old man, but a philosopher, and I can bear my misfortunes with grace, dignity, and honor."

"Well, great!" said the Prince. "What do you say we all go back to my throne room and have a chat?"

"But Prince Charming, Princess Purella is going to be sacrificed in three days," Lathan interjected. "We have no time to waste; we must leave here at once!"

"We?" said the Prince.

"Yes! You'll have to tell the Empress good-bye, and then we'll have to get some horses and go!"

"Of course, I'm really anxious to go," the Prince explained, "but unfortunately I've got this new job now, and to tell you the truth I've signed a contract and everything, and it's all very ironclad."

"But . . ."

"Just a moment Prince," Doctor Oldair interrupted. "Do you mean to say that they made you ruler of this Empire?"

"Emperor for Life," the Prince replied. "At least, that's what it says on my job description."

"Tell me," said the Doctor, "are there any philosophers in this country?"

"None that I know of," the Prince replied.

"That's tragic," said Doctor Oldair, "very tragic. By the way, is it true this country consists entirely of females?"

"Entirely, except for the three of us."

"They must feel a great yearning for philosophical enlightenment," said Doctor Oldair, "and, out of consideration for them, I'm more than willing to give them my philosophical assistance on a permanent basis."

"Well, you may have a point," Prince Charming replied. "Most of them probably don't know much about philosophy, because according to this census sheet I was given the average age in this country is 23.2."

"Oh, they'll need philosophy so much and I want to give it to them! Oh yes, yes, yes, yes, yes!" stammered a drooling Doctor Oldair, whose enthusiasm for philosophy knew no bounds.

"But Doctor . . . Prince . . ." said Lathan, "we don't have time to worry about this now; we've got to rescue the Princess!"

"Twenty-three point two!" the Doctor kept mumbling.

"The job's yours if you want it," said the Prince.

"As soon as we recover my specimens of Flaming Pink Chrysopata Scumatta of Phylum Fulvibrata (oh, and of course, the Princess) I would like nothing better than to spend the rest of my days imparting as much philosophy as I can to these young, impressionable women."

"Done," said the Prince, patting him on the back. Prince Charming led everyone back to the still-kneeling Empress.

"The prisoners are to be set free," he commanded. "Give them each a horse at once."

"But Your Awesomeness," pleaded the Empress, "those men are spies and . . ."

"Do as I command you!" said the Prince. He gave the Empress a harsh look, and then slapped her across the face.

"I'm sorry," the Empress sobbed. "I shouldn't have annoyed you like that."

"I'll let it pass . . . this time," he replied.

He reached down and raised her chin up with his hands. She looked at him with moist, pleading eyes.

"Now, now, don't cry," said Prince Charming. "I just want to tell you you're looking fine. Real fine."

The Empress smiled gratefully, and then rose to her feet and hugged her lord and master. She then light-heartedly ordered the horses to be made ready for the prisoners, and her orders were obeyed at once.

Lathan had never seen a woman struck before, and was actually beginning to rush up the stairs to defend the Empress until he saw her and the Prince quickly reconcile. The behavior of the Empress had Lathan utterly baffled, for she seemed to admire Prince Charming for hitting her, yet when Lathan came up to her and asked if she were all right, she called him an insolent wretch and told him to mind his own business. Prince Charming noted the expression of confusion on Lathan's face, and after the Empress had left to wash her face he spoke to Lathan in a confidential manner.

"That's the way you have to treat them," he said. "They're all alike, you know."

Doctor Oldair, who, unlike Lathan, had seen many women struck in his lifetime, sometimes from very close proximity (particularly during his twenty years of blissful marriage to Mrs. Doctor Oldair), agreed that it was a very effective method of reminding female upstarts of their proper place. Lathan frowned.

"Purella is a woman too," Lathan thought, "and if you ever dreamed of hitting her I'd knock you out cold, Prince or no Prince!"

When Lathan thought how close Prince Charming had come to marrying Purella, he shuddered. He decided he never wanted to see the Prince again.

The horses arrived, and soon Doctor Oldair and Lathan were mounted up and ready to go.

"Well, friends, have a nice rescue!" said the Prince in his most winning manner, "and remember, I'll be with you in spirit."

"Good-bye," said Lathan.

"Remember to keep the philosopher job open," Doctor Oldair reminded the Prince. "I have an urge to impart metaphysical happiness to your subjects that you'd find hard to believe."

"Oh, no, I believe it," said the Prince. "Farewell."

The two adventurers rode off into the distance, and soon left Prince Charming and the Amazons behind; Lathan with gladness and relief, and Doctor Oldair with some regret and intense philosophical frustration. They rode as fast as they could, but still watched helplessly as the sun plummeted below the western hills. It was two nights before the fatal day, and Purella was doomed to die.

Chapter XXII

An Embarrassingly Short Chapter, Which Nevertheless Contains Events Vital to This History

*P*urella's life in the Count's dungeon was not particularly gay or frivolous. One of the highlights of the day was her meal, which was always brought to her on a covered silver tray. A fumbling female servant would bring the tray in, place it on a chair with a clatter, and then would fumble her way outside.

On the night before the SIN convention the above-described event happened just as usual; however, when the servant had gone Purella noted that the meal smelled rather peculiar. Curious, she lifted the lid.

"Arf!" said her dinner, and the odorous repast jumped off the plate and onto her lap.

"Floppy, how in the world did you escape?!" Purella asked.

Floppy explained by illustrating to Purella, in pantomime, the fact that the kennel-sized dungeon for traitorous dogs was built to contain mastiffs and other large dogs, rather than small, unaffiliated mongrels such as Floppy. As it happened, Floppy hadn't been in the dungeon for five minutes before he discovered that he could squeeze in and out of the bars at will. For the next three days he snuck in and out of his dungeon every night, searching for Purella. Finally he discovered which dungeon she was in, and discovered where her food was prepared. He then switched himself with her meal, and here he was.

"We need to have you look around some more," said Purella as she doused him with a little water (he hadn't had a bath in quite a while). "The sacrifice is tomorrow, and I want you to find the idol of Moloch, and see if there's any way we can destroy it."

Purella had been so successful in her first attempt to ruin an idol that she was sanguine enough to think she could do it again. She regretted that she didn't have a bottle of Mr. Jack Crackback's famous BAP water.

"Here you go, Floppy," said Purella as she raised Floppy up to the barred opening of her door. "Jump to the ground, and then go find the idol. When you get back I'll lower my blanket through the window and you can climb up again. Now, get going."

Obediently, Floppy leaped through the bars, landed on the floor, and darted off in search of the great idol.

The Dark Castle was a maze of crooked hallways and twisting passages, and soon Floppy was hopelessly lost. Fortunately for him, most of the castle appeared abandoned, and he didn't have to worry about avoiding anyone. He wandered and wandered and wandered, until the sun rose on the fatal day. Finally, however, he heard the sound of several footsteps coming down a passageway in front of him.

Floppy crept forward into the passageway and hid himself in an unlit corner. The footsteps came closer, and soon six of the Count's men marched past, each man carrying huge hunks of beef, except for their torch-carrying leader.

"Move it!" he said to his men. "The members of the Society of Idolators and Necromancers are arriving in a few hours, and the girls are supposed to be sacrificed later today, so we've got to get this place ready!"

By the time he had finished speaking he and his men had passed out of sight. Floppy followed cautiously behind.

After winding down several more long passages, the hallway eventually opened up into a large, well-lit room. The room was stacked with posters and billboards which said things like, "*MOLD-A-GOD* works!" and "Ever have one of those mornings where you wake up and discover you need a new deity? Then contact *MOLD-A-GOD* today, and get your free brochure."

Passing through this room, Floppy walked into the gigantic indoor temple of Moloch, the scene of many a gruesome sacrifice, and the home temple of this year's Society of Idolators and Necromancers convention. Workers, too busy to notice Floppy, scurried back and forth, trying to prepare for the upcoming festivities. Monoliths were set up, incense was placed in strategic locations, and booths which would sell everything from pigs knuckles to portable pagan altars were set up throughout the hall.

At first, however, Floppy's eyes were glued only on the huge black and red idol at the far end of the temple, which continually had a stream of black smoke pouring out of its nostrils. The idol appeared to depict a creature half-man, half-goat, and it was lined with hundreds of blackened skulls, the remains of many a helpless maiden. In front of the idol was a massive sacrificial altar, where Floppy's beloved Princess was scheduled to be slain.

"We have to test the altar," said one of the Count's men. "Throw some of the meat on there and see how well it burns."

Floppy crept up to the altar. In front of it were huge stacks of meat, some of which was to be the preliminary sacrifice before the main event, and the rest of it to be consumed afterward by the voracious conventioneers. On the side of the altar were several black barrels. Floppy was walking over to investigate when suddenly some drunks came into the temple wearing bow-ties and funny hats. The conventioneers were starting to arrive.

"And this, gentlemen, is the altar of Moloch, custom-made from Deluxe High-Tone Ultra-Black Obsidian, a **MOLD-A-GOD** specialty."

With his deep, ominous voice signalling his arrival, the Count strode into the temple, followed by a large group of short, stocky men in funny hats, who had with them several flirtatious and slightly overweight bleached-blond companions, most of whom were named Gert, Pearl, or Ivie.

"Have a seat, and in a few hours the convention will begin," the Count informed his guests. "Feel free to drink excessively, and we have small rodents you can torture while you wait."

Soon more conventioneers began pouring into the temple, and the Count went over to Og to find out if the altar had been prepared.

"Duh, it seems to be burning a little warm," said Og, as he pointed to the charred bodies of the six men who had been trying to assist him.

"It does seem a little balmy," said the Count, whose skin was turning red, and was suddenly dripping with sweat. "You didn't put on any more than sixty gallons of oil, did you?"

"Sixty?!" said Og, "I thought you said six *thousand!*"

"Six thousand is a bit much," said the Count, while rapidly losing body weight.

The Count gave orders, and soon he had a detachment of men pouring buckets of water on the fire, until it finally cooled down to a bearable temperature.

"I have to get back to the guests," the Count told Og. "In a few hours, send some men down to get the Princess. Today she dies."

Og was pleased to hear it.

"And do you see those black barrels?' the Count continued, gesturing to the barrels next to him, as well as some barrels on a landing above the altar. "Make *sure* they don't get too close to the fire. We should have moved them yesterday. They're filled with liquefied Deluxe High-Tone Ultra-Black Obsidian, and if it catches fire there'll be an explosion you won't believe."

The Count walked away, Og walked away, and Floppy crept closer to the long row of black barrels.

"I hear several girls are getting it today, including a princess . . . try to get a good seat . . ." Floppy could hear voices say.

Floppy snuck close to the altar and looked carefully around. He crept closer to the black barrels that were about twenty yards from the altar; they were too far away to be in any danger of igniting.

Then Floppy looked up and saw the landing above the altar. The landing was lined with black barrels, and their spigots, which conveniently stuck out directly above the fiery altar, glimmered in the torchlight.

Floppy looked back at the temple entrance and saw the stream of conventioneers pouring in, and could hear a few of the Count's henchmen starting to hawk programs. He wanted to get to those barrels. He saw a small maintenance staircase that led to the landing, and bolted toward it.

"Hey, that's the Princess's dog!" he heard someone say.

Soon voices were shouting from all sides. Floppy raced up the stairs to the barrels. A spear clattered next to him. Some of the Count's men ran up the stairs behind him, and the Count, hearing the commotion from the far end of the temple, began running back toward the altar. Floppy ran to a barrel directly above the fire and clenched the spigot in his mouth. It wouldn't budge. As one of the Count's soldiers reached over to grab him, he gave the spigot one last, desperate pull.

Chapter XXIII

A Visit to a Perfect Republic

While Floppy was cavorting around the temple of Moloch, Doctor Oldair and Lathan had their horses stolen from them by bandits, were forced to wash dishes in a tavern in order to get some food, were fired for breaking a dish, were arrested for hitchhiking on a public thoroughfare, and escaped by leaping off the constable wagon and into a giant patch of star-thistles. They were tired and beaten, and still a few hundred miles from the Dark Castle with only ten hours to go before the sacrifice.

"Please get up, Doctor Oldair," said Lathan in a desperate frenzy. "We have to keep moving."

"I can't go another step," the Doctor replied as he picked some star-thistle out of his pants. "Let me just sit down on this rock and get some rest."

When the Doctor sat down Lathan heard a loud, pathetic groan.

"I know you're in pain, Doctor," pleaded Lathan, "but please, think about the Princess."

"Wait a moment," said the Doctor. "I didn't make that groan."

"Who was it then?"

Neither of them could figure it out until Doctor Oldair stood up and noticed that he had been sitting on a crumpled-up man.

The man looked up at the Doctor, said one sentence, and then rolled over and died.

"What did he say?" Lathan solemnly asked.

"He said, 'Sit somewhere else.'"

"What do you think happened to him?"

The Doctor shook his head.

"He's just another victim of a cruel and unjust universe," the Doctor replied, "a victim of the cruel savagery you and your alleged father call 'God.' O we are but aphids to the gods, they spray us for their sport!"

Before Lathan had a chance to be moved by this heart-rending speech, a scraggly-bearded man wearing an old hunting suit that was three sizes too small for him came out of a nearby thistle patch and asked Lathan if he had seen any dead guys around.

"Yeah, there's one right there," said Lathan.

"Thanks," the stranger replied.

"Behold, sir," said Doctor Oldair as the badly-attired stranger stepped toward him, "before us lies the body of a fellow mortal, who has suddenly been deprived of life by the amorality of the monumental void that holds the world in its sway."

"Well, actually I killed this guy myself," said the stranger, slightly embarrassed.

"You did?" said Doctor Oldair, in a quite different tone of voice.

"Yeah, it wasn't the monumental void at all. I just came back to get my knife."

"Well, at least I'm sure you had a good reason for doing it," said Doctor Oldair after a moment's deliberation.

The stranger gave a non-committal grunt, and then shrugged his shoulders.

"But why did you do it?" Lathan asked.

"You know, I really don't know," said the stranger thoughtfully, just as if he were thinking about it for the first time. "For one thing I didn't like his face, and then he started to make me mad on top of that, so I just let instinct take over and killed him. To be honest, the whole thing seemed . . . well . . . it just seemed like the natural thing to do."

Doctor Oldair must have been satisfied by this response, since he immediately switched the conversation to other topics.

"Are there any cities or towns nearby, or are we in the middle of nowhere?" he asked the stranger.

"You're in luck," said the stranger. "The Republic of El Limo is just on the other side of that hill."

"El Limo! You mean the fabled land where everyone is equal, and truth and justice reign supreme?!"

"None other," the stranger replied.

"I can't wait to see it!" the Doctor replied.

"Can we get fresh horses there to carry us to the Dark Castle?" Lathan asked.

"Of course," said Doctor Oldair, before the stranger could answer. "No one lacks for anything in El Limo."

The stranger, who was going in another direction, pulled his knife out of the dead man's back, shook hands heartily with the two Princess Rescuers, and wished them luck. After walking away for a short distance, Lathan and Doctor Oldair looked back and saw the stranger drag the dead man deeper into the thistles, and then walk casually away.

When they came to the top of the ridge in front of them Lathan and the Doctor beheld a large valley with a broad, pleasant stream flowing through it. They walked down to the stream and followed it until they came to a huge waterfall. From the top of the waterfall they could see an even bigger valley below them, which was part of the Republic of El Limo. They knew this because of a large wooden sign which said "El . . ." and the rest of which was obliterated by initials, hearts with arrows through them, and several obscure tips on how to find a good time.

"My boy," Doctor Oldair pontificated, "you are fortunate indeed to be visiting the land of El Limo. I've never actually seen this nation before, but yet I feel like I'm returning home. For many years I and my philosophical brethren have given aid and support to this land, where the most valuable parts of our philosophy have been put into practice. El Limo is a land where total equality exists, where a common laborer is considered the equal of a king, and where religion is no longer allowed to interfere with people's lives. It is a land of joy, of beauty, and of poetry in motion."

Doctor Oldair scampered down the ridge and into the valley, and Lathan, though stimulated by the hope that there was still a chance to rescue the Princess, could hardly keep up with him. Soon they reached the main highway at the bottom of the valley. Quickly seeing another wooden sign that said, "Cap . . . . . .ity," and then was obliterated by initials, hearts, and several awkwardly rhyming poems, they followed the direction of the sign in the hope that it would lead them to the capital city.

After following the road for a mile or two it became apparent (at least to Lathan) that the poetry of this noble land strongly resembled free verse, in that the country's rut-filled main road wound aimlessly back and forth for no apparent reason, all the surrounding fields were full of weeds and disarray, and the sides of the road were piled with litter, so that the whole country looked as if it had been abandoned to riot and confusion many years before. Lathan commented about this to Doctor Oldair.

"It's natural that you who have lived under the bondage of religious mania should at first glance find a truly free country unappealing," the Doctor explained. "You must realize that even the poorest cottage in this country is superior to the richest castle in ours, because that cottage sits in a land of equality, and its residents breathe free air."

With this stirring speech to inspire them they marched boldly down the road, avoiding the ruts, garbage, and fallen tree limbs as best they could. Looking off to the side of the road, Lathan thought he saw something shining. He went over to investigate it, and discovered that it was a pile of gold.

A moment later, while Doctor Oldair was stuffing this pile into his shirt (stretching that garment considerably), Lathan looked around and noticed little yellow piles everywhere: under every green tree, and on the sides of every hill.

"Doctor, this whole country is covered with gold nuggets!"

"Shh! Everybody doesn't have to know. Just grab enough nuggets to get us a good meal at the next tavern."

After piling themselves up with gold, rubies, and other precious metals, Lathan and the Doctor staggered down the road toward the capital city, delighted with their good fortune. Lathan was excited because now they could buy horses; nevertheless he knew that Purella was scheduled to die very soon, which made him sweat with anxiety, and pray that the sacrifice might be delayed. Doctor Oldair assured him that they would reach the capital city soon.

Sure enough, when they came to the top of the next rise they gazed down upon the capital city, which was the most magnificent collection of dilapidated shacks Lathan had ever seen. In front of the shacks (which the natives called "houses") a large wooden sign lay on the ground, its wooden supports having been stolen a long time before. Lathan and Doctor Oldair walked up and read it. It said, ". . . ital Ci . . ." followed by an assortment of the usual initials, hearts, and specimens of poetry, and our heroes realized that they had finally reached the capital of El Limo. Lathan commented that the city was not what he expected—the Doctor replied that perfection was often difficult for the untutored mind to grasp at first sight.

They walked into the streets, or actually, in between the houses, for there didn't seem to be any definite streets at all; the houses had not been placed according to any pattern, but haphazardly, facing in any direction. The houses themselves were uniformly drab and unkempt, with uniformly drab and unkempt people sitting in front of them, who stared ahead with stony faces, occasionally pausing to drink or smoke. The only lively aspect of the city was the children, who ran in and out of the houses, throwing rocks at each other, and occasionally swearing if they got hit.

"When there are no kings and big-shots telling you what to do, there's plenty of time for relaxing," said Doctor Oldair proudly, as a hand-sharpened rock whizzed past his face.

By this time the gold in their pockets was getting heavy, and they were anxious to find a tavern where they could eat and drink, as well as some fast horses that could get them all the way to the Dark Castle before the end of the day. With this in mind, Lathan asked one of the idle citizens whether there was a tavern nearby, whereupon this local Samaritan knocked Lathan down, stole his shoes, and ran away.

"Don't worry," Doctor Oldair explained. "It was just a misunderstanding of our language. I'm sure he must have thought you were a shoe salesman."

"Did he have to knock me down?"

"Maybe he thought it was a sale."

After meandering through the shacks a bit more, Lathan and the Doctor came to a place where the shacks were spread further apart, and were two or three stories tall. Correctly diagnosing this as a symptom of the business district, Lathan and the Doctor picked up their pace and soon spied a large tavern.

"Finally," said the Doctor.

"At last," said Lathan.

They walked eagerly up to the door and soon discovered a disconcerting truth: the front door was on the third floor. The first floor consisted entirely of windows unequal in size, and spread unevenly apart. The second floor also consisted of windows, out of which smoke poured out continually, apparently because the chimneys, rather than being on the roof, were located on the inside. The third and final story, from which the sound of grumbling patrons could be heard, had a wide front door with a sign above it which read, ". . . oon . . . ." The entire building was covered with the usual writing samples, except for a bronze plaque in front of the tavern, which read:

Designed And Erected
By The
Glorious Revolutionary Equal Opportunity Building Committee

———

May All Share Equally the Fruits of this Glorious Achievement

It was not immediately clear why this sign hadn't been defaced like the others; however, the two skeletons that sat next to it with marking pens in their hands and stakes through their hearts might have served as a discouragement to potential illustrators.

"Tell me, Doctor Oldair, why is the . . ."

"Door on the third floor?" the Doctor responded testily. "Oh please, spare me these ridiculous questions. Isn't it enough to know that everything in El Limo is done by committee, so consequently nothing is ever wrong?"

"Well, it may not be wrong to put the door on the third floor, but it certainly doesn't seem . . ."

"Let's just go inside and I'll explain later," the Doctor replied. "You're young now, but when you get to my age you'll realize I've been right about everything the whole time."

At first glance, entering the tavern appeared to be a considerable challenge for anyone under twenty feet in height, but on closer inspection Lathan and Doctor Oldair discovered a conveniently-placed ladder, and climbed up to the front door.

The interior of the tavern was unlike anything Lathan had ever seen before. There were bottles, chairs, and plates of half-eaten meals lying all over the floor, and everything was incredibly black and dingy. The bar patrons all stared numbly about like witnesses at an autopsy, and as many people sat behind the bar as in front of it. In fact, neither the Doctor nor Lathan could distinguish which person was the bartender, because everyone (both men and women) looked almost identical in their dusty black clothes, except for two men who sat in the far corner of the tavern. They wore silk shirts, and a sign on their table said, "Reserved for Members of the Committee."

Doctor Oldair, unsure of whom he should address, finally sidled up to the bar and, to no one in particular, ordered a roast turkey and a copious amount of their best liquid refreshment, which he hoped would be lemonade, but if it was alcoholic . . . well, he would just have to learn to bear it.

His order was greeted with stony silence.

"Perhaps it would interest you to know that I'm one of your benefactors," said Doctor Oldair, after an awkward pause. "You see, I'm Doctor Oldair, the greatest philosopher in the western world, and this is my servant, a young religious fanatic."

All the stony eyes turned toward Lathan at this singular introduction, and Lathan tried to oblige the Doctor by adopting a wild glint in his eye, in order to make the Doctor's introduction seem less strange. Still, everyone was silent.

"Oh, and don't worry, we have money to pay with," explained Doctor Oldair, as he slapped down a few nuggets on the counter.

Several people burst out laughing.

"Are you laughing because the food is free, and that in a glorious land like El Limo all the inns are completely financed by a generous government?" Doctor Oldair asked.

"No," said one of the men. "With the inflation we've got it would take you ten tons of that to buy a dinner here, and besides, who says it's yours anyway? We don't have private property here."

With that, several men jumped over the bar and stripped the Doctor of all his valuables, throwing aside the gold and rubies, and keeping his comb, his ring, some tea bags, and various other trinkets.

"What are you doing? You can't take my things!" Doctor Oldair protested.

"It's a free country," the men said, "and everything's as much ours as yours."

"This is an outrage," said Doctor Oldair, as a couple of guys turned him upside down and shook him. "I demand to see the person in charge."

"There *is* no one in charge," said the men as they started stealing from each other the things they had stolen from the Doctor.

No one bothered Lathan; he had dropped all his worthless gold onto the floor, and since he was the Doctor's servant, everyone assumed he had nothing of value.

"Don't you have a king, or emperor, or chief?" asked Lathan.

"Everyone's equal here, foreigner," one of the men said as he hurled a fellow patron out the front door. "We have no funny titles; the lowlier you are, the better you are, that's our motto."

"Give me back my things at once!" Doctor Oldair demanded.

The gentleman who had just spoken responded by grabbing the Doctor by the collar, and giving every indication that he planned to throw him out the front door. Lathan, heroically inspired by a certain coin in his possession, leaped on the brute in an effort to save his pedagogical friend, and soon the entire tavern was in an uproar, with Lathan fighting all comers, and getting knocked on his head repeatedly. The noisy clamor of the scene was too much for the pair of men who sat at the reserved table. They both rose to their feet and walked over to the bar, whereupon everyone sprang to attention, and the furor immediately ceased.

"I am Assistant Sub-Committeeman Merkins," said one of the men, with a pompous air. "You foreigners are noisy."

This was admittedly true, for Doctor Oldair was lying on the ground, groaning vociferously, while Lathan was wrestling ferociously with a chair, under the mistaken impression that it was a fellow human being. Eventually Lathan recognized his mistake, and sat up and looked sheepishly at Mr. Merkins.

"I'm sorry for causing so much noise, sir," said Lathan to the resplendent sub-committeeman, "but, you see, these people not only stole Doctor Oldair's things, but also attacked Doctor Oldair, the greatest philosopher in the western world."

The good Doctor responded to this introduction by groaning once more, and dropping unconscious.

"You have some misconceptions," Mr. Merkins explained. "In this country his 'things' are everybody's 'things,' and the fact that he's a doctor and a philosopher mean nothing here. Everyone here is equal, and we don't believe in titles. After all, I myself am just a humble Assistant Sub-Committeeman."

At the mention of his extremely humble office, all the people in the room bowed their heads respectfully.

"Well, I'm glad to hear that everyone is equal, and everything belongs to everyone," said Lathan, "because we need horses right away, and now we don't have any money to pay for some. So if you'll just point out where the horses are kept, we'll just take a pair and go on our way."

"Not so fast," said the Assistant Sub-Committeeman. "First you'll have to fill out a few forms."

The Assistant Sub-Committeeman's shirt was far more capacious than one might have thought, for he quickly reached inside that shirt and pulled out a bundle of papers, which, when stacked on the floor, stood about three feet high.

"What are these?" Lathan asked.

"Oh, just some requisition forms, a health certificate, a clearance waiver, insurance information, a personal history form, Statement of Disavowal, Identity Card, Blood Donor Recipient Card, Statement of Intent, Emergency Card, and a fifty-page survey about attitudes. The other stuff is pretty minor."

"It will take me hours to fill these papers out!" Lathan exclaimed.

"Twenty-three hours and fifteen minutes to be exact; that is, if you're a person of average intelligence."

Lathan didn't know what to say. He just stood there with his mouth hanging open, dumbfounded.

"In your case I'd allow for at least thirty hours," the Assistant Sub-Committeeman remarked.

"But we have to be at the Dark Castle in six hours, and it's a few hundred miles away!"

"All right, all right," said Mr. Merkins, "I'm not supposed to do this, but I'll let you skip parts B and C of the attitudes survey."

In apparent frustration, yet without provocation, Lathan attacked Mr. Merkins, and a ruckus began all over again.

Heavy footsteps could be heard coming up a staircase below them, and several people shouted for silence.

"Now you've done it," someone said. "You've bothered the Temporary Janitor."

Everyone stood hushed in silence, looking at a back door which apparently led to the staircase. Soon enough the door swung open, and a large man with greasy black hair and a seersucker suit marched into the room, followed by two nubile, giggling young ladies.

"What's all this noise about?" said the Temporary Janitor as he walked up to Lathan and the still prostrate Doctor Oldair.

Assistant Sub-Committeeman Merkins bowed low and scurried back to his corner of the room.

"Good evening, Mr. Temporary Janitor . . . fine day, Mr. Temporary Janitor . . . foreigners, Mr. Temporary Janitor," intoned several bar patrons in a servile tone.

"Foreigners, eh?" said the Temporary Janitor intelligently, as he eyed our two heroes. After giving them an appropriate period of perusal, he looked Lathan squarely in the eye and said, with a flourish of his hand, "I am the Temporary Janitor."

"Hello," said Lathan. "This gentleman on the floor with his tongue sticking out is Doctor Oldair, the greatest philosopher in the western world, and I'm Lathan, robust shepherd lad and son of 'Trollkiller' Sven Svensson."

"I'm very sorry to hear that," the Temporary Janitor replied. "No doubt in your country it's a good thing to have a respected father, but in our country everyone is equal, and they are judged on their own merits. Do you want to know what my father was? He was a drunken liar, who beat all his kids and never did an honest day's work in his life!"

The bar patrons oohed and aahed appreciatively.

"That's terrible," Lathan said.

"Worse than terrible," said the Temporary Janitor with a grin, "and my mother was a woman of the streets."

"Oh, no."

"Oh, yes, and she tried to sell me and my sister into slavery at least three times," the Temporary Janitor continued enthusiastically. "We'd go for days at a time without a scrap of food, sometimes even weeks!"

The Temporary Janitor was so affected by the prospect of his own lowliness that he began swaggering around the room uncontrollably.

"I considered dirt sandwiches a delicacy."

The bar patrons applauded each little detail of the Temporary Janitor's hardships, and were simply awed by the man's tremendous inferiority.

"I can't help it," one woman said to a nearby girlfriend. "I just adore an uneducated man."

"Yes," her friend replied with a sigh. "I must admit it, he's extremely common."

"We didn't own a mattress, so I just slept on a pile of nails."

"Please Mr. Temporary Janitor, I'm sure your youth was highly fascinating . . ."

"I shovelled snow, even in summer."

". . . but the Doctor and I need horses right away, and we'll pay you back for them someday, I promise."

"So you see, having respectable parents means nothing. My parents were scum."

"About the horses . . ."

"I'm not ashamed of it. Go ahead, it won't bother me, tell me to my face what my parents were," the Temporary Janitor demanded.

"Well . . ."

"Come on, what were they?!"

"Your parents were scum," said Lathan.

"You're darn right they were!" said the Temporary Janitor, beaming. "You know, I think you'll get along in our country very well."

"Thank you," said Lathan, "and now, about the . . ."

"And as for your friend being a Doctor and a philosopher . . . well, that doesn't mean much here. Why, I can't even read," the Temporary Janitor shamelessly bragged. "In fact, I'm not even very good with coloring books."

His countrymen responded to the Temporary Janitor's comments with expressions of awe and reverence, and all appeared cowed by his enormous humility.

"By the way, did I introduce you to my two friends?" the Temporary Janitor asked, gesturing to the two nubile young ladies who flanked him. "Like your friend, these are also Doctors. This is Doctor Sizzler, and this is Doctor Trotter; they're both brain surgeons."

The two physicians giggled, and sidled up a little closer to their humble friend.

"Very glad to meet them I'm sure," said Lathan. "And now we need a couple of horses right away."

"Have you filled out the forms?"

"We have no time for forms! The Princess will die in six hours!"

"A princess! Let her die," said the Temporary Janitor. "We hate princesses here."

"Princess Purella is the kindest, sweetest, nicest, and most virtuous person on earth!" Lathan passionately blurted.

"Let her rot," said the Temporary Janitor. "I hate these princesses with their fancy manners and their fancy clothes. I'm better than her: my father was scum, and my mother was a tramp!"

His fellow countrymen cheered boisterously.

Courage, like many other character traits, can be dangerous if overused, or applied at the wrong time. To illustrate this point, let's examine Lathan's response:

"You?! Better than the Princess?! She's better than you could ever dream of being!!!"

Everyone gasped. Imagine, talking like that to a Temporary Janitor!

"Being poor doesn't make you good, and being rich doesn't make you bad; it's what you are inside that counts. The Princess would still be better than you if she were born in the greatest palace or the dirtiest hole. And as for your parents being scum, I'm sorry to hear it, but it's easy for me to see the family resemblance. All I can say is that if you have a son, he'll have plenty he can be humble about too, believe me."

Now this speech, courageous though it was in defense of Purella, did nothing to enhance the appeal of Lathan's next statement, which was:

"Now, can we have those horses?"

The Temporary Janitor whispered something to one of the brain surgeons, who immediately disappeared and came back with two men wearing white suits.

"There can only be one reason for you to think that a princess is better than me," said the Temporary Janitor, as the two men stepped forward.

The commotion had finally roused Doctor Oldair back into his senses, and when one of the men came toward him he climbed to his feet, cleared his throat, and said, "I am Doctor Oldair, the great philosopher," whereupon the two men in white gave each other a knowing look, handed Lathan and Doctor Oldair each a candy cane, and tied their hands together with remarkable skill and quickness.

"But what about the horses?" Lathan asked.

"Don't worry, there are plenty of horsies at the Farm," said one of the men, as he patted Lathan on the head.

Quickly Lathan and Doctor Oldair were led out the front door, down the ladder, and out into the streets, and soon the tavern, the Assistant Sub-Committeeman, the brain surgeons, and the Temporary Janitor were all far behind.

Chapter XXIV

Further Adventures in El Limo, and One Last Chance to Save the Princess

I'm Senator Cragmore, and this is Senator Yackworthy," said one of the men in white, as they led our heroes forward. "We work at the Flowery Fountain Farm for the Relatively Twisted. It's only a few miles away."

They made good progress between the various houses (despite being occasionally stopped by a panhandling Chief Justice or Nobleman) until they arrived at a hundred-foot-wide golden highway. A huge golden plaque on one side of the highway said:

Erected by the Glorious Revolutionary Equal-Opportunity Super-Highway Construction Committee

Lathan and Doctor Oldair were led along this glorious highway for about 300 yards, until the highway happened to run into a gigantic and somewhat less than glorious brick wall.

"This super-highway doesn't go anywhere!" Lathan exclaimed.

"Yeah, but look at how *wide* it is!" Senator Yackworthy replied.

The two Senators then led our heroes back into the maze of houses, through which they wandered in and out for the next hour. Finally they made it out of the city limits, and were led up a long country lane. At the end of the lane was a large blue house with a white picket fence, and a large number of rocking chairs lined up on the front porch. The building was guarded by several burly guards, who wore ill-fitting white jackets, and looked half-asleep. This house seemed out of place in El Limo, for it was painted all one color, had evenly-spaced windows, a chimney on the roof instead of in the basement, and the front door on the first floor.

"What kind of place is this?" said Doctor Oldair. "I demand to know."

"Now don't get excited," Senator Cragmore said. "If you're very, very good we'll give you each a great big lollipop."

"This is a nightmare," said Doctor Oldair. "It's times like these that make me wish I had never left my garden."

"Do you like gardens?" Senator Cragmore asked. "We have an excellent garden here. Let me show it to you."

Senator Cragmore led the Doctor and Lathan to one side of the huge house, and proudly presented to them a large patch of weeds.

"Well, what do you think?"

"This isn't a garden," the astonished Doctor replied. "It's just a patch of weeds. It doesn't look like it's ever been cultivated."

"Cultivated?" said the Senator. "You foreigners certainly have some unnatural ideas. In this country we just put the seeds in the ground, and let the plants' instincts take over, and nature take its course."

"I'm not feeling very well," said Doctor Oldair.

"I don't think the plants' instincts are very pleasant to look at," said Lathan, after vainly trying to appreciate this handi-work of nature.

Senator Cragmore and Senator Yackworthy gave each other a grave look.

"They're much worse than I thought," Senator Cragmore whispered.

Soon Lathan and Doctor Oldair found themselves wearing straitjackets in a padded cell, and with at least one of them be-moaning the fate of Purella, who was scheduled to be burnt alive in less than two hours. Lathan, whose self-esteem had been boosted a great deal by his recent adventures, now felt lower than ever before.

"Try to control yourself," said Doctor Oldair. "When you get to my age you'll realize that . . ."

Just then a key turned in their cell door, and a balding man carrying a tray of food shuffled inside.

"Good evening gentlemen, I'm Professor Zweistein," said the balding man. "I'm an inmate like you, but they pretty much let me do what I please, so I thought I'd bring you some dinner and answer any questions you might have."

Like hundreds of thousands of professors before him, Professor Zweistein wore a bow-tie, adjusted his glasses after every third word, coughed after every seventh word, and spoke in an undefinable foreign accent.

"I am Doctor Oldair, the greatest philosopher in the west-ern world," said the Doctor, with a dignified inclination of his head (shaking hands being difficult, if not impossible, in a strait-jacket).

"I've heard of you!" Professor Zweistein exclaimed.

"Really!"

"Oh, certainly. Let me see . . . you're rated number six in the eastern world, aren't you?"

Doctor Oldair grew strangely quiet.

"Help us get out of here!!!" Lathan said to the Professor, by way of introduction. "If I'm not two hundred miles away from here in about forty-five minutes the most beautiful princess in the world will die!!!"

"What do you mean?" the astonished Professor asked.

Lathan, using about 79,000 fewer words than I have used, and with a marked reduction in polysyllabic verbiage, recounted the entire story to the Professor in the space of one and a half minutes.

"Oh, now I see what you mean," said the Professor.

"O, if there were only some way we could get to the Dark Castle in less than an hour!"

"Completely impossible," said the Professor, shaking his head. "Unless, of course, you were to take the new flying machine I've invented. In that case it would take you about thirty minutes."

"Flying machine!" Lathan exclaimed, practically jumping out of his straitjacket. "Take us to it!"

"Well, normally I wouldn't do it, but seeing as there's a princess in danger, I guess it's my duty to help out."

Professor Zweistein set down his tray, wiped his brow, and released our two heroes from their straitjackets. He then led them out of their cell and took them to another ward. When they arrived at the Professor's room, the solid oak door opened for them automatically.

"Just a little invention of mine," the Professor explained.

On one side of the Professor's chambers was his bedroom, which consisted of a bed and a nightstand, and on the other side was the Professor's study. The Professor's study, like professor's studies everywhere, consisted of a large, paper-strewn desk surrounded by stacks of dusty books, a few diplomas from foreign countries on the wall, a chalkboard scrawled with indecipherable formulas, three bowling trophies on a shelf, and a large skeleton in the corner, which had been a part of so many chemical experiments that it was completely psychedelic in color.

"Have a seat, gentlemen," said Professor Zweistein.

Lathan and Doctor Oldair hastily sat down in two swivel chairs ("Another little invention of mine," said the Professor) and the Professor handed them each a cup of lemonade, cooled by ice made in the Professor's own ice machine ("A trifle," the Professor insisted).

"Interesting inventions," said Doctor Oldair. "A man like you must be highly respected in a country like this."

The Professor smiled.

"It's true I had some respect once," he replied. "At one time I invented a drill that was powered by the sun's rays, and when they found they could use it for dental torture, they wanted to make me an Assistant Garbageman on the spot. But, I don't know, I guess I'm old fashioned, but I thought I'd just stay a plain old ordinary professor."

"But tell me, how did you ever come to live here?" Doctor Oldair asked.

"I was committed for life. They didn't like my new automatic clothes washer and dryer because it would put the Dry Rock suppliers out of business, and they didn't like my invention of artificial lights because it seemed like a putdown of everybody who had used torches in the past. But the end for me came when I suggested they use the old method of putting the front door of buildings on the first floor rather than the third. That was the last straw for them. Of course, I can somewhat see their point; after all, it is much easier to see the door when it's up high."

"I know this all very interesting," blurted Lathan, "but please Professor, where is your flying machine?!"

"Flying machine? Oh yes, the flying machine! Now where did I put it? Hmmm . . . I always . . . Oh yes! Why, it's outside of course," the Professor concluded after rummaging through some papers for it. Professor Zweistein was very much like professors everywhere.

"Have a look out the window," the Professor suggested.

Lathan and Doctor Oldair did have a look, and saw on the lawn below them a strange conglomeration of scrap metal, which a scientific mind would have easily discerned as a rudimentary flying machine.

"Care to go down and see it?" the Professor asked.

This question didn't really apply to Lathan, because he had already leaped out the window and had landed on the lawn two stories below, so the Professor directed it to the Doctor, who replied in the affirmative. They took the civilized method of walking down a staircase to get to a lower floor, and soon were on the lawn with Lathan, inspecting the flying machine.

"I built it and tried to sell it to the government," the Professor exclaimed. "I told them flying machines might be the wave of the future, but they just laughed at me. They said flying would just be a passing fad. What they really wanted me to develop was a horse with a fifth leg."

"Tell us how to fly it, Professor," said Lathan. "We must leave at once! And don't worry! We'll fly it back as soon as we rescue the Princess!"

"I hate to mention it, but there is a slight problem with that plan," said Professor Zweistein, "The flying machine only has room for one person."

Lathan, who was salivating in expectation of instant departure, started to climb into the machine.

"Lathan," said Doctor Oldair, stopping him. "If one of us must go, that someone must be me."

"But Doctor, please, I . . ."

"Lathan, rescuing Princesses is a job which requires a great deal of mental ability, and, as I have stated before, you are young and consequently foolish, and I am old and consequently wise.

This is not a job for a robust young fanatic; this is a job for a philosopher."

"Please, please, Doctor, I beg of you . . ."

"No more arguments," said the Doctor. "I'm going and that's the end of it."

"Excellent," said the Professor. "Of course, this machine has never been tested before, and I don't know how well it lands, but I'm sure I can set the controls so it will come down close to the Dark Castle."

"On the other hand, there's a lot to be said for youth," Doctor Oldair commented.

"If you want young Lathan to go instead, you can always stay here with us for a few weeks until he gets back," said the Professor. "It'll be a lot of fun. There's an all-night Checker Tournament tonight, and next week we're having a denture cleaning competition."

"Don't just sit there, strap me in," said Doctor Oldair.

He vaulted inside the flying machine, put on a helmet that looked like it might have once doubled as a fishbowl, and soon was ready for flight.

"Let's see, the usual time for sacrifices is 6:00, and the time now is 5:15," said the Professor. "If the Doctor leaves in one minute, he should arrive at the Dark Castle in approximately thirty minutes, which will leave him fifteen minutes to rescue the Princess."

The Professor then handed the Doctor a book of wiring diagrams, system maintenance, and troubleshooting procedures, and told him to consult Tables 1A through 13F in case he ran into any difficulties during the descent.

"Please start the machine, Professor!" Lathan pleaded. "The Princess's time is running out!"

While the Professor searched through his pockets for a match so he could start the engine, Lathan gave some parting words to Doctor Oldair.

"You're her only hope! Do anything you can think of to save her!"

"Of course," said the Doctor.

"And tell her I've been very worried about her, and I've been searching after her, and I'll never give up . . . and . . . and . . . tell her her parents are worried about her too!"

"Sure," said the Doctor. The Professor had finally found the match in his pocket and started to light up the engine.

"Tell her I miss her, and . . . and . . . tell her I luh . . . tell her I luh . . ."

"Tell her you luh?"

"Oh, she'll understand . . . just . . . just hurry!!!"

Even as this admonition was ringing in the Doctor's ears the Professor's match lit the engine, which started up with a roar.

Professor Zweistein stuck his head inside the machine and adjusted some of the controls.

"There you are, Doctor," said the Professor as he stuck his head back out again. "Now all you have to do is push the yellow stick forward and you will fly directly to the Dark Castle."

"Good luck!" Lathan shouted.

Doctor Oldair reached for the yellow stick.

"Oh, and Doctor, don't forget that you also want to get back your seeds of Flaming Pink Chrysopata Scumatta of Phylum Fulvibrata!"

"Don't worry," said the Doctor with a smile.

Doctor Oldair pushed the yellow stick forward, and the flying machine darted along the ground and right into a brick wall.

"I knew I forgot something," said the Professor with a chuckle. "It needs to travel for at least a hundred yards before it can get into the air."

Lathan and the Professor ran over to the flying machine and discovered that it was battered but unbroken; the Doctor was in somewhat worse condition. Still, when the Professor asked him if he wanted to try again he appeared to mumble yes. Lathan and the Professor turned the flying machine forty-five degrees so it faced in a direction where it could travel forward unimpeded. The Professor readjusted the controls, and he and Lathan wished the Doctor good luck once more. This time Doctor Oldair actually had luck, for when he pushed the yellow stick the flying machine zoomed forward and eventually began rising into the sky. It headed directly toward the Dark Castle, and Lathan climbed up onto the brick wall and watched it until it faded out of sight.

An hour came and went, and Purella's time was up. Lathan remained on the brick wall, clutching tightly his magic coin, and praying that Doctor Oldair had made it in time to save her. He was still sitting on the wall long after the sun went down, when Professor Zweistein wandered out from the Checker Tournament.

"Well, young man," said the Professor, "do you think your Princess has been saved?"

"One thing's for sure, Professor. I'll never find out sitting here."

Lathan jumped down off the wall and shook hands with the Professor.

"Thanks for everything, Professor. You're a very great man, and I'm sure that someday you'll not only invent a five-legged horse, but maybe even a six-legged one as well."

With that Lathan climbed back up on the brick wall and leaped to the other side. Soon he crept away into the nearby woods, and continued his weary march to the Dark Castle.

Chapter XXV

Lathan Travels North, and Things Hit Rock Bottom

*T*hrough fields, through brush, through briars; over hills, down valleys, through plains; past lakes, past rivers, and past streams, Lathan walked on and on and on, then rested for a couple of hours, and then walked on and on and on again. He wandered farther and farther north, while the trees grew sparser and the wind grew colder. Oblivious to the soreness of his feet, and the fatigue of his body, Lathan could think only of Purella, and he agonized over the possibility that the Doctor had not arrived in time to save her. Every so often these thoughts would force tears into his eyes, and compel him to run wildly forward, until finally his weary body could take it no more, and he had to slow back down to a tired, painful walk.

After five days of this desperate forced march, Lathan arrived at a broad treeless plain, in the middle of which was a road leading north. Lathan could make much better time on the road than cross-country, and he gratefully followed it northward.

The plain seemed to go on forever, and Lathan half-walked, half-jogged briskly forward, hoping to see the end of it over each little rise, and always being disappointed. He saw no signs of life, very little vegetation, and, what started to become a more important concern, no sign of water. Lathan could only spit the dust out of his mouth and push his battered body forward.

The trees grew stunted, the skies grew darker, and the wind grew colder. Lathan was sore, and weary, and thirsty. Finally his strength gave out. He dropped down to his hands and knees and tried to crawl forward for a while, and then, while his brain was spinning with thoughts of Purella, he collapsed in a heap.

Some time later, while he was still lying in the middle of the road, he thought he heard a scream.

"Purella! I'm here!" he said, scrambling to his feet.

He looked around in all directions, but saw no one. He heard the sound again, and realized that it was a male voice, bellowing in the distance. Looking down the road in front of him he saw, hundreds of yards away, a man mounted on a horse, riding across the road, perpendicular to Lathan. The man was apparently beseeching his horse to do something, but Lathan couldn't hear what it was. Suddenly the horse turned and began galloping directly at Lathan. Lathan was afraid that the rider would ride past, so he waved his hands at the rider in hopes that he would stop and give him some help. Unfortunately, as soon as the rider came close to Lathan he suddenly stopped, turned his horse, and inexplicably began galloping away from the road.

"Well, if I see one person I'm bound to see more," said Lathan. "I can't be far from the Land of Doom now."

Lathan started hobbling forward. After progressing for about ten minutes, he once again heard hoofbeats, this time coming from behind him. He turned around just in time to see the same horse and rider gallop at him from the opposite direction, and roar right past him. The horse continued galloping for a hundred yards beyond Lathan and then stopped again, and began grazing on some bunch grass on the side of the road.

Lathan walked toward the rider, and when he got close he saw that the horse was a highly-bred charger, and that the rider, who had his back to him, was opulently dressed in a beaverskin jacket, and the finest silk clothes.

"Excuse me, sir," said Lathan, as soon as he approached close enough to be heard.

The rider turned around.

"Doctor Oldair!!!"

Sure enough, it was the wrinkled visage of the venerable philosopher that gazed down on our hero. The aforesaid visage turned several shades of color in the next few moments, ending up very much toward the red end of the spectrum.

"My boy!" said the Doctor, after a few false starts.

"Why are you here?! Why are you dressed like this?!! Didn't the flying machine make it to the Dark Castle?!!!"

"Oh yes, it made it easily," said the Doctor. "It was really rather fun—you should try it sometime."

"Then where is Purella?! What happened to the most beautiful girl in the world, the object of my most sincere devotion, and the summit of feminine excellence?!!!"

"Well, she's . . ."

Just then the Doctor's horse began galloping back toward the north.

"Uh, you look a little thirsty," the Doctor shouted back to Lathan as the horse sped madly away. "There's a tavern a couple of miles ahead . . . I'll tell you the whole story over a drink."

By the time the Doctor had gotten this out of his mouth he and his horse were practically out of sight. Lathan raced madly after them.

The plain which the road traversed had been consistently flat, so Lathan was surprised to discover that a mile ahead the plain had a large depression in the middle of it, and he suddenly found himself standing on the edge of a ridge. The road continued to stretch onward toward the north, but only a few hundred yards ahead of him Lathan could see it being intersected by another road coming from the west. Just beyond the intersection was a ramshackle wooden building with a sign on it that said, "Last Chance Eat and Swill." In front of this establishment Lathan could see Doctor Oldair's horse, standing placid and riderless. About ten feet in front of the horse Lathan could see Doctor Oldair, stuck head first into a water trough, almost as if some mysterious force had thrown him there. Lathan ran down to meet him, pausing only momentarily to look at the signs at the road intersection. The sign to the north said, "To the Land of Doom—3 miles." The sign to the west said "Scagabash—190 miles." And the sign to the south, from which Lathan had come, said, "To Various Kingdoms and At Least One Perfect Republic—200 miles (More or Less; Your Mileage May Vary)." After assimilating all this information Lathan raced over to the Doctor, who had just climbed out of the trough, and was now trying to squeeze the water out of his shirt.

"You must have been really thirsty!" said Lathan.

"Huh? Oh yes, right."

"Now please, Doctor," said Lathan, eagerly grabbing the Doctor by his beaverskin jacket, "what's happened to the Princess?!!"

"Let's go inside and get a drink first," said the Doctor dizzily. "I can't concentrate out here."

The "Last Chance Eat and Swill" tavern would not receive a particularly high rating in most travel books, despite its colorful nomenclature. It was dingy, dirty, and often frequented by small furry animals. There were holes in the walls, the floor, and the ceiling, and the wood had a particularly black and brittle appearance, suggesting that the establishment had been partially burned down on more than one occasion. The novelty items that were scattered around the main room, such as deformed skeletons, old knives, and black-and-white paintings of famous executions, did little to enliven the gaiety of this isolated watering hole.

The owner of the tavern was a huge pink-skinned man who looked like a pig with a serious thyroid problem. He was also the bartender, and when Lathan and Doctor Oldair entered he squeezed behind the bar and asked them what they wanted.

"Triple Snake-Killer with a twist," said the Doctor. Within four seconds the bartender had it in the Doctor's hands.

"Now how about you?" the bartender asked Lathan.

"I'll just take a cup of cold water," said Lathan, which put the bartender into some confusion, and caused him to waddle off in search of his Bar Guide.

"Now tell me, Doctor," said Lathan feverishly, "what has become of Princess Purella, the epitome of pureness, the quintessence of kindness, and the most beautiful creature that walks upon the face of this earth?"

"She's dead."

Lathan fainted at the word, and Doctor Oldair spilled some of his Triple Snakekiller on him to rouse him back to consciousness.

"Purella dead!!!" stammered Lathan as he jumped to his feet. "Oh, how did it happen?!! Oh tell me, what happened?!!!"

"Well, first she was partially disemboweled, and then she was fried alive on a gigantic pagan altar. I arrived while she was still sizzling, and it really had me upset. I must have moped around for over an hour. Finally I decided to take one of her charred bones as a memento of her, but they had burned so many girls after her that I couldn't tell which bones belonged to which."

Lathan crumbled slowly back to the floor, groaning pitiably. The only other patrons of the bar, four oversized men who sat at a table in the far corner, looked at Lathan with contempt, having never seen such a disgusting display of emotion in their entire lives.

"But don't worry," Doctor Oldair continued, "I really gave Count Zandar a piece of my mind. I told him I didn't like what he was doing with these girls, so he apologized and promised never to do it again. Then he gave me a nice horse, and these fine clothes, and sent me on my way. Now I'm on my way to the Empire of the Amazons. I can't wait to give some private philosophy lessons!"

Lathan could barely hear the Doctor over the sound of his own sobbing. For an instant he started to reach for his magic coin, as he had grown accustomed to during moments of distress, but his arm dropped listlessly to his side and his groans redoubled when he thought how even the magic coin couldn't save Purella. He was shocked to realize that you could own a magic coin and still be miserable.

"Now, now, bear up my boy, bear up," said Doctor Oldair, as he leaned over and gave Lathan a hearty slap on the back. "You don't see me breaking down over this, do you?"

"Oh Doctor, I loved her, I loved her so much!!!"

"This is all the fault of your religious fanaticism," the Doctor explained. "You have to look at this more objectively. It was ridiculous for you to love the Princess in the first place, because you're just a peasant wretch. And it's ridiculous for you to worry about it now, since all that's left of her is a pile of black bones. I mean, what's left to love?"

"Oh Doctor, Doctor!" Lathan sobbed.

"You just have to comfort yourself by remembering that everything is born, blooms, and drops dead. That's what life is all about."

"That'll be three farthings for you and your friend," the pig-like bartender said to Doctor Oldair. The bartender had managed to scoop a cup of water out of the trough for Lathan, but Lathan was too upset to drink it. Doctor Oldair slapped the money on the counter while still looking thoughtfully at his young friend.

"Hey, what's the big idea?" said the bartender. "What are you giving me these seeds for?"

Doctor Oldair turned quickly around, snatched up six flaming pink seeds off the counter, and shoved them back into his pocket.

"Sorry, wrong pocket!" said Doctor Oldair.

He pulled some coins out of the other pocket, quickly slapped them on the counter, and then turned and looked sharply down at Lathan. When he saw that Lathan had been too distraught to notice the exchange, he relaxed.

"Well my boy, there's no point in us staying around here," said Doctor Oldair, hopping off his stool. "We might as well start heading south. When we get to the Empire of the Amazons I'll write my letter of resignation to the King, and you can carry it with you back to Hoodahooda."

"Go back?" Lathan said, "I can't . . . I don't . . . I don't know what to do . . ."

"I don't know why you'd want to stay, but you'd better decide right now one way or the other, because I'm leaving."

Lathan picked himself up off the ground and gloomily sat down on a bar stool.

"You go, Doctor Oldair," he said shakily. "I've . . . I've gotta think."

"All right then," said Doctor Oldair, as he headed for the exit. "So long, and remember, 'Think Happy.'"

"So long, Doctor," said Lathan, "and thanks for all your help."

"Oh, it was nothing," said Doctor Oldair with a smile. He quickly went out the door, and soon Lathan could hear Doctor Oldair's horse galloping madly around the building six or seven times, and then finally heading south.

Lathan pulled the magic coin out from under his shirt and stared at it ruefully.

"Your Doctor friend already paid for the drinks," said the bartender.

"Oh," said Lathan, "I wasn't gonna pay. I was just looking at this magic coin."

"Magic?" asked the bartender.

"Yeah," said Lathan. He sadly put the coin back inside his shirt and shuffled outside.

The wind blew heavily, blowing brush and dust everywhere, and the whole world outside the tavern seemed as black and empty as a desert. Lathan didn't know which way to go, or what to do, and even longed for the time when he thought Purella hated him, for at least then he knew she was alive. Now Purella was gone, and he stood at the crossroads and looked at the three forks disappear into the distance, thinking that each direction and each road was equally empty and meaningless, for Purella was not at the end of any of them. Lathan reached for his magic coin, held it for an instant, and then took his hand away, sickened by the feel of the once precious object. The sky thundered.

Zombie-like, Lathan staggered slowly up the northern road, toward the Land of Doom, only because that was the way he had always been bound. The thunder boomed in the distance, and soon rain came pouring out of the sky in thick, icy sheets. Neither the cold, nor the wind, nor the rain bothered Lathan as much as the emptiness he felt in his heart.

Suddenly Lathan felt a sharp pain at the back of his neck which dropped him to the ground.

He regained consciousness a few moments later, and felt himself being dragged by several sets of strong arms.

"Where is it?"

"Around his neck," he could hear voices say over the noise of the tempestuous weather. Someone pulled the magic coin off from around his neck.

"Got it!"

"You really think it's magic?"

"He said it was, didn't he? Besides, why else would he keep it on a chain around his neck?"

They dragged Lathan a short distance further and dumped him into a ditch.

"Wait till the other guys see this," one of them said. They abandoned Lathan and started sloshing away through the rain.

Lathan lay still, with his eyes closed and his body soaked with rain. He felt as if he would never have the strength to stand on his feet again.

Chapter XXVI

Wherein the Reader Meets an Old Acquaintance

Fortunately, all the bad moments on this earth, like the good moments, are certain to pass away.

The night came and went, and when the sun rose the next morning the rain stopped as suddenly as it began. Lathan still lay motionless, wondering how long he would have to lie there before he died of natural causes, when suddenly he felt a large furry animal nudge against him. Lathan, wide-eyed with fear, scrambled wildly to his feet. Standing before him was a large furbearing animal, partially resembling a pony, and partially resembling a very large dog. This beast, once he realized that Lathan was a living being, and not a particularly interesting subject for scientific inquiry, looked a little disappointed, and then walked away.

Lathan was stunned. Sometime, somewhere, he had seen this strange beast before. Suddenly he remembered the identity of this singular creature, and immediately began to follow him.

The pony (the name by which this particular beast was most often referred) wandered up and down several gullies until he came to a little ridge. At the edge of the ridge there was a grove of fertile trees, and in the grove was a log cabin with white smoke coming out of the chimney. On one side of the cabin was a stable and a little pasture. The pony walked into the stable, while Lathan gazed dreamily at this cheery abode, so near to the Land of Doom. On the side of the cabin was a huge wagon, piled high with goods, with a sign on it which said "Oddities." There was a straight, narrow path that led right to the cabin; Lathan looked back and saw the same path coming out of the mountains in the distance, and realized it might very well be the same path he and his friends had abandoned so long before. Lathan staggered down to the cabin, went up to the front door, and gave it a feeble knock.

"Coming!" said a cheery voice from inside. The door swung open and the cherubic face of Mr. Jack Crackback appeared, accompanied by his equally cherubic body.

"I'm sure you probably don't remember me, Mr. Crackback, I . . ."

"Why, of course I do!" said Jack with enthusiasm. "Come on in and have a seat, Frank!"

"It's . . . Lathan."

"Oh, yes . . . sure . . . Lathan, of course," said Jack as he steered Lathan through the door and into a comfortable seat. "You just stay here, and I'll fix you something to eat and drink."

Jack's cabin was incredibly snug and warm, with thick rugs on the floor, a blazing fire in the fireplace, and various "oddities" decorating the walls. Lathan, however, was oblivious to almost everything. He sunk into his seat and stared at the floor, while from the adjoining pantry Jack chattered to Lathan about various subjects, none of which was remotely relevant to anything that has happened in this history, and he consistently referred to the robust shepherd lad as "Nathan." Finally Jack reappeared from the pantry, with a plate piled high with bread and cheese, and a big cup of cold water. As he brought it over to Lathan he noticed the look of gloom on Lathan's face. Gently Jack set the food on the floor in front of Lathan, and sat quietly down in the opposite chair.

"She's dead, Mr. Crackback," Lathan moaned. "The Princess is dead, and I want to die too."

"Dead?" said Jack. "I don't see how that can be."

"Oh it's true, it's too true," said Lathan, sobbing. Lathan, between moans and sobs (and the occasional groan), recounted for Jack everything that had happened since the day that Jack had accidentally smashed the new idol. He told about how Purella was captured, and how he was the son of "Trollkiller" Sven Svensson, and how he was given the magic coin. He then told of his adventures with Prince Charming and Doctor Oldair on the way to Scuttleton, and how he escaped the spiders, and how he got a boat and sailed to the island of Lump.

"The Oracle said that to save the Princess I needed something magic, an army of Wabonian dwarfs, and the advice of a great philosopher. I had a magic coin already, and when I found the dwarfs and Doctor Oldair, I had all three. But then I lost the dwarfs, I lost the Doctor, and then last night I lost the coin, and now Purella is gone too. Everything I've cared about and believed in is gone, and I don't see much point in living any longer. It's like Doctor Oldair once told me: life is meaningless."

Jack looked thoughtful.

"Life can be odd, but never meaningless," he said, "and that's why you've come to the right place."

"What do you mean?" Lathan asked.

"Don't you remember? Jack's the name, and oddities is my game. Potions, powders, lotions, chowders, most of the questions, and all of the answers are in my wagon, ready and at your disposal."

"I'm afraid you don't have any answers that can help me," said Lathan.

"I'm not so sure about that," said Jack. "I think I should go outside and take a look."

Jack walked out a side door and went to his wagon. He came back a few moments later, carrying a newspaper.

"I keep telling the paper boy not to throw the paper into the wagon, but he keeps doing it anyway," said Jack. "Still, I don't mind this time, because it gives you the answer you need to hear."

"What answer?"

"This answer: the Princess isn't dead."

Lathan straightened up and looked Jack in the eye for the first time.

"What do you mean?!"

"Have a look," said Jack, as he tossed the newspaper to Lathan.

The paper was called the "Land of Doom Moon-Times," and the main headline read, "Pugnacious Pup and Princess Torch Dark Castle—Pup 'Not Sorry.'"

Lathan hastily read the article, which ran like this:

Dark Castle (LODP)—The Society of Idolators and Necro-mancers (SIN) convention was cancelled this week due to an immense conflagration which broke out in the main temple chamber. Scores of people were singed, and several fortyish bleached blondes (who virtually all claimed to be 29) had to be rushed to the hospital to get their hair re-bleached. All the human sacrifices and other festivities were cancelled.

The blaze began when a tiny dog, the property of one Princess Purella, 18, climbed up above the altar and pulled the spigot out of a barrel of Deluxe High-Tone Ultra-Black Obsidian, a highly inflammable material used in the construction of idols. The volatile liquid spilled onto the altar, causing a tremen-dous explosion. Several witnesses vividly described the scene.

"Duh," said Mr. Og, 32, the Count's personal assistant. "It was as if it got really really hot."

"I knew that little dog was up to no good," said Miss Gert Winterbelly, 29. "I saw him walk over to those barrels and I said to myself, 'Gert Winterbelly, that dog is no good.' That's just what I said. If I said it once I said it a thousand times, 'Gert Winterbelly, that dog is no good, that dog is no good, that dog is no . . .'"

"I just think it's a disturbing trend," said Mr. Shane Graftman, 52, treasurer of SIN incorporated. "If this princess didn't want to get sacrificed, she shouldn't have let herself get captured. By blowing up the temple and stopping all the executions she's essentially forced her views on us, and I think that's terribly unfair. If we went to her country, her people wouldn't let us rape, pillage, and commit all the human sacrifices we'd want to do, would they? Of course not. But now because of this one princess all the sacrifices, all the torture exhibitions, our demon seminar, and even our exhibit floor to promote the advancement of evil had to be cancelled. I hate to say this, but I think a lot of good has come out of our convention this year."

"Skip down to the last paragraph," said Jack.

Lathan, whose eyes appeared on the verge of popping out of his head as he read the first part of the article, hastily turned his attention to the last paragraph.

Count Zandar suffered third-degree burns over 40 percent of his body during this unfortunate incident, and, according to local medical authorities, must remain in bed for approximately a week. However, admirers of the Count will take comfort in his undaunted spirit, as exemplified by the words he spoke just as he was being carried into his sick room.

"I'm in bad shape now, but when I get out of here next week you just wait and see what happens! Sure, I let all the other young maidens get away, but I'm leaving that princess and her pooch locked in my Laboratory until I recover, and when I get through with them they'll be begging to be sacrificed, but it won't happen!!"

The paper slipped out of Lathan's hand, and he sat there shaking, half with excitement, half with fear.

"She still might be alive," he said breathlessly. "It's been six days since the sacrifice!"

"Looks like you've got to get going," said Jack.

"But no! This paper has to be wrong! Doctor Oldair said he saw the Princess being sacrificed!"

"That's strange," said Jack.

"Yeah, this paper must be wrong," said Lathan uneasily, as if he were trying to convince himself, but couldn't.

"At any rate there's a chance that she's still alive," said Jack.

He hopped out of his chair and slapped Lathan on the back.

"Good-bye, young man, and good luck!"

Lathan stood up and moved awkwardly toward the door.

"Of course, Doctor Oldair might be right," he said feebly.

"There's still a chance," said Jack. "Go!"

Lathan took three miniature steps toward the door and then sadly turned around.

"But . . . but . . . don't you see, I can't," he stammered. "The Count is very tough, and he has hundreds of men, and I don't have my magic coin anymore!"

"But what about the Princess?"

"But the Oracle said I needed Wabonian dwarfs, and a philosopher, and something magic, and I don't have any of them!"

Lathan flopped helplessly back into his chair. Jack looked at him thoughtfully.

"You know, I don't think you're really the son of 'Trollkiller' Sven Svensson after all."

"What do you mean?" said Lathan. "My grandmother told me I was."

"There's more to being a son than you think," said Jack. "A true son has more than just the same appearance as his father; he has the same spirit as well. A real son of 'Trollkiller' Sven Svensson isn't someone who looks like him, it's someone who has the same kind of heart."

"But I do have the same kind of heart," Lathan whined.

"Would 'Trollkiller' Sven Svensson be in here feeling sorry for himself, or would he be out rescuing the Princess?"

Shame forced Lathan up out of his seat again, but fear kept him from walking out the door.

"But the Count has hundreds of men! Without my magic coin and the Wabonian dwarfs I don't have a chance. Besides, I can't do anything without Doctor Oldair's advice, because I am young and consequently foolish, and he is old and consequently wise."

"No one gets old enough to be wise," said Jack.

Lathan shuffled toward the door, and opened it.

"Even if the odds were ten thousand to one, I guess old 'Trollkiller' would still try," said Lathan sadly. "So even if the odds are ten million to one, I gotta try too."

"From what I've heard, even if the chances were ten million to *none,* 'Trollkiller" would try," said Jack. "He would try, and make a chance."

Jack patted Lathan on the back once more.

"Remember, Lathan," he said, miraculously remembering Lathan's name for the first time, "you may not have your magic coin, but if you have the spirit of 'Trollkiller' Sven Svensson in your heart, you have something better than any magic could ever give you, because then 'Trollkiller' Sven Svensson will be with you always. Do you really believe it was magic coins and faith in Oracles that made 'Trollkiller' Sven Svensson a great hero? No—it was faith, faith in God. That's the first step, because if you don't have that you don't have anything. I think you lost sight of that for a while, but don't worry—I'm sure God has never lost sight of you. Who knows, maybe throughout all the disasters you've been through, 'Trollkiller' Sven Svensson has been watching you and secretly helping you the whole time, only you've never known it."

"Thanks, Mr. Crackback," said Lathan softly. "I still wish I had the advice of a great philosopher though."

"I wouldn't worry about it," said Jack.

Lathan took one last look at Jack Crackback, his snug room, and his blazing fireplace, and walked back out into the morning air. However, Lathan's mind had been too preoccupied to look at any of these things closely. If he had, he might have noticed that above the chimney, burned proudly and deeply into the bricks, were the initials T.S.S.

Chapter XXVII

Adventures at the Dark Castle

From Jack's cabin, the Land of Doom was not hard to find. Lathan merely climbed up the little ridge above the cabin and looked down. Looking back below him he could see the highway he had been following, and the place where his magic coin had been stolen. About a half-mile beyond that point the road passed under a large gate above which was a dark, metal sign which said:

LAND OF DOOM
VISITORS UNWELCOME

Lathan took a deep breath, hiked down to the road, and walked through the gate.

As he walked the wind began to blow hard against him, and the rain began to fall more heavily than before. The stunted trees along the roadside, which twisted weirdly into fantastic shapes, all seemed to gesture back toward the south, so that all of nature seemed to be telling Lathan, "Go home . . . go home . . . go home."

Lathan walked on.

A few hours later the road gradually disintegrated into a mere trail, and finally disappeared altogether.

Lathan walked on.

His feet became painful after alternately walking over the ashy soil and the cold patches of snow that lay all around him. He tried to rest more than once, but each time he did little swarms of red-eyed bugs would start to gather around him, and he'd have to limp painfully away.

Finally the rain stopped, and was replaced by a dark, heavy mist. Suddenly Lathan's attention was roused by a faint rumbling noise which came from somewhere in front of him. Fearful that it was another little army of bugs, he moved cautiously forward, but after a short distance he came to a little hillock and saw, not an army of bugs, but the fog-shrouded Far Northern Sea, which stretched before him toward the frozen wastes of the north. Below him, on a rocky, wind-swept promontory, lined by the most barren and grotesquely shaped trees that Lathan had ever seen, lay the Dark Castle, a massive, black stone fortress.

Lathan instinctively reached for his magic coin at this fear-inducing sight, but alas, there was no coin there to touch. All he could do was put his hand over his heart, the heart that made him a true son of "Trollkiller" Sven Svensson, whisper a prayer, and then stumble down the slope toward the castle.

At the front of the castle, nestled among the bizarre trees, was a huge wrought-iron gate set into a low stone fence. In front of the gate a couple of the Count's men were sitting on the ground with their spears beside them, throwing dice. Lathan, eager to avoid the gaze of the sentries, crossed down to the stone fence about fifty yards away from them, in a spot where the trees were the thickest. With some difficulty, he managed to flop over the stone wall and onto the castle grounds, and the knowledge of where he was filled him with eerie feelings of dread. And his feelings didn't improve much when he felt someone tapping him on the shoulder.

"What took you so long?" a voice said.

Lathan jumped into the air, landed, and then spun around to see six Wabonian dwarfs, with tattered clothes, battered faces, and underfed bodies, all grinning broadly.

"Bingo!" said Lathan, while ecstatically grasping the dwarf's leader by the hand, "we thought we lost you for good in that jungle!!! How did you make it out?! And how did you get here?!"

The dwarfs chuckled modestly.

"Oh, you know, it just took a little plotting, that's all," said Bingo, in the most off-hand way he could. "It was nothing, really."

The other dwarfs were smiling like six-year olds who were about to eat a chocolate cake.

"Please tell me what happened. I want to know," said Lathan.

"Well," said Bingo, "when we were in the jungle, do you remember those eyes that were watching us wherever we went, but that you never saw?"

"How could I remember them if I never saw them?"

"Well, I saw them, but I was too sly to say anything about it."

The other dwarfs looked at their leader with admiring eyes.

"Well," said Bingo, "the eyes turned out to belong to a tribe of man-eating pygmies, and after we threw out the longer vine to pull you out of the quicksand they captured us and took us to their village. Fortunately, because we're dwarfs they could only use as appetizers, so they left us in the village while they went out hunting for a main course. They tied us up, but they left a fire smoldering next to us, and Plottle brilliantly jumped into it and burned off the ropes, along with most of his clothes and some of his skin, but I'm sure he'll be able to sit down again in a few days."

Plottle smiled sheepishly, and Lathan noticed that he was wearing a borrowed pygmy costume, rather than the usual Wabonian clothes.

"Anyway, we agreed to rescue your Princess, so that's what we had to do. It took us a few days to get out of that jungle, and then we had to find our way to the Dark Castle. When we finally reached a town we went to a tavern and told everybody we needed to get to the Dark Castle as soon as possible. Fortunately, there were some men there from the Land of Doom, and they took us up north with them and got us some swell jobs in a salt mine. Of course, we didn't really want these swell jobs, but they were very insistent that we stay. However, we very slyly were totally incompetent, so they kicked us out of the salt mine and left us on our own. Soon we found out the direction of the Dark Castle, and here we are. You see, it was all very simple."

The dwarfs couldn't conceal their delight in their own ingenuity.

"I should have never doubted you," said Lathan happily. "Now all we have to do is slip past the Count's soldiers."

"Taken care of," said Bingo, amidst several half-stifled chuckles. "They marched out about an hour ago. The guards at the gate were the only ones left, and as we've been talking I saw them get up and go looking for the others."

"Amazing! How in the world did you get all the soldiers to leave?" asked the astonished Lathan.

"It was very simple—we don't have the slightest idea," said Bingo. "They just got up and left. You see, when our plotting starts working everything falls into place."

"Incredible!"

"Oh, and look what Rex just found over by one of the campfires."

Bingo pulled the magic coin out from under his shirt.

"The magic coin!" said Lathan as he snatched the precious relic off from around Bingo's neck. "Those were the Count's men who stole it from me, and now you've stolen it back!"

"Hey, what can we say?" said Bingo, amidst hearty Wabonian chuckling.

"Now, with the magic coin," Bingo added, "you might have the power to defeat the Count."

Lathan gave Bingo a thoughtful look, and then handed the coin back to him.

"You keep it, Bingo. I'm the son of 'Trollkiller' Sven Svensson, and I've got the faith of 'Trollkiller' Sven Svensson—I don't need the help of a magic coin."

Reluctantly, Bingo put the magic coin back around his neck.

"Now all we need is a plan to rescue the Princess," said Lathan.

"Don't worry, I've already got one," said Bingo as the dwarfs gathered round. "Now listen carefully: first we need a salami . . ."

Meanwhile, inside the Count's Laboratory deep in the recesses of the castle, Purella and Floppy were sitting on one side of the room strapped into two giant, metal chairs. Tons of obscure laboratory equipment lay piled around them, and hideous-looking devices lined the walls. Near the center of the room, below a huge ventilation shaft, was a fire pit, with a huge metal pot in the center of it. Floppy didn't like the look of that pot at all, and began chewing frantically on the straps that held him to his chair.

Purella heard footsteps. The door to the Laboratory swung open and Og squeezed inside.

"Duh, here they are, just where you said to put them," said Og, calling back behind him. "They've been here the whole week."

Another set of footsteps could be heard approaching the door. Soon Count Zandar entered the room, walking with his usual menacing strides, though slightly limping due to the bandages that covered forty percent of his body. His face and hair looked a little singed, but his moustache still retained its curl, and his eyes their look of hate. He walked across the room toward the two prisoners, and Floppy chewed on the chair straps with redoubled energy.

"Fools," said the Count ominously as he gave each of his captives a long look. "Such fools."

He then gave Purella a very long look, a very thorough long look, and then laughed fiendishly (which, I must admit, was the only way he knew how).

"So, did you think you could destroy my temple and get away with it? No, my dear, it's not that easy. Do you know what I'm going to do to you now?"

"Arf, arf," said Floppy, offering a couple of very mild suggestions, neither of which had much chance of being embraced by the Count.

"Silence, mutt!" said the Count sharply. "Soon you will be silenced forever, my adventurous little friend. In a few moments you will be skinned and fried alive."

This prospect appearing to be not the most pleasant, Floppy dropped all further attempts at conversation and resumed chewing on his straps.

"Are you going to kill me, too?" Purella asked.

The Count smiled wickedly.

"Something worse will happen to you."

"Are you going to fry me alive?"

"Worse," the Count replied with a slobber.

"You mean . . . you mean . . ."

"Yes! Yes! I'm going to have you boiled!"

Purella let out a sigh of relief.

"I've heard of people hating fried foods, but this is ridiculous," said the Count with a befuddled look. "What would you rather be, flame-broiled?"

"You're a coward," said Purella fiercely, impolitely chang-
ing the subject.

"What do you mean?!" said the Count ferociously, his gigantic but highly fragile ego hurt by her accusation.

"You pretend to be so fearless," said Purella, "but I know
better. You're afraid of Floppy and me, because you know we're
innocent and good, and innocence and goodness are the two
things in the world that make you shrink in terror."

"That's a lie!" the Count bellowed. "Right here in the middle
of the floor is a trap door that opens up to a pit full of alligators.
I could throw you in there right now! However, I have a few
new torturing devices I want to try out on you first."

"Please God, and spirit of 'Trollkiller' Sven Svensson, no
matter what happens to me, keep Lathan safe, wherever he may
be," Purella silently prayed.

The Count sneered with delight, and was turning to get his
torturing devices when Floppy chewed through his last strap
and leaped out onto the floor.

"Run, Floppy, run!" Purella shouted.

"Arf! Arf! Arf!" said Floppy with customary elocution. Without further comment he raced between Og's legs and out the
door.

The Count was furious.

"Og! Go stop that mutt!" he ordered.

"Duh, all right," said Og.

Floppy raced out into the labyrinthine hallways, searching
for an exit, while Og bounded after him.

Floppy found a staircase and eventually made his way up to
the ground level of the castle, with Og rapidly gaining on him
because of his tremendous strides. While racing down an enormous hallway Floppy spotted an open window and ran toward
it as fast as his little legs could go. Just as he was leaping out to

freedom, Og caught up to him and snatched him up in his gigantic right hand.

"Duh, I'm sorry, little pup," said Og, "but now I must crush the life out of you."

Just then there was a knock at the front door. Og dropped the pup and dutifully went to answer the door, and Floppy took the opportunity to leap out the window to freedom.

Chapter XXVIII

Lathan Battles the Count in This, the Most Astounding and Phenomenally Exciting Chapter of Them All

Og opened the massive front door and beheld an unusual man. He was about seven feet tall and swayed uneasily from side to side. Og thought he was some sort of strange foreigner, but a more discerning observer might have thought he looked suspiciously like two dwarfs standing on top of one another, the lower dwarf hidden by a long white overcoat, and the upper dwarf wearing a false moustache and a chef's hat.

"Excusa," said the upper dwarf with a Neapolitan accent, "Is-a the lady of-a the housa homa?"

"We don't have a lady of the house," answered Og.

"Ah, there musta be a mistake. We have an order from-a the lady of-a the housa for theesa pizza," said the dwarf, suddenly producing a large, Wabonian-style pizza.

"I don't think so," replied Og, confused.

"Hey buddy," replied the dwarf, excitedly, "you no get outa theese so easy. Somebody ordered theesa pizza, somebody she's a going to pay for theesa pizza!"

The upper dwarf punctuated this comment by poking Og in the ribs.

"Don't get mad at me," Og stammered. "I tell you we didn't order any pizza!"

"I wanta to talk to your boss. Maybe he's-a ordered the pizza. I gotta twelva kids, twelva little bambini I gotta to feed, and I ain't a-going withouta my money!"

He would have said more, but he started swaying so badly he almost fell over.

"My boss is killing a princess right now, but I'm sure he can come up and pay you in a little while," said Og, trying to appease the hot-tempered dwarf.

"I gotta no time!" the fiery pizza distributor bellowed. "I wanta my money now!"

"Duh, all right, take it easy," said Og. "I'll go down right now and check with my boss."

Og bounded back to the Laboratory. The instant he disappeared from sight the dwarfs lost their balance completely and toppled to the ground. The lower dwarf, who could easily be identified as one Tripper, crawled out from under the overcoat, earnestly rubbing his sore head. Shortly after this little spill Lathan and four other dwarfs came bursting through the still-open front door.

"Help them back into position," said Lathan. "I'll follow the Count's man to where the Princess is, and then I'll hide while he brings the Count up here. You've got to stall him while I rescue the Princess."

Lathan then darted stealthily after Og.

Meanwhile, Count Zandar was standing in front of Purella with a huge six-bladed torturing instrument in his left hand, and a plain, ordinary gigantic knife in his right.

"Hey, did you order pizza?" said Og as he squeezed into the room.

"No, I didn't order any pizza!" the Count blurted, his concentration ruined.

"There's a guy up there who won't go until you pay him," Og meekly replied.

"Oh, all right!" murmured the frustrated Count.

He turned back to Purella.

"Take this opportunity to say your prayers, because when I come back you die!"

The Count set down his knife and followed Og out of the Laboratory. They climbed up a nearby staircase, not seeing the figure of Lathan crouched secretly in a dark corner of a connecting hallway. As soon as they walked past him the resourceful shepherd lad darted down to the Laboratory and burst inside. There, across the room, his bloodshot brown eyes met Purella's radiant blue eyes, and all four of these orbs swelled with joy and exhilaration.

"Purella!" Lathan joyously cried, "I have come to rescue you!"

On this triumphant note Lathan began bounding across the room, but he had only gotten halfway before he stepped on a trap door and went crashing partway through it. The wood of the trapdoor had been rotten; now it was smashed completely, but fortunately Lathan didn't fall all the way through and was able to pull himself to safety. Purella breathed a tremendous sigh of relief.

"Oh, Lathan, please be careful! That pit is full of alligators!"

Lathan looked down into the pit. For the first six feet down it was only about four feet wide, but after that it opened up into a huge, dark chamber. Lathan couldn't see the bottom, but he could easily hear the restless motion of the alligators swimming in the water below. He gulped, and then, remembering what he had come for, raced over to Purella and, using Count Zandar's knife, set her free. Her big blue eyes bulged with emotion.

"Oh, Lathan, Lathan, Lathan!" she intoned sweetly.

"Oh, Purella, Purella, Purella!" Lathan replied.

Admittedly neither of them was a memorable conversationalist, but at that moment even ten thousand eloquent words couldn't have expressed the richness of their feelings. But alas, happy moments in this life are oft short-lived. At the entrance of the Laboratory Lathan and Purella heard a hideous laugh, and then six Wabonian dwarfs came tumbling headfirst into the room, coolly followed by Og and Count Zandar. Count Zandar grinned diabolically.

"I suspected as much," said the Count as he gazed on Purella and her robust rescuer. "The moment I smelled that pizza I knew it was a trick. I never order a pizza unless it has extra anchovies, and plenty of chocolate chips."

Neither Lathan nor the dwarfs looked well, but it was difficult to determine whether this was because of their predicament or their assessment of the Count's diet. The Count turned his attention to Lathan.

"You peasant wretch," he said, glaring, "how dare you try to contend with me! You will die a horrible death for your insolence."

The undiluted evil and icy malevolence of the Count's glance would have made even the bravest and most experienced warrior afraid, yet Lathan was not afraid. All that his grandmother had told him, all the adventures he had gone through, and all that Jack Crackback had said to him gave Lathan a courage that could not be shaken.

"I am Lathan, robust shepherd lad and son of 'Trollkiller' Sven Svensson," he said, staring boldly at the Count. "I have no fear of you anymore, because I have learned in my adventures that evil can't win for long, and that if we only have faith, good will triumph. You called me a wretch, but I think you're the one who's a wretch, and with faith in God and the spirit of

'Trollkiller' Sven Svensson to help me I cannot fail to defeat you!!!"

"I can't stand it any longer!" said Bingo, as he pulled the magic coin out from around his neck, and held it in his hand. "Lathan, let me give you back your magic coin! I know the Count is tough, but he's also a liar, a coward, and a nincompoop, and with your faith in 'Trollkiller' Sven Svensson and this magic coin in your right hand, you cannot fail to defeat him!"

Bingo punctuated this last line by thrusting his hand high into the air, which unfortunately caused the coin to slip out of his hand, hit the floor, and bounce into the alligator pit.*

Lathan and his friends stared thoughtfully at the broken trapdoor through which his magic coin had fallen. A definite attitude of gloom pervaded the scene.

---

* I think this is as good a time as any to say a few words about the history of the Wabonian dwarfs. Pliny the Elder tells us (in his famous work, *Pleasum Buymi Historium*) that, according to a Theban donkey merchant of his acquaintance, there was a heavily populated but infertile land somewhere in the southern hemisphere known as Wabonin. Whether this "Wabonin" is to be identified with modern Wabonia is a point of some dispute. Scholars have historically taken widely differing view points, but currently there are only two major schools of thought. One school says one thing about it, and the other school says something else. However, in my opinion, the real answer to the Wabonian question lies in the writings of St. Fuddleston.

According to St. Fuddleston (although some hypercritics claim this part of his works to be apocryphal) the Wabonian dwarfs were originally a people of normal size who were subject to the ancient kings of Pantaloonia. The Wabonians wanted their independence, but the Pantaloonian kings refused to give it, and would punish the Wabonian rebels by having their heads chopped off by the King's guillotine. The Wabonians, because of their famed ability as plotters and thorough knowledge of modern genetic theory, formulated a brilliant plan. They realized that the King's guillotine was built to accommodate (or, more simply, cut the heads off) men who were six feet tall; if they could somehow shorten themselves to four feet tall the King's guillotine would be useless.

"So," said the Count, turning to Bingo with barely controlled rage, "I'm a wretch, am I? I'm a nincompoop, am I?"

"Did I say that?" Bingo hastily replied, still staring pathetically at the opening through which the coin had dropped. "I mean, those weren't my exact words, were they? Of course you realize I was kidding."

All the dwarfs began to show evidence of shaking. The Count strode toward them with murder in his eyes.

"Just . . .just having a little joke," Bingo explained. "You didn't take me seriously did you? Oh, but how could you? Why

---

To achieve this goal the Wabonians decide to use a new theory they called "Evolution." One of the most difficult aspects of the plan was getting the evolutionary cycle going in the first place, and this indeed had them baffled for some time. Eventually they started a "Think Small" campaign, which included everyone spending at least one hour a day on their knees, and pregnant mothers being shown pictures of tiny baby mice by way of encouragement. Soon the plan started working and the children became shorter and shorter. Unfortunately, due to the whims and vicissitudes of the evolutionary process (which in itself is subject to much scholarly debate), by the time the average Wabonian was four feet tall approximately two million years had gone by.

The years in between were very unpleasant for the Wabonian dwarfs, due to their decrease in stature. For several thousand years the Wabonians killed by the King's guillotine were cut off at the chin; four hundred thousand years later they were cut off at the eyes; and for the last hundred thousand years they were scalped. Finally, however, the average Wabonian shrunk to four feet and the King's guillotine was rendered useless. The current King was so impressed by the Wabonian's ingenuity that he granted them the independence which they retain to this day.

That, according to St. Fuddleston, is the history of the Wabonian dwarfs. Of course, he doesn't explain why the Wabonians aren't still growing shorter, or for that matter (since they've stopped their "Think Small" campaign) why they aren't growing taller again. But since these appear to be complicated scientific and metaphysical speculations they are probably of little importance in our story, which, if we don't hurry back to it immediately, will proceed without us.

you're one of the finest Counts I know. You know, now that I think about it, I was talking about a completely different Count."

"Stop!" said Lathan, and before the Count could get to Bingo, Lathan had leaped on the Count's back. The Count brushed Lathan to the floor as if he were a bug.

"You've annoyed me for the last time," said the Count.

The Count picked Lathan up and threw him to the floor once more. With Og blocking the exit behind them, Purella and the six dwarfs stood huddled in a corner, helplessly watching this horrifying scene.

Finally, after smashing Lathan into the floor a third time, the Count picked up his huge carving knife off the floor and stalked toward the unfortunate lad.

"Now you die!" he bellowed.

Lathan was lying next to the alligator pit, battered and helpless. For an instant he entertained the wild thought of leaping into the pit and taking his chances with the alligators, but then he thought of "Trollkiller" Sven Svensson, and when the Count's vicious knife thrust came down toward him, he leaped nimbly out of the way.

The Count turned and faced him again, knife in hand, and vowed that he would never escape.

"I am the son of 'Trollkiller' Sven Svensson!" Lathan called out proudly. "Kill me if you can!"

The Count lunged at him again and missed. Lathan's faith gave him energy, but as the Count slashed and Lathan dodged it became apparent that the rigors of his adventures had taken a heavy toll on Lathan. His feet were sore, and his legs felt battered and weak, and with each knife thrust the Count came closer and closer to hitting his mark. Purella and the dwarfs looked on this scene with horror, their eyes transfixed on the murderous knife. Og was so excited he suddenly left to go to the bathroom. As soon as he left the Laboratory, Bingo had an idea.

"Lathan!" he cried, "hit him with the pizza!"

Any weapon was better than none, and Bingo slid the pizza across the floor to Lathan. Lathan, with a last desperate burst of energy, lunged for the pizza as the Count charged at him one last time. Then, as the fates would have it, Count Zandar inadvertently placed his foot on the pizza, and, since this was a Wabonian pizza,** the Count's feet gave way on the slippery cheese. He flew up into the air, gave a final maniacal roar, and then plummeted straight down into the alligator pit. Immediately a splash was heard, then swimming noises, then a scream, then chewing noises, and finally a very loud burp. Lathan, Purella, and the dwarfs gathered around the pit, looked thoughtful for a moment, and then burst into cheers.

"Look!" said Plottle, pointing into the pit. There, hooked onto a nail a couple of feet down, was the magic coin. Lathan pulled it up, and, with a smile, put it around his neck.

"I told you," said Bingo. "When the plot starts working, everything falls into place."

The dwarfs smiled broadly. Just then Og re-entered the room.

"Duh, where's my boss?" he asked.

"Quick," Bingo told Og excitedly. "Your boss is getting a free meal down there and told us to have you join him right away!"

"Duh, all right," Og answered.

He happily leaped into the alligator pit; a splash was heard, then swimming noises, then chewing noises, and finally a very, very, loud burp. Lathan, Purella, and the dwarfs gathered around the pit, looked thoughtful for a moment, and then burst into cheers. Then, with tears of joy on their faces, they turned to go.

Just then Og climbed up out of the pit. He was picking his teeth with a little piece of wood.

** The Wabonians are notorious for putting too much cheese on their Pizzas and not cooking them long enough. Thus, the cheese exhibits considerable movement over the surface of the Pizza, and more often than not will end up in the consumer's lap, rather than his mouth.

"That was a swell meal," he said, "but I still didn't see my boss."

"Well, did you swim down to the bottom and wait for ten minutes like I told you to?" Bingo asked helpfully.

"You didn't tell me that," Og answered, somewhat confused.

"Didn't I? Gosh, I must have forgot. He said to wait for him on the bottom of the pool for at least ten minutes. Oh, and he wanted you to take this along with you."

Bingo cheerfully handed Og a large anvil.

"Golly, thanks a lot," said Og.

He leaped back into the pit and was never heard from again.

The happy group cheered once more, and then left the dreary Laboratory behind them. Lathan's adventures had left his body one giant bruise from head to toe, but Purella's gentle hand proved to have remarkable medicinal powers, for when she took Lathan's hand in hers his aches and pains seemed to completely disappear, and he felt as if he were walking on clouds rather than ordinary ground. Soon they stepped out of the Dark Castle, walked through the main gate, and were as free as the air once more.

Chapter XXIX

Contains Several Reunions, Happy and Otherwise

For a little while Lathan, Purella, and the dwarfs walked aimlessly in circles, too joyful to think about where to go or what to do next. Finally, however, they decided to head back to the highway on which Lathan had come, and soon they were marching happily homeward. They had not gone far before they came across the Count's army, each member of which was tied up, and hanging upside-down by his feet in a large grove of twisted trees.

"Hey, let us down!" the men shouted.

The dwarfs laughed at them, while Purella and Lathan looked thoughtful, and then started laughing too.

"What happened?" Bingo asked one of the dangling men.

"I don't know," the man answered. "This afternoon a weird-looking pony came to the castle gates with a mysterious message in his mouth. The message said that an army was marching on the castle and we'd better march out to meet them. So we did. But before we could find the army we marched into this grove of trees and came across an old man in a wagon. We started to hassle him, but then—this is the strange part—one minute we were about to kill him and steal his wagon, and the next minute he had us all tied up and hanging upside-down from these trees. I'm not sure how he did it, but I'll say one thing, he must be awfully quick."

"Did you say it was an old man with a wagon?" Lathan breathlessly asked.

"No, no. I wouldn't say he was old," said another soldier, whose face was quite red from embarrassment. "He was more like early middle-aged."

"Yeah, and he had at least fifty guys with him," another soldier added.

"No, no, it was just one old man," the first soldier countered.

Soon all the soldiers were arguing at once, and generally claiming that there was no old man, and that they were lucky to be still alive, since they were so badly outnumbered.

"Please tell me," Lathan asked the first soldier, "did the old man look like . . ."

"Lathan! Princess!" Bingo shouted from up ahead, "I hear something coming."

Lathan, Purella, and the dwarfs ran ahead to see what it was, and soon beheld a large army marching toward them. The semi-staggering gait of many of the soldiers made the army's identity unmistakable. At the head of the army, on horseback, was the huge red-faced figure of King Lars XIV, and on his lap the inimitable pup, Floppy. The army of Hoodahooda had arrived.

"Father!" Purella cried joyfully, and ran happily toward him.

The King dismounted. As he stood watching her run toward him, his body did not sway, and his eyes did not vacantly roam, but they fixed themselves on her, and the glaze that long had covered them was washed away by tears of joy. When he finally held his daughter in his arms once more, it was such a moving sight that even the King's army (who were a little disappointed to see the Princess alive and well, considering that they had looked forward to a little killing and maiming) burst into half-hearted applause.

"Oh father, I knew you would come to save me! I knew it!" said Purella, while cradled in her father's brawny arms.

"If it wasn't for a shepherd lad we would never have made it here," the King explained. "When the Count kidnapped you, an imposter took your place, and soon I was, as usual, drunk. But then a robust shepherd lad came to me and told me the true story of how you were kidnapped; at first I didn't understand him, but long after he left, his words sank into my heart and I left the Great Table and locked myself into my room. I was determined to be sober again, and I stayed in there and didn't eat or drink for three days. For the first two days I wanted a drink so badly I thought I was going to die, but on the morning of the third day I came out of my room sober, and a King once more. I knew that you couldn't cure yourself of perpetual drunkenness in three days, or even three years, and that strong drink would always be a temptation to me, but I vowed that for me there would be no turning back. That very day I banished all liquor from my kingdom, and gathered the army you see before you, to rescue you from that diabolical Count, and to bring you safely home."

The King's army seconded his account by giving various coughs and grunts, and looking generally woozy.

"Father, that same brave shepherd lad that told you of my plight is here before you, and it is he who has rescued me from the clutches of that vile Count."

Purella then brought Lathan before the King and described in vivid detail all of Lathan's heroic achievements, much to the embarrassment of the robust shepherd lad, but to the great delight of everyone else.

"My boy," said the King, "you are the strongest, bravest, wisest, and certainly most robust shepherd lad in my entire kingdom. I can think of no person more suitable to be the husband of my daughter."

Lathan looked startled for a moment; then he and Purella looked at each other awkwardly, and then they giggled, and then they embraced enthusiastically, while their Wabonian friends cheered and grinned as if they had been plotting the whole thing from the very start.

Just then a carriage rolled up from the rear of the army, and out stepped a slim, serene, middle-aged woman, accompanied by four maids, who were chatting with their respectable-looking mistress with easy familiarity.

"Darling," said the King joyously, "come meet Lathan, our new son-in-law."

The slim, serene woman, who was none other than Queen Gertrude, tripped nimbly up to the slightly battered shepherd lad, hugged him, and earnestly insisted that she was delighted to meet him.

Since Lathan had last seen her the Queen had changed her hair style and her dress, but most shockingly, her attitude. Her sudden transformation had come about shortly after Lathan, Doctor Oldair, and Prince Charming left Purella, and it happened in the following way.

The Queen had been so busy cleaning up the Great Chamber for a new wedding ceremony that she was thoroughly shocked when her husband appeared before her after his three-day drying-out period not only sober, but also ordering everyone around as if he were actually in charge. She promptly ordered him to go back to the Great Hall, and leave her alone, whereupon he not only ordered her to go to her room, but picked her up and carried her there as well. Once inside the room the Queen ordered him to apologize, after which the King ordered her to never order him again, as that practice had cost them their daughter, and almost ruined their kingdom.

The King spent the next few days sobering up his courtiers and organizing his army, while the Queen remained locked in her room, having an unending temper tantrum, relieved only by lengthy bouts of crying, wherein she cursed her husband loudly, but secretly felt some admiration for his sudden return to forcefulness. She began to remember what it was like in the first years of her marriage, how happy she and Lars were, and her mind slowly began to fill up with tender feelings and regrets. Soon her thoughts drifted toward Purella, and her regrets began to turn very big indeed.

When the King finally opened her door three days later, he had hardly stepped inside before the Queen apologized to him, and when he looked at the svelte, sad-eyed figure before him, he felt guilty, kissed her warmly for the first time in many years, and told her he was sorry too. The Queen replied to him that all she wanted from now on was to be a good wife to him, and then, rapidly adapting to the situation, did so many kind, sweet things in the next couple of days that she soon got everything she had ever wanted from him in the first place, and was even allowed to accompany the army on their way to the Dark Castle. In short, in the space of one week she became the cheery advisor of her maids and the darling of everyone. The result of all these things was that King Lars XIV had complete control of his kingdom again, his Queen had considerable control over him, and everyone was very happy.

While Queen Gertrude hugged her daughter warmly (which gave Purella indescribable joy) the King turned to his ever-sober Steward.

"One more thing remains," said the King. "Bring the prisoner before me."

Another carriage, this time a dingy and battered one, rolled up to the head of the army. Two burly guards opened the door, pulled a spidery figure down from the carriage, and shoved him before the King. To Lathan's astonishment, the spidery figure was none other than Doctor Oldair.

"So, Doctor Oldair," said the King sternly, "when we met you on the road, you claimed that you saw my daughter roasted to death, and insisted that we all return home; how is it then that my daughter stands before us very much alive?!"

"He said the same thing to me!" said Lathan, as he stared at the cringing Doctor. "I wouldn't ever have rescued the Princess if Mr. Jack Crackback hadn't shown me the truth, and encouraged me on my way!"

"Well, Doctor," said the King, "what have you to say for yourself?"

All eyes stared at the Doctor, who stood there with his new clothes soiled, and his body contorted with excessive cringing. He gazed around at all the sets of eyes that bore down on him, and instead of stuttering an excuse, dropped all pretence of servility and let out a snarling, contemptuous laugh.

"You're a bunch of fools and I hate you all!" he said, and finally revealed himself to be the villain he truly was.

Everyone gasped.

"I've always despised you, you drunken idiot," he said to the King. "You and your battle-ax of a wife, and your oh-so-sweet daughter! I wish she were dead!"

The Doctor swung his arms wildly and paced from side to side, and everyone was too astonished to respond to him.

"And don't pretend that you haven't hated me too! You've hated me from the start! All of you! And why?! Because you saw my advanced gardening skills, and knew you couldn't do the same!!"

While the King looked Doctor Oldair sternly in the eye, Doctor Oldair shook a bony finger in his face.

"Oh, but soon your jealousy of my advanced gardening techniques went too far! It was you who sent those religious fanatics to destroy my garden! I knew!! I knew!!"

Doctor Oldair danced wildly about, enraged even at the memory of these atrocities.

"But you couldn't stop me!" the Doctor continued. "I knew that if I got the last five seeds of Flaming Pink Chrysopata Scummatta of Phylum Fulvibrata I could once again make my garden the greatest in the world. I tracked those seeds all the way to the Dark Castle, and in exchange for a promise to tell everyone that the Princess was already dead, the Count gave me these!"

Doctor Oldair reached into his shirt and pulled out the last five seeds of Flaming Pink Chrysopata Scumatta of Phylum Fulvibrata and held them out proudly for all to see.

"These five beauties are worth a thousand of your cursed daughter!"

The King unsheathed his sword, his eyes blazing with righteous indignation.

"Not so fast, Mr. 'King,'" said Doctor Oldair contemptuously. "You know the international law: anyone who kills a top-ten philosopher for any reason is to be punished by death and the confiscation of all his property."

The King, whose recently dried-out brain remembered such a law, paused.

"That's smart," said Doctor Oldair with a sneer. "And now I'm leaving you all and going to the Empire of the Amazons, where I'll be tending my own garden, which, with these new seeds, will be the greatest in the world!!"

"Doctor Oldair," Lathan calmly interjected, before the King could respond, "I let you advise me without question, and you deceived me and betrayed my trust. Now let me give you a little advice. I've learned in all these adventures that you can't tend only your own garden in life, because there are many people in this world, and we are all children of one God, and all of us are interconnected, and all of us depend on each other. What happens to you affects me, and what happens to me might affect everyone else, so unless we get together and learn to help one another the world will fall to pieces. You were just concerned with your own garden, and your selfishness nearly caused the death of the Princess, the death of all our hopes, and maybe the end of Hoodahooda itself. You can't just tend your own garden, Doctor; you'll have to help out in other gardens as well, or like a plant out in the sun with no other trees to give it shade, you'll wither and die alone."

"I'll handle all the garden metaphors, thank you!!" said Doctor Oldair. "And I'm not gonna sit here and be advised by a stupid little shepherd!!!"

The Doctor, with a melodramatic flourish of his hand, turned to go.

"You will never see my face again," said the Doctor. "Before long I'll be in the Empire of the Amazons, teaching philosophy next to the flaming pink flowers and purple and blue stems of Flaming Pink Chrysopata Scumatta of Phylum Fulvibrata."

"Did you say flaming pink flowers and purple and blue stems?" a voice asked.

The voice belonged to one of Count Zandar's soldiers, who had been cut down from a tree by the King's men and brought over for interrogation.

"That's right," said Doctor Oldair. "Flaming pink flowers, with purple and blue stems."

"And do they grow about three feet tall?"

"Very close to it."

"In that case, I've seen quite a few of them around here."

"Impossible," Doctor Oldair scoffed. "My five seeds are the only ones left in the world."

"Well, you can see flowers just like that from the top of that hill," said the soldier. "Let me show you."

Everyone climbed up the little hill to look. When they reached the top they saw, stretched out before them in every direction, and as far as the eye could see, a solid mass of three-foot flaming pink flowers with purple and blue stems.

"You see, they look just like the ones you described," said the soldier. He reached down and scooped up about thirty seeds off the ground.

Doctor Oldair sunk to his knees, and as he knelt there, with his mouth hanging open in shock, the five seeds slid slowly out of his hand.

"How . . . how . . . how . . ." was the only intelligible thing he could utter.

"Yeah, this stuff grows like you wouldn't believe," said the soldier. "People around here try all kinds of ways to kill it, but it just keeps coming back. Pretty soon it'll take over everywhere."

The expression on the Doctor's face might have provoked sympathy in some situations, but in this case it inspired derisive laughter.

"There goes your glorious garden, Doctor," said the King. "You left my daughter to be killed just to gain possession of a few worthless weeds."

The laughter and scorn heaped on the Doctor roused him to respond.

"Curse you all!" he said. "At least I have the satisfaction of knowing that nothing worse could happen to me."

Just then the sound of a paper boy could be heard.

"Paper! Paper! Read all about it! The new philosopher's ratings are in! Check out the top ten! Paper! Paper!"

"Come here, boy," said Doctor Oldair eagerly. "Gimme one, quick!"

He tossed the boy a farthing and then snatched up the paper like a hawk snatching up a mouse. The lists of the top ten philosophers in the eastern and western worlds were blazoned across the front page, and it didn't take long for Doctor

Oldair (and soon everyone else) to notice that his name had been dropped from both lists, and that his position had been taken over by Mrs. Greta Finkel of West Wimpley, Puddlesworth, authoress of the self-help classic, *You Are Basically a Good Person!.*

Doctor Oldair crumbled to his knees once more, let out a bitter cry, and then looked back at the paper just long enough to notice the following headline:

AROMATIC EMPEROR SACKED

Amazonia (LODP)—Emperor Charming the 1st was deposed yesterday by a huge throng of his hearty, female subjects, who could no longer tolerate the noxious odors which emanated from his body.

"I thought he smelled divine when I first met him," said the Empress, (age undisclosed), "but now he smells like a tropical sewer."

Reportedly, the Empress became concerned about the Emperor's health when a greenish slime began to cover his body, which could not be washed away, and gave off an extremely foul odor. Doctors speculate that it is the residue of many years of excessive perfume application, and can never be washed away.

Reports now circulate that ex-Emperor Charming has since been banished from his Empire, and was last seen in a hut in a nearby jungle, accompanied by a fat native girl dressed in white, an old woman crying, and an older man with a badly-wrapped wedding present in one hand and a spear in the other. Reportedly, the former Emperor did not look well.

Likewise, Doctor Oldair did not look well. His facial features were contorted into a picture of the most extreme gloom, and his body was twisted and bent as if it had just been punctured by hundreds of arrows.

"I hope you've learned a lesson," the King said sternly.

"Curse you all!" the unrepentant Doctor burst forth with a scowl. "I don't need to hear your self-righteous ravings! There are other kingdoms to philosophize in, and my precious garden can be rebuilt!"

"I will spread the word so that you will never work as a philosopher again," said the King. "I will make sure you're hounded from kingdom to kingdom, searching for rest, but finding none. You have my word on that."

Doctor Oldair sneered. He started to stumble away, but then stopped to take a last look at Lathan and Purella, who stood together, hand in hand. His eyes shone with hate.

"Curse you all!" he said, and then walked off through the blighted and bizarre trees that dotted the Land of Doom. Lathan watched his hunched and stooped figure as it stumbled into the distance, until finally the Doctor blended in so perfectly with the twisted trees that Lathan could no longer distinguish him.

Chapter XXX

A Short Chapter, Which is the Very Last One

*T*he trip back to Hoodahooda was one long, joyous celebration. The soldiers, exhilarated by the heady sensation of being sober, sang happily as they marched, and the King, the Queen, Purella, and Lathan all got to really know each other, and discovered that they not only liked each other, but loved each other as well. The only sad part of the trip was when the Wabonian dwarfs had to leave for their own country. Lathan and Purella thanked the crafty plotters with tears of gratitude, while the King showered on them many expensive gifts, which the dwarfs tried gamely to refuse, but not persistently enough to be rude.

The crossing of the ocean was uneventful and very smooth in the three huge galleys the King had commissioned for the expedition. The ships landed at Scuttleton, and because the King was worried about his unprotected kingdom the army began marching back to Hoodahooda immediately. Because of this

Lathan had no time to find Miss and thank her, but he sent a messenger to thank her, tell her what had happened, and invite her to the wedding.

The arrival back at Troddleheim was the scene of another joyous celebration, with everyone gathered in the town's main square. The Head Coachman, because he was one of the King's only employees known to be regularly sober, had been in charge of the kingdom during the King's absence, and he (guided by the profuse advice of his ever helpful assistant) had done a remarkable job of keeping everything safe and running smoothly. Thus the King rewarded him and his assistant handsomely, which caused the townspeople to burst into cheers; then the King announced that his daughter was going to be married, which caused the townspeople to burst into cheers; and then the King announced that his daughter was going to marry Lathan, which caused the townspeople to stare blankly, and then applaud politely. Everyone was in a very good mood, and when the King announced that idols were banned in his kingdom, and that he and his family now belonged to the religion of "Trollkiller" Sven Svensson, the crowd cheered lustily, and not a single groan could be heard.

For Lathan it was an incredible day, but before his joy could be complete there was still one person he had to see. It was Sunday morning, and he knew his grandmother must be on her way to the humble church of "Trollkiller" Sven Svensson.

Lathan ran down the little dirt path that led to his grandmother's cottage. He had been down that path many times before, but never had it looked so beautiful to him, and never did he enjoy the forest so much. He darted along the trail until it started to cross the little meadow where Purella had been kidnapped. He stopped short. In front of him, hobbling slowly up the trail, was his grandmother. He ran up to her as fast as he could go.

"Grandma! I did it! I did it!" he shouted. "I rescued the Princess, and now I'm going to marry the Princess! I nearly lost my magic coin, but then I found it again, but then I nearly lost it again, but then I found it again, and that Count didn't have a chance! You were right, grandma! The blood of 'Trollkiller' Sven Svensson flows through my veins, and there's nothing I can't do!!"

His grandmother gave him a wise, mysterious smile.

"Lathan," she said softly, "you're not really the son of 'Trollkiller' Sven Svensson."

"What do you mean?!" Lathan asked.

"You thought I meant he was your actual father, but I only meant he was your father in spirit," she answered. "You've always been a good, true-hearted boy, and even though you thought so little of yourself, I always knew that if you had faith in God, you could be a hero just like him. Well, I made up the story about that being Trollkiller's coin just to help you believe it too. Your real father was an honest shepherd, Lathan, just like I told you before."

Lathan pulled out the magic coin.

"You mean, it's not really magic?" he asked brokenly.

"Oh, heavens no. I never told you it was magic, Lathan," she gently replied. "That coin belonged to your real father. It didn't say 'Trollkiller' Sven Svensson' on it, it said 'Troddleheim Shepherd's Convention,' and that's not a picture of an old man with a bushy beard; it's a picture of a sheep. Your father won it in a 'Best Baa' competition. It's the only thing he ever won."

"But . . . but . . ."

"Don't you see, Lathan? You didn't need a magic coin to give you courage; that courage was in you already. There's no such thing as magic, but when you have the faith of 'Trollkiller' Sven Svensson, and let his spirit guide you, there's nothing in the world you can't do. It wasn't magic that rescued the Princess, it was you. You're the real hero, Lathan. It was you the whole time."

Two months later (after Lathan came out of the coma he fell into upon hearing this news) Purella and Lathan were married, and, needless to say, lived happily ever after.

> Farewell Princess, and shepherd lad,
> And faithful dog, and stinking cad,
> And pompous Doc, and woozy King,
> And dwarfs, and Miss, and each strange thing.
>
> Now there's some who'd like to quarrel,
> "You haven't given us a Moral!"
> I've got too many! But for fun,
> To please these folks, I'll give you one.
>
> That Moral is you should aspire
> To lofty goals, or even higher.
> If you have faith, I think that you
> Can be a robust shepherd, too.
>
> And now that we have reached the end
> I bid a fond farewell, my friend,
> And hope the last lines of my poem
> Will send you wise and happy home.
>
> That's all there is, no more to tell,
> The story's done, and so farewell.

The End

To order additional copies of

THE SHEPHERD'S ADVENTURE

—OR—

A PRACTICAL GUIDE TO PRINCESS RESCUING

Have your credit card ready and call

(877) 421-READ (7323)

or send $15.95 each plus
Shipping & Handling*

Your choice: $5.95 - USPS 1st Class
$4.95 - USPS Book Rate

to

WinePress Publishing
PO Box 428
Enumclaw, WA 98022

www.winepresspub.com

* Add $1.00 S&H for each additional book ordered.